Also by Alexander C. Irvine
A SCATTERING OF JADES
UNINTENDED CONSEQUENCES

ONE KING, ONE SOLDIER

ONE KING, ONE SOLDIER

ALEXANDER C. IRVINE

BALLANTINE BOOKS · NEW YORK

A Del Rey® Book
Published by The Random House Publishing Group

Copyright © 2004 by Alexander Irvine

Grateful acknowledgment is made for permission to reprint poetry excerpts from "Barbarian," "Farewell," "Bliss," "Sisters of Charity," and "Vigils" from *Rimbaud Complete* by Arthur Rimbaud, translated by Wyatt Mason. Copyright © 2002 by Wyatt Mason. Used by permission of Random House, Inc.

www.delreydigital.com

Library of Congress Cataloging-in-Publication Data

Irvine, Alexander (Alexander C.)
    One king, one soldier / Alexander Irvine.—1st ed.
      p. cm.
    ISBN 0-345-46696-9
    1. Rimbaud, Arthur, 1854–1891—Fiction. I. Title.

PS3609.R85O54 2004
813'.6—dc22

                                        2004049317

Manufactured in the United States of America

            1   3   5   7   9   8   6   4   2

            First Edition: August 2004

        Text design by Julie Schroeder

For my brother Andrew

Long after the seasons and the days, the living and land,
   A flag of flesh, bleeding over silken seas . . .
                              ARTHUR RIMBAUD, "Barbarian"

Somewhere along the line I knew there'd be girls, visions, everything; somewhere along the line the pearl would be handed to me.
                              JACK KEROUAC, *On the Road*

The whole lost land coming out to meet this soldier
Sole dier in a land of those who had to stay alive . . .
                              JACK SPICER, "The Book of Galahad"

ACKNOWLEDGMENTS

Thanks first to Beth for putting up with long nights when I wasn't home.

Also to the Cambridge SF Workshop for careful reading; Chris Schluep for persistence, more careful reading, and picking up my slack when the pool gods turned against me; Colleen Lindsay for indefatigable enthusiasm and scheming; Eben Weiss for timely intervention; and my anonymous copy editor for some very fine catches.

Also to Graham Robb, Charles Nicholl, Alain Borer, and Jean-Luc Steinmetz for books about Rimbaud that made the man at least as interesting as the poetry; Joyce Johnson, Dianne di Prima, Lewis Ellingham and Kevin Killian, Dennis McNally, and all the other biographers and memoirists of the Beat writers, the San Francisco Renaissance, and the Berkeley Renaissance; Black Sparrow Press for issuing a collected Jack Spicer; Bob Kaufman for existing; Graham Hancock for writing utterly cracked but seductive and entertaining books; Sam Hamm for giving me an excuse to come up to San Francisco and wander around (plus an excellent dinner); Jim Minz for a prophecy in a smoky stairwell; and Rick Wormwood for lending me a book that I still haven't given back.

Also to Rimbaud for illuminations, and Spicer for Martian radios.

ONE KING,
ONE SOLDIER

PROLOGUE

It began with a question about an uncle he had never met.

He was a small boy, six or seven, and his parents were arguing. From the flurry of words, one stood out: *l'Africaine,* spat with his father's icy sneer. It roused his mother to pale fury, and Arthur understood almost nothing of what she'd said. When she finished, his father turned without a word and retired to the study where he spent his furloughs scribbling over dusty books. The next morning Captain Rimbaud rejoined his regiment.

The days that followed were quiet. Arthur's mother spent the first week of the Captain's absences reinforcing the order she believed eroded by his presence, and the boys—Frederic was a year older—soon learned to stay out of her way or suffer discipline to crumble a legionnaire. When they tired of playing at service in the Captain's regiment, protecting French garrisons from the Algerian hordes, Arthur poked around in his father's study. He shifted the thick leaves of the manuscript, written half in his father's hand and half in a sinuous script he did not recognize, all curves and dots; he frowned over detailed commentaries on military actions in places he'd never heard of; and he avidly devoured his father's reports on Africa.

By Christmas no letter had come from the Captain, and Arthur's mother gathered the boys. With baby Isabelle in her arms, she told them that the Captain would not be coming back. "Have the Algerians killed him, Mama?" Frederic asked. No, Mama said. But Africa has made him dead to us.

She began to insist that her neighbors call her the Widow Rimbaud, and methodically she began to remove all traces of the Captain from the house. The boys protested until she bloodied Frederic's nose, and then they resisted by hiding what mementos they could under the stairs. It was a great relief to them both when the next fall they escaped to school.

Two things happened before that, though, both of which seemed—at the distance of nearly thirty years—to have set Arthur on the course that had gotten him here, to the parched and famined hell of the Shoa, bargaining with a heartless tribesman over guns.

First he had asked who the African was.

Mama did not slap him, as she often did when he asked a question. "That is what the pitiable baboons in this town called your uncle Felix when he was alive."

Arthur risked another question. "Why?"

"Because he ran away to Africa when his European sins caught up with him," Mama said.

Arthur couldn't help it. "Like Father," he said, and then Mama did hit him.

In the spring a man none of them had ever seen before knocked at the door. Cold air came in when Mama answered his knock, and behind him Arthur saw a black horse lifting its left forefoot from the cobbles. Steam plumed from the horse's nostrils and curled around its ears.

"Madame Rimbaud," the stranger said. "I beg your pardon that I did not write ahead to announce myself, but my travel here was unexpected."

He stood in the doorway as Mama sized him up: curling black

mustaches; high black boots caked with mud that speckled the hem of his heavy cloak as well; hard eyes of a traveler in a young man's face. In his belt Arthur was certain he saw a pistol.

Take me with you when you go, Arthur thought. Take me with you to Africa.

Which was anywhere that Mama was not. Already Arthur was his father's son.

"What is it you want?" Mama asked.

"To be brief: your husband wrote a great deal about his time in Africa. I represent a learned society that would very much like to acquire those manuscripts."

Father's writings still lay on his desk because Mama hadn't yet gotten around to throwing them away; only a few days before, though, she had used some of the larger sheets to wrap vegetables. Now Arthur saw annoyance flit across her face, a look that when directed at him or Frederic meant they'd better duck their heads. How delicious it would be if she slapped this armed stranger across his mustache and sent him on his way!

But no, then he would be gone, and of course her annoyance was directed at herself, for ruining pages she otherwise might have sold. "My husband's belongings are precious to me now that the Lord has called him home," she said, not one lie but two in the same sentence, and each so absurd that Arthur nearly corrected her. Frederic pinched him to keep his mouth shut.

The traveler gave no sign that he doubted her. "Certainly, these materials are valued heirlooms of the departed Captain Rimbaud. For us, though, the Captain's knowledge would prove greatly useful." He unfolded a leather wallet from an unseen pocket. "Perhaps . . . ?"

Mama's eyes fastened on the wallet. So did Arthur's. "My children are a great burden," she said.

"We would be glad to arrange their schooling," the traveler said, "so they will make some use of themselves."

"And then how will I keep the house and the farm?" Mama

snapped. "You send them to school, I must hire laborers and listen to their filth though my kitchen windows."

The traveler had begun to slip bills from his wallet, one at a time, keeping them fanned in his fingers. Mama watched him, and held out long after Arthur's resolve would have failed. Take it! he thought, and immediately: and sell me too. Let me go with Father's papers and books.

The bills came more slowly, the tension exquisite and unbearable. Arthur had long ago lost track of how much money now rested in the man's fingers.

"Frederic," Mama said. "You and Arthur go and get your father's papers."

No, Arthur thought. The allure of the money vanished. He ran after Frederic, who was already in the study. "Frederic," he said. "Don't take them all."

Frederic did not look up. Dutiful already. "He paid for them all."

"He'll never know. Frederic, don't."

But Frederic was pushing past him, back toward the front door, where the stranger waited with an open saddlebag. Rain had begun to fall. Frederic set the sheaves into the bag, and the stranger buckled it shut.

"Don't take Father's papers," Arthur said suddenly, already feeling the bruises it would cost him later but no longer able to care. Mama whirled on him, but he went on. "We have nothing else of him."

The traveler squatted, bringing his face level with Arthur's. "It's hard, boy," he said. "But we need these. And a boy keeps his father here," he tapped a gloved hand on his chest, "not in words on paper." His attention turned to Mama, and he handed her a calling card. "If you turn up anything else, we would very much like to hear about it."

She took the card, and the traveler touched his hat. With a last look at Arthur he was gone. Arthur was crying when Mama shut the door, and he never saw the first blow coming.

BOOK ONE

——

I can laugh off truthless loves, and strike down duplici-
tous couples with shame—down below, I experienced a
hell women know well—and now I'll be able to *possess
truth in a single body and soul.*

ARTHUR RIMBAUD, "Farewell"

Carefully now will there be a Grail or a Bomb which
   tears the heart out of things?

JACK SPICER, "The Book of Merlin"

They are still looking for it
Poetry and magic see the world from opposite ends.

JACK SPICER, "The Book of Gawain"

LANCE

THE FIRST THING the doctor said to Lance Porter was, "March fifth, is that right?"

Lance didn't know what he was talking about.

"When you were wounded."

Wounded. So that was why he felt so shitty. Lance couldn't quite open his eyes all the way, but he tried to get a better look at himself. He was lying down, and his right leg hung from a pulley. Pain tolled like a distant bell in the leg, and in his hip. "What happened?" he asked the doc.

"Mortar shell. The guys at the MASH saved a couple bits of shrapnel for you. Your leg was broken, and there are some pieces missing from your hipbone on that side, but you should be okay. Surgery went well. Your war is over, Corporal Porter."

The MASH. That brought back some memories. Mostly lights, Lance trying to say something and a masked face snapping irritably at someone Lance couldn't see: *he's not out yet, for Christ's sake, put him out.* And before that, a muddy streambank. Shaking his head, trying to figure out what had happened.

"Reason I brought up the date is that it's the day Uncle Joe finally cashed in his chips," the doctor said.

The words took a long time to soak through Lance's skull. Uncle Joe. "Stalin?" he said.

"Stalin. Everybody's favorite despot. Had a cerebral hemorrhage, is what they're saying." The doctor flipped sheets of paper on Lance's chart, made notes. "A nurse will be in to see you in an hour or so. She'll top off your morphine if you need it."

"Thanks, Doc," Lance mumbled automatically, and was asleep again before the doctor got to the door.

He awoke to the whistle in his head of the falling shell, and remembered.

Just after dawn, when even the mud and tree stumps of Korea were beautiful. He'd been awake much of the night with a toothache, and had finally given up and climbed to the top of the bunker stairs to watch the sun come up. Mornings looked different, smelled different, when you'd been awake waiting for them, and on this morning Lance felt his spirits lift a bit as the sky brightened. Luke the Gook hadn't sent them any mail overnight, and he never attacked in daylight. All Lance had to do was wait for the morning jitters to pass on both sides, and then he could walk back down the ridge to the CP and get a ride back to have his tooth worked on.

Morning jitters: someone down the line to the east ripped off a long burst from a BAR, just on general principles. A few rifle shots cracked here and there. Across the valley that separated the 2/23rd Infantry from Hill 355, Luke greeted the dawn in his own fashion; Lance ducked back into the bunker as the clacking of a gook machine gun echoed from 355. The bullets didn't hit anything near him. After waiting five minutes for form's sake, Lance put on his helmet. "Sarge, I got a toothache," he said to the platoon sergeant, who was stirring in the corner of the bunker.

"Better take care of it," the sergeant said.

Lance climbed out of the bunker and walked down the back of the ridge, behind the line and away from Luke's Land. The trail switchbacked down the steep incline before following a stream to the CP, and Lance was just coming around a bend when he heard the whistle. Mortar, he had time to think, and then it hit him.

The blast erased all thoughts from his head, and it surprised him to find that he wasn't on the trail anymore. He was lying on his left side on a muddy slope, with his feet in the shallows of the stream. Automatically his hands started looking for his rifle. Rocks, mud, helmet. No rifle.

Pain rose in his leg like the brightening of dawn. He groaned, or thought he did, and realized he was deaf from the blast. And something was in his mouth; he worked it to the tip of his tongue and picked it out. His hand came away bloody, and between thumb and forefinger Lance held a triangular piece of metal about the size of his pinkie fingernail. Now how the hell did that get there? he wondered, probing around in his mouth, and he found a clean hole in his right cheek about two inches back from his front teeth. While looking around he brushed against the sharp stub of his aching molar, and the jolt of pain was much worse than the throb in his leg. I'll be damned, he said, and couldn't hear himself. Luke knocked out my bad tooth for me.

Okay, inventory. Hole in cheek, broken tooth that wasn't any good anyway, ears starting to ring, little stings awakening all up and down his right side . . . oh God.

He hadn't really looked at his leg yet, and when he did the pain rolled over him and he started to scream for real.

Broken, the doctor had said. So casual. Bullshit, Lance thought. Broken was when someone cut you on the football field, you heard a clean snap, the doc set it, and that was that. Lance's leg had been a hell of a lot more than broken. But there it was, apparently whole, encased in plaster and suspended from a pulley. The doc had said something about his hip too, and Lance instinctively reached down to check that his works were all still there. They were. He let out a long sigh.

The guy in the next bed started to laugh at him. "You too, huh? I did the same thing, buddy. Sonsabitches only shot me in the arm, but as soon as I woke up from the surgery I went looking after my Johnson too."

Lance let his heart rate settle down. The sudden motion had reminded his leg that it hurt like hell, and his head was clear enough to figure out that the morphine had about worn off. "How do you get the nurse?" he asked.

"You can ring, but they come quicker if you yell."

Lance found the button on his bedside table and rang.

"I gotta warn you, though, the more you bitch about the morphine the less they give you."

"Well, I haven't said a thing yet. They must cut you a break the first time, right?"

The roomie shrugged, and Lance noticed that only two fingers stuck out of the guy's arm cast. He saw Lance look and said, "I'm left-handed. Lucky me, right? I'm Morton Trecker." He reached his wounded arm out to Lance as if he really might want Lance to shake it.

Lance introduced himself, and the nurse came in. She was about fifty, with *career military* written all over her: ramrod posture, hair in a bun that an atomic bomb wouldn't shake loose, lines at the corners of her mouth, eyes bright and pitiless as a hawk's. "What can I do for you, Corporal Porter?"

"I think my morphine's worn off."

She checked his chart and gave him a shot. "Hey, what's the date, anyway?" Lance asked.

"Twelfth of March," she said. "Three forty-seven PM."

A week. He'd been wounded a week ago. "Where are we?"

"USS *Repose.*"

A ship? Lance held himself still, and couldn't detect any motion. Maybe the shell had done something to his inner ear.

She saw what he was doing and smiled. "It's a big ship, and we're not moving right now. Plus you had a severe concussion from the blast; you've been a little dazed since we got you, but you're coming around now. We're going to transfer you in a couple of days. Maybe if you're lucky we'll get a storm and you'll notice we're on the water."

The curtain parted again and a much younger nurse came in with lunch. The morphine started to hit Lance, and he'd barely touched his sandwich before he lost interest in it and fell asleep again.

Six weeks later his leg was still hanging from a pulley, but now the pulley was bolted to the ceiling of a room in the Oak Grove Naval Hospital in Oakland, California. It only hurt when he twisted his body the wrong way, and then mostly in his hip. The doctors said he'd make a full recovery, the halls were full of gorgeous candy stripers, Joe Stalin was dead, he'd turned twenty on March 20, and in general Lance was beginning to feel optimistic. Could have been a lot worse, he thought, looking out his window at the city and a tiny sliver of what must have been San Francisco Bay. Trecker lost fingers; I just lost a rotten tooth and a couple of pieces of bone that'll grow back.

While he was still on the *Repose,* a dentist had come around and done a root canal on Lance's broken molar. Now he had a gold tooth. It made him feel like an outlaw, somehow, a pirate or a gunslinger. His tongue wandered over it often, and then found the lump of scar on the inside of his cheek, and he caught himself wishing the gold crown was closer to the front so people would see it when he grinned.

One of the candy stripers came in with a canvas bag full of paperback books. She handed one out to each of the six guys in

Lance's room, and they all watched the switch in her hips as she left before seeing what they'd gotten.

"You got a science-fiction book," the guy to Lance's right said. "You like science fiction?"

"Not as much as you do, I guess," Lance said. He tossed the book over.

"Thanks, pardner," the guy said. He was from Texas, Lance remembered, but he'd forgotten the guy's name. He'd had the toes blown off his left foot, and was waiting to have a special shoe made so he could start walking again. All the guys in their ward had leg wounds.

"Wait a sec," Lance said as he opened his new book. "Mine's not right." He looked at the cover again, a guy with a gun and a fainting girl. It was right-side up, but the words on the page where he'd opened it, somewhere around the middle, were all upside down.

Without looking up, Tex the science-fiction fan said, "It's two books. They put 'em upside down to each other so you know when the first story's done."

Lance turned the book over, and sure enough it had another cover that aligned with the upside-down words. *Junkie,* it said. The other cover read *Narcotics Agent.* Strange pair, cops back to back with robbers, or cowboys with Indians. A Fed, Lance thought. That's a line of work I could get into if my leg heals up right. Probably a lot of ex-GIs doing it. He bent back the cover and started to read, trying to ignore the itch under his cast.

The next morning a different candy striper came in, this time with mail, and Lance's heart did a little skip when she handed him a letter from Ellie.

She'd written on the thirteenth of March, but the letter had probably gone all the way to his unit before being sent down to the MASH, then the *Repose,* and finally Oak Grove. He tore it open, thrilling a little to the sight of her handwriting.

Dear Lance,

By the time you get this, maybe you'll be home. Your mother told me as soon as she got the telegram, and I wrote right away. I don't even know how bad it is yet, but your Mom says not to worry. She's sure that you'll be okay. Here's my news: Dexter is closing in around me; I'm going to quit working for Mel Fricker and——are you ready for this?—— come to CALIFORNIA to meet you! I have a place set up in Berkeley, thanks to a friend of Jerry Kazmierski's, but I won't get there until Mel can find a replacement, so if you get discharged write and let me know where you are. If not, we're expecting another telegram from the army telling us where you're recovering, and I'll just come there.

I'm so excited to see you, Lance my love. But a little scared too. You see, I'm not just coming because I want to—— although God do I want to——but some people have asked me to come and talk to you about something important. It has to do with your family; Jerry came back from New York City looking for me, and he's talked to your mother, and there's some big secret they won't tell me. I'll get it out of them, though. They talk to me like I'm a little girl, and it drives me nuts.

This is important: don't go anywhere until I get there and we have a chance to talk. I want to tell you more, but it's not the kind of thing you should read in a letter lying in the hospital.

Not too terrible a request, is it, to hang around in San Francisco for a while waiting for me? I hope not. Get well, get completely well, and I'll see you soon.

Love, Ellie.

He read the letter over again, making sure he hadn't missed anything. Below her signature was an address in Berkeley.

Ellie was coming to California to meet him, and she wouldn't tell him why except it was about family. "Hey, Tex," he said to the science-fiction fan. "Where's Berkeley?"

Tex pointed out the window. "Right over there eight or nine miles. North of Oakland, across from San Francisco. That's where all the Reds go to college around here."

Sweet Jesus, Lance thought. Was Ellie a Red? Was that why she was being so mysterious? She couldn't be. Her parents wouldn't allow it.

Dexter is closing in around me, she'd written. If she was a Red, she wouldn't be able to stand Dexter, Michigan, that was sure; even though it was right next to Ann Arbor, it wasn't a place where a commie would find much sympathy.

"Is everybody at Berkeley a Red?" he asked Tex.

"Just about. Why would they go there if they weren't?"

Don't be crazy, Lance told himself. This is Ellie you're talking about. She's as American as any girl. She's no Red.

The worry stayed with him, though, as he went back to his book and read about Maurice Helbrant's crusade against dope fiends and degenerates.

He didn't get his cast off until the first week of June, and by that time he'd come close to tearing it off with his toothbrush, just to scratch the ten million itches that crawled along his leg. The itches in his head were worse—try as he might, he couldn't shake the fear that Ellie had gone Red, and he couldn't figure out how to ask her about it, so in the end he didn't try to get in touch with her at all. He read the newspapers to get a sense of what Berkeley was like, and what he saw, especially in the *Examiner,* confirmed all his suspicions. So he let it sit while he figured out how he could feel her out without actually confronting her. If he did, she'd either deny it and be hurt or admit it and try to turn him, and if that happened Lance didn't know what he'd do.

The docs had him stand up, squat, raise his leg, pivot his torso back and forth while they watched. Then they assigned him physical therapy, and suggested a transfer to the Great Lakes Training Center in Chicago. "You're from Michigan, right?" one of them said. "Closer to home."

It was, but Lance asked if he could do the therapy there in Oakland. After some consultation, they decided he could, over at the VA hospital. Lance caught the implication right away: if he didn't take the transfer, they were going to discharge him.

He jumped at the chance. He had three months of pay piled up, after all. That would get him a long way if he decided to kick around San Francisco waiting for Ellie. Two days later an army doctor at the VA hospital gave him a physical and pronounced him fit to leave the service. Two days after that he had his discharge papers in his pocket and his service duffel between his feet, and he was standing outside the base wondering what to do next. The bag had only arrived a week before, and he hadn't even looked in it yet. It would have his gear and whatever personal effects he'd left in the bunker. Since he hadn't seen any of it in three months, Lance figured he could wait another couple of hours to take inventory.

What he couldn't put off was Berkeley. The place had worked into his head, a collage of lines from newspaper articles, scenes from *Narcotics Agent,* and the insinuations of his fellow patients at Oak Grove. It was unanimous: Berkeley wasn't fit for a girl from Michigan. It was damn suspicious of Jerry K. to have set up Ellie there. But Jerry K. was crazy; who knew if *he'd* finally gone Red?

And where was Ellie anyway? She should have been around to see him by now. She hadn't even written him again, which struck Lance as mighty strange given how urgent her letter had sounded. The only thing to do was head up to Berkeley and set things straight.

Lance walked to the nearest bus stop and asked the driver how to get to Berkeley. The driver told him to hop on, and Lance tried to, but he couldn't put enough weight on his leg to walk up the stairs with the bag. Right away the driver leaned over to take Lance's burden. Gritting his teeth against the humiliation of being a goddamn cripple, Lance stepped slowly up onto the bus, taking all his weight on his left leg and swinging the right up after it. The seat right behind the driver was empty, and he slumped into it, amazed and disgusted at the weakness of his body. Twenty years old, and he'd come up the stairs like an old lady. Thank God Ellie hadn't been there to see it. What would she think when she saw him, thin and scarred and limping? He tried not to think about it, but he was sunk in a morass of self-pity, no two ways about it, and he stayed sunk until the bus driver said, "Buddy, didn't you want to get off in Berkeley?"

The bus was stopped at a shelter plastered with handbills, in front of a pharmacy. "Yeah," Lance said.

"Well, here it is. You want a particular stop?"

"This is fine, thanks." Lance got up, painfully, more aware of his leg than he'd been since first seeing it in the cast, and got off the bus without asking the driver how to find the address Ellie had left him. The letter was buried in his pocket, and he hadn't wanted to stand there at the front of the bus with the other passengers watching him dig around in his pants. Look at the crippled GI, poor bastard. Doesn't even know where he's going. The bus growled away and Lance looked up and down the street, catching a sign at the corner: Telegraph Avenue. He was reminded of Telegraph Road back in Michigan, running through Dearborn; once on a school trip to the Henry Ford Museum, the bus driver had gotten lost and they'd gone up and down Telegraph, Lance thinking all the while that they were a lost signal on the wide concrete wire. Strange thing to remember right then, but he guessed the bus had something to do with it. And this part of Berkeley looked a lot like parts of Ann Arbor. State Street or South University, a campus neighborhood: coffee shops, diners, record stores. He didn't see any bars, though, which was different from Ann Arbor.

A sign under the road marker at the intersection confirmed his intuition: UNIVERSITY OF CALIFORNIA, it said, above an arrow that pointed up Telegraph.

He could go into the pharmacy, look at a map, and find Ellie's address. Simple. He'd be talking to her in half an hour. The idea made him nervous. All his determination had melted away the moment he ran aground on the steps of the bus back in Oakland; he just felt scared that Ellie might pity what he had become. The last time he'd seen her, he'd been almost nineteen, a solid five-eleven and 170. Now he was just turned twenty, with a limp and a spackling of scars on his right side, his wounded leg atrophied to a stick. He couldn't face her, couldn't face wondering what she would think when she saw him again.

But he could walk. He could force his leg to move and re-member that it used to be strong. The docs had said he'd recover, and Lance intended to recover. He'd do what Ellie asked him, he wouldn't go anywhere, but she'd understand if he needed a little time to . . . well, to get his feet under him again.

While he did that, he could get a sense of what she was get-ting into. Here he was in Berkeley, breeding ground for commies and other bleeding hearts. While he was here he could do a little reconnaissance. He put himself into gear, concentrating on walk-ing evenly, even though his hip groaned at every step and the muscles of his thigh were trembling by the time he'd gotten to the campus. He paused near the bottom of the broad stone stairs leading up to the library's front doors. A lot like Ann Arbor, he thought. Same leafy quad, same big proud buildings, same peo-ple killing the summer throwing a football around on the grass or reading a book under a tree with a plaque at its base. All of it redoubled the feeling that he'd been thrust away from this whole way of living; once you'd used an MRE box for a crapper because there were snipers outside your bunker, you couldn't look at a dozen happy-go-lucky people your age without getting a little resentful. Ellie was part of it all now, or soon would be, a college-bound girl with a boyfriend from back home by way of Korea. She was probably reading philosophy somewhere in one of the coffee shops he'd passed back on Telegraph Avenue. Different state, but the same kinds of people and the same kinds of places.

"Need directions, soldier?"

Lance turned around. Sitting on the lower library step was a stoop-shouldered tweedy guy maybe ten years older than Lance, with thinning hair and a face that pouched along his heavy jaw. Something about him put Lance on guard, and the fact that he had no reason to be on guard made him even more jumpy.

"How'd you know I was a soldier?" he said, and right away knew it was a dumb question.

"Well, you're carrying a bag with your name stenciled on it, and those boots aren't Buster Browns. And something recently poked a hole in your cheek, there. I'm guessing it wasn't a chopstick. Also, you're limping a little, which I'm guessing isn't a trick knee from football. I'm Jack," the guy said. He stood to shake Lance's hand, and the limp handshake put Lance's hackles up all over again.

"I'm looking for my girlfriend," Lance said.

"You don't say." A grin showed Lance that Jack should have taken better care of his teeth. "If I had a dime for every soldier who showed up here looking for his girlfriend . . ." He shook his head. "The registrar is right across that way." Lance followed Jack's pointing arm and saw the building. "They'll tell you where to find her."

"Thanks." Lance took a step away.

"Listen," Jack said. "You're new in town, and I'm always game to buy a soldier a beer. There's a place in San Francisco called the Black Cat. Right off Columbus and Montgomery in North Beach."

A civilian beer. It sounded good even if there was something about this Jack guy that Lance didn't trust. "I might just do that," he said. "Appreciate it."

"Least I can do." Jack nodded at him and went up the stairs into the library.

The registrar's office would have a map, Lance thought, and

was wrong, but the student union—which he'd walked right by on his way to meeting Jack—did. He fished out the letter and traced the way to Ellie's address. It was maybe a mile from where he stood—much closer to a bus stop on Telegraph, just down from the stop where he'd gotten off earlier. Now he knew. He could find her whenever he wanted, and knowing that made him feel a little better. If she was looking for him, she'd be there, and when he was ready he'd go find her.

Right then, though, his leg was raising hell and whatsisname, Jack, had put the thought of beer into his head. He could taste it. A civilian beer.

Later. The recon wasn't done. He didn't know nearly enough about what Ellie was up to, and his leg could goddamn well scream. He was going to work it more.

Lance went back outside and spent the afternoon eyeballing the suspicious characters of Berkeley. Professors, beards, girls in sandals. It was a wonder Tailgunner Joe didn't send a fleet of trucks to round up the whole bunch of them. Lance Porter stuck out like a sore thumb in this crowd. His frustration about his leg, and Ellie, this sense of not belonging, started to make him feel violent. If Ellie had turned Red, he swore to himself, and he found the guy who had turned her . . .

He had killed six men in Korea, which was a lot for the spring of 1953. Just his luck, to be with one of the units that saw action even as the diplomats argued over the fine print of the cease-fire. He hadn't done anything wrong; every guy he'd lined up would have done the same thing to him; but he wasn't happy about it either. It was one more thing that Ellie would eventually ask him about. One more thing he'd have to justify. And it sure wouldn't make things easier if he caught the guy who had first given her Mao's Little Red Book. That guy would be one dead son of a bitch. Lucky seven.

A group of girls walked by, laughing, their hair bouncing over their shoulders. It was hard to keep up a homicidal mood when pretty girls came by. Out of reflex Lance scanned their faces, on the off chance that Ellie was one of them. Then he wondered what he'd do if he saw her. Follow her? See what she did, who she talked to, where she drank her coffee?

What the hell was he doing? What was this all about?

When you started asking questions like that, it was time to call it a day. Lance pushed himself up off the bench where he'd been sitting for the past hour. There must be a bar somewhere on Telegraph, he thought.

And there was, but it was a long damn way from the campus, and by the time he got there his leg was way past healthy fatigue. The place was called the White Horse, and it looked like it must have been a restaurant in the not-too-distant past. A bar took up one wall, but the rest of the room was cluttered with tables, and in the back there was a fireplace with chairs and even a couch. At the end of the bar, a doorway opened onto a big empty room. Dance floor? Lance didn't care. Beers were fifty cents, and when the first one hit the back of his throat, he decided on the spot that it was the best four bits he'd ever spent. He kept at it until the beer had soaked up all his emotions except a sullen self-pity. Once in a while he noticed other people in the bar, students and older people, mostly men, and as it grew later Lance kept dim track of time by how many arguments he was hearing about poetry. Fucking poetry, which anyone with sense forgot all about when they weren't in a classroom, and here he was in Berkeley goddamn California listening to a bunch of people bickering about T. S. fucking Eliot. *Let us go, then, you and I,* he caught himself thinking as his next beer arrived, and was enraged at himself for remembering his own recitation for Mrs. Welch. Yeah, let's go, he thought, and was standing up when someone clapped him on the shoulder and said, "Soldier. Didn't I see you on campus today?"

Lance turned and focused on the gargoyle who had given him

directions earlier. "That was me," he said, and tried to keep moving, but the gargoyle was in his way.

"Didn't work out like you planned, did it?" he said with a not-quite-sympathetic smile. Lance had a brief urge to knock him on his ass. But the gargoyle was waving at the bartender, and another bottle appeared in Lance's hand, and he was being hailed at a corner table, soldier, soldier! What the hell, free beer, he thought, and sat down.

"We were just talking about you," the gargoyle said.

It took Lance a minute to figure out that this meant they'd known he was there. All of his swimming brain was devoted to remembering the gargoyle's name, which he couldn't do. "Is that so," he said.

"It is. Do you play baseball?"

Another minute spent grappling with the change of subject, then Lance nodded. "Sure." Who didn't? He'd been a half-decent second baseman, better arm than bat, better glove than either, visions of Charlie Gehringer in his head. Which had shit to do with anything.

"I thought so," the gargoyle said, and nodded to his friends at the table. "Didn't I tell you?"

They all agreed that he had. Lance's beer was empty already, man was he throwing them back tonight, and he started to get up, but one of the other guys at the table was at the bar. The gargoyle kept talking.

"Baseball is our rite of spring," he said. "A game based on completing a circle, dying in the fall with the crowning of a new king and then resurrected when the trees are starting to bud. Played on a field that's bounded only on two sides. And the players, they're our real kings. You think Eisenhower's ever going to be as loved as Joe DiMaggio? Ever hear of the Fisher King?"

Lance hadn't.

"The Grail stories, King Arthur and the Round Table? The

Fisher King is wounded, and the Grail will heal him and restore fertility to the land. You were wounded in Korea, right?"

"Nothing wrong with my fertility, bud," Lance said, and for some reason heard Morton Trecker, his roomie on the *Repose*, guffawing in his head. You get enough beer, and the ocean motion comes to find you, he thought, then his head cleared and he realized that the laughter was coming from all around him at the table.

The gargoyle made placating gestures. "Not what I meant. It's a symbol. The King is a symbol, the Grail is a symbol, all of it." His eyes shone, his gestures were becoming jerky—he was drunk too, which relaxed Lance a little. Even playing field.

"Where were you hit?" one of the gargoyle's friends said, like he was reciting a line from a movie.

Here we go, Lance thought. How many times was he going to hear that? "Leg. Leg and hip mostly. Lost a tooth too." He felt vaguely ashamed to be talking about it, like he was admitting to having seen his parents having sex, but the feeling evaporated when he saw the reaction he'd gotten.

"You're kidding," the gargoyle said. Everyone else at the table was stone silent.

No way was Lance going to tell them the whole story. It wasn't something you talked about. He swallowed more beer. "Teeth are a fertility sign, too," someone said.

"Oh for God's sake," sighed the gargoyle. "Everything's a goddamn fertility symbol if you look hard enough."

"Not that it makes any difference beyond the academic, to us." More laughter, and outright hilarity when someone added, "No *fish*."

Somewhere in the middle of it Lance put something together. "Wait a minute," he said. "You guys are queers."

Milton Berle couldn't have gotten a bigger laugh. "As a three-dollar bill, soldier boy," the gargoyle said when the ruckus calmed a bit.

"Jesus Christ," Lance said. He'd gone looking for his girl-friend—well, sort of—and ended up in a bar full of queers.

"Don't be afraid. You're safe with us," the gargoyle said. "What's your name? You didn't tell me this afternoon."

Jack, Lance remembered. What a name for a fairy. "Lance," he said, against his better judgment, but again it was worth it when he saw Jack's reaction.

"Lance?" Jack repeated, and his jaw actually dropped. Never saw that before, Lance noted absently.

"As in Lancelot?" one of the other queers asked.

Jack ignored him. "You can't stop there, Lance. What's your fish's name?"

Lance didn't follow. "Fish?"

Jack held his nose. "Your girlfriend. Her name wasn't Elaine by any chance, was it?"

Which was when the whole thing stopped being funny, stopped being even bearable. "Fuck you," Lance said. He stood. "Don't you fucking joke with me."

Leaving them there, he banged out of the White Horse and walked down Telegraph Avenue, limping a little and only wondering an hour later where he would be able to spend the night. In the end he ran out of steam near a park and sat drowsing on a bench until the sun came up and he heard the buses running on Telegraph again. He got up, his drunk faded to a barbed-wire hangover, and made his way by city dog over the bridge to San Francisco. He'd looked at it enough across the bay, and there was sure as hell nothing for him in Oakland or Berkeley; time to see what the San Fran mystique was all about.

He got off the bus on Market Street and put his feet to work, loosening the leg and loosening his mind too. Twenty minutes later he was captivated: people, restaurants, streetcars, music and voices from open doorways, the smells of coffee and fresh bread, pretty girls walking dogs, men with beards and short-skirted women on a street called Columbus. A place that knew itself, was what it felt like. He saw a bookstore and went in. It had just opened, and Lance wasn't sure he even wanted a book, but he did want to distract himself from thoughts of Ellie. The only other option was to call his mother, and he had no idea what he'd say to her. If she was shocked about his leg the way Jack had been, the way he was afraid Ellie would be, Lance was going to hitchhike to Mexico and drink margaritas on the beach for a year.

The bookstore was all paperbacks. Lance noticed several copies of the book he'd gotten from the candy striper, and picked up two titles from the same rack, just to buy something. Back out on the street, he looked around. The next cross street was Broadway, and he spotted a diner. Hungry, he thought; he hadn't eaten in nearly twenty-four hours. In the diner he polished off three eggs and a short stack, drank enough coffee to set him straight, read enough of a newspaper to worry all over again what was going to happen to Ellie in Berkeley, generally gathered himself for what he knew had to come next.

Call Mom, he finally told himself. She'll have gotten letters, she'll know I'm home. Shouldn't let her worry.

He left the diner, and as he shouldered his bag he realized that what he wanted right then more than anything else was a place to put it down. Ten minutes' search located a fleabag called the Lombard, which had to be better than a bunker on the MLR, and it only cost $4.50 a week. He paid for two weeks and spent twenty minutes showering away the night outside and the beer smell coming out of his pores. Already a civilian again, he thought. One night on a park bench and I need to be steam-cleaned.

He couldn't duck it any longer. He got a dollar in change from the front desk and found a phone booth a few blocks away. A primly dressed Negro woman was inside the booth, patiently explaining something to someone on the other end of the line; Lance couldn't catch her words, but she seemed deeply annoyed—no, angry and trying to hold it back—from the roots of her graying bun of hair to the soles of her sensible shoes. Once more she went through whatever complex argument it was she was mustering against her telephone adversary, making the same hand gestures as the previous time. She's talking to her son, Lance thought. She's gotten a wire asking for money and she's explaining why she can't send it. Or won't. Was her son a soldier too? Lance had known plenty of Negroes in Korea, more than he'd ever met back home. He'd heard, too, that wounded soldiers got addicted to morphine and turned into junkies back in the States. The platoon sergeant who had okayed Lance's trip to the dentist had just six months before been court-martialed for stealing morphine from the infirmary. Was that this woman's problem? Lance imagined her son a junkie, pacing back and forth in front of a pay telephone in Chicago or New York, walking around the block when the police passed by and praying that the hurried detour wouldn't make him miss the call from Mother, the call that might answer his prayers for a fix via Western Union.

The woman hung up the phone, hard. As she brushed past him Lance saw tears in her eyes. "Hey," he said, but either she didn't hear him or she just had no time for soldiers.

What he'd meant to say was *It'll be okay.*

His mother answered the phone on the second ring, and immediately Lance could picture her in her plaid chair. The lamp would be on because, since his brother Dwight had disappeared, she never opened the curtains. The phone would be on the table to her right, book open on the left arm of the chair, her favorite ashtray on its stand next to the table. The radio would be playing Nat King Cole or Burl Ives, and since it was summer she would have a glass of iced tea on the table. A powerful ache rose in him, to be home again, in the town where he'd grown up, sharing a root-beer float with an Ellie Patterson who had never thought of going to California.

"Mom," he said.

"Lance! Good Lord, where have you been? Are you home? I'll

come get you. Why didn't you call me before now? I know there was this thing with Ellie, but my God, son, I'm your mother."

"Yeah, I know, I've been, I don't know. A lousy son. I'm sorry."

"Lousy son, don't you say that. Where are you?"

"San Francisco."

"San Francisco? What for? I got your discharge papers."

"Yep. I'm a civilian again. The docs patched me up and let me go. I just figured since I was here . . . well, no, there's more to it than that. I can't talk to Ellie yet, Mom."

Silence, heavy with disapproval. "Have you met another girl?"

"No, it's not that." He changed the subject. "Listen, Mom, I'm going to stay out here for a while. Get used to the world again, enjoy being a civilian."

When she responded, the warmth had left her voice. "I'm not sure that's a good idea, son."

"It's not forever, I just want to see the sights. This is some place, and who knows when I'll get out here again?"

"Lance, I think you should come home. Find Ellie and come home."

Now her tone was bothering him. "Something wrong, Mom? Are you okay? You seeing a doctor?"

"Never mind that. You should come home. That's not a good place for you to be."

"It's a vacation, Mom. Just a vacation. I'll be home soon. Okay?"

A long pause. "Well, you're free, white, and eighteen. You can do what you want. But that doesn't mean you have any sense. There are strange people in San Francisco."

He laughed.

"I mean it. Have you seen Elaine?"

He almost lied to her, but the truth jumped out of him. "Not yet."

"Well, you should. She came all the way out there to see you."

"About what, Mom? What's the business with this letter and all the mystery? She said she'd talked to you. And what's Jerry K. got to do with anything?"

"You're going to have to hear that from Ellie. You be careful, son. This is not the time to be associating with the wrong people. Promise me you'll be careful."

Lance ground his teeth. "I promise. Now I have to go, okay? I want to go see the Golden Gate Bridge. You know, they let you walk across it."

"Can you walk that far with your leg?"

Truth was he didn't know, but that wasn't the kind of thing you dropped on your mom long distance. "Sure. Like I said, the docs patched me up good as new. Now I'm off to ride a streetcar. I'll write you a letter every day."

"No you won't. But you should."

"I love you, Mom." Just rote, but he meant it.

"You're my only son, Lance. I love you too. Take care of yourself."

"I will." He hung up and left the booth, and right there across the street was an alley, and at the mouth of the alley was a sign that said THE BLACK CAT. Sometimes the world was just too damn small.

He did get on a streetcar, and he did get to the park at the base of the Golden Gate Bridge, but he didn't walk across it. Five miles round-trip seemed a little much, even though he'd walked more than Johnny Appleseed while he was in the army. Instead he got takeout fried chicken and a carton of milk, and killed the day in the park looking at the bridge. It was beautiful, that was the only word. It fit where it was, making a low arch over the water between the city and the hills to the north of the bay. The only thing he could compare it to was the Ambassador Bridge in Detroit, which was big and impressive but you didn't get any kind of pleasure from looking at it. Come to think of it, that was the difference between Detroit and San Francisco right there. San Francisco was fine to look at, and Detroit just wasn't. Lance tried to conjure up some kind of regional pride, but it wasn't there. In Dexter right now it was probably ninety degrees and humid enough to drown, and the people on Main Street still spent their days off from the Ford plant in Ypsilanti bitching about Truman firing MacArthur. Maybe Ann Arbor was different, but there was no place in Ann Arbor where you could sit and watch the Golden Gate Bridge.

Lance was no pinko, but he liked California, liked being there in a way he'd never enjoyed being in Michigan. Now I can see why so many people come here, he thought. Whatever else is going on, you can get up in the morning and look at the bridge and the hills and the water, and it all seems right. He started thinking about a job. Maybe he couldn't be a cop or a G-man because of his leg, but he could sure do something. Hell, maybe he could go to college; Congress was extending the GI Bill to cover Korea vets. It was something to consider.

Something else to consider was how come Ellie hadn't said why she was looking for him. His mom had seemed strange on the phone, too. There was something they didn't want to tell him, and he was damned if he could figure out what it would be. *Family*, Ellie had written. But his father was dead, and Dwight was gone too. He got a cold lump in his gut thinking about his brother. Had they found out what happened to him? Was that what this was about?

After eight years, Lance didn't want to know. You got used to the steady weight of guilt after a while, the occasional start when you thought you'd seen him or heard his voice. And you got used to holding onto that tiny branch of hope that you were wrong, that after all this time a grown-up Dewey would turn up safe, still with his lopsided grin and the white patch in his hair over his birthmark. Either way, knowing the truth would rob you of something.

Stop. Every time you do this it just twists you up.

He got out the letter again and read through it, gnawing at the spaces between the words. Again he felt like heading to Berkeley, and again his leg, stretched out in front of him on the grass, brought him up short. A little time, that's all he needed, to get it shipshape again. If Ellie was starting to get pink around the edges—and that was still his leading explanation for the furtive tone of her letter—there would be hard times ahead. He loved her, and he believed that she loved him, but some things weren't open to compromise.

Before they got to that, though, he'd let her be for a while. Give them both some time. Maybe he could soak up some of whatever was in the San Francisco air, and the next time he went to see her some of the soldier would have rubbed off.

The afternoon wore on, and like someone had flipped a switch the park was full of couples holding hands. Just what I need, Lance thought. He'd been sitting by himself long enough now. Time to go someplace where he could talk to people. The first place he thought of was the Black Cat, and as soon as the idea occurred to him he remembered that Jack had known Ellie's name the night before. That fag son of a bitch, he'd probably gone right to the registrar and found out who Lance was looking for, and then followed him to the bar, what was it called, the White Horse, as a prank on the soldier new in town. Probably hates me because the army wouldn't take him, Lance thought.

That's what he would do. Wander back through the city, stroll into the Black Cat, and if Jack was there, Lance had a couple of questions for him.

What happened, though, was Lance got to the Black Cat a little earlier than he'd meant to, and they had a beer called Rainier for thirty-five cents, and by the time Jack and his buddies came through the door Lance was drunkenly preoccupied with the name of the place. White Horse, Black Cat; somewhere in San

Francisco there was probably a place called the Purple Rhino. Take a color, take an animal, presto—you had the name of a bar.

"Well, if it isn't Lance," Jack said. "You aren't still mad, are you?"

"Hell no," Lance said. "You got nothing better to do than pull pranks on strangers, that's your problem."

"Pranks?" Jack looked puzzled. "You mean your fish—sorry, your girlfriend—her name really is Elaine?"

"Oh, give it a rest."

"No, I mean it." Jack sat on the stool next to Lance. The rest of his group settled at a table near the back wall. "I did say it as a joke, but it was just a play on the Arthur story. Lancelot's wife, or paramour depending on which version you read, was named Elaine."

Lance looked at him. He didn't look like he was joking. If anything, he looked too serious.

"Well, forget it. Yeah, her name's Elaine."

Jack bought a round for both of them. "My condolences."

"Ah," Lance shrugged. "I'll talk to her soon enough, get things straightened out."

"Maybe," Jack allowed. "Depends on the story."

"Story, hell. This isn't about a story. It's about me and her."

Jack pointed the neck of his bottle at Lance. "That's where you're wrong. It's definitely about a story, all of it. Look." He pointed at a mural that ran around the Black Cat's walls near the ceiling. Lance didn't recognize most of the names, but he picked out some that he did: Twain, Hemingway, some others. Then there was Nietzsche, Bierce, Steinbeck, Joyce, Pound, the list went on. "Story," Jack said. "That building right over there"—he pointed toward the door—"is called the Montgomery Block, or Monkey Block if you live there. Nobody much does anymore, a few artists, and the city's probably going to tear it down soon. But right there in that building, people have done as much to change the world as they have at the UN, that's for sure. Twain hung out there, Bierce lived there, Sun Yat-sen wrote the Chinese constitution there, Indian revolutionaries plotted to overthrow the Raj there. The world has centers, vortices, where things happen, where things are generated, and that's one of them. This is an important place. Did I tell you last night that I'm a magician?"

This threw Lance. He was still trying to figure out how Sun Yat-sen had gotten into the conversation. "What?"

"Poets are the only magicians left. I'm a poet. We've always been magicians, all the way back to Orpheus and Thoth. Here. Watch this. You ever have your fortune told?"

Lance thought about it. "Don't think so."

A pack of cards appeared in Jack's hand, expertly fanned out. "Pick one," he said.

"Don't you have to lay them out or something?"

"If I'm right about you, Mister Lance the Soldier, all it will take is one."

Right about what? Lance wondered. Probably another joke, but he didn't care. Might as well see it out, just to get the punch line. He took a card and turned it over on the bar. There was a figure on it, a guy dancing under a tree with one leg up in the air, waving something in each hand. Lance didn't spare it more than a glance.

Jack didn't say anything for a while. Finally Lance had to prod him. "Well?"

"I'm going to be serious now," Jack said. He killed his beer and waved for two more. "You're into something very big here."

"Shut up already. You're just jerking me around again."

"No. Last night I was, a little. But right now . . . listen. You were wounded in the leg."

"You knew that. Fertility, right?"

"More than that. Story. You were wounded in the leg, your name is Lance. When's your birthday?"

"March twentieth."

"Of course."

"Of course what?"

"Spring equinox. Horus' birthday, when—wait a minute. I ask you this in all seriousness. Are you a twin?"

The question blew a storm of memory up from the bottom of Lance's mind: Dewey nine years old pulling his own tooth because he was afraid to let their mother do it. Dewey eleven years old, coming around to score from first on a single in a Little League game. Dewey crying after Lance blacked his eye the day before they were going to have school pictures taken.

Dewey twelve years old, gone, his shoes and shirt left in the grass. Police at the door. The swish of curtains closing out summer sunlight.

"I had a brother," he said, voice barely above a whisper. "He's dead."

"No, he's not," Jack said. "I'll bet your family comes from France."

"I'm going to tell you this once," Lance said. "My brother is dead, and we never knew our father, and my mother's name is Porter. You decide if that's French, and then we aren't ever going to talk about this again. Read me?"

"I read you. You bet I read you." Jack's grin was back, and Lance caught the joke.

"Fuck you and your stories," he said.

"It's a lot to take in, isn't it?" Jack said. "There's magic in the world, Lance. You're part of it, right in the middle. And before you say something you won't really mean, remember that you were angry at me last night too, and then you wanted to talk again tonight. You know something's going on."

"What's going on is I don't want to talk to you anymore," Lance said. He put another dollar on the bar and left.

Banging on his door woke him the next morning. He rolled off the sprung mattress and shuffled across the floor, still wearing his pants.

Jack was waiting in the hall.

"What, did you follow me home? I told you I didn't want to talk to you," Lance said.

"You have my card," Jack said.

"No I don't."

Jack pointed past him. Lance turned and saw the card on the floor next to his bed, on top of his shirt.

"Okay." He picked up the card and held it out. "Here's your card. Now beat it. I don't like queers."

"A soldier who doesn't like queers. Boring." Jack made no move to take the card. "Lance, I don't apologize very often, but I am sorry for rushing you last night."

"Nothing to rush," Lance said. "You and I aren't going anywhere."

"That's not what I mean. It was all a little too much to drop on you all at once." He studied Lance's face. "You want to hit me? Here." He took the card. "Now you have both hands free."

It was tempting, but Lance didn't bite. He let his hand drop and waited for whatever Jack was going to say.

"Marvelous restraint." Jack put his hands in his pockets. "Seals are playing today. Want to go?"

"Seals?"

"Baseball. The team of DiMaggio and Lefty Gomez. They're no good now, but once a fan . . ." Jack shrugged.

Lance ran aground on the idea that queers liked baseball. "If you're asking me on a date, I'm going to bust you in the mouth."

"Lance, I know you're just out of high school, but try to get your head around this idea: I don't want to be your boyfriend. Not every fag in the world lusts after you."

"Good, 'cause you can't make me queer."

"Can I make you go to a baseball game?"

Going to a baseball game with a queer poet who thought he was a magician. San Francisco was different all right. Lance cracked a smile, recalling his mother's warning about associating with the wrong kind of people.

"Is it a day game?"

"You've got time to get your boots on. Shirt too, if you hurry."

Seals Stadium was about half the size of Briggs, where Lance had seen a double handful of Tigers games. Come to think of it, the Seals' park reminded him of what Briggs had looked like when it was still Navin Field in the early forties, before the upper decks were added. Lance's first ball game had been a 3–1 Tigers win in May of 1941. Sitting in the stands now, he was taken back: hot-dog mustard on his mitt, the seventh-inning stretch, a long home run by Mickey Cochrane that won the game in the eighth, he and Dewey chattering on the way back out to the car. They'd gone with a friend from school and his friend's father, and looking back on it Lance wished he'd had a father to take him. At the time, though, he hadn't noticed. He and Dewey, they didn't need a father. They had each other.

He cracked peanuts and watched the Seals fall behind early to the Seattle Pilots. Jack was so wrapped up in the game that he didn't bug Lance about magic or stories or poetry or any other bullshit, but it was too good to last, and with two outs in the Seattle half of the sixth he said, "You pay attention in English class, Lance?"

"Enough to pass."

"A poet named Shelley once said that poets were the unacknowledged legislators of the world. That's what I was trying to get at, telling you about the Monkey Block. Shelley was right. Legislators write laws, and you may think you live under the laws of government, but you don't. You live by the laws of poets you've never heard of. What do you know about Egyptian mythology?"

"Nothing."

"How about the Knights of the Round Table?"

"They were looking for the Holy Grail, right? Get to the point."

"The Grail, right. Because it would cure the Fisher King's wound. The King Who Dies is a symbol of his land; as long as he's wounded, the land is wounded. Famine, pestilence, the whole nine yards. If he's cured, the land will be fertile again. Be nice, wouldn't it, if everything was so simple? Find the Grail and voilà! Everything is better."

"Sure," Lance said.

"But it's all myth. It's all symbol. The Grail is a symbol for this beautiful unattainable ideal, the light switch that will turn on the perfect society."

Lance's impatience boiled over. "Jack," he said, "what the hell does this have to do with baseball?"

"We substitute. One ritual for another, one symbol for another. Poets make those substitutions, they dictate the terms. Poets are magicians, like I told you."

Which didn't answer Lance's question. "You're a magician, right?"

"I told you that too."

"You just run across this magic? Teach yourself?"

"It's all about knowing where to look. Symbols, Lance."

"Right, symbols. I heard you. Get specific with me here. My English teacher senior year was Mrs. Welch. Who's your magic teacher?"

"Arthur Rimbaud," Jack said.

ARTHUR

HE HAD LONG since stopped looking for his father, but events had in the end brought him to Africa, which had marked Uncle Felix and obsessed the Captain, his father. At thirty-three he was more African than European: a trader sitting among his camels laden with rifles; a seeker consumed by the secrets of Abyssinia; a white man who taught bits of the Koran to street urchins when the Emperor's spies weren't watching—which was, of course, never. Around him, dusty hills threaded with hyena dens. Children in this part of Abyssinia didn't stay out after dark.

Menelik's *hazage,* the chief steward and general busybody, emerged from the main hall at the center of a compound walled off from the rest of Entotto. "Mister Rinboo come inside," he said, and held the door. The deliberate mangling of Arthur's name was one of the *hazage*'s little games; Arthur often played, but not today. Already the caravan's profit potential had all but evaporated; Jerome had sent Arthur to Ankober to settle the affairs of a former associate, Pierre Labatut, who had gotten Arthur into the gunrunning business. Jerome was concerned that certain sensitive information might be inscribed in Labatut's records, and Arthur, without knowing exactly what Jerome was worried about, had burned all of Labatut's journals—over the violent protests of Labatut's Abyssinian widow, who had then bogged

Arthur down in a series of legal actions to recover debts Arthur ostensibly owed Labatut. It had taken weeks to settle it all, and in the meantime Menelik had conquered Harar. He had returned to Entotto more or less simultaneously with Arthur's arrival, and Arthur had waited days to finish the deal for the load of guns he'd brought for the putative emperor.

Who waited for Arthur on a silk divan in what he called his council chamber. Attendants stood around in various attitudes of boredom, among them two Italians Jerome had told Arthur not to trust and a Swiss, Alfred Ilg, who had Jerome's approval. *Ilg knows everything,* Jerome had told Arthur, *and he will go to any lengths to keep it that way.*

"Good day, Rimbaud," Menelik said, in Amharic. Arthur had picked up enough of the language to do business in it; he replied in kind. Careful, he reminded himself. Ilg may know everything, but Menelik sees everything. He had the bright cold eyes of a broker in human lives.

"Your Majesty," Rimbaud said. "Your recent success fills me with pride for the people of Abyssinia."

"And no doubt with anticipation that I will be easier to do business with than the emir."

"Your honesty is beyond reproach," Arthur said. A lie obvious to everyone in the room; Menelik was in fact a pure swindler, and he proceeded to rewrite every provision of the agreement under which Arthur had trudged across the Shoa with his load of rifles. The guns were antiquated, would explode in the faces of his prized soldiers; Labatut owed Menelik money for which Rimbaud was responsible (this again, and Arthur could only grit his teeth); the expenses of transporting the arms and paying the workers had to be deducted; and so on. When it was done, Arthur stood before the Lion of Judah, heir to the Solomonid dynasty, wishing he had a pistol and a fast hand to draw it.

"It seems to me, Rimbaud, that I have paid enough for these decrepit rifles already. You will leave them with me, and I will see that you and your men arrive safely back at Harar," Menelik finished.

Arthur found his voice, with difficulty kept it civil. "Your Majesty's expenses have of course been burdensome. Who would argue this? But surely," and then he was off into a futile defense of the deplorable Labatut situation, the difficulty of even getting the caravan from Tadjourah across the Danakil to Entotto, the irresistible strength the new rifles would provide Menelik's formidable army. To Ilg's credit, he concurred with each of Arthur's objections, and Arthur made a note to stay on Ilg's good side. Menelik heard them out, and with his typical calm dismissed the issue. It was clear, he said, that the value of the guns in question was barely equal to the sum of debts and expenses Menelik had incurred to get them there.

Unless . . .

"Leave us," said the Lion of Judah, and the council chamber emptied. Only Ilg remained, and Menelik waved him away as well. The Swiss left slowly, puzzled and angry. When he was gone, Menelik fell silent for some time, as if weighty issues had for the moment distracted him from haggling. Arthur waited as patiently as he could. Eventually Menelik said, "The rains fail. And the Italians' cattle die of rinderpest and spread it to the herds of my people. Famine, Rimbaud. The land dies."

Arthur said nothing. This was dangerous ground.

Menelik gauged Arthur's silence. He sat forward on his couch. "There is a valuable service Rimbaud alone might provide."

"I am of course at your service," Arthur said.

"My service and others'," Menelik said. "I know something of your father's work. A tireless seeker after certain truths, your father. And his friend, your mentor, this Jesuit Jerome."

This is when the guards come to take my testicles, Arthur thought.

Menelik saw his anxiety, and smiled. "Be at ease, Rimbaud. Jerome is not the first to seek what he seeks in my country. I do not begrudge him his quest. You are in my country, though, and in my country you must work for me. So from this moment his quest, your quest, is my quest. Do we understand each other?"

How does he know this? Arthur wondered. The answer presented itself: the Italians. Their country hungered to make a coffee plantation of Abyssinia, and it was after all Italy, where nothing happened without the knowledge of the Holy See. Jerome could not keep all his secrets.

"We understand each other," he said.

"Down the hill from Entotto is a hot spring called Filwoha that heals those who bathe in its waters. This will be my capital city when I am Emperor of Ethiopia, and I will call it Addis Ababa, the New Flower. Do you understand this, Rimbaud? This new city founded on water and the life it brings?" Menelik was watching Arthur closely, and Arthur felt as if he were being weighed.

"I understand."

That gaze rested on Arthur for an interminable moment. "Your services will be rewarded, of course," Menelik said, and called in the *hazage* to draw up the note.

It was another two weeks before Arthur could leave Entotto, and nearly the end of May before he reached Harar. Immediately Arthur wrote to Jerome, and they met on the first of July. The situation had changed, that much was clear; Jerome made two decisions. One was to give Menelik every indication that they had accepted the necessity of working according to his terms; the second was that Arthur must be told everything. "You have a lively mind, Arthur," Jerome said, pacing the empty rooms of Arthur's house in Harar. "Surely you have some idea of what we're looking for."

"Some idea, yes. Would it be incorrect to call it the Grail?"

"It would, if by the Grail you meant the cup that caught the blood of Christ. No such artifact exists."

"Then what is it?"

"It is what will complete the Ark of the Covenant, and restore its Old Testament power. What it looks like I do not know, but my suspicion is that it is a piece of stone. It may be part of the Tablet of Moses; it may be a fragment of the Emerald Tablet of Thoth; it may be what the Egyptians revered as the head of Osiris; it is possible that those three things are one and the same. The Grail is that which restores power. Solomon mistrusted his bastard offspring, your Menelik's namesake, and hid it beneath the stone the Arabs call Shettiyeh, below the Temple in Jerusalem. Menelik stole the Ark, just as Solomon had feared, and the Grail lay there in its crypt until the Knights of the Temple discovered it during the Crusades. They tried to return it to the Ark, but could not, so to keep it safe they held it first in Cyprus and then in a number of places around Europe. But it was never safe; its story drew searchers, and after the suppression of the Templars in 1307 the survivors determined that it should leave Europe entirely. Where it went then, we do not know."

Jerome sighed as if relieved that at last the knowledge was no longer his alone, but at the same time he seemed to have diminished during his brief tale. It was all he had, Arthur realized; in sharing it, he surrendered much of himself.

"I pass this to you, Arthur Rimbaud," Jerome finished. "Your father's work brought us much of the distance we have covered this last fifty years. He told you nothing of your family, did he?"

Arthur shook his head. Jerome sighed. "It should not fall to me to tell this, but things are as they are. *Rimbaud*—a word meaning rogue, outcast. Did you never wonder who was the first in your line to bear this name, and why?" Of course I did, Arthur thought. There were days in Paris when I thought of nothing else, when Verlaine in one of his fits of agonized puling threw it in my face.

Jerome was reading his expression. "This uncertainty, at least, I can assuage. Your forebear, the man who gave you your name, came to France in the year of our Lord eleven sixty-five. From where, you want to ask? From here." Jerome stabbed one of his long fingers at the dusty earth beneath his feet. "He came with a delegation of Abyssinians who begged the Pope to suppress the Knights Templar, but this is not the last marvel. Your ancestor, the man whose name you bear and whose mission you continue, was a spy. He was the usurping Emperor's man, a Zagwe wormed into a party sent by the outcast Solomonid dynasty to thwart their goals. Having arrived in France, he remained behind to do the Templars' work even as the Solomonids waged their quiet war against the Order."

Arthur burst out laughing. Jerome too smiled, and said, "Yes, I've read that line as well. You called yourself a nigger once, and now you find it's true. Your line is one of poets and kings, ambitious beyond their station perhaps but possessed of immense will. In the records of Chartres one finds that a certain Canon Raimbaud contributed to the reconstruction of the cathedral after its terrible fire in eleven ninety-four. What one does not find in the records is the canon's responsibility for that terrible event."

"An ancestor of mine burned Chartres?" Arthur said with incredulous delight. It was too perfect, the kind of family story he would have reveled in at seventeen and which even now gave him a thrill of misanthropic pride. Not just an Abyssinian in the family tree, but an arsonist responsible for one of the great disasters of the twelfth century.

"The original cathedral was built on a grove sacred to the pagans of the area, and later became a shrine to a relic of the Virgin, which of course was fake. The power of belief is a marvel in itself, though, and the canon realized it must be destroyed and rebuilt to his purpose. From the ashes rose the famous book of stone, sculpted with the stories of the Patriarchs, and with the story of the Ark." Arthur had seen the north porch of Chartres. He was nodding, face still split by a grin of near delirium. "The canon helped finance this reconstruction with gold from the Templar coffers, and he acquired a French name. He married, or at any rate begat children, and seven hundred years later his descendant has returned to his ancestral home.

"Your father's work. You must take your place in the line, and you must complete the task. Fail, and the Grail falls into the hands of those quiet Italians you see flanking Menelik on his couch; or it falls to Menelik himself. Either would be a disaster. You must find the Grail, Arthur, and having found it you must give it up. Return it to the Ark. This is what we work for. This is what we have died for. This is what you must do."

His father's work. Arthur could not but accept. Go to Cairo, Jerome said. In Egypt stories live like flies in amber, unchanged. There is much we do not know, but we believe that the truth of the Grail's location can be found in Cairo.

LANCE

"SO WHAT THE HELL does this have to do with anything?" Lance asked when Jack had finished his story.

"I'm trying to tell you what this is all about. Rimbaud knew it; it's all through his poetry, he knew even before he knew, and when he went to Egypt he hadn't written a line of poetry in fourteen years. Martian radio, Lance. The voices come from the Martian radio, and when they talk you listen."

"Don't tell me about dead poets and the Holy Grail, Jack. If you're a magician, tell me about my brother."

"I am," Jack said, and when he wouldn't say anything else Lance left the park and wandered around the city trying to think of a reason not to just get drunk and forget about the whole thing. In the end he went back to the hotel and stared at the cracked ceiling, head empty except for a formless worry that the world was full of lunatics and he himself had lost any way to tell what was real.

Every morning for a week, Lance got out of bed, ate eggs at one diner or another, and sat on a park bench writing his mother letters that he never sent. He wrote them carefully, trying to let her know he was okay without saying too much about what he was doing, which was mostly trying to figure out how much of Jack Spicer's magic show was just show. Tarot cards, random lines of poetry, nonsensical references to Egyptian mythology, and this Rimbaud that Spicer kept harping on about—somehow Spicer wanted Lance to believe it all had something to do with him, and with Dwight. Lance was afraid that if he decided to mail his mother one of the letters, he wouldn't be able to keep himself from saying something about Dewey. His mother was not a woman to indulge false hope; if he told her he was starting to wonder if maybe Jack was right, she'd have him locked up. Out of self-preservation she'd decided a long time ago that Dewey was dead, kidnapped and murdered by one of the hoboes who rode the rails that cut through Dexter near the old house. Search parties had combed the woods and dragged the river for weeks without finding Dewey's body, and in the end the police had decided that he'd run away. Twelve-year-old boys did it every day.

But the shirt and the shoes . . .

Dewey's dead, Lance told himself. Jack is a drunk who believes in Tarot cards. Why do you let him get to you?

It came back to Ellie. If she hadn't written him that letter, he'd already be back in Michigan. He'd never have met Jack Spicer, and all of his carefully walled-in guilt about his brother would have kept its distance.

Time to go see her. He'd been walking almost all day, every day, for more than a week, and already he could feel the muscles of his leg coming around. His hip didn't hurt as much either. The doctors were right. He was on the way back, and it was time to sit down with Ellie so they could get to know each other again. He'd tell her about Spicer, and she'd laugh, and all the business about magic and poets would be so much pie-in-the-sky bullshit again.

He'd get his feet back on the ground.

The day's letter was done. He folded it into his pocket with the others and headed down Columbus to the station where he could catch the F train to Berkeley. Along the way he got hungry, and he detoured into a diner to grub some eggs. He was eating so many eggs that he was going to turn into a chicken, but that was one of the things he'd missed in Korea, real eggs and the time to sit and eat them.

San Francisco was seeping into him. He was no longer surprised by the bums who wandered in and out, or the sight of groups of Chinese eating pancakes, and it didn't even faze him when the guy next to him at the counter had tried to pay for his eggs and toast with a poem. "Goddammit, Bob," the counterman said. "I told you not to try this shit again. You want to eat here, you bring money."

Bob hit him with a long spiel about pure exchange, poem as sustenance, money as the force that alienated one man from another. The whole exchange left Lance purely joyous at being in a place where things like that happened. He'd have to put it in tomorrow's letter, and maybe he'd send that one just to be able to grin at the vision of his mother's reaction. Already he was chuckling to himself over the yolky smears on his plate.

Then Jerry Kazmierski walked in and said, "Jesus fucking Christ. Where have you been?"

Jerry looked old, was Lance's first thought. Old and scared. He was losing his hair, and what was left stood out from the sides of his head in wild red tangles. The lenses of his glasses were nearly opaque with dust and scratches. He smelled like bourbon. Jerry K. had never been a prime physical specimen, but two years had turned him into a sallow, shambling wreck. A sallow, shambling, angry wreck. He sat next to Lance and said, "Did you not pay attention to the letter? What the hell is wrong with you?"

"Nothing's wrong with me, Jerry. I just wanted a little time to get myself together. What the hell's wrong with you? You look like you woke up dead this morning."

"I wake up dead every morning." Jerry lit a Pall Mall and asked the counterman for coffee. "Today more than most. You want to know why?"

Lance didn't.

"Because Ellie's gone, shithead, and it's because of you," Jerry said. "She was waiting for you because you didn't come see her and the army didn't know where you'd gone, but you've been crawling up your own asshole for the past week and now she's gone."

"So I'll go home and find her," Lance said. "No need for you to babysit us. What are you, matchmaking?"

"You'll go home and find her." Jerry snorted out a cloud of smoke. "She didn't go back home. She's gone. As in not of her own accord, Einstein. Somebody didn't want her to talk to you."

"Jerry. Listen to yourself. Ellie got sick of waiting around for me, she's pissed off, she went home. I don't blame her. I'll go home too, and we'll patch it up. And it's none of your business anyway. Who asked you?"

"Ellie asked me. Your mom asked me. You think I've enjoyed wandering around here for a week? I hate California. Everybody's so goddamn happy here. Fucking suffocates me. I can't wait to get back to New York."

"You live in New York?"

"Wouldn't live anywhere else. You give me a chance, I'll tell you why. But not here. Come on. Time for you to step up and go after your lady love."

"She's in Michigan, Jerry. I'll call her house today and apologize. Butt out."

Jerry threw up his hands. "You know, I should. I should just forget about this whole mess and go back to New York. Wash all this sappy sunshiny happiness off. And I would too, but you're already starting to talk to the wrong people."

"You sound like my mom."

"That's because your mom and I both know more about this than you do. You run into a guy named Jack Spicer, by any chance?"

"What if I did?"

"If you did, it means that people are starting to notice."

"Oh no," Lance said, with all the sarcasm he could muster. "Lord help us if they notice."

"You think it's funny, but Spicer's shtick about magic isn't all bullshit. He knows something about what's going on. Not as much as he thinks he does, but something. He do the Tarot business with you?"

This startled Lance. "Yeah, why?" he said, adding the question before he could stop himself. He didn't really want to know. If Spicer was just making a pass, he thought, I'm going to black his eye for him next time we meet.

"What was the card?"

"I don't know, some kind of tree thing."

Jerry nodded. "Figures."

"Figures how? He probably had a whole deck of them. He was just showing off for his friends."

Now Jerry stubbed out his cigarette and folded his hands. "He ask you if you had a brother?"

And that was it. The whole conversation, the whole crazy business of Jerry K. dragging himself out of whatever hole he'd found in New York just to drive across the country and hassle Lance about Ellie, wasn't funny anymore.

"If there's one thing I'm not going to talk about, Jerry," Lance said, keeping his voice as even as he could, "it's Dewey. You ought to know that."

"And you ought to know that it's way past ordinary coincidence that the day you walk away from the army, you run into a guy who starts asking you all kinds of questions that are more than a little similar to the things Ellie came out here to talk to you about. Unless you're either too dumb or too far gone pitying yourself about your fucking leg. Is that what the problem is here? Poor you, got blown up in Korea so you're going to crawl into a hole and pull it in after you?"

Lance got up. He wasn't going to listen to this, especially not from a certified loony like Jerry Kazmierski. "The army's got shrinks, Jerry. I don't need this from you."

"Oh yes you do," Jerry said.

"Leave me alone," Lance said, and left. Jerry didn't follow him.

He walked, working the leg, heading south out of the part of the city he'd gotten to know over the past week. An hour later he was lost, and liking it. Back where nobody knew him. That morning he'd been basking in North Beach; now Jerry K. had come along and ruined it for him. Lance debated just keeping on, walking south out of the city and down the peninsula, thumbing his way down the Pacific Coast Highway to Los Angeles or San Diego or Mexico. Anywhere to get away from people coming out of the woodwork to drop loads of mysterious crap about Dwight. If Ellie wanted to talk to him, fine. He'd call her when he was damn good and ready. But Spicer and Jerry could go to hell and take their diarrhea of the mouth with them.

The bag was back at the hotel, though. If he was going to hitchhike to Mexico, he'd need a change of underwear. Oh well. Today he'd settle for just being left alone.

On his left, a row of warehouses ended in a huge railyard. Rusting boxcars sat in long strings on dead-end sections of track, weeds growing around their wheels. Lance's grandfather had died in a railyard like this one, bleeding out on a track after an engine had backed into the flatcar whose linkage he was cleaning. It was the one thing he knew about his family. His mother never talked about his and Dewey's father, and she'd never had much to say about her mother either, so he clung to the fact of his grandfather's death because it added certainty to his life. Railyards were like shrines to him. Every time he saw one, he stopped and thought of his grandfather, and the fact of tracks and weeds and rusting boxcars had come to feel like a family tree. Even in Korea. Train yards looked the same everywhere.

And Lance had always suspected that whoever had taken Dewey had come off the tracks that ran through Dexter. It was an instinct, nothing more, but it had never left him. Train tracks seemed like secret highways to Lance, and all the hoboes who rode them carried secrets. A hidden America, with the truths of Lance's history clanking through its night.

He crossed the street and walked along the tracks, tapping his hand along the sides of the cars and wondering where they'd gone before being abandoned here. What they'd carried, why they'd been left. Did anyone still know about them? Was there a guy in an office somewhere who ran across a file in his desk once in a while and reminded himself oh yeah, I should do something about those?

A little way ahead of him, a guy was sitting in the open door of a boxcar, a hobo if ever Lance had seen one: skinny, sprung boots, flannel shirt, canvas pants the color of old grease, and skin much the same under a straggly beard. "Hey, buddy," the guy said. "Good thing you're here, 'cause I make it a point not to drink alone and I was just about to compromise my principles." From a pocket he produced a pint of whiskey and held it out to Lance. "Care for a snort?"

After the morning he'd had, Lance did indeed. He hoisted himself up onto the car, reached out for the bottle, unscrewed the cap, and took a long pull. Perfect. It burned down his throat and bloomed in his stomach, and Jerry K. melted away along with Spicer and Ellie and Dwight and his damn leg that let's face it would never work the same way again.

The hobo took a drink of his own, swinging his heels against the car's undercarriage, ka-thump ka-thump ka-thump. "Like to see a young man who enjoys his whiskey," he said after he'd wiped his mouth.

"Whiskey's got a lot going for it," Lance said. He'd acquired a taste for liquor while on leave in Seoul. It was cheaper than beer, and easier to carry when one of your buddies picked a fight and got you kicked out of the bar. Plus boom, it hit you, no deliberation like drinking beer demanded. You wanted a topic change in your own internal conversation, whiskey did the trick, no questions asked. He hit the bottle again and handed it back.

"Sure does," the hobo agreed. "What brings you down trackside?"

"Just taking a walk. Some days everyone you know has gone nuts, and you just have to take a walk. Be by yourself for a while."

"I'm with you," the hobo said. "People don't make no goddamn sense. Especially family, you know what I mean?"

He looked at Lance. "Family is a bitch for sure," he concluded, and reached into his pocket, Lance figured for cigarettes, but the hobo came out with a knife and right then as the whiskey was just getting to his head Lance turned into a soldier again. He stopped seeing the knife, saw only the arc of the arm that held it, and still sitting he pivoted inside the thrust, one hand coming down to clamp on the hobo's forearm and the other hammering into the hobo's neck just under the jaw. His momentum carried them both off the edge of the boxcar floor, and they hit the ground together, faces close enough to kiss. Lance caught the hobo's beard and forced his head back. The hobo hit him on the side of the head, hard enough to blur his vision, but Lance got him with a knee and in the fall the hobo had lost his knife. Say goodnight, Gracie, Lance thought in the voice of his drill sergeant from basic. Bigger man gets in close, fight's over. He threw his weight to the right, rolling both of them over, and let go of the hobo's arm to clamp both hands around his neck. The hobo was hitting him, but leg or no leg Lance's hands were still strong, and there under the summer sun Lance strangled the man, letting go only when the hobo's arms had fallen limp and the blood vessels had burst in his eyes. He sat there straddling the body, breathing hard, his mind slowly returning to California.

Seven.

He had to get out of there. Cover his tracks and get out. He stood, staggering as he straightened from his crouch, and caught the dead man under his armpits to drag and shove him underneath the boxcar. The knife still lay in the weedy gravel near the furrows dug by the dying hobo's heels—but he wasn't a hobo, now was he? *Family's a bitch,* he'd said, and winked. Jesus, Lance thought. Ellie. He threw the knife under the car next to the body, kicked the bottle away, walked in a tight circle, mentally beating himself for his pure stupidity. Beyond coincidence was goddamn right. Jerry was right. *Something* was going on. Whoever the dead man was, he'd followed Lance, and for all Lance knew he'd followed Jerry too. And Ellie.

"No no no," he said, and dropped to his knees to go through the dead man's pockets. Nothing. A cold feeling cut through the whiskey fuzz in Lance's head. This guy had been an assassin, anonymous whether he succeeded or failed. Somewhere someone was waiting for him to report back. Somewhere someone wanted Lance Porter dead.

Put it together, he thought. Think. You come home, there's a letter from Ellie saying she's got to talk, Spicer's waiting for you on the library steps, Jerry K. appears out of nowhere, and they're all hinting that something's going on but none of them will give it to you straight. Spicer and Jerry could both be written off as crazy, but Ellie? What an idiot I am, Lance thought.

The dead man had a tattoo on his wrist. A square cross, each arm thickening away from the center. Like the German Iron Cross, but not exactly. Nazis? Lance wondered. What the hell would they have to do with him? Could be nothing, just a guy with a tattoo.

Idiot. Nothing was nothing right then.

But none of it squared, either. All he had was odd coincidences, and the only way he could fit them together was to put Jack right in the middle of it. Jack had known something about him. No way he just *happened* to be there on the library steps when Lance got off that particular bus and got cold feet about talking to Ellie.

Time to get gone. Even an abandoned railyard had people

moving through it. Lance's bag was at the flophouse; he had to get it, and get gone from San Francisco.

But before he left, he had to talk to Jack.

He was in and out of the hotel in ten minutes flat, including a fast shower. Digging around in the bottom of the bag for clean clothes, Lance got a surprise: his service rifle, the trusty old M-1, lay underneath everything else, cleaned and disassembled and wrapped. On an impulse, he rummaged through the rest of his gear, and damn if there weren't four shells rattling around one of the pouches of his web belt. It was illegal as hell, not to mention a violation of fifty or so army regulations, but at that point Lance was ready to kiss whichever absentminded quartermaster had forgotten to collect his weapon. Next time someone tried to kill him, he'd be ready.

The guy at the desk was glad to see him go, especially when Lance didn't ask for a refund on the extra week he'd paid for. Lance got on a streetcar, took it up over the hill, got off near the foot of Powell Street, and spent the day kicking around the piers, trying to stay with crowds and breaking into a sweat every time he saw a cop. He ate a cheeseburger at a grill overlooking the Embarcadero, and then he started walking back toward North Beach. No telling when or if Jack would show up at the Black Cat, but if he was there tonight Lance had to make sure not to miss him.

By the time he got to the Monkey Block, it was almost dark, and evening fog was creeping up out of cracks in the sidewalk. Lance paused in one of the Monkey Block's overhung doorways and set about working up a plan. He could wait for Jack, try to intercept him before he got into the bar, but if Jack had lots of friends around he'd start playing to his audience, and if he did that Lance figured he just might belt the guy.

What decided him against passive surveillance was the simple fact that he had to take a leak. One of the things Lance had sworn to himself in the hospital was that after Korea he'd never void bladder or bowel outside again, and what the hell, it wouldn't make any difference if Jack came in and found him there. He went into the Black Cat, straight to the men's, and pissed for what seemed like three days, thinking the whole time of the last time he'd been in the bar, when Jack had as much as told him that Dewey was alive. Jack had been right about overloading him, but now he'd had time to think it over, and now Ellie was gone, and Lance was damn well going to find out what Jack knew about what.

When he came out he ordered two shots and a beer, and buried the shots one right after the other. A day like this, a guy had a right to get shitfaced, what the hell. The world was full of liquor, and he needed to wash the taste of killing out of his mouth and his mind. He drained the beer and ordered another.

At the back of the room a skinny and acne-scarred guy with a wispy bit of beard was reading short poems, one after another, dropping the sheets on the floor as he finished each. The first one Lance heard was just three names: "J. Edgar Hoover, Dwight David Eisenhower, Joseph McCarthy," the poet said, and with a wink added, "I call that one 'Symptoms.'"

Laughter from some of the audience. The poet went straight to another:

> In the oven rising
> Between one war and the next
> Mushroom Cloud Soufflé.

More laughter, and the poet held up a hand. Someone brushed against Lance, leaning up against the jukebox. He glanced over and saw a girl, tall and slim with dark hair that washed over her shoulders, wearing a flowing skirt in some kind of bright pattern. She felt him looking and gave him a smile, and he didn't mean to, but he smiled back as the poet flipped aside a sheet and read his next:

> Soldier coming home
> Bleeds his way over oceans
> Doesn't know the way.

Something broke loose inside Lance, and tears started in his eyes. That's me, he thought. That poem is about me. It was a shock like he'd never felt, a churning blend of loneliness and frustration and gratitude, and in the troughs between waves of feeling he had the thought that Spicer was right, that he'd just become part of the story. All over the world people go through their lives never knowing this, he thought. I might have missed this, I might have just gone on not knowing that someone understands.

The girl touched his arm, and he swiped a sleeve across his eyes before looking at her. "You okay?" she said, and he nodded. "That's the thing with haiku," she said. "A hundred in a row are stupid, and then there's one like an arrow straight into your soul."

"Haiku," Lance said. So there was a name for that kind of poem.

"I'm Gwen," the girl said. "What's your name?"

"Lance." *I killed a guy today,* he wanted to say. *With my bare hands. But he was going to kill me.* The urge to confess was a physical need.

"You don't look like a local, Lance. What brings you here?"

He was still so overwhelmed by the day, and now by the poem, and a little by this girl Gwen who apparently didn't feel embarrassed to start conversations in bars with men she'd never met, that the question stumped him for a moment. Then he snapped back into focus. "You know Jack Spicer?"

Gwen wrinkled her nose. "Don't tell me you're looking for him."

"Yeah, I am. He——"

As if summoned, Spicer appeared at Lance's elbow, opposite Gwen. "That last one got you, didn't it?" he said with his squinty grin that Lance already hated. "Superficial sentimental bullshit in an old man's form that doesn't even work in English, and you lap it up with tears in your eyes. That's not fucking poetry, that's posing. Poetry is about truth, and it's never obvious. What you're feeling right now is exactly what Mildred Bronski of Dubuque, Iowa, feels when the girl gets married at the end of *Guiding Light*. It's fake manipulative crap, and you should know better. Here's real poetry: 'Long after the season and days, the living and land, / A flag of flesh, bleeding over silken seas'——that's you. Forget this idiot. Rimbaud will tell you what you need to know."

"You just can't stand to see anybody happy, can you, Jack?" Lance said.

"Happiness is fake too. Nobody who really thinks about anything can be honestly happy. I just don't believe in pretending."

"What a load. You're a miserable asshole, so you want everyone else to be miserable too."

Jack shrugged, and Lance noticed that Gwen was gone. "Have it your way, soldier. Doesn't matter; you'll find out soon enough."

"Find out what?"

"How fake everything is when you think you're happy. But like I said, forget it. You come down for the reading? Getting to be quite the 'gone cat' for a soldier boy from Michigan, Lance Porter."

Lance let it all pass. He'd stored the poem away, and right now he needed to get some answers about Ellie. Not to mention keeping the cops off his back. "I came down here looking for you. Come on."

"Come where?" Jack said, putting a little flirty lilt into it. "Lance, I thought you said——"

"Jack, don't fuck with me right now. You come with me right fucking now or so help me God I'll put you in the hospital."

"My goodness. This is way too much emotion to be about baseball, so hmmm, let's see . . ." Jack's puffy face lit up with theatrically malicious delight. "You want to talk about your fish, don't you? Isn't that always the way. Guys like you don't have the time of day for us pansies until you want us to decipher your girlfriends for you. What's the matter, Lance? She swim away? You worried someone else got a hook into her?"

Lance hit him, flush on the mouth. Jack hit the floor, and around them people erupted in shouts, drowning out the poet who had followed the haiku artist. Jack's friends came out of nowhere to shove Lance toward the door. He pushed them away and started to go after Jack again, but someone hit him over the head and his legs went out from under him. Through doubled vision he saw Jack sit up, still wearing that goddamn smile.

"There's other fish in the sea, Lance," he said, and the next thing Lance knew he was outside, on his ass in the street with his bag next to him and the bartender shouting from the doorway.

"You don't come in my place anymore. Ever! You want to pick on fairies, do it somewhere else!"

The door slammed, and Lance waited for his head to stop spinning. Time passed. The fog thickened. People walked around him on the way to wherever they went when they had places to go. Okay, Lance thought. I made a mess of that. But Jack is goddamn well going to talk to me.

He was getting to his feet when the door opened behind him, and a woman's voice said, "You sure made Jack's night. He loves it when someone gets mad enough to take a swing at him." Gwen steadied Lance as he shouldered his bag. "Buy a girl a drink?"

What else was he going to do? "Sure," Lance said. They walked around the corner and down Columbus to a place called Vesuvio's. The waitress came and Lance, after a double take, ordered Gwen the whiskey sour she asked for and a Rainier for himself. "Kind of an old man's drink, isn't it?" he said. "Whiskey sour? I think of golf courses."

"Where are you from?" Gwen said playfully. "I drink them all the time."

Maybe it was the blow to the head, maybe just the echoes of death he still felt in his hands, maybe just simple loneliness, but Lance began to have visions of what he'd heard referred to as free love. Unlike many of his comrades in the army who'd spent leave time in Seoul and Tokyo, he was still a virgin, and he was glad there was a table between him and Gwen. Was this the girl? he thought. She came right up to me in the Black Cat, and now she's drinking whiskey with me on the same day that I find out Ellie split, and if that wasn't fate, what was? It struck him that Ellie didn't want him anymore. Whatever Jerry said, she'd made that clear by leaving. He was free.

Gwen was looking at him. "What is going on in your head?" she asked. "Your eyes were practically crossing."

"Just thinking how strange all this is. I didn't know for sure that Spicer would be at the Black Cat, and then he had to say the one thing in the world that would piss me off enough to deck him, and then there you are to pick me up off the sidewalk."

"If you say the word *coincidence,* I'm leaving," Gwen said. It was exactly what Lance had been about to say, but he didn't want her to leave, so he kept his mouth shut. "Coincidence doesn't really exist. It's just a word people invented to deal with their expectations being wrong." She looked at him over her glass. "Be where you are, Lance. I asked you to buy me a drink, you did." She finished it. "Now I'm hungry. How about Chinese?"

They walked to Chinatown. Lance made a show of offering her his arm, and Gwen laughed as she took it. "My hero! My knight in shining armor." Walking with her through the fog, Lance thought he was going to explode from the pressure of his lust. Now this isn't right, he chided himself. Ellie's your girl.

Over lo mein and General Tso's chicken, Gwen talked incessantly, telling him about her childhood (boring, mostly in Oakhurst, Illinois) and her trip to San Francisco (a long train ride and men wouldn't leave her alone, but she was determined to make her mark somehow in the big city). "What do you plan to do?" Lance said.

"Who knows?" she said. "I haven't been here very long. Something will come along. It's just a matter of knowing, and grabbing the chance when it comes."

Maybe it was just the context, the fact that they were the only white people in the restaurant, but Lance was struck by the way Gwen suddenly looked Oriental. Something about the planes of her face, the glossy black of her hair . . . he didn't know, but the surroundings were getting to him. It seemed strange to be speaking English. He kept expecting her to answer him in Chinese. Well, there were plenty of Orientals in California; maybe the gardener had planted more than tulips somewhere a couple of generations back. Wasn't the kind of thing you could ask someone about, though, and he wasn't sure he wanted to know. It was enough to be here, talking to this exotic stranger whom he'd met through two coincidentally related coincidences and soaking up the atmosphere of Chinatown. It struck Lance that this was the first Oriental food he'd had since leaving Korea. Had he been avoiding it, afraid of the memories yellow faces and slanted eyes might generate? He'd never seen the guy who loaded the shell that left him with his limp; he could have been Korean, Chinese, even Russian.

Besides which, the closest he'd ever come to dying was earlier that afternoon.

Gwen was looking at him again, something sharp in her eyes behind a playful expression. "Am I boring? Your eyes are crossing again."

"No, sorry. I just—" The confession was on Lance's lips: *I killed a man today, but he was going to kill me and I don't know why.* He opened his mouth again and was surprised at what came out. "I just, you know, was sitting by myself on the curb and all of a sudden this beautiful girl comes up and we have a drink and now dinner, and . . . man, it's kind of like a dream. Something you'd see in a movie. The Mysterious Stranger."

She laughed and put a hand to her mouth as she swallowed a mouthful of noodles. "Not so mysterious, really. Just a girl in the big city who got a laugh out of seeing Jack Spicer planted on his ass. Whew, I'm full," she said, pushing away her plate and patting her mouth. Dainty mouth, bottom teeth showing just a bit, the curve of the lips pronounced like a pinup girl's, reminding Lance of how alluring the rest of her was. "So what are you doing here, Lance?"

Now that was a tough one. Looking for my girlfriend, he could say. She's disappeared and an old friend of mine from high school says it's my fault. Or he could tell her all about Jack's Holy Grail obsession. "Just out of the service, thought I'd travel around a bit," he said. "That poem I heard tonight got me thinking, you know? I'm that guy who doesn't know the way. Guess I'm just kicking around until I figure it out." He put down his chopsticks and took a drink of water, leaning his head from side to side as he tried to articulate his next thought.

"The problem is," he concluded, not knowing how else to say it, "you can kick around a place like this for a long time, and still not figure out what you're looking for."

Gwen was looking at him very seriously now, her eyes wide as they drank in the sight of him drinking in the sight of her. She moistened her lips with her tongue, and muscles twitched all up and down Lance's spine.

"Well, even if you weren't looking for me, I'm glad I was there," she said. "You're not what I was expecting."

"How's that?"

"I thought you'd be, I don't know. More of a soldier, I guess. I just asked you out because you punched Jack. But as it turns out . . ." Her voice dropped to a near whisper, and all her city bravado vanished. "I kind of like you, Lance."

She sounded nervous, and just for a moment Lance saw

something tender under the gone-girl front. A sweetness. He realized that he liked her too.

Then the tough-girl mask was on again. Her eyes met his, all boldness and mischief. "Well, Lance, it's getting late for a single girl in the city," she said. "How about if I show you the way as far as my apartment?"

Back on the street again, Lance thought dimly through his intoxication with Gwen that there was an awful lot of San Francisco he'd never see if he spent all of his time in bars. He lost his train of thought as Gwen rested a hand on the back of his neck. "Where are you staying?" she said. "I don't want to take you too far out of your way."

"No, it's okay. I'm just down the street here. Crashing with a friend for now until I decide whether or not I want to stay." Lance opened his mouth and words came out, but the entire focus of his being was her hand—slender, long-fingered, ringless and without nail polish—on his neck, and the gentle bump of her hip against his as they walked. *Is what's happening what I think is happening?* he thought, and what felt like a magnetic wave rolled from her hand down into his groin. His balls felt like they weighed a ton apiece. *Give up*, he thought. *Stop trying to put it all together, stop thinking. She's right. Be where you are.* It felt good to let go.

They got off Columbus and Lance quickly lost track of where he was as she cut through alleys and across small parks and squares. Gwen's apartment building was new, if the elevator was anything to go by, and Lance enjoyed the feeling of lift under his feet—oh, what tremors the elevator's start set off in his balls, and oh, what equally tremulous thoughts tangled in his twenty-year-old mind. Gwen leaned against him as they rose, giggling, "Hoo boy, whiskey sour." Lance dared to put his arm around her, and she actually snuggled into his side. He was saved from having to speak by their arrival on the tenth floor. Her building was shaped like a capital *H,* with the elevators in the crossbar. "It's ten seventeen, down here," Gwen said, leading him around to the left. She left the door to her apartment open and disappeared into the dark. Lance shut the door and locked it before turning around. He wished he had a coat to take off.

Gwen turned on a lamp and dropped her purse on the end table between a red couch and a brown leather easy chair. Behind the chair a doorway opened onto a kitchen, and past that, to Lance's right, a hallway lined with framed pencil sketches. Gwen went into the kitchen, took a bottle of wine from the refrigerator. "Drink?"

"Sure," Lance said. He sat on the couch, dizzy with the newness of it all. This was the first apartment he'd ever visited with a woman who had no worries that her parents might come home early. What did you do in a situation like this? Did you let the girl make the first move? Gwen had approached him, gone to dinner with him, invited him into her apartment; when would she expect him to pick up the hint and take over? What would she do if he didn't? Oh God ohgod ohgod, Lance thought, the nerves in his fingers crackling with the imagined texture of her skin.

She sat next to him and put the bottle of wine on the coffee table. He took a glass and she raised hers. "To chance meetings." Their glasses clinked and Lance drank, feeling the heat of the wine roll down his throat and settle between his legs. He had no idea what time it was, what day. The only thing in his world was Gwen with her black hair and long legs and dress that shifted on her hips as she walked.

"I want to kiss you," he blurted.

"All right." She smiled and shifted to face him. "Better put your glass down first."

He did, and then he kissed her, first brushing her lips and feeling the taste of them, holding himself back. Her tongue flicked against his, and he forgot to breathe, and then he lost his grip on the last slippery rock of self-control. The hand he'd held the wineglass with tangled itself in her hair; she made a sound low in her throat and ran her hands down the sides of his neck onto his chest. Lance mimicked her. Gwen was braless, and he moaned back to her, feeling the smooth weight of her breast in his hand, the perfect size of it. She undid the four buttons that ran from the neck of her dress down its left sleeve, then guided his head to her. He took her nipple in his mouth, brown leaf on sea-foam, and felt it rise under his tongue. Her other hand trailed down his stomach and gripped his erection. "Ohh," he murmured into her breast, and opened his hips to her.

"Stop a second," she whispered. She took a drink, stood to shrug out of her dress. Naked, she drank again and said, "Undress for me, Lance."

He unbuttoned his shirt, stood as she had to take off his pants, and then had to sit again to unlace his boots. He felt clumsy and somehow powerless, struggling out of his clothes when she'd disrobed so gracefully. At last he got his shoes and socks off, then stripped off his pants. Gwen came to him, kissed along the line of his jaw and down his neck while her hands roamed across his back. She found a scar and ran a fingernail across it, moved down to his hip and the top of the jagged crescent that marked both wound and surgical scar. Lance jerked at her touch there, and she murmured "Ssshhhh" into the hollow of his throat as she traced the scar from above his hipbone down to where his leg narrowed above the knee. "Such a terrible wound," she whispered, and knelt.

Lance cried out softly, feeling her lips brush along the length of the scar. Her hair slithered around his penis before falling against his thighs and he shut his eyes, suddenly afraid that if he looked at her she would disappear. "Gwen," he said.

"Mm."

I killed someone today, he wanted to say. Instead the admission: "I've never done this before."

Her lips reversed direction, moved from leg to hip to stomach and on up until she was facing him again. She was swaying slightly from side to side, the hair below the curve of her belly brushing the head of his penis, and Lance almost wanted her to stop in case he embarrassed himself. "Your first time shouldn't be on a couch," Gwen said, and took his hand to lead him down the dark hallway.

She drew back the covers on her bed and lay back, keeping her hands on Lance's hips as he followed. Her mouth found his, kept him steady as she guided him between her legs. He thrust and she lifted her hips to meet him, breaking the kiss and whispering into his ear, "Remember me, Lance, remember me," and he wanted again to stop because even now he knew that when it was over he'd never have another first time, but her hips were moving, and the heat and smell of her surrounded him and her hands gripped the big muscles of his ass, and he bunched the sheet in his fists and drove into her until at last but too soon he came with a series of small gasps like weeping.

"Gwen," he said when he could speak again.

"Lance." He started to withdraw but she held him in, rocking against him. Lance followed the motion, rode with her, his eyes open now as hers closed, and her jaw fell open and little beads of sweat appeared on her nose and her hair fell like shadows across her face and finally she said, "Oh. God. Lance," three distinct words, and bucked so hard against him that he pulled the sheets loose. Shrouded and held against him, Gwen rode her orgasm, face against his chest and nails digging into the small of his back. Lance held her, marveling, the newness of touch and smell and sound driving itself into him as he thought *Yes I will, Gwen. Yes I will remember you.*

At last she was still, and they settled into the bed. Lance lay his head between her breasts, sweat slick on his cheek. Gwen's fingers moved up his back to stroke his hair, and for some reason he remembered that he needed a haircut.

"Now we're bound together," Gwen said.

Lance felt the words in her chest. "Bound together," he repeated, and thought of Ellie.

He was absolutely tranquil, as if the marrow of his bones had exploded out of him with his orgasm. It seemed like he should sleep, but he'd never been so aware of every part of his body: the quiet weightlessness in his groin, the faint chill of sweat evaporating from his back, the ever-present throb of the war in his hip. He grunted, shifting next to her so he could lie on his back and relax away from the pain, and Gwen's hand found the scar again. "Does it always hurt?" she asked.

"Yeah," Lance said, and then realized that it wasn't true. His hip hadn't hurt at all when he'd walked into Seals Stadium, the first time. The pain had just gone, and then come back the next morning when he'd been trying to write a letter to his mother.

And it hadn't hurt while he was strangling the tattooed hobo in the train yard.

"Terrible, to be always in pain," Gwen said, her fingers touching here and there along the scar: here where his femur had split skin and muscle to dig in the mud, there where a piece of steel large enough that the doctors could read the name of the factory on it had buried itself in the hollow of his hipbone. "Maybe you forgot for a minute?"

That sweetness again. Lance nodded in the dark. "Maybe I did," he said.

He woke before dawn, thrust from sleep by guilt so acute he was out of bed and dressing before he'd made any kind of conscious decision. Gwen stirred and called softly from the bedroom. "Where are you going? Stay with me, Lance."

"I still have to talk to Jack," he said, which was true even though it had nothing to do with anything right then.

He heard her slide across the bed, and then she came out into the living room to sit next to him on the couch while he tied his boots. She stroked a palm along his back. Outside, the sky was just lightening, and the coming day filled Lance with a terrible fear of having to live with what he'd done. He couldn't think; apologies to Ellie flooded through his mind, every way he could come up with, and none of them meant a goddamn thing. Gwen laid her head on his shoulder, and he sat with his shirt bunched in his hands, wanting to throw her off or tear the shirt into shreds, or just fall back into the couch and scream at the intolerable mix of exhilaration and remorse that twisted inside him.

"There are some things we should talk about," Gwen said.

Lance sat still a little longer, then slowly brought his shirt up and slipped it over his head. Gwen moved, and he finished dressing.

"I can't talk, Gwen," he said. "I have to get going. Talk to Jack."

"Lance. Lance, look at me."

He did, seeing her in the clean unbearable light of dawn. When he'd sat on the couch, he'd been barely a shadow to himself; now, minutes later, morning light picked out the lines of her face, and she was too beautiful to leave. So he stood up, it was the only way to save himself, and he said again, "I have to talk to Jack."

"I know you do," she said. "But you should know that he's lying to you. He doesn't know it, but he is."

"Lying to me about what?"

"Jack knows enough to think he knows everything, enough to figure that what he doesn't know he can fill in with his own personal mythology. That's what he calls poetry, or magic. He fills in gaps with what he wants to be true."

Too much like what Jerry had said the day before. "I don't know what that means, Gwen."

"It means that he's right about you."

I'm supposed to ask, Lance thought. *Right about me how?* But he didn't want to hear whatever her answer would be, so he just said, "If he's right about me, I should listen to him."

"Listen to him, yes," Gwen said. "Believe him, maybe not."

"When you say we need to talk, do you mean about this King Arthur thing?" Lance asked.

"Not really. Kind of. I can't explain it sitting naked on my couch, Lance. If we're going to talk about this, let me get dressed and let's sit down and talk about it."

"What is this, Gwen? Does everybody in San Francisco believe in the tooth fairy and Bigfoot too? I'm not a king. I'm not a knight. I was a corporal in the army, and I have a hole in my leg. That's it. I—" He caught himself, considered what he was about to say. "I would like to see you again. But right now I have to talk to Jack. It's about family."

She was nodding as he finished. "Yes, it is," she said, and from her inflection Lance guessed she meant it differently than he had. But she didn't pursue it. "Jack probably went home with Terrence, the boy he was with last night. Terrence lives just down Montgomery from the Black Cat. His door is next to a shoe store, toward Columbus. They're probably still there."

Lance waited for her to go on, but she'd put the ball in his court. Me or Jack, she was saying, but what she didn't know was that meant her or Dewey, and that was an easy call.

"Thanks," he said. "For the directions and for . . . for last night."

"Your first time should mean something," Gwen said, with a sadness that made Lance feel like he'd used her even though he hadn't meant to. She was looking away from him, and he had the feeling it was so he wouldn't see her cry.

He bent and kissed her forehead, feeling awkward and insufficient. "It did mean something. It did. Can I see you again?"

She nodded without speaking and without looking him in the eye, and Lance went quietly to her door. Then she said, "Remember Lancelot always tries to fight his way through everything. That's what gets him in the end."

What was there to say to that? Lance shut the door softly behind him.

It took him long enough to get his bearings and find his way back to Montgomery that by the time he'd found the shoe store he was nearly in a panic that Spicer had gotten away from him. He could always go to the university, or stake out the Black Cat again—he knew enough about Spicer's routine that finding him wouldn't be hard. Still, he'd gotten himself into a situation he should have avoided, and now everything was more complicated than it should have been. Nothing, he told himself, nothing good comes of loneliness and aggressive girls.

As soon as he thought it, though, it all washed over him again. He smelled Gwen on his skin, could recall every touch of her lips and fingers as if it were happening to him right there on the street. The visions were branded in his memory. So assured last night, so quiet and sad this morning, he thought, and didn't know what it meant.

There was an all-night diner across from the shoe store. Lance settled himself at its counter, ordered coffee, and waited. His stomach hurt, and he had to keep looking at his hands to make sure they weren't shaking. Finally gave virginity the old heave-ho, he thought. Now I'm sitting alone over coffee waiting to button-hole a nut who might know what's happened to my brother and my girlfriend. It wasn't supposed to happen this way.

It was supposed to be Ellie. I've made a terrible mistake.

To pass the time he started reading *Junkie,* but it didn't hold his interest. He had no experience with drugs, no real desire to get any, and no real sympathy for anyone in the book, these beat losers with their habits and misery and their excuses. Every couple of pages he looked across Montgomery to the doorway he'd pegged as Terrence's, whoever Terrence was, and after a while he put the book down and just stared out the window at the empty street. Once in a while a lone figure straggled past; a few of these wanderers doubled back and came into the diner, or cut across the street to linger a little longer in his field of vision. Night-hawks, appearing on the sidewalks like they were born from the fog. He watched them, wondered how he was different, felt a wave of loneliness as he realized he was becoming one of them, just another disconnected traveler with no place to stay and no idea what he'd be doing tomorrow.

"What kind of book is that?" the guy two seats down the counter asked. Lance hadn't registered his presence before, an older colored guy with salt-and-pepper stubble and a pin-striped railroad engineer's cap sitting high on his forehead.

He stuck out his hand. "Harrison Reese. Ex-brakeman, retired. You expecting company?"

"Nope." Lance put the book down and shook. "Lance Porter. Damn fool traveler."

"Traveler?" Reese's graying eyebrows raised. "Where you traveling to? Los Angeles, that's where I'm going."

"Never been there," Lance said. "Just here."

Reese nodded. "This is a nice place. That fog, though . . . brrrr. Especially in the winter. LA's nice all year round." He felt in his pocket, came up with a frayed cigar, stuck it in his mouth and popped a match on his thumbnail. "You gonna go on the road this time of year," he said around the cigar, "you should smoke. Keeps you warm, especially if you ride the rails."

Lance tried not to think of Dewey. "Is that so?"

"Yes, it is. So, Lance Porter, why you traveling? I don't mean to pry."

Lance turned on the stool, facing Reese. "Looking for my girlfriend."

"Ah." He took the cigar out of his mouth, jabbed it at intervals toward Lance. "That's the only true reason a man ever do anything, for a woman. Unless you a fruit. And ain't no soldier boy like you a fruit." He puffed on the cigar, then said, "Mm. That's not true. I've known some men who was pansies and they was in the army. So let's just say it ain't likely."

"Fair enough." Lance was starting to like Harrison Reese. "You ever in the army, Harrison?"

"No," Reese said easily, "I was just too young to join up for the

Spanish War and just too old for the first one over in Europe. Plus I had my girls by then."

"Just too young for the Spanish War?" Lance sat up. "How old are you?"

"Seventy this year. Don't look it, do I?" He laughed, a gravelly chuckle that put Lance in mind of his grandfather Porter, but with that recollection came the dead hobo's face, the burst blood vessels in his eyes. "How 'bout you?"

"Just turned twenty," Lance said, and rolled his eyes. "Spent my last birthday in a hospital across the bay."

"So you seen Korea."

"Yeah, only for about five months. Then Luke the Gook sent me home."

"Where you get hit?"

"My hip, mostly. Broke my leg too, and knocked out one of my teeth. But it's the hip that still bugs me sometimes."

"So your hip's broke and you're just back from the war, and instead of enjoying this fine town you're off to look for a girl who didn't care enough to wait around for you." The old man rested both elbows on the counter and let out a low whistle. "She must really be something."

"Yeah," Lance said, feeling it. "She is."

The counterman came by, sick of serving them coffee. Lance ordered a breakfast he didn't want, and thought what the hell. "Whatever he wants, too," he said, pointing at Harrison Reese, who ordered steak and eggs, hash browns, pancakes, and more coffee. Lance picked at two eggs and toast while Reese plowed through his feast. When they'd sat back from the meal, Harrison started to dig handfuls of change from his coat pockets. "No," Lance said. "I'll get it."

Harrison shook his head. "Don't take charity," he said. "I work for my money, and I pay for my meals."

"It's not charity," Lance said as he picked up the bill. "This might sound strange, but I was kind of losing track of what I'm doing, you know, and talking to you put me straight. That has to be worth breakfast." He took the check to the cash register and paid. Harrison Reese was getting up, too. Lance shook hands with the old man, who still reminded him of his grandfather. "Stay warm, Harrison."

"Get me to LA, and warm won't be no problem." Harrison touched the brim of his hat and walked out. About half an hour later Jack and his boyfriend appeared across the street. They went into the diner next to the boyfriend's apartment, and Lance gave them a couple of minutes to settle in before heading across.

They were sitting in a booth, Jack facing away from the door. Lance stopped and leaned on the table. "You guys mind a third?"

Terrence looked like he'd just stepped in dogshit. "We certainly do."

"No, sit down," Jack cut in. He was expansive, one arm flung out in welcome, still—or again—stinking drunk.

Lance sat next to Terrence, who gave him a lot of room. Spicer's eyes were puffy, and grease shone in his hairline. His upper lip was split from Lance's punch; the lower was swollen. Through it all glittered a desperate humor. "This isn't a happenstance meeting, is it?" Jack said.

"I said we needed to talk. We need to talk."

"About your fish."

Lance didn't bite. "Where is she?"

"Jack doesn't know where your girlfriend is," Terrence said.

"Shut up, Terrence," Jack said without looking away from Lance. "Maybe you should go back to *your* girlfriend. I imagine she's waiting for you. As Lance's Elaine apparently is not."

From the corner of his eye Lance saw Terrence stiffen, then collapse. A young man, blond and chiseled, coming off a night that he thought had changed his life, and now he was kicked to the curb like an empty beer can. In that moment Lance understood a great deal about Jack Spicer. He liked ruining happiness. Put that together with this Tarot-card bullshit, and who knew what he would say where Ellie was concerned?

"You're just a sad lonely fairy, Jack," Terrence said. He pushed at Lance, and Lance got up to let him out of the booth.

"Terrence. Please. You're talking about yourself."

Terrence stopped in the aisle to get in the last word. "LF, Jack. There's a million like you. When you've crawled into a bottle and died, Carol and I will be living in Marin with three kids and a new Buick. Suck on that, faggot." He walked out of the diner.

Jack settled into the booth with a dismissive flip of his hand. "One of my students. They're a little flighty at that age."

Lance had no interest in any of it. "I killed a guy yesterday, Jack."

"Here's hoping he's the last," Jack said, but something about his expression turned it into a lie. It took Lance a minute to figure out what he saw percolating through Spicer's wiseass expression, and then he pegged it: Spicer was scared. Of what, Lance didn't know. Queers probably spent a lot of time scared; it went with the territory. Lance felt a flash of pity for Spicer. It had to be hard to carve your own way the way he was.

So what did Spicer know that scared him? Did he really believe all the whoppers he'd spun out about Lance's wound, poets, the Holy Grail, and all the rest? Gwen thought he did, but she also thought he was wrong. Like deciphering a code, and wondering if the other guy knew you'd cracked it and was feeding you misinformation.

Consider the kind of guy you're dealing with, Lance told himself. He hooked this kid Terrence just so he could have the scene over coffee the next morning. A guy like that, who knows why he does anything?

You knew it was a snake when you picked it up, was what Lance's mother would say.

"Talk to me, Jack."

"You know why baseball fucks them up?" Jack said. "On a

baseball field, it's always spring. In spring things are impossible to control. Death is easy to control. Life isn't, and spring is life. April is the cruelest month because April brings rebirth, and no one can know what is going to happen with all that new life in the world. In baseball you're always trying to get home, but every time you do the score is different. Uncertainty is cruel, Lance. Use that. That's the only advice I'll give you."

"I don't need advice," Lance said. "I want you to tell me what happened to Ellie."

"Well, if I had to guess, I'd say what happened to Ellie is that you didn't ask the question. That was Galahad's error. He was right there in the Grail castle, and the Grail passed before his eyes, and he didn't ask the question."

"Enough King Arthur bullshit. Give me the truth."

Spicer laughed. "The King Arthur bullshit *is* the truth. A version of it, anyway." He paused to sip his coffee. "The Seals are playing this afternoon. Meet me there, where we sat the last time, and I'll give you the story as I know it. It's the truth, but no truth is ever the only truth." He leaned forward and spoke in a conspiratorial whisper, slopping a little coffee onto the table. "Baseball is like jamming their radar, I think, and there are worse people than cops looking for people who can do magic. You found that out yesterday."

Lance was speechless. How much did Spicer know?

Sliding out of the booth, Jack winked. "Hope you don't mind picking up the coffee. Terrence said he would, but you can't count on those kinds of people, can you?"

Then he was gone. Lance sat. The waitress came and went. Then the bell over the door rang, and Gwen sat where Jack had been five minutes before. "I figured you'd be here," she said. "Jack always comes here."

"You just missed him," Lance said.

"That's how I like it. He gives me the creeps."

That makes two of us, Lance thought. The bell rang again, and he looked over his shoulder to see Jerry Kazmierski. What the hell, Lance wondered. Was he wearing some kind of homing device?

"Lance, Jesus, *her?*" Jerry said. "There's half a million women within twenty miles, and her?"

"And who is this?" Gwen asked.

"Jerry, Gwen. Gwen, Jerry. Jerry's an old high-school friend."

Gwen was eyeballing Jerry like she didn't like what she saw, which was understandable. Jerry was a mess, even worse than yesterday. He smelled bad, and he looked like he'd slept in a storm drain. "Tell me you didn't fuck her," Jerry said.

"I don't have to listen to this," Gwen said. She got up. "Lance, you know where to find me when you've thought things over."

"I bet he does." Jerry stood too close to her, and she backed away. Then she stepped around him and left. Jerry stayed where he was. "You did fuck her, didn't you?"

"Hey," the counterman said. He pointed his spatula at Jerry. "Watch your mouth."

"I don't know what I'm going to tell Ellie," Lance said. Which was true in all kinds of ways.

"Well, yeah, there's that," Jerry said. "Plus she's Dwight's girlfriend."

This time when Jerry said *let's go* Lance got up and went.

Jerry wouldn't say another word until they were in his dusty green Plymouth, over the Bay Bridge, through Oakland, and up into the hills. Lance held out as long as he could, and finally said, "Jerry, if you don't tell me what the hell is going on here, I'm going to jump out of the car."

"Ha," Jerry said. "That'd simplify things."

Lance exploded. "Goddammit! You said she's Dwight's girlfriend, now you tell me what that fucking meant!"

"It meant she's Dwight's girlfriend."

A crack of the emotional whip flung Lance out of his anger and into a bone-deep shock. "Dewey's alive," he said, just to say it. Just to believe it.

"Yeah, Lance," Jerry said. "He's alive. Dead guys don't send people thousands of miles on idiot errands." He paused. "Usually."

Dwight was alive. Lance let himself steep in that for a long time, as they rolled down the other side of the Oakland Hills into the Sacramento Valley. "If this is a joke, Jerry, tell me now. If I find out later, I'm going to come after you, and so help me God I'll kill you."

"No joke, soldier boy. Your brother is alive and well, and before you get all weepy you should know that when he sent me to find you he put you right in the crosshairs."

Which did nothing to stop the tears. Too much, Lance thought. Put it in order. "I can't take this right now," Lance said. "Ellie's gone. I can't go see Dwight right now. I have to find her."

"You don't go see Dwight, you'll never find her," Jerry said. "Spicer might think this is all some kind of poet's game, but other people take it a lot more to heart. You are a serious monkey wrench in a very old plan, buddy. From here on out, you've got only one good option, and the trouble is, nobody knows what it is."

Lance rode out his crying jag. It went on longer than he wanted it to, and he started to feel ashamed of himself even though it was only Jerry K. driving. When he'd finally gotten himself under control, he said, "Plan."

"Plan," Jerry agreed. "It's a long story, but what the hell, we've got a big country to cross."

"Start with the Grail," Lance said, and Jerry did.

GEORGE

Pitchers are obviously not human. They have the ghosts
of dead people in them.

JACK SPICER, "Four Poems for the
St. Louis Sporting News"

"MAHONE BAY? Where the hell is Mahone Bay?" Ev Tillbury
yelled. He was near six feet five inches tall, and when he spat into
the gaps between the train platform's planks, the brown stream of
tobacco was as long as a normal man's arm.

George grimaced. He liked a cigar once in a while, but chew
was another thing altogether. Around him, the rest of the team
shuffled back and forth, already in uniform, Charlie Spencer leaning on his bat to take the weight off his leg that had been spiked
the day before, covering first in the game against the coloreds
from Shelburne. I want out of Canada, George thought. George
Gibson don't belong on no barnstorming nine called the Catskill Maroons. He belongs playing center field for the Detroit
Wolverines or the St. Louis Brown Stockings. And he would be;
hadn't Chris Von der Ahe himself told him he wanted George to
tour with the Maroons so other National League clubs wouldn't

spy him out and sign him away? A summer wandering around backwoods New England and Canada was a small price to pay, if it meant he would be wearing brown socks next summer.

The station manager held out his hands. "Now don't get sore at me," he said to Ev. "I didn't make you get off here."

Ev glowered at him, working his chew in time with the pulsing vein at his right temple. "We was told the game was at Lunenburg."

"Loonie-burg, more like," Ben Fink grumbled, glaring out over the small hilly town with its tiny waterfront like a boy's model of Boston Harbor. The manager glanced over at him, then glowered silently up at Ev, arms folded and shoulders hunched, looking for all the world like a woodchuck hunkered at the entrance to its den.

"All right, goddammit," Ev finally said. He dug out his chew and flipped it onto the tracks behind him. "There a hack around here we can hire to take us?"

The wagon that transported them to Mahone Bay, five or six miles up the coast, clearly had once been a brewery shuttle. Midway through the trip George decided that an hour-long ride in it would dry out the most committed of drunks. They got there in one piece, though, creaking to a malodorous halt on a dirt track bisecting a grassy field. On one side was a farmhouse, a few chickens poking around in front of its barn and a single horse gazing placidly at the arrived players. Newly mown grass extended from the other side of the road to a strip of beach thirty yards or so to the south. Across a narrow channel, an overturned rowboat lay on the shore of a small island.

Wonder if that's Oak Island, George thought. The porter on their car from Yarmouth to Lunenburg hadn't been able to stop talking about buried treasure and pirates skulking in and out of the million secret inlets perforating Nova Scotia's Atlantic coast.

George looked up at the sun setting over a line of low hills back the way they'd come. He wouldn't have time to look around today, but maybe the train to Halifax wouldn't leave until the next afternoon. Be easy to swim that channel and have a look at this Money Pit.

The chickens scattered with a collective squawk as a group of a dozen young men trooped out of the barn. "We thought you wasn't going to come," one of them called. "And we spent all morning mowing the field there."

"Some field," Ben grumbled. "Like to break my leg and get shot like a lame horse."

"You're a lame horse already," Charlie said, and George laughed out loud.

Ev met the opposition as they approached the wagon. He introduced himself and asked who their captain was.

"That's me," volunteered the freckled redhead who'd first spoken. His hands were nearly the size of the glove Fred Schmidt used to catch, engulfing even Ev's knobby paws. "Walt Wallace. This here's all my land."

"Where's the fans?" Ev asked. "Thought you said the whole town'd show up."

"They did," Wallace retorted. "But you didn't say they'd have to wait all the damn day, and most of 'em went on home." As he spoke, though, people were beginning to trickle out of the farm-house, mostly young boys and girls who must have been sweet on one Mahone Bay player or another.

Ev watched them come, and George could see him thinking *No money to be made from this bunch. Good thing we're playing four games in Halifax.* "All right then, Walt, let's play. We're burning daylight."

"You owe me two dollars," the wagon driver broke in. Ev produced two silver dollars. "Whyn't you stay and watch?" he said.

The driver snorted through his mustache, the sound oddly like his horse's constant complaints. "That'd cost you five."

"What, you don't like baseball?" Charlie Spencer interrupted.

"No, you gotta stay, Virgil," Wallace said. "We need an umpire."

"Hell, then, *that'll* cost you five."

"Okay. You got a dollar and a half, Mister Tillbury?"

"Reckon I can find it." Ev dug in his traveling case. "Go on, the rest of you. We got a game to play. George, you're pitching again."

For the first part of the game, the two teams felt each other out. The Mahone Bay pitcher wasn't much, but the boys behind him knew how to catch the ball, and they hit all right for a bunch of farmers. They couldn't hit George, though, and George could sure as hell hit them. In the bottom of the third inning he beat out a slow ground ball to third, his second hit in as many tries. "Better get a little more of it next time," Wallace said as he tossed the ball back to his pitcher.

"Oh, I don't know," George answered. "Way he throws, I guess I could do this all day."

Truth to tell, though, he was angry at himself. The batter's box faced out into the bay, and he'd found himself paying more attention to the island than the jug-eared coal miner on the mound. It occurred to him to ask Wallace about the treasure story, but before he could Kelly Robinson slapped the ball over his head and he took off running, still looking at the island as he rounded second and bore down on the third baseman with an arm like George's grandmother.

In the fifth, George cranked a long fly to right center that cleared the beach and splashed into the channel. "That more what you had in mind?" he said to Wallace as he rounded first. Wallace's answer was to spit on George's shoes.

With this in mind, George didn't think Wallace would be of a mind to converse when, after his third base hit of the day—this one scoring Charlie and Ben ahead of him—he trotted into first. After all, the Catskill Maroons were ahead 9–2, and those two both came in on a bobbled fly ball for which George had nearly decked Ev between innings.

What the hell, he thought. "So how about that island over there?" he said, a thumb aimed in the general direction of the up-ended rowboat.

"How about it?" Wallace said.

"Ever go treasure hunting?"

Wallace looked at him. On the mound, the coal miner was engaged in a heated discussion with the noodle-armed third baseman. "You heard there was treasure, eh?"

"Porter on the train couldn't talk about anything else."

"Well, I don't know about treasure, but I can damn sure tell you there's a ghost."

"A ghost?"

Wallace nodded. "Seen it myself. Man in a white suit. Always sailing a little boat around the bay, and every time he goes around to Smith's Cove—that's where your treasure's supposed to be—he disappears. Honest to Christ."

"That so?" George said, and took off for second as the coal miner threw a pitch so laden with spit that it bounced over the catcher's head.

Five hours later the moon was directly overhead and the Catskill Maroons were raucously drunk in Walt Wallace's hayloft. To their credit, the Mahone Bay boys hadn't taken their defeat to heart, and a fine batch of home whiskey had long since dissipated any residual ill will. Men from both teams played cards and jumped from the loft to the pile of hay below, enlarged just for this occasion. Hanging lopsidedly against the swaybacked horse George had noticed earlier, the jug-eared pitcher was the only one lacking in good cheer.

George wondered how things would have turned out if his

grandparents had never immigrated from Quebec to Michigan, and then on out to Colorado in the sixties. Grandpa Taillandier, himself the son of immigrants from France, had fought in the War Between the States, and somewhere in Virginia he'd met a fur trader who swore Taillandier could make his fortune mining in the Rocky Mountains. Grandpa had come back from the war in the summer of 1865, sold everything they owned, and headed west with his wife and daughter, Anna. The year after they'd come to Colorado, Anna Taillandier had fallen for a gold miner named Everett Gibson, and George, her second son, had made his squalling way into the world in 1871. But I could have been born up here, in Three Rivers or Montreal, George thought. I could have been a Frenchman, a lumberman instead of a baseball player. I could have spent my nights raising hell in logging camps and barns like this one.

On the whole, he was happy Grandpa Taillandier had gone west.

All the racket was making George cross, though, since he was trying to write a letter to Martha and the whoops and crashes of bodies hitting the barn floor kept distracting him. He'd drunk enough to be convinced that one of the girls along the foul lines that afternoon was really a cleverly disguised scout from the Boston Beaneaters.

Dear Martha, he wrote. *Sorry I haven't been writing so regular, but we're playing every day and sometimes I'm just too*—he almost wrote "drunk"—*tired.* He told her about the previous day's game against the colored nine from Shelburne, shaking his head over the fact that a colored preacher had actually been allowed to umpire.

I will write sooner than I did last time, George said to finish up. *Sure wish you'd had your photograph taken at the fair last year, Martha. There aren't no girls up here near as pretty as you.*

He signed the letter and looked up to see Charlie wobbling toward him. "Cripes, Charlie," George snorted, "you look like you can't decide which leg hurts."

"Ain't none of 'em hurt," Charlie said, and slumped down next to George.

Charlie's arrival reminded George of what he'd been thinking earlier. "That fellow Wallace says there's a ghost on that island over there," he said.

"A ghost," Charlie repeated, nodding as if he'd known it all along. "Where's treasure, is bound to be ghosts. That Wallace cheats at cards."

"Think I feel like a swim." George stood up, took a deep breath, found that his balance was not too badly impaired. "Come on, Charlie. I ain't never seen a ghost."

"They cheat at cards, too," Charlie groused, but he got to his feet. "Okay. Swim. Nice night."

"Anybody else feel like chasing ghosts?" George scanned the loft. Other than him, Charlie, and the now unconscious Mahone Bay pitcher, everyone was playing or kibitzing on five-card stud. "You go on ahead," Ev Tillbury said around a cigar.

Charlie promptly fell out of the loft, but when George made his way down, he found the wiry second baseman up and full of sudden energy. They made their way down to the shore and, surprising an occasional crab, out to the end of the spit pointing toward the island. It was a bit farther away than George had thought, probably close to three hundred yards. But tonight, he thought as he stripped to his skivvies and tied his shoes around his neck, I could swim right back to Maine.

Mahone Bay was cold as hell, but no colder than Clear Creek in the early spring, where since he was a boy George had waded out to catch trout while his father dug gold out of the Rocky Mountains. He swam slowly, keeping Charlie in front of him, letting the sharp salt ocean wash away the game's sweat and the whiskey fog. The night was calm, the moon full, the water disturbed only by his and Charlie's steady strokes.

Even if there's no treasure and no ghost, George thought, this is worth it. When I make the National League, I'm going to bring

Martha out east, and after we're married we'll live right on the ocean. If I could swim like this every day, I'd live forever.

And if there is treasure, I'll be the richest damn baseball player around.

They reached the island in a few minutes, coming ashore near the boat landing George had been looking at in the third. He'd missed a steal sign staring at that landing.

A dirt track led from the shore back into the woods. "That the ghost road?" Charlie said as he struggled into his shoes.

"Wallace said it leads to the other end of the island." George started into the woods, Charlie cursing softly at the mosquitoes that found them as soon as they left the shore. They passed an old clapboard house, then skirted a small cornfield and snuck past two more houses, breaking into a run when a huge black dog barked from the yard of the last house.

"I hate dogs," Charlie panted as they ran. After the house with the dog, the island seemed empty. They didn't pass any more houses.

"We'll catch a ride back with the ghost," George said when they'd slowed to a walk again. *Or take his boat and let him float back,* George was about to add, but then he saw lights ahead through the trees and stopped short.

Charlie had seen them, too; he slowed and crept forward. They could hear voices now—speaking French? Well, it was Canada. And now they could see a group of men moving around in the light thrown by a circle of torches. Moving closer, George saw a square hole in the ground maybe ten feet across. Six men stood around the pit, three of them holding a rope wound through a block and tackle built over it. Two of the other men leaned on long-handled broadaxes, while the sixth remained a little apart, his face hooded by a heavy cloak. A hoarse shout came from the pit, and the three belayers started hauling on the rope. Gradually a sling rose to ground level, supporting a young Negro, dripping wet and cradling something in his arms.

Charlie caught George's eye, and George could tell what he was thinking. There was treasure, and they'd missed it.

But why dig in the middle of the night?

The one man without rope or ax said something, and the Negro reached out a hand and said something back. George didn't understand any of it, but it was easy enough to figure out: *Let's have it. Sure, but give me a hand up first.*

"*Oui,*" the cloaked miner said. He reached out and caught the Negro's wrist, pulling him to the lip of the pit, and then he flicked a thin knife from his sleeve and slit the Negro's throat.

"Oh Jesus!" Charlie cried. He leapt to his feet and dashed back the way they'd come, crashing loudly through the brush. George started to go after him, but he heard the miners shouting and froze where he was. The three belayers dropped the rope and sprinted out of the clearing in the direction Charlie had headed. The two with axes each knocked out a leg of the frame, and the block-and-tackle collapsed, jamming in the mouth of the pit and dropping the dying Negro out of sight. The rope, too, jammed in the pulley as the two axmen followed after Charlie's pursuers.

George hunkered down in the brush as footsteps pounded past him. Go, Charlie, he thought. If you get to the water first, you might get away. Forget about your leg and fly.

The remaining miner, the one who'd stabbed the Negro, kicked at the tackle frame but couldn't break it loose. He swore, or that's what it sounded like, and walked quickly away in the opposite direction, holding the canvas-wrapped bundle he'd grabbed from the Negro.

George heard shouts from the forest, but none he recognized as Charlie's voice. Keep going, he thought again. Now what do I do? Maybe they'll all just leave and I can sneak back. Or maybe—

The broken tackle frame creaked and a black hand reached up out of the pit to grip the rope just below the jammed pulley. The Negro was alive, George realized, and at that moment a despairing scream echoed through the woods, cut off as soon as it began.

Oh dear Lord, Charlie. George stood, panicking and uncertain which way to go—back to the cornfield, or somewhere else to hole up until daylight?—and he saw the Negro's face at the lip of the pit. Before he could think about it he ran to the pit and squatted. "Give me your hand," he hissed.

"I can't," the Negro said calmly, an accent in his voice George didn't recognize.

"Come on, nigger, those Frenchmen are coming back! Give me your damn hand!" George hauled on the Negro's shirt collar, soaking his hands in blood.

"Take this," the Negro wheezed. Blood bubbled from his mouth as he heaved a small leather bag out of the pit, then caught George's forearm. "Take it and go."

"Shut up and come on," George said, even as another part of him was yelling *Go, go! He said to go!* "Come on," he repeated, trying to lift the Negro clear of the pit.

"You have no time." The Negro sucked in a breath like a dying fish. He choked on the blood in his windpipe and said, "Go."

The smell of blood on the Negro's breath flooded George's mouth and nose, and he gagged from both the stench and the feeling that something was crawling like hot water into his nose and down the back of his throat. He let go and fell back, ears roaring at the sensation of something filling his sinuses, and at the same time the Negro released his arm and fell out of sight. George felt like he was falling too, and with the sound of a distant splash came the frantic conviction that it was him drowning in his own blood in cold black trapped ocean water.

Go.

He hadn't spoken, but the voice had come from inside his head, a voice faint as if it were bridging the void between the living and the dead.

George grabbed the leather bag and ran away from the clearing, not back the way he'd come but to the south, scrapping through the thick underbrush until quicker than he'd expected he was on a thin strip of beach. Clear moonlight fell over the ocean and the trees on the mainland. Walt Wallace's farm was out of sight around the western end of the island. George tried to calm his breathing, listen for sounds of murderous Frenchmen in pursuit, but his lungs hauled in gasp after shrieking gasp, and his pulse hammered against his eardrums.

Swim. He'd have to swim. Couple of miles, back around the island, or a few hundred yards straight to the near shore. He stepped into the gentle waves rolling onto the beach. The Frenchmen hadn't seen him, didn't know he'd seen them kill the colored boy. If he got to shore, he could forget the whole thing. Fellas back at the barn would be asleep by now. Bad dream. Teach him to go treasure hunting.

The ocean pulsed over his knees. A few more steps and he could swim.

Into the water. Quickly!

The thought snapped up out of his mind as if it were his own, but it pushed at him, nearly moved his limbs before he'd made the decision to go. The nigger, George thought. The nigger's in my mind.

Something hit him hard in the back, just under his right shoulder blade. George's breath seized and he stumbled, arms flailing into an agonizing crawl as his feet left the bottom and he swam straight out into the bay. Right away he knew he wasn't going to make it; at every stroke the muscles in his back tore a little more, and he didn't seem to be able to draw a deep breath.

George Gibson, you are dying. We are far enough out now. Let go.

Far enough? George thought. Far enough from what?

No. He was not dying. Would not die. He would play center field for the Brown Stockings and marry Martha. He would swim to shore with one goddamn arm if that's what it took.

George rolled onto his side, tucked his right arm against his chest, stroked ahead with his left. The only light was the moon, and he could no longer see the shore. Seawater slapped into his mouth, and when he coughed too much fluid came up. Blood, he thought. Tastes just like seawater.

His head was underwater. No, he thought again, and forced himself back to the surface. Strength was leaving his legs. Another cough tore through him, and the pain spiked through his chest and right arm.

We are far enough out. Let go or he will not come.

Too many questions. Water closed over George's head again, and all he could think was: we?

He got a hand out of the water, grasped at the surface that wouldn't hold him. The moon gleamed wavy and huge, and his hand would not reach it. He could hear himself grunting, holding his mouth closed.

He has come.

A tearing sound in the water. Something blotted out the moon, and George thought he saw his hand reflected in the halo left behind. Then the reflected hand caught his, and *yes,* George thought, *let go,* and he opened his mouth to let the water in.

BOOK TWO

But I've nothing more to crave;
All my life is now its slave,

Spell that took me flesh and soul,
Dissipated every goal.

ARTHUR RIMBAUD, "Bliss"

Fooled by nature, I
Accepted the quest gracefully
Played the fool.

JACK SPICER, "The Book of Gawain"

LANCE

"So how do you know all this?" Lance said.

"Some of it I know, some of it I'm guessing. But I'm a good guesser."

"Right. Jerry, somebody tried to kill me yesterday," Lance said, "and here you are telling me ridiculous bullshit stories that have nothing to do with anything. So this guy George Gibson was a good baseball player, and he went out to this Oak Island and never came back. So what?"

"You know what?" Jerry said. "I hope I'm wrong about you. No one as fucking stupid as you are should be important."

"Kiss my ass," Lance said. Crazy Jerry K., Dexter High School's resident lunatic genius, the guy Lance and Dewey had always let come along to the movies or the river because he kept them laughing, and that was worth being associated with a kid who clearly wasn't right in the head. Now that he was moving, doing what Jerry wanted—and what Jerry said Ellie wanted—Lance was already suspicious. How had Jerry known he would be here? A week ago he would have said it was a coincidence, but now he was hearing Gwen in his head: *Coincidence doesn't really exist. It's just a word people invented to deal with their expectations being wrong.*

Revelations, wild stories, as they blasted along Route 6

through the suffocated brown hills of Nevada, Lance feeling already like runoff from the Sierra, destined to evaporate somewhere in the vast American interior. "In the end," Jerry said, "it's all about belief, or maybe I should say in the beginning, but that's not the way to start." He pounded on the steering wheel, keeping his own time and coating the dashboard in cigarette ash. "The way to start is to tell you what's not right. The Grail isn't the cup Joseph of Arimathea supposedly caught Jesus' blood in. But so what if it was? A cup. Big deal. Other people think that the Grail's a symbol, a clue that will lead to proof that Jesus had kids with Mary Magdalene."

"Are you kidding?"

"No. And they're probably right. Jesus was a Jew, man, and Jews don't stay single, especially then. But that's not what the Grail is about."

"Jesus had kids? With Mary Magdalene? She was a whore."

"So? Would she be the first girl someone came along and made an honest woman of? And this is all two thousand years ago; who knows whether she was a whore or not? I sure as hell wouldn't trust Peter on the topic."

"Okay. So the Grail isn't a cup and it doesn't have anything to do with Mary Magdalene. Why is Spicer so excited about my leg?"

"Belief. Did you know that people who go to church live longer than people who don't? Did you know that half the time people given placebos in the hospital do just as well as people who get real drugs? Belief makes things happen. Jack calls it magic. Well, so do other people, but you asked about Jack. Shit, capitalism is magic."

"Is that so."

"You bet it is. Look, you've got one society that protects its weak by making sure that everybody has enough, and another predicated on competition, which ensures that someone will lose. Capitalism doesn't work without losers. Now who in their right mind would prefer a system that might make a loser out of them over a system that guarantees they'll always be able to get by?"

Jerry was a Red. Lance was glad they were in the car, where nobody could overhear them.

"Americans, that's who," Jerry went on. "The American Dream is to get ahead, right? To climb the ladder, get on top of the heap, cock of the walk, all that Sinatra bullshit. And even though the vast majority of people will never get to the top of the heap, they're all still trying. And their belief makes this system work even though it fucking guarantees they'll never realize the dream that makes it all work. Belief!" He saw the look on Lance's face and laughed. "Go ahead, turn me in. Hoover'd have a field day with me. I'd tell him some things that would get his panties in one serious bunch."

Lance imagined Jerry K. in an FBI interrogation room telling J. Edgar Hoover about the Holy Grail, and he couldn't help it. He cracked up.

"Except he already knows some of it," Jerry said, and Lance stopped laughing.

"Some of what?"

"The Grail. The only reason it's still hidden is that so many people are looking for it. Belief, man—they all believe they're looking for a golden chalice or a fucking birth certificate, or some other medieval story. Every government in the world including ours is looking for it, and so is the UN. Dag Hammarskjöld thinks he's the new Solomon, presiding over the division of the world like Solomon and the baby. He goes to bed every night believing tomorrow he'll find the Grail in the morning. FDR used to go up to Oak Island and look around, but he was too late. I could go on and on. The point is that some people want to use the Grail, a few of them want to destroy it, but everyone's looking for it, and because they're all so invested in what they think it is, they're all barking up the wrong tree in the wrong part of the forest. Which is lucky for you."

"But you know the truth," Lance said.

"Part of it. What I know is this: there is a Holy Grail, an actual physical object. It is a real thing. It is very old. And most of the people who know where it is don't know what to do with it. That's where Dwight comes in."

"How?"

"If I told you, I'd get it wrong," Jerry said. "You'll have to hear it from him. I don't get involved in other people's family issues."

"Okay, fine, but you still haven't told me why Spicer's so interested in my leg."

"Because he thinks you're the Fisher King, dope. He thinks you can find the Grail. The times, as they say, are ripe. Joe Stalin is dead—and did you know that he had a deformed foot? You better believe *he* was looking for the Grail. But he's dead, and Roosevelt's dead, and Truman doesn't give a shit, and Dag Hammarskjöld is too caught up in being a sorcerer, and nobody in Red China can be bothered with the whole mess. There's a hole right now, a vacuum waiting to be filled. On the surface, we Americans are all busy spitting out kids and moving to Levittown so we can watch Jackie Gleason with all our neighbors, but underneath people are looking for an answer."

Jerry stopped, as if he'd realized he was losing some of his sarcastic armor. "Belief," he said after a while. "We all go to church, we all give ourselves ulcers worrying about the next promotion or the communists in the Rotary Club, but deep down inside I think we know that's not the point. There's something bigger out there, and we want to know what it is so we can believe in it."

They stopped to leak and get some sandwiches for the road. Maybe it was Nevada, maybe Utah already: a clutch of four buildings calling itself a town, with wire fences radiating out in all directions, spokes of the western compass under a half moon bright enough to read by. Lance saw his first tumbleweed and caught himself looking around for cowboys. Inside the square white-washed general store—post office—gas station, a wiry old bird who looked like the only survivor of Little Bighorn sat reading a newspaper. Another weathered denizen nursed a beer in a chair by the shuttered postal window. Jerry stayed outside to fill the Plymouth, and the Indian fighter glanced out the window. "Hope you boys don't need your oil checked."

"No, I think we're fine," Lance said. He bought salami, bread, mustard, beer, remembered at the last minute to replenish the Pall Malls that Jerry smoked at the rate of fifty or so a day. They pissed around the back of the building, climbed back into the car and roared off again, in silence until Jerry had decided on his next disclosure.

Somewhere in the mountains, the road snaking away beyond the headlights, a bottomless gorge on one side and rockfall debris on the other: "The Oak Island thing gets weirder and weirder. FDR didn't get polio until he was thirty-nine, after he'd spent summers digging around up there. Get that, GI Joe? He goes to Oak Island hale and hearty, then after sniffing around the Grail for a while his legs are wrecked, but he's elected president even though he's a cripple. And Uncle Joe Stalin, the Man of Steel, had a birth defect, one of his feet was screwed up. What do you want to bet that Churchill has something wrong with his legs? What about Hitler?" And away across the Great Basin, where the water didn't know which way to go, and down the lee side of the Rockies, Jerry expounded on Roosevelt's cabinet, the eye on the U.S. dollar. "It all ties together, man. Solomon put the Ark of the Covenant between two pillars because he was a wizard, just like Melchizedek and all the way back to Thoth, and the Emerald Tablet of Thoth was hidden in one of two pillars at Thebes. Re-telling. Emerald tablets, tablets of the Law, it's all the same thing, man. The Templars built little replicas of the Temple all over Ethiopia."

Just like that, Lance lost track of the conversation, all the sub-

terranean connections, all the misdirections and fake illuminations, ciphers and poetic bread crumbs scattered in the dark
woods of history. Still he listened to Jerry, heard about cathedrals
and sacred groves, severed heads that spoke and ritual sex,
Solomonids and Zagwes, Prester John and Menelik, Rimbaud and
Spicer, grails and grails and grails. The Plymouth's tires thrummed
on the pavement, Jerry's palms hammered the steering wheel,
they drank the last of the beer and the clinking bottles on the
floorboards chimed along. The night passed, and they were running out of steam. Jerry's cigarettes burned down unsmoked.
Lance lolled against the headrest, his skull bouncing against the
window as Jerry with heat-seeking accuracy found every frost
heave on Highway 6.

My turn, Lance thought.

"The doc on the hospital ship said I was wounded the day
Stalin died." He almost didn't want to tell Jerry, but something in
the whole kooky story was starting to hang together. What if he
was this Fisher King, or could be? Stalin with his twisted foot,
FDR's polio, Lance Porter's broken thigh. Wouldn't he do a better job than either of them? Wouldn't he? The war's over, he
thought. It's like the world is pausing for breath, Jerry's right
about that. I'd be a good King. I know what's right. I could heal
the land, like Spicer said the King does when he gets the Grail.

"Jesus," Jerry said. "Jesus H. Christ. Doesn't that just figure.
Are you starting to get this yet?"

I'll be King, Lance thought. And Ellie will be my Queen.

"Yeah," he said. "I'm starting to get it. So Dwight's supposed
to tell me where the Grail is?"

"Like I said, I don't know what Dwight's going to tell you.
I—listen, I don't want to talk about Dwight. There are too many
things I shouldn't say."

Family issues. Lance yawned, a real skullcracker. His eyes
started to slide closed. "Okay," Lance said. "Keep it to yourself,

I'll try to figure it out. Let me guess: the first Fisher King was Jesus. Nails in his feet, right?"

Jerry snorted. "Hell no. Jesus has nothing to do with this. The first Fisher King, if you want to call him that—and it probably goes back farther than that—was Osiris."

ARTHUR

HE WAS ARRESTED in Massawa, waiting to board the steamer. Grim French officials marched him to the police office, where an official whose name Arthur didn't bother to remember grilled him about his lack of papers, his reasons for going to Egypt, his citizenship, and not least the belt of gold he kept under his tunic. Arthur grew curt: how could any papers survive a two-year caravan through the bandits of the Shoa? Must every businessman disclose the secrets of his trade? And who could he trust with the forty thousand francs in gold that Arthur carried belted around his bony hips? Contact Jerome, he said at last, and endured his house arrest until some days later the official returned, all silk and gladhanding, commiserating with Arthur on the miseries of the European in Abyssinia, offering him chilled port wine, and all the while interspersing wheedling and tiresome inquiries about investing in Arthur's audacious ventures. Arthur remained as polite as he could, but he couldn't board the Red Sea steamer soon enough.

Cairo in September: flies and dust, djellabas and pith helmets, low buildings of bleached mud brick, British soldiers with rifles and shoes shining blackly in the pitiless sun. English and French and Arabic in the streets. Waiting for Michel. He had been there two weeks, enough leisure for a comfortable trip to Gizeh, looking at the Pyramids, dithering away an afternoon deciding whether or not to carve his name in one of them. Not at all like one of Jerome's missions. When Jerome sent Arthur somewhere, he had an itinerary, a rigid clockworks of investigations and appointments; but now Arthur was acting on his own, and while waiting for Michel he indulged his natural curiosity.

It was late evening, and he had been gazing at the Sphinx since after lunch. Silent all these centuries, like him. Ages had passed since it had spoken. Nostalgia tickled the back of Arthur's mind, for poetry of all things. Ten years ago he'd written his last poem, in Java, and then he'd thrown it into the ocean. Then had come Jerome, and Arthur had found his life's work. Once he'd thought poetry was his birthright, a forced and welcome destiny; now it seemed the diversion of a boy insensible to the world's demands and opportunities. At intervals he heard from Paris that his poems were being republished, or that he was believed dead. It was all the same to him. A published poem was a dead poem. His real reputation had still to be made.

Speak, Sphinx, he thought. For all the gold on my body, speak. I will scatter your words and my gold in the sand for the beggar boys, and leave Egypt forever.

The Sphinx declined his offer. Even so, he considered unbuckling the belt of gold from around his waist and leaving it as an offering to abandoned belief. An act of anonymous charity, and one that would unburden him of ten kilos. He'd begun wearing the gold out of a simple mistrust of Abyssinian banks, such as they were; but gold was pure, and he'd come to think of the belt as an enforced symbolic chastity, a ward against the snares that lay in his path. Menelik was a snare; Michel might be; even Jerome's guiding hand might at any moment tighten into a fist. Decisions were at hand. Alliances would form and crumble during the coming months.

And Jean-Nicolas Arthur Rimbaud was at the center of it. His father's work.

"Rimbaud," a voice called from the Sphinx's paw. Michel had come. Arthur followed him around to the rear of the Sphinx, a much less popular view with tourists, and there at the ass end of a great stone lion with the head of a woman and a missing nose, he plotted to change the world.

"Jerome suggested you were the man to deal with the Menelik situation," he said.

"The proper way to deal with the Menelik situation would be a quiet knife in his liver," Michel said.

"So then you could deal with Johannes and the Ras Makonnen," Arthur said. "Johannes is old and the Makonnen his brother's cat's-paw. And perhaps you should find out how Menelik knows what he knows before you talk of knives."

"Perhaps I have no need of a degenerate boy poet to tell me the Order's business," Michel replied mildly. Arthur let the slur pass. Warmth bled from the sand, but already he could feel evening's chill in his ears. He was right, and Michel knew it. He waited, and Michel continued. "You are correct, though, that it is time to act."

"Then let us act."

"Let us indeed. But let us consider who else may be acting. Does Menelik trust you to follow his orders? That is the first question. The second involves the Italians. The Order is old, Rimbaud, and like all dynasties it is rent by schism. The Italians would just as soon let Menelik have the Grail, and then take Abyssinia to control him. Whether they can do this is uncertain, but the Holy See believes it can be done. Others—I am here speaking of myself—have a different perspective. We have the blood on our side, and can take the Grail for ourselves, but the time is not propitious. Abyssinia is at war, and will be at war; the British and the French wrangle over Egypt and the Sudan; Leopold baits the French and the Germans in Central Africa. It will be many years before it all sorts itself out, and prudence argues that the Grail should not return to Africa when such action would endanger it."

So it was not in Africa. Knowing that alone justified the trip to Cairo. Not in Chartres, not in Cyprus, not in Africa; where, then?

"The best course of action is to remove it from its resting place and keep it somewhere until the time is right to restore the power of the Ark," Michel said. "But even this course is not without danger; I have twin sons, eleven years old, who already contend to succeed me. Whatever is done must happen before they gather enough strength to make a serious attempt, and before those others who know the location of the Grail arrive at the conclusions I have reached. So this task I give you: send your Galahad. We will have him bear the Grail to France, and we will keep it there. Once it is found to be missing, eyes will be on Axum, but we will outwait them."

A thought coalesced in Arthur's mind, from a diffuse cloud of ambition and desire he'd begun to feel after Jerome's revelations of the previous months. *Blood on our side,* Michel had said— Michel who did not know that Arthur too shared that blood. Neither did Menelik know. I am the Zagwe spy again, Arthur thought. This is my father's work.

"Like Banquo," Michel mused, "I will sire kings though not be one myself. Some men knowing this would kill their sons. I make the Grail a gift to whichever of my sons is stronger. They love each other as brothers, and I do not believe either will kill the other. When I am gone, one of them will be King in my stead. This is enough for me."

Which confirmed for Arthur that children brought only madness. "My Galahad," he said. "Where shall I send him?"

"To Chartres. Send him in the spring; the equinox is an auspicious date."

"The Grail is not at Chartres."

"I will tell him where the Grail is, not you. And I will go with him to recover it. You are Jerome's man, and possibly Menelik's; if I must lie down with dogs, I will take care to cleanse myself of fleas."

Arthur made his decision, in the sudden nightfall of Cairo in autumn. He would play the role; he would seem just overambitious enough to arouse suspicion, but not so grasping as to endanger his life. To make it work he needed a Galahad loyal to his Arthur, a Galahad who was a Jew. The people of the Ark—surely one of them can bear the Grail. There was a boy in Harar, a Falasha named Yishaq. He was bright, and determined, and Arthur had bought him from slavery on the way back from Entotto. Smirking at himself, Arthur thought: all I need now is to fashion a Round Table in my house at Harar. But his silence had gone on too long to be pique at Michel's insult.

"What is the Grail?" he asked, the stupidest question he could think of.

Michel spat in the sand. "No living man knows. Think of it as the cock of Osiris; perhaps that will make you desire it all the more."

LANCE

"So this Rimbaud was queer?" Lance asked. "No wonder Spicer's such a big fan."

"You're a dipshit. This has got nothing to do with who people like to fuck," Jerry said. "The story is that while Isis is in prison she gives birth to Horus on the vernal equinox, a kind of Immaculate Conception, and then when she gets out she's headed back to get the bastard who killed Osiris—that's Seth, who is Isis' half-brother—but before she can get to him he finds Osiris' body, cuts it into fourteen pieces, and throws them all in the Nile. Isis eventually finds them all except his dick, which was eaten by fishes. Makes you wonder what the Fisher King is really fishing for, doesn't it?"

Jerry laughed, and then the cigarettes got to him and he started coughing and pounding on the steering wheel. When he'd gotten his lungs back under control, Lance almost asked him about the way Spicer used the word *fish,* but he didn't want Jerry to have an aneurysm and die while he was driving. Plus he wasn't sure he wanted to hear the answer.

They slept in the car somewhere in Wyoming, got to Indiana before crashing out again, and were tearing across Pennsylvania when Jerry veered north instead of going on toward New York. "I thought you lived in New York City," Lance said.

"I do. But you can't go there, so I have to take a bus the last bit."

"I can't go there?" As he said it, Lance was thinking about his mother's radio, the introduction to the *Grand Central Station* radio program that was her favorite thing on the airwaves next to *The Guiding Light* and Burl Ives: *the glitter and swank of Park Avenue, and then Grand Central Station . . . crossroads of a million private lives.* The Empire State Building, and next to it the Chrysler, mismatched towers over the American cathedral of Manhattan. Bridges and tunnels, the wakes of ships on the Hudson River, all the names that had come up in conversations among Jack Spicer's writer friends back in California: who was this Ginsberg, this Kerouac, these guys everyone talked about and who supposedly knew the guy who had written *Junkie,* whose name wasn't really William Lee at all and who had supposedly killed his wife while playing William Tell in Mexico? Times Square, Lance thought, with news-reel footage flying through his head along with William Lee's deadened descriptions of the junkies and hustlers. Eric the Fag banged up against Nathan Detroit in his head, and both of them stumbled over the Yankees and the Giants, Mantle and Reese and Snider and Robinson. Pure tourist awe, the Michigan boy's open-mouthed amazement at his first sight of the Big Apple.

And Jerry said he couldn't go there, casually, like he was talk-ing about a traffic problem. Then Jerry was off on the Grail again, endlessly talking about the Philosopher's Stone and the Crusades and Dag Hammarskjöld again and again until all of human history turned into a procession of magicians with bum legs. For empha-sis he'd hammer the steering wheel and shout, "It's all bullshit! All of it!" Just like he had across Wyoming and Nebraska and Iowa and Illinois and Indiana and Ohio and Pennsylvania and now upstate New York.

Twenty-nine hundred miles by the odometer—so far—with Jerry yammering every second in a '49 Plymouth that rode like a hay wagon. "If we're not going to New York," Lance finally said, just to hear Jerry talk about something else, "where are we going?"

"You're going to drop me off in Cooperstown," Jerry said. "I always wanted to see the Hall of Fame."

"You're going sightseeing?"

Bam bam bam, Jerry pounded the steering wheel. "When are you going to stop thinking you know everything when you don't know shit about shit?" Jerry yelled. "Goddammit, Lance, haven't you heard what I've been saying?"

"I hear what you're saying, and you're saying you're going to Cooperstown. What do you think that sounds like?"

"Baseball. I need to look into some things. They have records from the minor leagues there, and I'm going to see what they have to say about George Gibson."

This was good sense, at least within the framework of lunacy they were dealing with, and Lance didn't feel quite so brash anymore. "Okay," he said. "I'm sorry. You're right. If you say I can't go to New York, I can't go to New York, and if you have to go to Cooperstown, okay. Look, you have to understand that this all sounds nuts."

"Sure it does. If it sounded sane, too many people would pay attention."

When Jerry finally pulled up to the curb at the Baseball Hall of Fame in Cooperstown, Lance got out of the car coated in ashes and feeling like he'd just as soon have his leg amputated and be done with it.

"This better not be a wild-goose chase, Jerry," he said, stretching. "If you dragged me all the way here and I lose track of Ellie, I'll break both your legs and you can be two kings."

"You don't *have* track of Ellie, tough guy." Jerry was crossing the street. Lance followed him as far as the front door, and he considered spending the day looking around at all the old pictures. Cobb would be there, and all the other old Tigers. It would do him good to take his mind off things for a while.

Jerry stopped before they went inside, though. "Okay, it should be safe to say this here. Spicer told you about Rimbaud, and I bet he gave you some of the whole Thoth and Osiris bit, but he's too hung up on that Tarot crap and magic to see the big picture. Kingships are about families. The Fisher King is supposed to be a descendant of Solomon, but history is long, and usurpers creep in. Did Spicer tell you that one of Rimbaud's ancestors worked on Chartres Cathedral?" Lance nodded, but Jerry went on anyway. "An Ethiopian guy, showed up in France with a note supposedly from Prester John complaining that the Templars were building churches all over Abyssinia, making little replicas of the Second Temple in Jerusalem. So they sent this letter, but one of the guys who delivered it was a spy for this usurper crowd called the Zagwes."

"An Ethiopian spy with a French name?"

"He got the name later. It just means scoundrel, outcast, something like that. He stayed, picked up this nickname I'm guessing because he started chasing the local girls in between adding a bunch of ciphered sculptures to the cathedral after he burned it down so he could get the message out that the Ark of the Covenant really was in Ethiopia."

"You lost me," Lance said.

"And right about that time," Jerry went on, "you get the first mention of the Holy Grail in the literature of the time. Written by a guy who'd spent time in that part of France, and when he died it was probably finished by another guy who grew up in a town called Troyes, which is like fifty miles from guess where?"

"Chartres," Lance said.

"No. Charleville. Arthur Rimbaud's birthplace. So right there, where Rimbaud could go on a school field trip and see it, is the story of the Ark of the Covenant, put there by one of his ancestors while the Knights Templar were building models of the place they set up as their headquarters during the Crusades. Is this starting to add up?"

"Rimbaud really had an Ethiopian guy in his family?" Spicer had mentioned this, but Lance had written it off as too loony to believe. The past couple of days, though, seemed to have lowered his loony bar, and now Lance caught himself thinking that there was no reason not to believe it.

"He sure did. Probably so do you."

"What?"

"Ah, shit, I should shut up. This is all about family, man, I told you that. This is where Spicer is right even though he doesn't have all the details, and where the Freemason wackos are right even though they're crazy. It's another version of Seth and Osiris, and it's about the King's bloodline."

And suddenly all Lance could think about was Gwen just happening to be in the Black Cat, and just happening to take him home with her, and just happening to be Dwight's girl, and just happening not to believe in coincidence. "Solomon," he said.

"No! Not Solomon! The fucking Zagwes, man, pay attention! Think!"

Lance did, and Jerry opened the door. "Jesus, Jerry. You can't just leave now," Lance said.

"Dwight's in a town called Peggy's Cove, Nova Scotia," he said, and tossed Lance the keys to the Plymouth. "Get moving. Good luck, man."

"Nova Scotia? How do I get there?"

"You drive my car, and you buy a map. It's a small town. You'll be able to find him when you get there."

Jerry disappeared into the Hall of Fame. Lance went back to the car and sat at the wheel. His hands were shaking, and he was alone again, and he'd betrayed the two people who were closest to him in the world, even Dewey who he'd thought was dead for eight years now, and he hadn't made an inch of progress toward finding Ellie. Plus he'd killed a guy in San Francisco, and now that he'd run away the cops wouldn't think much of his story.

Go, he thought. Do something. Move. Follow the one lead you have.

He dropped the Plymouth into gear and looked for a way to turn around and head back to the Thruway.

GEORGE

NIGHTS OF SUCH BEAUTY, one thought they must come directly from the river. A night for lovers, that was certain, or astronomers. Yishaq had a brief vision of naked astronomers, swimming coupled in the chilly Seine while their telescopes swayed from moon to stars and back again. Even as he smiled at the image, he pinched himself, hard, on the inside of the elbow. Paris made quite an impression on me, he thought. I can't even keep a thought in my head since going there.

Or perhaps it's just the cathedral, that great book. All its mysteries, the stories told by its cornices, its sculptures, its very shape, telling themselves to one they think might listen. Yishaq felt gooseflesh ripple up along his dark skin. He was no longer in Paris; the dominant bulk of Chartres Cathedral told him that. And he knew it was the correct day, that much he could keep straight. And the moon told him that midnight must be fast approaching.

"The moonlight when the bell was chiming twelve," Rimbaud had said six weeks before, quoting himself. *Peculiar, what I knew when I thought I knew everything.* Yishaq patted the book of Rimbaud's poetry he had purchased at a stall in Paris. He had found the line three days before, and underlined it carefully. It seemed to him that there must be other lines in the book that he should note with equal care. When so much remained unknown . . .

Yishaq wished to be home, with the high plateau of Ethiopia under his feet. Harar, Axum, back in the caravan dying of thirst in the Shoa, anywhere but under the dead gaze of this cathedral at midnight as winter turned to spring.

He'd started walking without realizing it. Now his feet carried him away from the shuttered cafés and shops facing the cathedral's south porch, across the street and beneath the looming towers to the steps leading up to the north porch—"the door of the initiate," Rimbaud had called it. North, Yishaq thought. How much longer must I go north? Slowly he made his way up the steps, his mind seized by a fragmentary image of a man on the deck of a ship, awaiting the sight of land, fearful of what lay in the hold below.

The vaulted north porch was dominated by three groups of statuary, each like a gathering of vigilant ghosts in the near darkness. Yishaq began to shiver; that someone had known, seven hundred years ago . . .

On the left, the Virgin cradled her infant Son, while prophets clustered about them like so many eager fathers. Directly ahead, the sorcerer Melchizedek held a cup to his breast as if he too had an infant to suckle. Standing with him, the Patriarchs—Abraham, Moses, Samuel, David—turned their blank gazes outward, away from the Grail in Melchizedek's hands. To the right stood Makeda, the Queen of Sheba, her head turned slightly to the left as she listened to Solomon. At her feet crouched a child-size African slave, holding in an upturned palm some kind of orb or stone.

The truth of the situation, Yishaq thought. Run away, little slave, before your master, too, proves to you that all white men are hyenas. Even though they be poets, their fangs can't stay hidden behind words. And the gifts they bring from the north, beware.

A column stood between Melchizedek and the renegade Queen. Yishaq's eyes were not acute enough to penetrate the darkness of the vaulted porch, but he knew that the Ark of the Covenant itself was depicted there—in a carved tableau, as it was carried away from Israel to the remote monasteries of Ethiopia. Yishaq's mind fixed upon another image, a ragged line of Africans roped together, pulling the Ark over the stone blocks of a Roman road. When a figure stepped out from behind the column, he let out a short bark of fright.

"Be easy, my African friend." The white man held out his hands, palms out. "It was you, after all, who arranged this meeting. Rimbaud is in Aden?"

Yishaq nodded, swallowing to get some moisture back into his mouth. *"Oui,"* he said. "You are Michel?"

"Luckily for you. You must be careful, you know. An African in Chartres . . . well, let us just say that your presence has been remarked upon. By certain parties whom we both wish to keep in the dark regarding our project."

"I—"

Michel waved a hand. "You are naive, I understand that. It is not your choice that you have become involved. But, what is choice? Careful, always, from now on; in particular with Rimbaud. He must continue to believe that you intend to retrieve the—object—for him."

Yishaq waited silently, confused and stung by Michel's patronizing tone. Michel was leaving him an opening, expecting him to make a choice. Yishaq did not know how to respond, and realized that his silence might already have failed some test. He fingered the book in his pocket, wanting more than ever to be away from the cathedral, from France, from the north. Wanting the whole unholy business finished.

The flare of a match blinded him. He closed his eyes, waiting for the afterimage to fade. When he opened them, he could see the Frenchman's face clearly: long jaw, longer nose, mournful mustache. Steady and solemn as the prophets carved into the walls. Michel was speaking, not French but the short glottal syllables of Hebrew, and with his eyes closed Yishaq could swear that the statues in the room were murmuring a response. Oh God, he thought, I am so far from home. Stones speak in the language of prophets.

The match burned down, and Yishaq blinked, able to see a bit again. "Sorry," Michel said. *"Let there be light,* you know. I had a question that needed answering, and you weren't helping. Now: take this."

Yishaq reached out, and Michel slapped a folded sheaf of papers into his hand. "You must bear this, you know," Michel said, his face pale as the spirits Yishaq's mother had conjured to frighten him when he was a child. A trace of sympathy softened the Frenchman's tone. "We must speak no more, now that the statues are awakened; but I would wish you luck. Do not look at what I have given you until you are safely away from here. I will meet you when you arrive."

With that Michel disappeared into the darkness, gone as silently as he'd come.

Echoes of the Patriarchs' whispering seemed to linger in the stone crevices, and Yishaq thought that Makeda and Melchizedek had actually shifted, turning their faces toward him. Examining this interloper, weighing his motives on the ancient scale of history and belief. At the Queen's feet, her slave's mouth had split into a mocking grin. *Now only sand in all directions,* the slave said silently. *Long time will pass before you see another road.*

Door of the intitiates, Yishaq thought again, the words coming to him in Rimbaud's voice. And what madness have I taken rites for tonight, meeting an apostate Templar here on the eve of the equinox?

I could destroy these instructions. Or simply leave them here. Tuck them into the stone fingers of Moses and have done with it.

But what if what Rimbaud said was true? Yishaq saw him again, limping across stone floors in his rooms in Harar, the money belt always around his waist as if gold were what kept him alive. The awful hunger in his face when he said the words aloud.

Fisher King.

And if he could really be healed, his health restored . . . *Must I be Lancelot?* Yishaq found himself shivering again.

From darkness, shapes begin to resolve. A boat, on an ocean smooth and gray as smoked glass. George struggles out of the dream, sits up, shakes his head, catches his breath expecting the pain in his back, which does not come. He turns to his left and sees that the boat is docked, and that the dock goes straight and level as far as he can see. Walking toward them on its salted planks, a man in a white suit with the head of a bird. So he's still dreaming, and that's why his back doesn't hurt. He's at a hospital, they've given him drugs and he's dreaming like a Chinaman with a head full of opium.

Then he raises his hand without meaning to, and the hand he sees is skinny, with a crooked pinkie—and black.

It all crashes down on him. *Oh Christ I'm a nigger,* George thinks. *A dead nigger.*

"George Gibson," Yishaq says, and it takes George a moment to realize that he's speaking aloud, "I tire of your slurs."

Sorry, George says. *This is kind of a shock, you know.*

"No more of a shock than when I found myself attached to a white man. When I was a boy, I was told that white men have the blood of hyenas. Would you want to be in the mind of a hyena?"

George can't make any sense of this. Dreaming still?

The bird-headed man in the white suit climbs back onto the boat. "I got your book," he tells Yishaq, handing him a small leather-bound volume with French words on the cover. "The bookseller will pass the message along."

Yishaq puts the book in a small leather purse looped into his belt, George's belt. George feels the motion and is repelled when he can't resist it, can't change it at all. The thought that all this might be real is too much. Yishaq murmurs quietly, "This will not last. As soon as Michel hears about the book, he will know someone has the Grail. What he does then is his concern; what you must do is complete the task I was assigned."

What task, George wants to know. *How can I do it if I—Jesus God, I'm dead, Yishaq.*

The bird-headed man sits at the boat's tiller and unbuttons his suit coat. It is a small sailboat, its sail limply twisting around the mast, but as soon as he sits the boat begins to move, away from the end of the endless dock out onto the endless water. *Who is he?* George wonders, and the bird-headed man looks up as if he's heard the question.

"James," he says. "James Pitblado. Long time ago I worked with Michel, trying to prevent what happened here."

But you're helping us now . . . ?

"Michel can't be trusted anymore," Pitblado says simply.

Michel. The guy who killed me, George thinks. *The Templars have guys with birds' heads working for them?*

"Thoth puts his mark on those he uses," Yishaq says. Pitblado seems to have lost interest in the conversation. He looks out over the water. From time to time he adjusts the tiller, to no effect that George can see; the boat leaves no wake, and there are no stars in the sky to guide them.

Some time later, if you can call it time, George is walking . . . Yishaq is walking along the surface of the ocean. Far below them, ghostly lights wink, moving in the complex pattern of a dance; is this still the sea, George wonders, or are we in the air now, flying over some city of the dead?

"Good question," Yishaq says. They are sinking, walking ahead as they fall slowly to the bottom of the sea.

Where are all the fish? George asks.

"Good question," Yishaq says.

Where'd Pitblado go?

"Dead men marked by the gods have their own errands. You will find this."

They walk. Or rather, Yishaq walks. George watches. Should they have been there by now? Wherever *there* was?

Are we close? he asks.

"We will get there when we get there," Yishaq says. He is tiring, to judge from his voice, and George adds another worry to his list. What if Yishaq isn't strong enough to complete the journey? What will happen to George Gibson if his host simply stops, simply gives up in the middle of this endless midnight ocean?

"You will die, George Gibson." Yishaq's voice is grim and ragged. "But I will not give up. I crossed this ocean living, I will cross it dead."

As if hearing Yishaq's words, a sharp cliff thrusts itself up out of the darkness, its face fading away downward beyond the limits of vision. George whispers a prayer as Yishaq's foot finds thick mud, and he feels as if his bearings are returning. Yishaq stops to rest, and George can feel fatigue like the dying notes of birdsong in his limbs.

"If you were dead," Yishaq pants, "I would not have to carry you."

Are there others here? George asks.

Again words seem to have some power over this world. Ahead of them, a vast outline uncoils from the shallowing darkness, a head larger than Yishaq's field of vision brings its gaze to bear upon them.

"The Swallowing Monster," Yishaq says in greeting. "Eater of the Dead."

"It is well that you know me." The Leviathan's voice is more felt than heard.

"Why are you not the creature I have seen pictured?"

"You are two," the Monster says. "One gives me name, the other form. Thoth and Osiris: one cannot be born, one cannot die."

Yishaq named it, George thinks. So I gave it form? Why this? The beast before him is Leviathan, the great sea beast of the Bible, rising to life from his memories of Sunday school in Central City, Colorado. Who are Thoth and Osiris?

"Will you eat us? I carry a living man with me."

"If he is here, he is more dead than living," the Monster growls, appetite speaking in every word. "I eat who would pass."

"I would pass," Yishaq says, "and you must let me." He holds up the leather bag.

"What token is this?" the Eater murmurs, its voice like an earthquake rolling up from the bottom of the sea. The vast muzzle draws near, nudges the bag with the gentleness of great strength, withdraws. "The Bearer," says Leviathan, reluctantly. "The Bearer must pass."

Yishaq lowers the bag, and George can hear the gratitude in his voice. "Your mercy."

"Mercy," the Monster snorts. "I do what is commanded of me. I fulfill my role. Before you pass, I have a question for the one you carry." Again the great mouth glides by, the seemingly endless sweep of scaly jaw. An eye like the moon comes to rest at the level of Yishaq's face.

"My question, George Gibson," Leviathan says, and George shudders at its mention of his name. "When you fish, will you cast your line for me?"

Then it is gone, and the rumble of surf leads them up onto an alien shore.

Naked hills under a faintly starlit sky. A great estuary flows around them, a river mouth as broad as any George has ever seen. "This was half our journey," Yishaq says. "The water is behind, the land ahead."

Where are we? George asks.

"Still in the land of the dead. But this land I know. Africa: I have come home." Yishaq kneels, buries his hands in silver sand. Then he gasps, tries to stand, and George sees that another pair of hands have grasped Yishaq's. Yishaq pulls, and a woman rises from the earth, sand running from her naked body like rivulets of water. George hears the word in Yishaq's head before it is spoken: *Mother.*

She stands before him, his height exactly, her son's hands held in her own. She speaks his name, echoes his words. "Yishaq, you have come home. Return to your land. Leave this white man."

George's vision blurs with tears. "My errand, Mother. I do not know if he is strong enough."

"If he must, he will," she says. "Have you not done enough? Is not dying for your errand enough, this errand that you did not seek? Can you not be peaceful even in death?"

"Mother," Yishaq sobs. His longing is tangible, the tidal pull of love. George fights against the surge, struggles not to be lost in the maelstrom of Yishaq's emotion.

There is one thing to do.

"No, George," Yishaq is saying, but beneath the words George can feel the upwelling of hope, the gasping joy Yishaq feels at the prospect of being relieved of his burden.

You saved my life, George says. *I give you your death.*

What is that in the bag, Yishaq?

All the stars go out, sucked into Yishaq's mouth as he throws his head back to cry out for joy. The sound of his voice is the sound of Leviathan, the Swallowing Monster, saying *When you fish, will you cast your line for me?* and the sound of the surf rearing up to plunge against the current of the river. George hears all these voices, realizes that they are the same voice, realizes that he has opened himself up to the world. All the voices, all the cries of pain and shouts of joy, whispered love and murmured hate, the bright green glee of a budding flower and the tired despair of a leaf falling in autumn—all of these are his now.

Was this your burden, Yishaq?

"No," Yishaq answers. He has fallen into his mother's arms, and George hears his voice through her mouth. "Your burden, George Gibson, is greater than mine, because in asking after the nature of the Grail, you ensnare yourself in its pursuit. Rimbaud still lives, and he has touched the Ark. The Grail is his to claim. Be on your guard: the only way Rimbaud can assume the Kingship is to kill you, and he will not scruple about it. Neither will Michel. When Pitblado bought the book, they were thrown off the scent. But they will find it again—they will find you again. I was sent to bring the Grail to Rimbaud, and I betrayed my errand. You must as well. You must return the Grail to its resting place; you must complete the Ark of the Covenant.

"Go to Axum, to the monastery where they keep the Ark. If you can return it, my errand and yours are discharged. But if the Ark will not take the Grail from you, and it may not, then your choices multiply afresh."

George is seeing Yishaq from the outside now, as if he is regaining his own body. *Not yet, not yet,* he thinks; *if I am bodied in the land of the dead, how will I ever return to the living?*

"This is not your fear," Yishaq says. He pushes forward, and his body begins to melt into his mother's. "You have given me back to my land, George Gibson, and for that I give you back to the living. Go now; we will not speak again."

Yishaq disappears into his mother's body, and before George has time to be afraid of the awful burden he's shouldered, he feels himself exhaled from the land of the dead like a last lingering breath.

When George could open his eyes again, he was kneeling in the sand at the mouth of a great river, a small leather bag tied to his right wrist and a group of terrified natives fleeing from him into the dense jungle. His back hurt when he straightened, and when he reached back to examine the pain he found the hilt of a knife. It came loose, and he felt the wound begin to close and itch as it healed. The Grail, he thought. It's real. He nearly opened the bag to look at it, but Yishaq had said it was part of the Ark of the Covenant, and George remembered his Sunday school well enough to know that you didn't look at the Ark of the Covenant. Get rid of it, he thought. Yishaq saved your life, and you don't want it anyway. So do what he asked you to do.

The knife was simple, double-edged with a wire-wrapped pommel. He put it in the purse at his belt, heard it clink against something that sounded like money. Closing his eyes, George reached tentatively into the bag. Inside, it was divided into two pockets. The larger pocket held the knife, the little book of poems, and a handful of coins. He took out one of the coins and looked at it. On one side was a human figure, separated ever so slightly at every joint, as if it had been dismembered and then laid back in the shape of a man. On the other side was a man with the head of a bird.

He closed his eyes again and put the coin back, careful not to reach into the other pocket.

I don't have to do this, he thought. I could just throw the whole goddamn works into the surf and walk to the nearest white settlement. Get working passage on a boat to Europe, then back to America. Keep the coins, maybe. Forget the whole thing.

But Yishaq had saved his life.

Just so I could clean up his mess, George thought angrily. Hell with him. Let the Templars do what they're going to do. What do I care about the goddamn Knights Templar? It doesn't affect me.

That didn't hold up either, though, when he thought about the knife. That yellow bastard, George thought. He stuck a knife in me and watched me drown. Right there is reason enough to put this Grail back where it belongs, just to get a thumb in his eye. And if I ever see him, he better watch out.

Fresh determination propelled him to his feet. He looked around again, and saw Africa. The jungle absorbed his gaze and reflected nothing back. He took in a breath, felt the liquid, steaming air in his lungs like a cough, exhaled and was surprised that he couldn't see what was coming out of his mouth. Sweating already, he pulled his collar away from his neck and blew down his shirt. To his left, a tiny fort squatted behind timber walls between him and the ocean, and a disorienting wave swept over George as he realized that he was looking west across the Atlantic Ocean. He was really in Africa. Stanley and Livingstone, Burton and Speke had struggled across desert and jungle, fought natives and wild animals, died of diseases and venomous bites and cannibals' stew pots here. And I thought I was really traveling when I went to Canada, George thought. He tried to remember how Africa looked on a map; if he was in the west, and Ethiopia was in the east, he still had some traveling ahead of him. Maybe the soldiers in the fort there would be able to help him out.

Walking toward the fort, George felt the landscape begin to fall into place around him. He felt better when he could imagine New York facing him across the sea, better still when he could imagine the hilly eastern United States giving way to the Great Plains and then the Rocky Mountains, in whose foothills Martha still waited for him. Was she thinking of him right then, while she was cooking in the back of her father's Black Hawk tavern or throwing a stick for her black-and-white mongrel dog? George wondered if he could post a letter from this fort, wherever it was, and how much it would cost. He touched the bag at his wrist to reassure himself that it was still there and that he still had a little money.

And the Grail. A sharp surge of energy ran up George's arm, the way he thought electricity must feel. I am no different, he thought. I carry the Grail, but I'm no King, I'm no Arthur. Saint George, though, maybe?

He laughed out loud.

"Hello!" he called, pounding on the fort's gate. "Anyone there?"

A soldier appeared on the wall above his head, aiming a rifle more or less in George's direction. He shouted a demand in what sounded like French.

"Was that French?" George said. "I don't speak French. My girlfriend does. *Parlez-vous anglais?*" It was the one phrase of French he remembered.

"Anglais?" The soldier disappeared, came back a moment later with a second.

"Are you English?" the second man asked.

"American."

"American?" A quick burst of French between the two soldiers. "What are you doing here, American?"

Hm. That was a good question. Best to get right to the point, George decided. "I have to get to Abyssinia."

The English-speaking soldier laughed. "Oh, you do? Abyssinia is four thousand kilometers away, my American friend. How do you think to get there?"

George shrugged. He didn't know what a kilometer was. More or less than a mile?

Still laughing, the soldier said something in French to the first guard, who waved over the wall. The gate creaked open and George strolled into the fort.

The soldiers turned out to be Belgian, keeping a small outpost on this side of the river, across from the main settlement of Banana on the north side of the Congo River estuary. George went up onto the walls and saw the small town to the north, across miles of brown water. In the other direction, the jungle crept to the very edge of the ocean; if humans lived there, no sign escaped the endless devouring green.

"How can I get to Abyssinia?" he asked the lieutenant on duty, one DeSailly.

"You can't," DeSailly said. "Impossible. Mountains, jungle, no roads, fever. Madness."

"Still, I have to go," George said. "Can I take a boat?"

"As far as Leopoldville, yes. But after that you would be on your own. Nobody goes from here to Abyssinia. Stanley himself is trying for the Sudan right now, and he will die in the attempt."

George thought about this for a few minutes while an off-shore breeze blew across his face. This wind came from America, he thought. Across all that water. I came from America, too, but not quite the same way. At this he smiled ruefully and wished Yishaq were there to offer some kind of guidance. Sorry, friend, he said silently. I didn't mean all those things I said.

"Well, hell, Lieutenant," he said to DeSailly. "I said I'd do it. And I don't lie."

LANCE

COMING UP to the customs checkpoint at St. Stephen, New Brunswick, across the river from Calais, Maine, Lance got a cold sweat from realizing that the Plymouth's registration wasn't in his name. He wasn't sure he was up to lying to a customs official. Could always just spill the whole story, he thought, and hope they just lock me up. Then I'd be rid of the whole problem. Let it all blow over, wait until Spicer and Jerry and Gwen all forget about me.

But this was Dewey. This was his brother.

He pulled up to the inspection booth, radio on but not too loud, arm hanging out the window, duffel bag in plain view on the back seat. Just a guy out for a drive, crossing borders, nothing to hide.

The guy in the booth was bald and wide in the hips, with a prissy little mustache. "Citizen of?" he asked without looking at Lance.

"U.S."

"Coming from?"

"New York."

"Destination?"

"Nova Scotia."

"Purpose?"

"I'm going to visit my brother. Haven't seen him since I got out of the army."

That got a glance from the border guard. "You in Korea?"

"Just got home a couple of weeks ago," Lance said.

"How long do you plan to stay?"

"Couple of days, maybe three. Long enough to catch up."

The customs guy made a note on his pad. "Enjoy your time in Canada," he said, and forgot all about Lance.

He pulled off the road to sleep when he'd made thirty or forty miles into Canada. When he woke up, sweating inside the car on a brilliant morning, he felt like he'd lost his memory. Wasn't he in New York? Wasn't he in San Francisco? Wasn't he on a ship in the Sea of Japan? Too much traveling, felt like he'd left little bits of himself all across North America. He got out of the car, stretched, stomped back into the trees to take a leak—so much for vows about indoor plumbing—before hitting the road again. Seeing Dewey would put him square on his feet again.

New Brunswick looked a lot like Maine. Pine forests gave way to black-water muskrat bogs full of dead trees gave way to pine forests. He passed through a town here and there, but mostly the roadside was trees, interrupted by occasional small houses with cars pulled up in their yards and signs advertising small-engine repair or woodwork or Authentic Maritime Crafts! By the time he got to Saint John, he'd seen only half a dozen stoplights, and New Brunswick's capital wasn't much bigger than Dexter, from the looks of it. Maybe the size of Ypsilanti. He was through it in five minutes, and on around the Bay of Fundy across the Nova Scotia peninsula, bearing away from Halifax to the southern coast. He started to see signs for Lunenburg and Mahone Bay, and remembered Spicer's story of George Gibson. Was there really a farmhouse across from Oak Island? Maybe he'd go see after he talked to Dwight.

Talked to Dwight. After eight years, he was going to talk to Dwight.

At last Lance let go of the idea that his brother was dead, and as he let go of it his last memory of Dewey tore Lance loose from his twenty-first year and left him sprawled on the banks of Warrior Creek in the summer of 1945, where he lay weeping because he hadn't *been there*. Whatever had happened to Dewey would have been different if Lance had been there.

He'd told Dewey he was going down by the river to catch some frogs so they could gig for pike out on the lake that weekend, and Dewey had wanted to come along, but the truth was that Lance was going to meet Ellie. I'll kiss you if you meet me at the Tree of Many Roots, she'd said. Tomorrow morning at nine. He couldn't tell Dewey, couldn't tell anybody. He had to keep it all to himself until it had happened. If he talked about it, she might change her mind; these things were fragile, bound up with the strange magic of girls, and any disturbance might ruin his chance. So he put Dewey off, said he wanted to go by himself, and when Dewey pressed him Lance got sharp: Look, I don't always want you around, I just want to go by myself, okay? And then he'd gotten on his bike and split for the Tree without looking to see the hurt he knew was on his brother's face.

The Tree of Many Roots was a huge oak that grew out of a slope above the creek. Years of erosion had exposed the downhill part of its root system, and you could crawl in under the giant trunk, earth behind you and living tree above, with the roots like a woven curtain hiding you away from the world. They'd all been going there since they were old enough to explore the woods on their own, Lance and Dwight and Jerry K. and even Ellie and a couple of other girls once in a while. The hollow under the Tree had been Tom Sawyer's treasure cave, the dungeon of the Man in the Iron Mask, a hideout for the Lone Ranger and Tonto, Superman's Arctic fortress, and any other secluded place they read about or heard on the radio. Their imaginations lived there, and now Lance imagined it the lair of a dragon, himself the knight and Ellie the damsel he'd just rescued who would reward him with a kiss. He flew out Dexter-Pinckney Road past the fork that led to Chelsea, then down an old dirt track that petered out north of town, on land that had been logged over sixty years before and then left to grow wild again. The frog pail clanked on his handlebars, and his breath came hard, but more from anticipation than exertion because he was twelve and could do anything. He dropped the bike at the side of the track where a narrow footpath disappeared between sumac bushes, and dove into the woods, thinking only of Ellie. And she was there, watching him come breathless up the path toward the Tree, resting her hand on one of its roots, thick as Lance's leg, that arched out and then dove into the earth at her feet. She was wearing a plaid skirt, canvas shoes, a white short-sleeve blouse. A wide blue band held her hair back from her forehead. He stopped in front of her, unsure of what he should do next. Were you supposed to take her in your arms? He'd kissed girls playing spin the bottle, but this was different. This was real, and he had no idea what he should do.

Her hands found his, and the touch calmed him. The magic of girls, they always knew what to do, or at least Ellie did and that's why he thought he loved her. She kissed him, softly, closing her eyes and tilting her head a little so their noses didn't bump, and at the first brush of her lips Lance closed his eyes too. Something minty tingled on his mouth—she'd brushed her teeth, oh God and he hadn't, but she leaned into him a little and brought his hands around to the small of her back. The pang of mortification left him and he let his hands open, feeling the waistband of her skirt below his fingers, the swell of her hips. A long, long moment passed, the sensation of her lips on his, the smell of her shampoo, the trilling of cicadas somewhere in the trees, and then she brought his hands back to his sides and broke the kiss. Her eyes were dancing, like shafts of sunlight falling into the river, and Lance thought he might never speak again.

She did, though. "Come back tomorrow and I'll give you another one," she said, backing away a step, and then she was off down the trail, running with astonishing grace.

Lance floated to his bike and rode back into town. The world was a brand-new place. He crossed the bridge by the carhop stand and was suddenly bursting with desire to tell Dewey. Before it happened, the kiss was like a wish too cherished to reveal; now he couldn't wait to let Dewey in on it.

Late in the afternoon he saw a sign for Peggy's Cove and swung onto a winding two-lane road that paralleled the coast. He could see the water through breaks in the trees, the Atlantic Ocean. It looked just like Lake Michigan, but through the Plymouth's open windows came a crisp salty tang that reminded Lance of San Francisco. He pulled into a gas station ("petrol" here in Canada) and filled the Plymouth. It occurred to him to wonder about money, since his VA checks were going to Michigan and he didn't know how long he'd stay in Canada, but he still had two hundred bucks or so, and he would worry about that problem when it became a problem. Right now he'd done the right thing, and when you did the right thing, problems took care of themselves.

Looking for someone to take his money, Lance went into the garage and saw a pair of legs sticking out from under a shiny red Buick set up on jacks. Curses ricocheted out of the Buick's engine compartment.

"Excuse me," Lance said to the boots.

"Oh," the boots' wearer said. Something clanged on the floor and he rolled out on a low carriage, wiping his hands on the exact same blue rag that Lance had seen in the coverall pocket of every mechanic he'd ever known. "Sorry about that," he said, his vowels clipped and rounded. "Get carried away turnin' wrenches. Need directions?"

"No, I got some gas. Petrol."

"Okay." The mechanic—Lyle, according to the patch over his left shirt pocket—led Lance to the cash register. Lance paid for the gas and bought a Dr Pepper from the vending machine outside. Then he went back in and asked Lyle if he knew of anyone named Dwight Porter in the area.

"Sure do," Lyle said, nodding and still wiping his hands. "Lives right down on the water 'tween here and West Dover. Past the lighthouse. From the States, this fellow you're looking for?"

"Yeah, an old school friend. Thought I'd come up here for a vacation."

"Couldn't have made a better choice." Lyle got enthusiastic, digging at his cuticles and then polishing the snaps on his coveralls. "Wife and I went to the States once. Got as far as Boston and turned around. Too many people. Maine's all right, I suppose. I don't blame Dwight for comin' up here."

Lance wondered what stories Dwight told people, who he'd become since coming to Canada. Had he just showed up here, twelve years old, and settled into the town without anyone thinking it was strange? Couldn't be. Had he been somewhere else for a while? It crossed Lance's mind to ask Lyle, but he couldn't very well do that and still keep up the pretense of being an old friend.

"Yes sir," Lyle went on. "God's country, this is. Weather gets prickly once in a while, but I wouldn't live anywhere else." He looked Lance up and down, his gaze lingering on the army cap and boots. "Soldier, are you?"

"Just back from Korea," Lance said.

"Guess you need a vacation, then, don't you?" Lyle laughed, then got serious again. "Can't abide communists. Somebody had to do something."

But why me? Lance thought. To Lyle he said, "Yeah, I guess so. Suppose you could give me directions to Dwight's place?"

• • •

Wearing only a pair of cutoff corduroy pants, Dwight was painting a boat when Lance pulled the Plymouth into the gravel half
circle that served as driveway. His house was smaller than Lance's
mother's garage, a white saltbox much more in need of a paint job
than the overturned skiff. A bicycle leaned against the wall near
the front door, and a clothesline was strung from the eaves,
drooping between one downspout and a scrubby pine tree ten
feet away. Twenty feet beyond the tree, a sagging dock poked out
onto the water, missing planks and flaking rust from every bolt
and post. Dwight looked up at the car's approach, then stood as
Lance cut the ignition and slowly got out, favoring his hip. Leaning back in the passenger seat was one thing, he was up to that,
but hours of driving locked up the joint but good. He shut the
door and started to walk around the front end of the car, all the
while meaning to say something but muted by the mass of words
that gathered on the tip of his tongue.

Dwight started to say something, then turned to set his paint-
brush across the open can. He wiped his hands on his shorts and
looked out over the ocean, where a broken line of clouds was retreating toward the Outer Banks. As Lance got close to him, he
looked back, and they regarded each other. Lance wanted to
touch him, embrace him, but couldn't quite believe he was real.

Dewey did it for him, and in his brother's embrace Lance remembered the rest of the day he'd lost him.

He banged through the screen door, annoying his mother.
"Gadzooks and little fishes, kid, you'll break that door, and then
who's going to put it back up?" she said.

"Where's Dewey?" Lance was already running down the hall.

"Said he was going to catch frogs," she called after him, and
Lance stopped at the door to Dewey's room. A little of his exhilaration dissipated at the thought that Dewey might have followed

after him, only to discover that Lance had lied and gone somewhere else. Even though they were twins, Lance had always felt like the older brother, like it was his responsibility to look after Dewey; he was disappointed in himself that he'd left his brother lonely. He'd apologize, and he wouldn't do it again. When he told Dewey why he'd lied, Dewey would understand.

The best frog spot within biking distance was a pool in Warrior Creek, upstream from the Main Street bridge, and Lance crashed his way through the brush until he couldn't hear the cars in town anymore. Where the trees grew tilting and close together, the low weedy bank made for prime frog territory. He came out of the brush and saw a pair of Chuck Taylor sneakers and a white T-shirt, and then all he could remember was the police and the nets dragging the creek all the way up to the Huron River and the worry on his mother's face becoming awful sorrow. Lance would never get to tell Dewey about Ellie's kiss, would never get to explain to him why he'd been hurtful when all he'd wanted was to fall in love.

All this in the time it took Lance to feel the life and strength in his brother Dewey, feel the pain spark and recede as the muscles in his leg loosened, and step back to arm's length to really see his brother, alive and tanned, hair a little too long and streaked with blond from the salt air.

"Been a long drive, probably," Dwight said finally. "Come on in."

Molsons in hand, they settled around a wooden table in the middle of the room that served Dwight as kitchen and living space. A small stove, refrigerator, and sink took up one wall. Across the small room, a couch rested under a window looking out onto the road, where evening fog had crept around the Plymouth's running boards. A doorway opened onto a short hall with a bedroom at one end and a mudroom at the other. In between was a bathroom almost big enough to do a jumping jack in.

"This place yours?" Lance asked. He was relaxing after the trip, still feeling that sense of rightness about everything, and taking no small pleasure in the cold beer. Dwight's house smelled of the sea and old wood, along with wafts of the beef stew simmering on the stove.

"I rent it from an old woman in town. Her husband used to fish, but he had a stroke and she moved back in with her daughter. Thirty bucks a month, can you believe it? Canadian."

"What do you do?"

"Oh, whatever needs doing. During the season I go out on the boats once in a while, dig some clams, mend nets. You know. Winter, I mostly sit around. Tried brewing beer, but it didn't come out. I have a lot of time to read. Think." Dwight leaned back in his chair and rolled his bottle between his hands. "I think about going back to the States once in a while, but not yet. I'm invisible here, and for a while that's okay. Things are good here." He paused.

Dwight motioned toward Lance's leg as he put his beer down on the table. "You know I have to ask this, right? How it happened?"

"You don't have to," Lance said.

"No, I do. How did it happen, Lance?"

It wasn't something you talked about, but this was his brother. So Lance told him the story: the sunrise over the line of hills, earned after a long night on watch with a throbbing molar and fatigue like ground glass in your eyes. Snow still clinging to the shady patches and rocky overhangs, the cold fighting it out with the tentative greening of spring. The whistle of the shell, the very first of the morning, and the blast that threw him to his left over a line of sandbags to skid down the muddy hillside toward the reedy marsh. The icy water, so much colder than the air.

Blood in your eyes as you crawl out of the water to lie in the mud and look at your femur, bits of grass clinging to its broken edge, so white against the shredded mess of your thigh. The feeling you can only get when you're screaming for a medic but you don't really want him to come because then he'll see that you've shit yourself from shock and fear.

Dwight didn't say anything when he'd finished.

"It's pretty much healed," Lance said after a while. "Bit of a limp, and the docs at the MASH said they didn't have time to get all the shrapnel, so I feel that every so often. But you know— could have been a lot worse."

"Oh, man." Dwight's fingers kneaded his face. "Oh, man, I never meant . . ."

"Dewey," Lance said. "Hey, little brother." Dwight wouldn't look at him, and Lance let him stay like that for a long moment, elbows on the table, fingers working at his face.

Meant what? Lance wondered. Meant to sit here in Canada while I went halfway around the world to leave pieces of myself in the mud? *Meant*, hell. It *happened*. I didn't run, I didn't hide, I just did what I was supposed to do. He was gloating, lording Dwight's guilt over him, and when he realized it Lance was ashamed of himself. He didn't know what Dewey had been through, why he'd done what he did. This was family.

"Dewey," Lance said softly. "I don't blame you. I wouldn't have come all this way just to blame you."

"That's not what I'm talking about," Dwight said, his voice muffled. Lance couldn't see if he was crying, didn't really want to know because right then it had all gotten to be too much. Dewey was alive, and instead of celebrating they'd found themselves tip-toeing around all kinds of emotions grown too hot to the touch. Enough, Lance thought. We don't have to do this all in one night.

Outside, the sun had gone down and the fog was climbing over the Plymouth's roof. "It's been a long trip," Lance said. "I'll crash on your couch."

• • •

He woke up with the feeling that it had been light for quite a while. Sun came in the window over the couch, and Lance, after a slow moment's figuring, realized that it must be after noon. He stood, found his boots, carried them around while he sleepily bumped into the table and the hall door frame. In the bathroom he dropped the boots and took a leak that made him feel like he'd just slept twelve hours—which, if his guess was correct, fell four or five hours short. He flushed the toilet, sat on it, and laced his boots. In the kitchen a pot of coffee was still warm on the stove. Lance filled a Mason jar and went out to look at the ocean.

Dwight sat relaxed but erect at the edge of his dock, feet swaying in the gentle swell of St. Margaret's Bay. He was still wearing the cutoff corduroys and still holding a Molson in his right hand, and a light offshore breeze lifted sun-bleached curls away from the nape of his neck. Lance walked onto the dock, sorry now that he'd put on his boots. A little dip in the North Atlantic would be perfect to shake the half-a-day-in-the-sack lethargy. Like a swim in Lake Michigan, only salty. "You sit out here all night?" he said.

Dwight shook his head. "Watched the sun come up," he said. "Haven't had a good reason to move since then." He tossed the bottle over his head, back toward the house. "Don't worry over me, meatball. I didn't sit up all night feeling guilty." Standing, Dwight stretched, then dove off the dock. He came up thirty feet or so away, shook water from his hair, and said, "I have bread, if you want some toast."

"Good idea," Lance said. Yeah, he was hungry. It had been nearly twenty-four hours since he'd eaten. He started to say something else, but Dwight ducked under the water and reappeared farther out, stroking smoothly across the rolling face of the ocean.

The toast was better than it had any right to be, crisp and buttery and perfect with the strong coffee and the slight tang of the breeze. Lance sat at the table, glancing at the spines of the books stacked at one corner: Jung, Frazer's *Golden Bough*, Nietzsche's *Beyond Good and Evil*, some paperback science fiction. And Suzuki's *Introduction to Zen Buddhism*. "Heavy reading," he said as Dwight walked in, breathing heavily and dripping on the floor.

"You don't know the half of it," Dwight said, and went into his bedroom. "It's a good thing you brought a car," he called. "Let's take a ride."

Half an hour later they were walking along the Halifax waterfront, where Dartmouth Cove broadened into Halifax Harbour. Clear sunlight shone on the water, highlighting the wakes of fishing boats as they moved like a migrating pod into the estuary from open ocean. Coming the opposite way, a drawbridge slowly lowering behind it, a coal freighter warned them away with deafening basso blasts of its horn. Dwight stopped at a restaurant small enough to have once been a fare booth for pleasure cruises and ordered fried clams and french fries for both of them, with lemonades to wash it down, and led Lance to a bench out on one of the piers that had been given over to tourists and teenagers. "How's Jerry?" he asked, a glob of tartar sauce sliding down his chin. He wiped at it, sucked it off a finger.

"Losing his goddamn mind," Lance said, before he could think of a more diplomatic way to put it. "Acted like there were Freemasons in his coffee grounds. That guy should be on the radio as an ad for the Joe McCarthy School of Human Relations."

"He's right, though," Dwight said, still grinning and swabbing another clam through the paper cup of tartar sauce.

"Right how?"

"Never mind. You done? Let's take a walk."

Ten minutes upriver, Dwight paused and made a sweeping gesture that took in all of the river and the white houses of Dartmouth on the other side. "Close to the end of World War One," he said, "an ammunition ship caught on fire around here. The crew couldn't put it out, and when they abandoned ship, it just floated a little ways downriver and blew up. This whole area"—he turned in a complete circle, his arm still held out parallel to the side-walk—"was flattened. I've seen pictures, and I swear to God it looked like Hiroshima, only not as big."

He dropped his arm and turned back to Lance. "Almost two thousand people died, and maybe a hundred of them had anything to do with the war. Reason I'm telling you this, meatball, is to let you know that I know something that I don't think you know I know. Wars happen, and when they happen, people get killed. Not all of them are involved. And—and this is really the point— it's true the other way around, too. Sometimes people who should have been there get away scot-free. That's me. You fake the draft board, or your number never comes up, or your dad is a congressman and pulls some strings, or you take your terrified ass out of the country. It all amounts to the same thing. What I'm say-ing to you is that I take responsibility for what I did, and Joe College whose dad knows someone in the State Department doesn't. So if you're worried that I'm feeling guilty about your leg, ease your mind."

Lance found that he'd been waiting to speak for some time. The question jumped out of his mouth and hung there in the late-summer Canadian afternoon.

"Why are you angry at me, Dewey?"

Which wasn't the question he wanted to ask.

"Come on, stop with the bullshit," Dwight said. "You want to know why I didn't come home, or why I didn't write. Spit it out, Lance: why did I let you think I was dead? Isn't that what you want to know?"

"No, it isn't. I swear to God I don't want to know that. I mean, I do, but if . . ." I don't want to hear the explanation and have it not be good enough, Lance thought. I don't want to have to feel that way about my brother. "Is that why you sent Jerry all that way to find me, so I could come across the country and hear you explain yourself? Please tell me there's more to it than that."

Dewey waited for Lance to say something else, then shook his head.

"You're holding out on me," Dwight said. "Before I tell you what's going on here, or as much as I know, I need you to level with me. Tell me everything you've done since you got home from Korea. Some of it I've already heard, I know you talked to Spicer and I'm guessing Jerry worked you over pretty good while you drove east, but I don't get much in the way of details. So spill it. You walk out of the army in Oakland, and what do you do?"

"First you tell me something. How'd you know to send Jerry to the diner?"

"Gwen told me you'd been talking to Spicer."

Gwen.

Tell him, Lance thought. Get it off your chest. Work it out. It's been too long to let a girl come between you now.

But a girl already had, a long time ago, when he'd gone to the Tree to see Ellie and left his brother behind, and it was too soon to let all that out now. When Lance opened his mouth, he meant to at least come clean about Gwen, but he did what Dewey had said, started from the beginning: discharge, Berkeley, meeting Spicer on the campus, talking to Ellie, Spicer again at the White Horse, and then San Francisco with its lotus-eater charms. Shaking himself loose to go look for Ellie again, running from cops real or imagined, finding Spicer, and then the shock of seeing Jerry K. at the diner. Somehow he skipped Gwen. Too many variables already, and something was different about Dewey—and even if Lance had been comfortable with everything else, shame had a way of gluing his tongue to the roof of his mouth.

Dewey took it all in, nodding here and there, cracking a smile at Spicer or Jerry. When Lance had finished, Dwight leaned back. "Okay," he said. "It's not as bad as I thought it might be. So let's start with this question: do you believe that you might be the Fisher King?"

It came across like a job-interview question—do you have any experience that might be relevant to our needs?—and for some reason Dewey's tone put Lance on the defensive. "Dewey, I don't even know for sure what a Fisher King is. Spicer says this, Jerry says that, both of them tell me stories about some baseball player who found the Holy Grail down the road from here, what the hell do I know?"

"Do you believe it?"

"I guess so," Lance said. "Everyone else seems pretty sure of it, and they all know more than I do."

"Good. Because in the end this is all about belief. Now, what would you say if I told you that I've been here these past six years waiting to become King myself?"

"What—are you—Dewey, Jesus Christ. Are you telling me we're rivals?"

"Now we are. When you came back from Korea with that"—Dewey pointed at Lance's leg—"you were marked. But before that they were grooming me."

And not you, Dewey didn't say, but it hit Lance all the same. He'd been left behind, with his guilt and their mother's drawn shades and drawn-out silences, while Dwight had been taken to await their birthright. And who would have done that but their father?

Eight years old, skipping through the Michigan Avenue crowd at the end of his first Tigers game, Lance had run and joked with Dwight until they'd gotten to the car, parked over on Trumbull Avenue behind a lumberyard. Playing catch in the parking lot, the smell of fresh-cut wood in his nose, Lance had gloried in a sudden hot defiance. Who needs a father? he'd thought, when you have a brother like Dewey—and after Dewey was gone Lance had carried that moment with him like a birthmark. Now he felt their father's choice with an eight-year-old's pure despairing disbelief.

Dewey had always been the favorite. And somewhere along the line their father had watched and weighed and decided that Lance wasn't as good as his brother. He looked at Dewey now, saw him tanned and healthy and confident while Lance had hobbled home lost and friendless, teased along with wild stories until he'd swallowed the whole thing. All for this, to hear his brother's calm voice telling him that their father loved him more than Lance. All this while I thought you were dead, he thought. I've spent the last six years killing myself because I thought I could have stopped it, and here you are telling me I've been a fucking dupe all along. He was too deeply hurt to cry.

"Is this what you got me up here to tell me?" he asked his brother.

"That's part of it," Dewey said. "Also I wanted to tell you that I don't want it. It's all yours, the Grail, the whole thing. I don't want anything to do with it."

You wouldn't, Lance thought. You know he picked you, and that's enough, isn't it? You can afford to give this away because you'll always know that it was meant for you.

Good, then. I'll take it, you goddamn bet I will, and we'll just see what I do. Dewey could sit painting his boat. Lance would be King, and their father would see he'd been wrong.

Lance took his anger and hurt and resolve, and he molded it into a small stone in his gut, just below his heart, where he could feel it with every breath. He felt cold and certain, as if the world had narrowed to the notch between the sights of the M-1 broken down in the bottom of his bag.

"I'll take it," he said, and tried to smile. "So what do I do?"

Dwight watched him, his gaze sober and searching, but Lance was cool. The rules had been laid out, and from here on out he'd play the game.

"We'll get to that," Dwight said. "But first we should catch up, you know? How about we get a beer?"

BOOK THREE

But black alchemy and sacred studies
Repulse the wounded soul; pride's dark scholar,
He feels an unbearable solitude bearing down.
                    ARTHUR RIMBAUD, "Sisters of Charity"

It was not searching the grail or finding it that prompted
     me
It was playing the fool
                    JACK SPICER, "The Book of Percival"

ARTHUR

ARTHUR WISHED he still had Yishaq around to do things like paddle these damned papyrus-reed canoes. I could row a proper boat, he thought, but these woven weeds feel as if they'll shred at the first breeze. And if I fell in this water, Yishaq's errand wouldn't much matter. Except to the Templars.

It always came back to the Templars, sneaking their way about the wings of history. It was no accident, this Italian interest in Ethiopia. The Vatican pulled strings on both sides of the Mediterranean, and Arthur was certain of one thing—inside the Holy See, the hands on those strings belonged to men wearing the Red Cross. Let them call themselves Freemasons or Knights of St. John; names were just that. Just words. The gift of the human species was not reason; it was the ability—not to mention the proclivity—to lie. As I am about to lie to this mad *kahen,* he thought. If poetry has taught me anything, it is man's desire not only to tell lies, but to hear them.

He let the *tankwa* glide onto the sandy shore of Tana Kirkos, a lumpy island in the eastern reaches of Lake Tana, far away from the Italian garrisons on the Red Sea coast. The garrisons that so annoyed Menelik, who still schemed to annex the whole of Eritrea and much of the Sudan. But certain other events had indirectly led Arthur here. And given him the groaning wound in his right leg that brought beads of sweat to his forehead as he stepped ashore and hauled the *tankwa* clear of Lake Tana's gentle waves. Limping along the beach, Arthur flipped a coin in the air, watching the faces of Osiris on one side and Thoth on the other as they glittered in the reddening sunlight. Wondemu would want to see this coin despite knowing of Arthur's transformation. It was a peculiar sort of currency, circulated by a peculiar and limited group of people.

Who do not yet know that I have touched what they have only sought after, Arthur thought. For all the damned Templars have discovered, in this one thing—the most important of all—I have surpassed them. And for my achievement I am slowly dying.

Such were the gifts of dreams.

Spell that took me flesh and soul, dissipated every goal, he had written once, seventeen years old and only able to name it bliss. And bliss it was of a sort; gold found its way to him as if he were a walking (limping now, ha ha) Philosopher's Stone, and both women and men acted like bitches in heat when he looked at them a certain way. The gift that eluded him, though, the gift that would cure him and give him the power to cure or kill . . . in search of this he had paddled the many kilometers from Bahar Dar, blistering his hands and driving the pain in his leg to the threshold of delirium. Wondemu, he hoped, could be duped into setting him on its trail.

The old priest appeared, hunched and knobby as the rocks flanking the path that led from his church down to the beach. Weathered as the stones that fell from that church when the winter rains blew across Lake Tana, overflowing it and causing floods that, five thousand kilometers downstream, fed the people of Egypt. In his black robe and toque he looked like an alchemist from a Renaissance drama, a "fantastical scholar" bent over elixirs and nefarious extractions. "Monsieur Rimbaud," he said in his whining French. "You have traveled far, knowing the danger to both of us."

Much more to you than me, thought Arthur, but he returned the greeting. *"Kahen,"* he said, "let this ease your mind." He flipped the coin into the priest's outstretched hand.

Wondemu's leathered face bunched around his beard as he studied the portraits. The coin had been minted in 1317, in the Vatican's own molds, just ten years after the great farce of the Templar suppression—the same year when the terrible three-year famine in Europe had finally abated. Fewer than one hundred of these coins remained, used as passkeys into dialogue that would otherwise be fatal to one party or the other. The *kahen* bit into the coin, looking for all the world like a stock moneychanger in another old play.

Crooked bite marks tracked across Osiris' sundered body when Wondemu held the coin up to the light. Smirking, he dropped it into a pouch at his waist and said, "Come."

"Menelik has been emperor nearly nine months," Arthur said. "Now is as good a time as any; if I can't get something moving, he'll tax me out of existence." They'd seated themselves on a bench before the immense and empty stone church that served Wondemu as both laboratory and retreat. Below them, at the bottom of a rocky slope, Arthur's *tankwa* lay beached between two outthrust bluffs.

"Nine months of your friend Menelik, and here you are," Wondemu cackled. "Another bargain he has not kept."

"With both of us," Arthur reminded him, irked by the *kahen's* tone. "I can still bend his ear, and I don't suppose he'd be fond of your laboratory in there."

Wondemu stood, no longer smiling. "You bring me gold, you threaten me. I am not one of your camel drovers, monsieur." He walked into the church, leaving Arthur to sit.

Annoying business, making threats, Arthur thought. If every-one just kept their bargains, it wouldn't have to happen. Now he would see if he'd judged Wondemu correctly, if a hint of coercion would succeed where negotiation had failed in freshening the trail that led to the Grail. The *kahen* wouldn't know that he had lied, that he could no more bargain with Menelik than with the slow death growing in his leg. Accompanied by the music of his thoughts, Arthur followed Wondemu into the old stone church.

The old man was in his laboratory, gently stirring an opalescent fluid in a glass bowl. "I'll come to the point," Arthur said. "I need to know where Yishaq is."

"He's a Jew," Wondemu answered, peering into the bowl. "They wander, no?"

"Well, this one had better wander back home. Please, *kahen*," Arthur said, forcing out the words, "I need your help. I sent him more than a year ago, and the last word I had of him was in France. I must know if he's made the journey to Canada; I must know if he has assumed his burden."

Wondemu scowled at the fluid, poured it into a drain in the floor. "What of this knowledge?" he said as he poured fresh water into the bowl. "It will not change your course of action, will it? You still must wait on him and hope that Menelik does not consolidate his strength before you are able to gather yours."

Arthur lost patience. "Enough dissembling, old man. You know damned well why I need to know."

Wondemu cackled again, his hands quivering as he plopped first a tiny skull, then three drops of a brown fluid, into the water. "Oh yes," he said. "If your Jewish boy has run afoul of certain bad elements, you had better make yourself scarce, no? You have said it before, Monsieur Rimbaud: the Templars know all, and what they don't know they will soon find out. You exist in the gaps in their knowledge, and you will be crushed when those gaps are filled. Do not forget that you need me at least as much as I need you." He stirred the fluid and it changed color, this time becoming a tawny brown rather than the milky mess of the previous attempt. When Wondemu stopped stirring, a live mouse scrabbled its way out of the bowl. He caught it before it could escape off the edge of the table. "Not such an old fool, you see," he said to Arthur, holding the mouse up by its tail.

"Oh, it's quite an accomplishment, your mouse," Arthur responded. "But does it speak? Will it tell me whether Yishaq is returning, or whether I should be running to Australia to live among the aborigines in the hope that the strange stars will throw the Templars off my scent?" He dug in his bag and produced a human skull. "Get her to speak, and you'll have another coin to buy your life when Menelik comes calling."

"Hm." Wondemu went to a bookshelf, muttering in Amharic or some other dying language and running his finger along the spines of his books, the mouse dangling from his other hand. He selected a volume and returned with it to the table after dropping the mouse in a hole in the floor. "Is she a Jew like your Bearer?"

"A Falasha, yes. She is Yishaq's mother. If anyone knows where he is, it will be her." Arthur fidgeted while Wondemu took the skull and placed it in a large basin of polished copper. There followed nearly half an hour of referring to the book, mumbling in Arabic and Latin, pouring various fluids, tincturing and catalyzing, and dropping lit candles into each mixture to see if they would float before the flame was extinguished. When the *kahen* was finally satisfied, he mixed a soupy black concoction into the basin, dribbling it slowly over the skull. "If I have done this wrong," he said as the basin filled to the level of the skull's empty eye sockets, "your leg had better not prevent you running. Head for the lake; the water will warn her away. Unless she drowned?" He cast a questioning look at Arthur, who shook his head and didn't bother to tell the *kahen* that the lake water warned him away, too.

For the first time since he'd actually been in the presence of the Ark of the Covenant, the last summer solstice, Arthur was afraid. I have touched the Ark, he thought, trying to calm himself. I have been in the presence of God or whatever lives within, and

I am alive, if not for very long. No dead black Jew is going to do me in now, and I can't run for the lake. It recognizes me as one who has touched it. A foreigner who has touched the Ark; the lake would drown me like an exhausted bird.

Arthur watched carefully as Wondemu hesitated over the copper basin, then went to the hole in the floor and felt around for the mouse. "I had other plans for you," the *kahen* said to the dangling creature as he returned to the table. "But things are as they are."

He lowered the mouse into the black fluid headfirst. It struggled briefly to the surface, paddling violently toward the skull's half-filled eye sockets as if shelter were there, but Wondemu's hold on its tail kept it away. "Go on, little one," he said. "Things are as they are." After a minute or so of gradually sinking lower, the mouse finally gave up, and its head dropped below the surface. Its rear legs flailed a few more seconds, then their motion subsided to a spasmodic twitching.

It took Arthur a moment to register the motion, so slowly did the skull float to the surface of the black pool. It stopped as its lower jaw drew level with the now floating mouse, which Wondemu released as he stepped back.

"A mouse?" the skull said, its jaw moving no more than a ventriloquist's. "You raise me with a mouse?"

Against all his instincts, Arthur wanted to laugh. "We use what materials are to hand," Wondemu said, adopting the wheedling tone he always used when asking Arthur for money. The skull clicked its jaw shut, spattering Wondemu's face with thick black droplets. The burnished mahogany of his skin paled to a fearful muddy gray.

"Do not patronize me, *kahen*," the skull said. "Ask what you will, and quickly. This small life shall not sustain me for long."

"*I* ask you, Zareh," Arthur said. A small wave crested over the lip of the copper bowl as the skull rotated to face him. "Yes, I address you by name. Do you remember me?"

"I do, Jean-Nicolas Arthur Rimbaud. Is it you who has torn me from the earth? Beware that you yourself do not make my journey sooner than you wish."

When would one wish to die? Arthur thought. Many times I've spoken of it, but never meant the words. "I did not raise you for warnings," he said. "I wish to know this: where is your son Yishaq?"

"Ah, your knight errant, your Bearer. Does he not answer the maimed king's call? I will tell you this, Jean-Nicolas Arthur Rimbaud. My son is farther from you than you suspect, and closer to me than I desire. And that is all the life," the skull said, "your little mouse purchases. Rimbaud, beware your rival." The last words seemed to break from bubbles that rose to the surface as the skull sank back to the bottom of the basin, resting there like a flooded ruin awaiting an explorer's ambition. Following the ripples that rebounded from the basin's edges, the dead mouse floated into the left eye socket.

"That was barely a minute," Arthur said to Wondemu. "How am I to learn anything in so short a time?"

"Bleed into the bowl yourself next time," the *kahen* replied mildly. "I would be happy to arrange it."

"Shit," Arthur hissed. He flipped another one of the coins into the basin; it clinked off the skull's forehead and disappeared. "Watch out she doesn't bite you, *kahen,*" he said. "I'll be back."

Rowing back across Lake Tana in the rickety *tankwa,* Arthur considered what Zareh's skull had said. Aside from the comment about rivals, which was to be anticipated—even if the Templars didn't know where the Grail was, they knew it was out there somewhere and would have prepared someone to receive it—the only thing of value was her answer to his query about Yishaq's location. *Farther from you than you expect,* she had said, *and closer to me than I would desire.* The answer was inescapable: Yishaq was dead, his Bearer selected from the Falasha, the descendants of the Jews who had returned with the Queen of Sheba and carried the

Ark—when the Grail was still within it—to the monastery in Axum where he had been allowed to touch it the previous summer. Arthur felt the same way he had when Menelik had swindled him out of the guns that he'd sweated, cheated, bribed, and nearly died to deliver three years before. Angry, exhausted, frustrated. And, despite it all, determined. Setbacks were to be expected; if he lived long enough he would overcome them all.

If he had miscalculated with Yishaq, left the boy vulnerable somehow to Michel—and what skulls did *he* have talking to him?—it was certainly a grave error. Not, however, insurmountable, not if he could find out who the rival was and intercept the Grail before the new Bearer could complete his errand. This is what I have come to, he thought. I feel death growing in my leg, and out of animal fear I betray my father's work and Jerome's trust. A turncoat, a double agent like my firebug ancestor.

Africa scourges the ideals from a man, Rimbaud thought, and stroked on across the hostile waters of Lake Tana.

He sent a message to Jerome outlining his needs, and while he waited for a response Arthur tried to lose himself in business: merchandise coming in from Italy, Egypt, even the occasional caravan trekking in from the Sudan, where Khalifa Abdullah's nomad bandits were still more numerous than officials of any government. Arthur passed the weeks cursing the incompetence of brokers, shippers, drovers, porters. He cursed the weather, the stinking monkey skins drying in the open square in front of Harar's mosque, the dogs that pissed on the skins in revenge for their poisoned brethren, the landless beggars who shit in the street and clustered around him as if they knew about the gold he carried around his waist. Lately he'd begun sleeping with the gold, believing that it attenuated the pain from his leg—and wasn't there also the possibility that it masked him from the Templars' prying (or scrying) eyes? Wondemu had said that gold hid a man's personality, obscured it behind a mask of purity. Arthur was willing to concede the effect, but the cause, he believed, had more to do with the fact that when he wore the belt he couldn't think about anything else. The one thing the gold could not do, it seemed, was grant him the single wish he desired with every particle of his diseased, exhausted, sunburned body.

It appears that I am in the grip of a canard, he thought, shooing beggars away and smiling inwardly as they pelted him with mishmashed cries in Arabic, Amharic, and Italian. His gold would buy him neither happiness nor freedom. And there was another old saying: a man should indeed be careful what he wished for.

LANCE

Drunk to the point of invincibility, Lance roared down the coast road in the Plymouth, Dwight slouching against the passenger door. The last twenty minutes, since they'd turned off the main road out of Halifax, neither of them had said a word. The garrulous part of the drunk was long past, back around twelve o'clock when the bartender had started chasing people out of the Waves Tavern. "Time to go home, yeah?" Lance had said, but Dwight had shaken his head as he drained his last beer. "We're not done yet," he'd said. "Still things to see."

Now they were barreling down this two-lane road in the middle of the night, for all the world like a couple of kids racing down Territorial Road just for the hell of it. Dwight hadn't said anything else about the war all night, and that was fine with Lance, but he wondered what it was Dwight wanted him to see. Another lesson like the exploding ammunition ship? Lance didn't think he could handle it. It was all well and good to walk his brother through guilt, but enough was enough. He needed some answers.

"Left here," Dwight said, and Lance slewed the Plymouth across the center line, not quite making the turn onto a side road. The car sideswiped a leaning oak tree, extinguishing one headlight and crumpling the right fender.

"Christ, don't kill me, soldier," Dwight said. "I'm a conscientious objector."

Both of them burst into raucous drunken laughter that intensified when they got out to inspect the damage. "Somebody," Dwight gasped, "somebody gave your car a black eye. Pow, oak tree wins by knockout." This set them off again, and they barely managed to push the Plymouth back onto the road. "Looks like I bought myself a car," Lance said.

"Plymouth's a fine automobile," Dwight said. He jumped up on the hood and shouted, "Big, beautiful, brilliant, and a powerhouse to drive!" Lance cracked up again, remembering the ad from when he was a kid. He shoved Dewey into the bushes and fell back into the car. Both of them were whooping as they set off.

The road, if Lance's sense of direction hadn't completely deserted him, led toward the coast. He drove with marginally more care, trying not to exceed fifty as they cruised by darkened houses with the flags on their mailboxes up, waiting for tomorrow to begin. At a stop sign Dwight pointed to the right, and Lance turned past a run-down diner with a single gas (petrol, he reminded himself) pump out front. A couple of miles farther on, he made a left onto a narrow packed-dirt road that petered out on a point of land sticking out into the water. "Crandall's Point," Dwight said.

Ahead of the car, across a channel, a low island was a darker blot against the nighttime water, a silhouette of absence in the starry sky. Dwight was out of the car before Lance could ask him why they were there, and Lance followed him down to the marshy shore where Dwight was untying a rowboat from a stake that had been driven into the ground above the high-tide mark.

"Your boat, Dewey?" Lance asked, even though he knew the answer.

"We'll have it back before morning."

"Oh, Christ," Lance said. "They couldn't build a bridge?" He sat in the stern while Dwight rowed across the short strait, then followed the curving shore of the island around to the left. A chilly breeze, hinting of fall, picked up as they moved out of the protected channel, and waves slapped at the boat's gunwales. Dwight pushed ahead, finally grounding the boat in a shallow cove. "Pull it over here," he said, pointing at a thick tangle of cut brush to their right. They draped branches over the little boat and Lance followed Dwight away from the water, skirting a small pond and passing piles of dirt and what looked like oil-drilling equipment.

Dwight stopped at the edge of a broad, shallow depression where the brush had been cleared away thirty or forty yards on all sides. "This is it," he said.

"This is what?"

"Moment of truth," Dwight said. He walked out into the center of the depression and squatted. "Under my feet somewhere is buried treasure. People have been looking for it since seventeen ninety-five. Errol Flynn and FDR got involved, and about sixty years ago this crazy baseball player named Gibson went out on the island in the middle of the night and apparently never came back."

"Gibson." That was the name Jerry K. had dropped back in Cooperstown, and everything else Dewey had said squared with Jerry's ramblings. For some reason, the idea that Jerry and Dwight saw things the same way worried Lance as much as anything else. It triangulated the whole business, made it seem solid and real.

"Yep," Dwight said. "Spicer wasn't kidding you, at least about that. This whole island is a trap; the original hole is designed to suck in seawater when people dig into it, and there are false leads everywhere—hell, whoever put this here built an artificial beach back where we landed the boat, with tunnels underneath that lead to the hole. And the whole thing just gets to be more and more of a snipe hunt. The first shaft collapsed a long time ago, when people were working with horses and hand pumps, and guys have even barged steam shovels out here looking for the real Money Pit. Who knows where the original shaft is now? But people still look, which is part of what Jerry was trying to tell you."

Lance didn't follow. He'd gotten to the tired part of his drunk, too tired to be angry or ambitious or anything but sad and a little lonely. He walked over next to Dwight and lay down on the cold sandy floor of the depression, glad that the breeze had blown all the mosquitoes away.

"I don't know about any of that, Dewey. Right now I just want to see Ellie."

"Which is exactly what some of them want."

"Some of who?"

"The Templars, or whatever they're calling themselves now. There's more than one horse in this race, and the guys who are betting on me would just as soon have you forget about this whole thing and go looking for Ellie. I'm betting that's part of the reason they're holding on to her."

"They're what?"

"Lance, they've let all this happen so far. They let you come to see me, they let Ellie go to Berkeley, then they changed their minds when you started talking to Spicer."

It was because of Spicer that Ellie was gone. I'll kill him, Lance thought. Just for that. "Where is she now, Dewey?"

"Wherever the Grail is. That's my guess, anyway."

Lance worked it over in his mind for a while, then said, "Is that what happened to you? Somebody got you out of the way?"

Dewey sighed. "Yeah. Something like that. Do I have to tell it?"

"I told you. Fair's fair."

Time passed. The mosquitoes found them again, and Lance was just about to give up and head back to the boat when Dewey said, "You get used to feeling important."

Lance thought of the greed he'd started to feel over the past few days, the sense that he deserved all this, that if Dewey didn't want it that was just fine, Lance would do the job better anyway. "Yeah," he said. "You do."

"Happening to you already, huh? Doesn't take long. Tell you what, I started to feel it right away. Here's the whole story. I'm guessing you already figured out that I was trying to find you the day I left."

"I wasn't trying to be mean, Dewey."

"Doesn't matter now."

"Yeah, it does. You remember the Tree of Many Roots? Reason I didn't want you along was that I was meeting Ellie there. First time we ever kissed."

"Was that it?" Dewey chuckled. "Ah, you could have told me."

No, I couldn't, Lance thought. But it was too hard to explain, so he said, "I know."

The fog was clearing, and the stars came out, hard and brilliant. Dewey popped Lance on the shoulder. "Like I said, forget it. And shut up for a minute so I can tell you this."

Lance shut up.

"I didn't find you at the creek," Dewey said, "so I figured, what the heck, I'd take a swim. I splashed around like hell so if you showed up all the frogs would be gone, but you can only do that for so long, and after a while I just swam around in circles until I got bored. When I came back to where I'd left my clothes there was a guy sitting there. I said hi, and he said, 'Dwight. Good to see you.'

"Well, I didn't recognize this guy, so I said, 'How do you know my name?'

" 'A father always knows his son,' the guy said, and I stood there staring at him like he'd said he was from Mars. Then I said, 'Dad?' and he stood up and said, 'Correct, kiddo. Come on.'

"I was suspicious, you know, all the stuff you hear about kids getting kidnapped because they're dumb, so I said, 'You're not my dad. My dad's dead.'

" 'Is that what your mother told you?' he said. 'Figures. She had to come up with something. Let me tell you, my boy, the story's a lot stranger than that. Come on, now. People are looking for us.'

"And that's when I started to get shaky, thinking that maybe he was our dad, and I kind of came apart. 'Where were you?' I said. 'Where have you been?'

" 'I've had to do some things,' he said. 'But I've been watching you, son. Your mother's had twelve years, and now it's my turn. Let's go.'

"So I went. I don't know why. The whole time I was thinking he might be some kind of a nut, you know, but then what if it was true? What if Dad had come back? We went into the woods, back to one of the old fire roads, and he had a car there, and we took off. I asked about you, and he said he was coming back for you later, that there was only time to get me right then, and I was just pissed enough at you to go along with it. I'm not going to lie to you, it felt good to have him come for me and not both of us. It's—I'm sorry about that. Always was."

"It's okay," Lance said, even though it wasn't. "I probably would have done the same thing." Which was another lie, or at least he hoped it was, he hoped he would have held out and said *No, I'm not going anywhere until you get Dewey, too. We're brothers, we go together.* But he'd never know now; he'd never had the chance to find out.

"He had me leave my shirt and shoes there, to give the cops enough to investigate but not enough to get anywhere. We went down the railroad tracks to a dirt crossing and walked to where he'd parked his car. Then we drove straight through to Halifax. He had clothes for me in the car, and when we got to Halifax we stayed for a couple of days while he arranged for a place to stay, and then . . ." In the darkness Lance felt Dwight's shrug. "He kept me here, and after a while he admitted he wasn't Dad. He worked for Dad, he said. Dad couldn't show himself right away in case Mom had sent someone to look for me; his name was Dave, and he'd be bringing messages from Dad and taking care of me. Dad would come see me as soon as it was safe. So I waited. Half of me figured it was just a matter of time before this guy Dave killed me or worse. Half of me believed him. I went through all the stages: I begged him to send Dad, I swore at him, refused to talk to him. After a while he told me what it was all about, a little at a time, and then he gave me a long time to think about it. And I decided it was okay."

That last sentence hung there, making Lance more sad and hurt with every second of silence. "A guy tried to kill me in San Francisco four days ago," Lance said.

"Yeah. That was only a matter of time. You're the wild card, big brother. All the people who have been angling to deal with me now have you to worry about, too." He paused, and then added, "What happened?"

"It was him or me," Lance said, and hoped Dewey wouldn't pursue it.

Dewey didn't. He'd always been more attuned to how people felt. Time passed. Mosquitoes whined.

"Where's Dad now?" Lance asked after a while.

"I don't know," Dwight said. "I never did see him. When I got old enough to have a place on my own, Dave started leaving me alone more. I thought for a while Dad was going to see you; fact is, I thought for a long time that he had you stashed away somewhere else, and I worried that he'd had someone tell you the same things Dave told me, but when I asked Dave about it he just said that there were different plans for you. Sometimes I believed it, sometimes I didn't, and once I just took off and tried to get back to Michigan on my own. That's when I found out that all the cops around here are in on the whole thing. They caught me before I'd been gone two hours, and Dave told me that if I got away there were people he was working for who would have you killed. I'm guessing they figured that if I told you about what was going on, we might make some kind of other plan, and these guys don't fool around. Dad's a big wheel, but there are bigger guys. Probably one of them sent the guy after you in Frisco. So after that I sat tight, and like I said, you know, you get used to the idea that you're going to be a King."

Dwight sat up. "And that's the story. I just wanted to tell you that. And I wanted to tell you that I'm out. I played along for eight years, and now I'm done. I sit on the shore, and I read books, and I think, and I've spent so long waiting that I'm used to it. Don't know what I'd do if all of a sudden I got what I was waiting for. So you're welcome to it if you want it."

If I want it, Lance thought. "What I want right now is to talk to Dad."

"See, I knew you'd say that. And maybe I have no right to stick my nose in after what's happened, but I'm going to anyway. I've been reading a little Zen, and there's this line I read in one of the books: *They seek the truth too far away from themselves, while it is right near them.* I read that line eight hundred times before I got it. It doesn't mean that there's no truth because everyone's version of it is equally plausible; what it means is that in making decisions, you need to steer by your own lights, right or wrong, not according to your idea of how someone else thinks." Dwight lay down next to Lance, and both of them stared at the stars. "You want to talk to Dad because you think he's going to change his mind somehow, either that or so you can tell him to fuck off once and for all, and okay, you're entitled. But before you do that, let me tell you something. When you showed up, I thought for sure you'd hate me once you knew the situation, and if you didn't hate me I thought you'd make some big show of absolving me, but you didn't do either. And then in Halifax today, the same thing, I threw it all in your face, and all you did was accept it. I wanted to be judged, expected to be judged, and when you didn't do it, right then—right then—I figured out that I'd been so caught up in blame and guilt that I'd started to think like a King, you know, calculating alliances and loyalty and all the rest. But you were just my brother, and that healed me. You healed me, Lance. Maybe that's why you came all this way and maybe it isn't, but you healed me. Maybe you're the only one who could have."

Throughout Dwight's speech, Lance lay suffocating. He couldn't think of anything to say in return. Maybe that was Zen, or maybe he was just too drunk for his lips to be reliable.

My hip doesn't hurt, he thought, and realized at the same moment that he was about to cry because he'd forgotten what it was like to have a night like this. Just two brothers together, and the unexpected realization that love endures.

"So is the Grail really buried here, Dewey?"

"Was, yeah. But there's all kinds of other theories. Most people think pirate treasure, probably Captain Kidd's. Others say Inca gold, or Francis Bacon's manuscripts of Shakespeare's plays, or hey, maybe it's the Holy Grail. Oak Island is as weird as you want it to be."

Lance thought about that, listening to the quiet surf and the rustle of a night breeze in the trees. All the stories converging where you found a brother you'd long since given up for dead. "If you have to find a grail, this is a good place to do it," he said, and fell asleep.

In the morning Lance found himself on Dwight's couch. Coffee was percolating on the stove, and Dwight was noisily chopping vegetables. "I took your car into town and got some groceries," he said when he saw Lance sit up and stretch. "Travelin' man needs a good breakfast."

"Am I traveling?" Lance stood and felt something grate in his hip.

Dwight waved a spatula at him. "Time to find your girl, big brother. You've been slacking long enough. I'm kicking you out."

This was a bit much, first thing in the morning. "How'd we get home?"

"Oh, between the two of us we got you back into the boat, and you made it mostly on your own back into the car. Spooky thing, though." Dwight paused in his omelet making. "I could have sworn that right when I pushed off from the shore, I saw ghosts."

"Pirates?"

"No, a guy in a boat out in the bay north of the cove, and—get this—a colored guy back up by where the Money Pit's supposed to be. He had this huge rip in his neck, but he wasn't bleeding. Light, I swear to God, was leaking out of it. He pointed out into the bay and then did this." With the spatula Dwight drew a finger across his throat. "And when I looked out where he'd pointed, there was this guy on a little sailboat, wearing a white suit. He was pointing back to shore and shaking his head. Craziest thing I ever saw. Heard all kinds of stories about the island, but this was the first time I ever saw anything."

Dwight sprinkled scallions into the skillet. "There's a bit in Wordsworth, in the *Prelude,* where he's a boy and he steals a boat, and while he's rowing across this lake he gets the feeling that the mountains are going to rise up and come after him." Beaten eggs followed the scallions. "Now I know how he felt. I kept waiting to see the guy in the sailboat float up next to me."

Poetry again, Lance thought. He walked over to the stove and picked bits of green pepper off a cutting board. "So now you're seeing George Gibson's ghosts."

"Yeah. Last time I go drinking with you."

Lance snorted. "Sure, blame me because you can't hold your beer." He munched green peppers, smelled cooking omelets and brewing coffee, and wanted very much not to leave. "I thought I might stay awhile," he said.

"No way," Dwight said. "You leave today. I hope you don't go looking for Dad. He's probably in New York, and Jerry's right that you shouldn't go there. What you should do is go see Mom. She's got some kind of plan, I don't know what, but she was the one who told Ellie to go out to San Francisco. Got any cash?"

"Enough to get by, yeah. Why such a hurry for me to leave, Dewey?"

"Because I love you, brother, but you've got to get this straightened out before it gets both of us killed, and Mom, and Ellie, and God knows who else. The people on the outside are trying hard to get in, and now that they know about you they're going to try harder. You've done what you came here to do. I've given you everything I know, and now we're brothers again. Right?"

"Right."

"Okay, good. Now listen. The shit is approaching the fan. I haven't told Dad about my decision, and when I do there's no telling what'll happen. That's why you should go see Mom. And here's what I'm going to do. I might be able to talk to Dave and convince Dad that if they let Ellie go you'll forget all about the Grail and take off after her. If that works, they'll tell Mom what they're doing because I'll tell them you're going to Michigan. If it doesn't work, they might figure I'm working an angle. Then they'll probably just kill me."

"Jesus, Dewey."

"That's the game, big brother. Somebody's already tried to kill you, and I doubt that was the last time. Pretty soon they'll decide it's time to make a clean sweep of the whole family. I can't get out of here, but they're still waiting to see which way you move." A grim smile crossed Dwight's face. "This is how royal types spend most of their time. Wondering who has the knife, and when they'll show it. This is what you're letting yourself in for, so remember one thing for me, will you? The story of the Grail is a story of transformation. Medieval alchemists thought it could transmute lead into gold, but what they were really talking about was a spiritual transformation. The Grail isn't about making you powerful or rich or immortal, it's about making you *better*. Everybody's forgotten that, but you can't. If you're going to have the Grail, you can't ever forget that. That's what will get Ellie back for you. Now eat your breakfast and go."

Lance went, but it wasn't until he'd crossed back into the States that he decided Dewey had been right. What else would he have done in Peggy's Cove, he thought as he drove down Route 9—the locals called it the Airline—through the hills and bogs of eastern Maine, but drink beer and watch the ocean? It was time to get things back together; it had been right to go, and now it was right to come back. He stopped in Brewer, across the river from Bangor, and ate pizza at a counter full of beer-drinking workers from the pulp mills up the Penobscot. Then he turned south to Ellsworth and picked up U.S. 1. He slept somewhere north of Portland, pulling the Plymouth off the road and dropping off to the sound of pine branches scratching on the roof, and when he woke up he'd made a decision. Maybe Dewey was right, but before Lance headed for Michigan he was damn sure going to put things right with their father.

GEORGE

THREE WEEKS LATER George trudged out of the jungle onto the muddy open ground of Leopoldville, the nominal capital of the Congo Free State. It had been raining steadily for the past three days, and he was soaked to the skin and thankful for every moment that passed without his contracting some fever. He'd had to walk ten days from Banana through the Lower Congo delta to the future railroad terminus at Matadi, bringing up the rear of a procession of sailors on their way to the Upper Congo to pilot riverboats. At Matadi a letter from Lieutenant DeSailly had gotten him through the garrison, and another ten days later he was here, grateful in an abstract way for DeSailly's kindness in offering the letter. But that gratitude had long since been pounded into the back of George's mind by what he'd witnessed during the previous fortnight. Everywhere he turned was pain. Black bodies shuffled along the trails chained together at the neck, black faces stared unseeing up into the rain, black backs cringed away from the wicked hippopotamus-skin whips called *chicotes*, black hands and feet hung smoked and dried in markets.

George didn't know all that much about what the European powers were doing in Africa, but he had been under the impression that the reason for imperialism was to stop the slave trade and civilize the natives. What he saw in two weeks of slogging through the Lower Congo shocked him at first, then angered him, then buried even his anger beneath an avalanche of despair that he seemed to inhale with every breath. To share the air with the rattling breath of the dying, to constantly hear their cries at the touch of *chicote* or rifle butt . . . This place will drive me crazy, George thought as he shouldered his bag and looked in vain for a place where his field of vision would be clear of human misery.

The Congo Railway was being built from both ends. George crossed a partially finished turning platform and went to the office of the local government, hoping to find passage at least to the Upper Congo. If he could get to Stanleyville, there might be an expedition going east. Arab traders, perhaps, plying the caravan routes that George had heard snaked all the way across the continent to Egypt.

He was approaching the door when two soldiers burst through it, dragging a native between them. Cursing in French and pausing only to spit on the terrified Congolese, they hauled him through the mud and bound him with oxtail ropes to a tree trunk. The native, a boy of perhaps fifteen, put up no resistance as the ropes were cinched above his elbows and drawn tightly enough that he was forced to kneel and hug the splintery bark. His face was empty of expression, no more animated than a wooden mask, and he made no sound until the two Belgians stepped back and, raising their rifles overhead like harpooners sighting in on the eyes of a whale, began methodically to crush his hands.

The boy screamed and flailed his forearms at first, but the soldiers simply broke his arms and then went back to work on his hands as he screamed into the bark of the tree. In less than a minute the soldiers had battered the boy's hands completely off, and he had fallen limp against his bonds with his forearms hanging crooked. Blood fell steadily from his wrists to pool around his severed hands.

"That's what sloth gets you here," a voice said from behind George.

Speechless, he turned to see a white-clad man in a pith helmet calmly tapping a staff on the porch. The man had spoken English, George realized dimly, and he tried to find something to say in return.

"I see you're a bit shocked," the official said. "I agree, it's a nasty business, but when you're dealing with a people as debased as these, you've got to make examples. Did you know they believe the skulls of the dead rise from the ground to attack travelers at night? You wouldn't believe what I had to do to keep the caravans moving after dark. Superstitious savages. I daresay they'll work now."

The soldiers, after cutting the boy loose from the tree, had come back to the office. They strode past George and the official and went inside.

"What." George swallowed, trying to force some moisture into his throat. "What did he do?"

The official pinned George with a gaze pitiless as the Eater of the Dead's. "We're building a country here," he said. "In the long view, it's for their own good." He touched the rim of his helmet. "Garrett Bryce Halliwell. I'm the Belgians' local attaché; better work than being a barrister at home. Did you have business with me?"

Still staring, George shook his head. "Right, then," Halliwell said, and went back into his office.

George went back down the steps and stood in the center of the muddy square. He felt as if he were falling away into himself, as if his soul were retreating from the madness that the world forced it to confront. Was all of Africa like this, from Banana to Cairo? Didn't anybody know? Wasn't anybody doing something?

He walked slowly to the native boy, lying in a puddle of bloody rainwater. The boy was dying; the exhaustion of it, the weary finality George had once seen in the eyes of a cow dying as she birthed a dead calf, dulled the boy's bloodshot eyes. George sat next to him and lifted his head out of the mud. The boy's eyes flicked down to his shattered arms, followed the steady pattering of blood down to the ground. "No," George said, and he started to cry. "Don't look at that." He searched in the leather bag Yishaq had left him and withdrew a silvery stone about the size of a fist. Or a baseball. "Look at this."

And George looked too, drinking in this first sight of the Grail, so unlike the jeweled chalice he'd read about in the Arthur stories of his boyhood. It seemed to welcome his gaze, even to invite it, and some of George's anguish drained away into it. He looked again at the boy and saw that the bloodshot gaze had seized on the stone, that some of the Grail's silvery vibrance had leaked into his eyes. The boy's breathing slowed, slowed, stopped, and his eyelids began to flutter as if George were telling him a bedtime story. George felt a gate opening, a bridge building itself into a place he'd been once before. Can I go this way? he asked himself. And if I can, can I get back?

In his mind he saw the soldiers' rifle butts rising and falling, and felt the shrieking agony of his own bones breaking, and one thought came through it all. *I cannot survive this.*

Was that his mind speaking or the boy's? It doesn't matter, George thought. Either one is right. How long can I breathe this in before it chokes me?

I'm coming with you, he told the boy. *Please, I can't stay here.*

And the light is still the same. There is a peculiar quality of undifferentiated distance between George's eyes, the ground at his feet, and the hills on the horizon like a line of low clouds from which the river condenses like dew. A sensation of déjà vu starts George involuntarily swimming, and only when he realizes that his arms aren't moving does it become apparent that once again he has no body.

"No. No, no. You will not use me anymore."

The twilight landscape tears itself apart, George's mind shudders with violent nausea as he protests: *I don't mean to use you, I don't mean to, I just need to get where I've got to go and don't you understand I couldn't stay there?*

"If you stay here, white man, it will not be on my back."

George's eyes are open, really open, and he has a head to turn and a mouth through which to draw a surprised gasping breath. And he can speak. "What did you do?"

The dead boy stands before him, feet wide apart, eyes distilling the diffuse light around them into a fierce glare, one accusing finger thrust into George's face. "I cast you out, devil," he says, his voice shaking with hate. "Devils took my name, took my body, took my life. You will not follow me here."

"No," George says. "I didn't take anything from you." He holds the Grail out for the boy to see, and with a rush of relief intertwined with embarrassment he realizes he is crying. "I just wanted to make it easier."

"Easier would have been to die without knowing that *you* were following. How do you think that felt, devil? White men take me from my home, stripe my back with *chicote,* smash off my hands with their guns and leave me to die, and even dying a white man follows me. No. I will speak to you no more. If you are not dead, find your own way to live."

"Wait," George pleads. "Please. Answer me one question. Am I dead? How do I get out of here?"

"I thought you wanted to get out of *there.*" The boy will not look at George, but he isn't leaving either.

"Yes, but I have to go back." George touches the Grail, feels its strange energy crackling in his fingers. "This is not mine. I'm just carrying it, and I have to give it back."

"So you have read the writing on it? It does not tell you?"

Writing? George frowns.

The boy's smile is cruel. "So it looks different to each who sees," he says. "What is it hiding from you?"

George shrugs. "I don't know," he sighs. "I don't know. I just have to get it back."

"Follow the river," the boy says, and now he is turning away. "When the river turns away from the mountains, cross the mountains. After that, the place will speak to you." He stops to deliver a parting shot over his shoulder. "But how you get out of here is up to you. I would not tell you even if I could."

George is silent while the boy walks into the river, reappears after a few minutes on the other side. "You're right," he calls to the retreating back, still streaked with pale *chicote* scars. "You don't owe me anything." There is no response, and the trees on the other bank swallow the boy in shadow.

First Yishaq, then this kid, George thinks. I drag them into my errand. They've got no reason to like me.

No, that's not quite right. I don't want anything from them but a little help, and I'm trying to help them too. If the wrong person gets the Grail, all of Africa will be just like the Congo.

And it's up to me to make sure that doesn't happen.

This is what the Grail does, George thinks. It forces you to feel other people like they were you. I didn't mean to apologize to that boy—hell, my old man would have split my lip for apologizing to a nigger—but the Grail did. And I couldn't handle everything I saw in Boma and Matadi and Leopoldville because the Grail was making me more aware. George wonders what he would have done if he'd had the Grail when he was a kid, and saw all those Chinamen coming through working on the railroad. How different was that from what was happening in the Congo? I didn't think anything of it then, he thinks, and now I can't remember.

Time to get moving, George thinks. When he'd come across the ocean with Yishaq, it didn't seem like it took that long, but months had passed in the world. Now he had to get all the way across dead-Africa by himself.

"Might be nineteen hundred by then," George says, and he starts walking along the banks of the starlight-colored river.

He awoke in a tent, lying on a cot draped with mosquito netting, sweating like he'd just run a mile in July. Rolling over, he saw a pail of water next to the cot. Someone outside heard him as he picked it up and started to drink; the front flap of the tent was thrust back and the official he'd spoken to before the boy's killing stamped in. "Well, you recover quickly, I'll grant you that," he said. "Most men don't shake off their first malaria fit for a week or so."

"How long," George started to ask.

"Just a day. You pitched right over by that young savage, and we laid you in here, and you've been in here all night. Can you stand up?"

George could, and did. His purse was on the cot between his feet; he retied it to his belt, then rubbed the cooling sweat from his face.

"Good," the officer said. "If you can stand, you can walk, and if you can walk, you can get the devil out of my district. I'm going to have no end of trouble with the niggers around here now that they've seen what you did. Go. I don't care whether you go up-river or down, just go. There's a steamer heading up to Stanley Falls tomorrow morning. Be on it."

The steamer pilot listened to George's story and fit him in on the deck, among piles and boxes of clothing, ammunition, scientific equipment, and building materials. "I'll work if you want," George said, and the pilot pointed to a rifle leaning against the steamer's aft rail.

"If you see a nigger with a spear, a bow, even a rock in his hand, use it," he said, and went into the cabin to ready the boat for departure.

A week later they reached Stanleyville. George left the boat grateful that he hadn't had to use the rifle, since he wasn't sure he would have. *If I was these folks, I'd damn sure shoot at any white folks too,* he thought. *But you can't fight bullets with spears, poor dumb bastards.*

The first thing he did when he got off the boat was follow up on what Lieutenant DeSailly had told him, all the way back down-river at Banana. He found the local sahib, or bwana, or whatever these Europeans called themselves around here, and asked him which way Stanley had gone. "He's disappeared into the Ituri" was the answer. "Gone from here almost two years now. Either he's found Emin Pasha, or the pygmies got him."

"Pygmies?"

"Little blighters, live in the jungle out that way." A careless wave toward what George thought was east, or northeast. "Only three feet tall, even the grown men. They shoot poisoned arrows at any white man they see. Nothing for it but to shoot them on sight; even Tippu Tib and the Arabs don't want them for slaves. Apparently they languish outside the jungle. In any event, if it's Stanley you want, you'll have to wait to hear where he's gone. Last we heard around here, he was following the Aruwimi hoping to get to Lake Albert and rescue Emin Pasha. Whoever that is." He shrugged and went back to directing a group of porters headed toward the falls.

"Wait a minute," George said. "Two years? What's the date?"

The officer stared at him for a minute. "It's July twenty-seventh," he said. "Eighteen ninety."

He was watching for George's reaction, but George didn't give him one. "Thanks," he said, and walked away. *Eighteen ninety? Two years after he'd swum out to Oak Island with poor Charlie? It couldn't be right.* He looked around him, at the mud and the settlement of shacks and animal pens, the surging river and the mist that came down from the falls. It was all real, but George couldn't feel it. It was like he had a callus over his mind, couldn't actually touch anything around him.

That'll happen when you die, he thought, and gave up trying to figure it all out. The Aruwimi. George had passed it, back downriver a couple of days. The moody Polack piloting the boat had pointed it out. Okay, he thought. I can get a ride to there, and then take things the way they come.

He found Stanley's track easy enough. Even the jungle couldn't erase the passage of five hundred men in just two years. The path along the Aruwimi veered occasionally into the jungle, and at the end of these detours George always saw the same things: ashes and bones. Village after village, erased from the face of the earth. The only people he saw were slaves, clanking in their misery toward the river from their homes—wherever Stanley had been, Tippu Tib's men soon followed to take up the survivors. George hid from them, ate from the stores that fell by the wayside when one of the slaves collapsed and spilled his burden into the brush. At times George thought he saw faces in the trees, and at each of these times he braced himself for poisoned arrows shot by midgets, and after some weeks in the Ituri jungle he began to pray for one of those arrows. He ate plantains when he could find them, beetles and grubs when he couldn't. His body began to fall away from him; he tied his trousers tighter with a vine and felt himself growing thinner. Spectral. At any moment, he started to believe, he might sink into the earth and come to rest back with Yishaq and the rest of Africa's ghosts. Living Africa and the land of the dead beneath it grew less and less distinct from each other. The underworld oozed up through the earth to claim this place where the dead so outnumbered the living, and it brought leeches and biting worms that left George with running abscesses on both legs and bleeding scabs that he couldn't scratch enough.

I could stop, he thought. Back to the big river, back to a boat, back to the ocean, back to America. Lay my burden down, here in the jungle where no one will ever find it, and walk away. It's too much. Not the bugs, not the worms, not the rain and the mud. Those he could stand. It was the death everywhere. He came to a halt in the middle of the trail and took the pouch's leather thong between his fingers. Nobody would hold it against him.

Even there and then, with relief at his fingertips, George couldn't escape one simple fact. You'd be dead yourself if it wasn't for Yishaq, he reminded himself. You owe him this. You've borrowed time from him, and this is paying it back.

He drew his only strength from shame, and went on.

How far had he come? How far to go? He passed a large camp, half a dozen white men and a few hundred Africans. Large fires burned, and the smell of roasting meat clenched George's stomach like a fist. Walk in, he said to himself. Eat. Find out where you are, how far there is to go. Talk to someone who isn't dead.

He'd been talking to Yishaq. Sometimes he tried out excuses for turning back, but mostly he just kept a kind of ongoing commentary on the bugs and the vines and the wasp nests and the bones and the strange compulsion he felt whenever he heard the clinking of chains and the soft moans of African agony. "I'm doing it, Yishaq," he murmured. "I said I'd do it, and I'm doing it."

Then he caught himself. Walking into the camp would be one thing—getting dragged in by a sentry would be something else. For all he knew, this group could be looking for him. They had guns, the long Enfields whose spent shells George had seen in how many villages since he'd gone into the bush from Stanleyville.

Stanleyville, the falls . . . George leaned against a tree. He had to rest. You could hear the falls for days before you saw them, and when you saw them it struck fear into you, because at any moment it seemed like the thunder and the trembling under your feet might crack the world wide open. And still they were beautiful, the way something was beautiful when you couldn't think of owning it, even approaching it, the way beauty sometimes froze your guts in fear and wouldn't let you look away. The mist in the air, clean and cool after the choked and sweating air of the lower Congo . . .

He startled himself awake. Something was happening in the camp. One of the white men screaming, an African woman pleading with him, now a new voice booming over them both—and a gunshot. The camp erupted, people running in every direction but mostly toward the shot, and George put it together. Bwana wanted somebody's wife, wouldn't take no for an answer, and the nigger shot him. Goddamn right, too, George thought. I'd do the same.

He crept closer to the camp perimeter. His mother had taught him not to steal, but she'd also have told him not to walk across Africa by himself, so he'd already be in the doghouse with her. He skulked past stacks of rifle ammunition, crates stenciled STANLEY, a couple of canoes. They were eating meat, they had to have tons of food along. There: tucked next to the canoes were man-size loads of roped-together canvas bags. Has to be food, George thought. He lifted one and waddled with it back into the jungle.

The firelight had ruined his night vision, and until it came back he couldn't find the trail. He squatted with the armload of what he hoped was food, letting details emerge from the darkness. And there was the trail, a ten-foot-wide track of packed mud. How you could miss something like that, George didn't know, but this jungle was *dark*. He'd only seen darkness like it in a mine. Even with his night vision back, it only stood out as a kind of emptiness, a gap in the midst of the impenetrable forest.

He made a mile or so before his energy failed—God, the bundle was heavy, how did the porters carry them on their heads?—and then he settled into a depression at the base of some giant tree. He was asleep again before he'd caught his breath, slumped against the canvas bundle, one hand cupped around the leather bag on his belt.

In the morning the passage of another slave convoy woke him. He sat perfectly still, counting the slaves the way he'd counted train cars when he was a kid. A hundred and seven, plus a dozen guards dressed like Arabs in white robes even though they were as black as their captives. The slaves' chains clinked in rhythm with their steps, like the clack of a train over a bent section of track. These people, George thought. Where do they all come from? The jungle's empty, and still Tippu Tib comes up with slaves. Doesn't anybody know about this?

He felt the weight of the Grail on his hip. Maybe this was what it was all about. Bring Arthur back from the island, Avalon, and put an end to it.

But Avalon was in England. If the Englishman Stanley was anything to judge by, Arthur wouldn't do your average Congo tribesman much good at all. Which would explain why Yishaq didn't want the Templars to get the Grail.

That damn Yishaq, he was just about always right.

The convoy passed, and George untied the bundle. Home run, he thought. Corn, jerky, dried apples for Christ's sake, more food than he could carry. Even a pencil stuck in the binding ropes; if he'd only had paper he could write to Martha. The book! He could write to her in the spaces around the poems and give her the book when he got back. Wouldn't that knock her for a loop?

George ate until he was just this side of puking, rested for a while, and then got the book out and found a page with a short poem and lots of space. He wrote:

Dear Martha,
> *Yes, I am in Africa, and I can't explain how I got here.*

Wasn't that the truth.

> *I was traveling with a friend, but now he's gone and I have to get from the Belgian Congo to Abyssinia on my own. The men at the fort back in a town called Banana—least the ones who speak English and not French—say that no one has ever crossed Africa this way. I'm finding out if they're right. I think about you at least a hundred times a day. If you hear of a man named Michel (he's French so has a name like a girl's) looking for you, RUN. Go hide somewhere until you hear from someone that I'm back.*
>
> *I am writing in this book because I'm in the middle of the jungle and don't have any paper. Maybe you can tell me what the poems mean when I get back.*
>
> *Love, George.*

He wasn't sure what else to say right then. If he went on, he was afraid he'd tell her about the boy with the broken arms, so he put the book away. Martha didn't need to hear things like that. George stuffed his pockets with food and set out again, feeling strong for the first time in weeks. Feeling like it was all real, like he could get through it, like there really was Abyssinia on the other side, with a monastery in the hills where he could put the Grail back where it belonged. "Told you, Yishaq," he said to the jungle. "I'll get this done." It all had to end sometime: the jungle would peter out, he'd be able to move faster, and then he'd head down the Nile and back up over the mountains to Abyssinia. For the first time since he'd come to Africa, he felt like he might actually be getting his old self back.

Then, on the second morning, the pit opened up and swallowed him again.

. . .

It was bright, or anyway as bright as the ground under the jungle canopy ever got, and George was loping down the trail at a good clip, well fed and determined to get this whole Grail thing over with so he could go home and play baseball again. The jungle was full of noise, birds and monkeys and some kind of weird chirping bug that when you ate it turned out to be full of the vilest green stuff you could imagine, and this strained kind of squalling behind it all, like a cat had just been looped up by one of those damn big snakes you saw hanging like vines from the trees. Jungle's a tough place even if you're a cat, he thought, and added for Yishaq, "That's one snake won't be coming after me, anyway." As he said it, he smelled smoke, and slowed his pace because smoke meant people, and George was becoming enough of an African to be leery of people who might be white.

The cat kept up its yowling, and George was just thinking *Come on, snake, put a little something into that squeeze, willya,* when he came around a bend in the trail and saw that it wasn't a cat at all.

In the middle of the trail lay a little girl, maybe a year and a half old. She was naked, and her hair was tied up in little balls that stuck out from her head, and her eyes and her nose and her mouth swarmed with fire ants that she no longer had the strength to get away from.

"Oh Lord," George choked out. The slavers. One of the women he'd counted like train cars was this girl's mother.

She heard him speak, and turned that awful face to him, and when she moved he saw that the ants were between her legs too. Her screaming changed in pitch, and maybe there were words in it, and she tried to reach for the sound of his voice but she was too weak.

George ran to her, saying *oh Jesus little girl hey it's okay oh Christ Jesus hey what am I going to do,* and even before he took her up in his arms he could feel the ants on him, worse than wasps, and he ran with her to the river. He splashed into the shallow part of an inside bend and swept her through the brown water. The ants came off in clumps, climbing over one another, and after them came blood that streaked George's arms as he went deeper and doused her again. The fire was spreading up his legs now, and he took another few steps and crouched down to duck himself completely under. When he came up the girl started to kick, there were still ants all over her, and when he glanced back to see how far he'd gone into the water George saw with pure horror that the ants were building a bridge of themselves, out into the shallows after him. He stumbled backward into deeper water, holding the girl in one arm as he flailed the other to keep his balance, and still there were ants on her and on him, and he slopped huge handfuls of water over her and rubbed ants out of wounds in her skin—and still they came out of her, and screaming he thrashed her violently through the water, and he didn't mean to or maybe he did but when he stopped she was limp in his hands, and all he could do was let go and watch the tiny black body drift away down the lazy current.

George was crying, and his throat hurt, and the ants had bitten all up and down his legs and arms. "I said I'd do it, Yishaq," he sobbed. "Why did you leave me?"

Later he found the village, burned out and silent. Numb, he shambled through it, seeing other small bodies but unable to look at them. He walked all night, praying to be relieved, to die if that's what it took. Some time after dawn he reeled off the path and slept. When he woke, her blood was still on his arms. He thought he could still see it when he came out of the Ituri onto the shores of Lake Albert a month later, and he thought he could still hear her, toddling after him at the head of an army of all the dead he'd seen and left behind.

LANCE

HE MADE GOOD TIME, and he'd been up with the sun, so Lance drove into New York City just after noon on the seventeenth of June. He crossed the 103rd Street bridge onto Manhattan Island and made his way downtown through midday traffic that reminded him of Seoul's except for the lack of bicycles and rickshaws. After a while he figured he'd come far enough. He left the Plymouth at a parking garage on Second Avenue, paying for a week, and stepped into a phone booth on the corner to page through the listings until he found J. Kazmierski on East 4th Street. He looked at the street sign and saw that he was at 23rd, then looked south. The blocks looked short, and the week's parking put a dent in Lance's remaining cash, so he started walking.

Along the way he thought about money. He didn't have much, and didn't have any way to get more, but there was always Jerry's place to crash at, and Lance didn't plan to be in New York for long anyway. As soon as he'd tracked down his father, he'd square things away and head home to see if Dewey had followed through and gotten Ellie loose. It was all backward, and he knew it. Right then he should have been on the road back to Michigan, back to his girl.

You don't just walk away from your father, though, he thought. Especially not now, not when your brother's been talking to him for the past eight years (okay, at second hand, but still) and you've still never laid eyes on him. One day. He'd give himself one day, and if Dad didn't turn up Lance would be off. That was fair.

First thing was to find Jerry. Lance walked down 4th Street, along a block of five- and six-story buildings with sunken courtyards in front of them. Bars and delis and butcher shops occupied the bottom floors, with apartments above, and Lance found Jerry's building right away. He walked up three flights of stairs and doubled back down a hall lit by a naked bulb that might almost have illuminated a refrigerator. Jerry's door was the last one on the left. It was a little open. Lance knocked and said, "Hey. Jerry?"

Something thumped inside the apartment, and then Jerry's face appeared in the crack between door and jamb. "You dumb bastard," he said. "I told you not to come here."

"I need to find my father, Jerry. Dewey said he's probably here."

"Lance, if you're going to live through this, you need to put away childish things, and that includes little-boy fantasies that you're going to reconcile with your dad and go play catch. Look, we can't talk about this here. The Yankees are playing right now. Go to the stadium, buy a scorecard, and sit up in the bleachers. I'll find you."

Jerry shut the door in his face. Lance raised his hand to knock, or maybe to knock the goddamn door out of its frame, but then he dropped it again. The game. Play the game. Okay, he thought. Yankee Stadium. I always wanted to see it anyway.

It was the top of the fifth by the time Lance got to the stadium. He'd gotten so caught up in his first subway ride that he lost track of the stations. Even apart from the crowd, the shuffling panorama of New York's people, Lance marveled at the subway tunnel. People had built that. Amazing. It was the same feeling he'd had looking at the Golden Gate Bridge, only something about the subway seemed perfectly New York–ish. Fast, packed under the city, removed from the landscape. San Francisco fit into what was there; New York imposed itself. Both cities simultaneously enthralled Lance and made him wish he was in a cabin somewhere in the Upper Peninsula boondocks. Then the train had come up out of the ground after the 149th Street station and Lance was amazed all over again. It came to a stop so close to Yankee Stadium that Lance thought he could have thrown a ball from the station into left field.

He managed to cram himself through the closing doors and get back into the world, coming down the big concourse right to The House That Ruth Built. Statues in the outfield, DiMaggio's fifty-six-game streak, all of it. Wow, he thought. Just wow. Spicer had crowed over the fact that DiMaggio had actually reeled off sixty-one games while he was playing for the Seals back in the thirties, but that was the minors. The Pacific Coast League was good ball, but still the bush; Yankee Stadium was as big-league as it got.

He bought a bleacher ticket and then had to look up and down the concourse to find a scorecard. Most of the vendors who sold them had already gone home. When he'd finally gotten one, he made his way up into the stands and picked out a spot above everyone else, ten rows or so below the back wall in center field. The Yankees were winning 4–3 over the Tigers, and Lance bought himself a hot dog and settled in to enjoy the game until Jerry showed up, about fifteen minutes after Lance's first bite of mustard-slathered ballpark goodness.

"Look, man," Jerry said as he collapsed next to Lance. "Forget everything I said on the road."

"Why? Makes a good story."

"It's also true. Every word of it. But it's not what you need to know, so forget it. Let me give you the short version, and don't stop me if you've heard some of it before because you need to hear it all at once. Okay. Within twenty years at the end of the twelfth century, an Ethiopian delegation visits Europe to complain about the Templars, Chrétien de Troyes publishes the first Arthurian Grail poem, the Templars lose Jerusalem to Saladin, and Chartres burns and is rebuilt with a weird little sculpture about the Ark of the Covenant on its north porch. Zip ahead a hundred years. In thirteen oh six another Ethiopian mission talks to Pope Clement the Fifth; the next year, he has every Templar in France arrested and run through the Inquisition. By thirteen twelve the Templars are officially suppressed, and King Philip spends the next two years burning every important Templar. The last one, Jacques de Molay, goes to the stake in thirteen fourteen, and the very next year crops all over Europe fail and millions of people die in a famine. Thirty years after that the Black Death kills off a third of Europe's population. If the Grail means fertility, health, all that, what does all that make you figure?"

Think like Jerry, Lance told himself. "The Grail left Europe," he said.

"Exactly. Now if you're the guy who has it, and the Inquisition's on your tail, and things in Ethiopia are too up in the air to take it back there, where do you go? Someplace where nobody will even think to look. Wolfram von Eschenbach, the guy who picked up the Arthur poems after Chrétien died, called the Grail's hiding place *Terra Salvaescha,* the land of salvation. Already when he was writing, the Grail was gone from Jerusalem, so where was he talking about? The next place where all the religious nuts in Europe thought they'd found the New Jerusalem: North America. At this point the New World is still a rumor to most people, but some important folks knew about it. One of them was Henry the Navigator. In the thirteen eighties he made a little stop in guess where, Nova Scotia, and when I tell you that Henry the Navigator was a Templar you should be able to figure the rest out all by yourself."

"So the Black Plague happened because the Grail had been taken out of Europe?"

"You bet it did. And not just the Black Plague. Between thirteen hundred and the middle of the nineteenth century, Europe went through a mini ice age. Snow fell in places where people had never seen it, there were famines all the time, the weather was screwy, and then beginning in about eighteen seventy the climate gets back to normal in Europe but you start to see famines in Africa. This is right about the time when the European powers get hot and heavy with imperialism, and right about the time that Arthur Rimbaud says the hell with poetry and starts wandering in the general direction of, where else, Ethiopia. Not too long after that, George Gibson has a bad night on Oak Island, and when Rimbaud dies in eighteen ninety-one a whole series of famines kills millions and millions of people all over Africa and India and China. What I'm telling you is that this isn't just some hoodoo story about a Christian relic. When the Grail situation gets fucked up, the whole world goes to hell. Now look at the twentieth century, Jesus H. Christ, you've got World War One, World War Two, Hitler, Stalin, the flu epidemic, the atom bomb, people starving everywhere . . ." Jerry trailed off, and when he spoke again all of the energy had drained out of his voice. "I'll tell you the truth, man. When I think about all this, I just fucking despair. Nobody can fix it, and even if somebody gets the Grail it won't be the right guy. Not even you. Somewhere way back in the twelfth century you've got a connection to the Zagwes, no doubt about that, but the Grail King has to come from the place where all this started. It goes all the way back to the first stories that the Egyptians heard. It goes all the way back to Africa, where we all first came down from the trees and said the hell with being monkeys, we've got stock markets and television to figure out. The Grail King's got to be African. It won't work any other way."

"Are you listening to yourself? If there's one of these Zagwes back in the family tree, that makes me African."

"I told you, man, the Zagwes were usurpers, they back-stabbed their way onto the throne and were gone after two hundred years. That's a blip. This has been going on for four thousand years. More."

"So you're telling me all this to let me know that I'm not up to the job."

"Oh, poor Lance. Did I hurt your feelings? For Christ's sake, I don't know if you're up to the job or not. I don't know if anyone is. What I'm telling you is that there are traditions here, and it doesn't look like you're part of them."

"Bullshit. You go back far enough, we're all African, right?"

"Maybe, who knows. For the sake of argument let's say yes. But along the way, certain actions disqualify people from holding the Grail, or make it clear that if they do get it, everything they do will turn to shit. Whoever's got it now sure has a lot to answer for. And your family, Zagwes and Templars and whoever else, hasn't exactly lived up to Galahad's example."

My family, Lance thought. These are real people.

"Then it's up to me to change that," Lance said. "It's up to me. How do I find my father?"

"Ask your mom, probably," Jerry said, and Lance felt like he'd been kicked in the gut.

Jerry saw the look on his face and said, "Lance, kid, you're being pretty dense here. She's got to know something about this."

"My mom is a Templar?" Dewey had hinted at this, but hearing it from Jerry made it simultaneously threatening and impossible. Lance didn't know what to think. His mom?

"You think it's funny," Jerry said, "but ask her about it next time you see her."

Meanwhile the game was going on, and Jerry fell into a dark mood, muttering under his breath, ripping the scorecard out of Lance's hand. "Fuck," he said. "Top of the sixth already. Now we might never know."

"Know what?" Lance asked, but Jerry was busy filling in the lineups.

"Fuck," he said again, and looked around. "Hey," he said to a gaggle of twelve-year-old boys in front of them, "lemme see your scorecard a second."

"Buy us a beer," one of the boys said.

Jerry looked at Lance, and Lance got up to go to the concession stand.

When he came back, Jerry had his scorecard filled in. Something he saw got him started talking, almost as if he was just spinning out a story in his own mind to see if it held together. "Okay," he said, "it's eighteen ninety, more or less the centennial of the ratification of the Constitution, which is a good time to get things done in the U.S., right?"

"Right," Lance said, but Jerry glared at him and he shut up.

"So a guy stumbles across something that he isn't supposed to stumble across. Happens all the time, look at history. No, don't look at history, that's exactly what you shouldn't look at. Look at what history doesn't tell you. Try this on: after eighteen ninety, empires started to fall apart, millions of people died in famines in Africa and India and China, two world wars, revolutions, fire-bombing cities, the fucking Bomb. I told you all that before."

Twice, Lance thought. On the field Hank Bauer lined a long double to right-center. Jerry noted it. "How it happens is this. Something that was keeping everything together is no longer there to keep them together. Simple cause and effect. First principles, man, and the firstest of them all is where we came from. Africa. Everything that happens, happens because of something in Africa. All patterns replicate the original pattern. So what's happening in Africa in eighteen ninety? Livingstone, exploration, colonies everywhere. Except for one place, right?"

Phil Rizzuto drove Bauer in with a bloop single to left, and Jerry's next words were drowned in the crowd's roar. "What?" Lance said.

"For Chrissakes, listen, man. Ethiopia. The only place in Africa that was never colonized, at least not until the thirties and by then it was too late for the Italians to get what they wanted. Way too late. But in eighteen ninety it was still possible, and that's why they tried to strike a deal with Menelik. But he kicked their asses. I'll lay it out for you as clear as day: who runs things in Italy? The Vatican. And who runs things in the Vatican?" Jerry looked away from the field and stared at Lance.

"The pope?" Lance guessed.

"Exactly what you're supposed to think. But no. Think back to right after the Crusades. Who were the most powerful people in Europe?"

Jerry was looking back to the field again, where the Yankees had just grounded into a double play. Lance wasn't sure if he was supposed to say anything.

"The fucking Knights Templar, man. They owned Europe. And they owned the Middle East, stabled their horses in the fucking Dome of the Rock. They were the world's first capitalists, ran banks, financed wars, the whole nine yards. Now history tells you that the pope got jealous of the Templars' influence and seized their property, had them suppressed. The truth of it, though"— and here Jerry looked at Lance again—"is that it was the other way around. The Templars figured out that they needed religious authority, political authority, that they wouldn't have if they were just a sect of crazy warrior monks with too much money. They needed to go mainstream, issue bonds, put on a suit and tie and infiltrate Wall Street."

Lance couldn't help himself. "Wall Street?"

"Shut the fuck *up,* man; it's a figure of speech." Jerry paused.

"Even if it's true. The point is, the Templars were running things when Italy put the moves on Menelik in Ethiopia, and after they got their whiskers singed, nobody else moved in until nineteen thirty-five. So what did Menelik have that the Templars didn't, and that they wanted?" The Tigers came to bat. Don Lund took an inside curve. "Think about it. The Dome of the Rock, where Solomon's temple was. Where the Ark of the Covenant was. Now what happened to the Ark of the Covenant?" Lance didn't say anything. Lund took ball two. "Nobody knows. At least, history says nobody knows. But it just falls off the face of the earth; it's there one minute in the Bible, gone the next. And nobody ever mentions where it went, or even that it's gone, except in a code that the Templars left for the right people to figure out. Chartres Cathedral: a great big puzzle box, carved reliefs, messages in cipher, the whole nine yards. It's all there, the Queen of Sheba going to Solomon, having a son, going home with that son, and stealing the Ark to take with her. And where did the Queen of Sheba come from?"

Jerry stared at Lance again. Humor him, Lance thought. "Ethiopia?"

"Now you're starting to pay attention." The boys in front of them got up and moved over toward left field. "The freaking Ark was in Ethiopia this whole time, and the Templars knew it, and that's what they wanted when they got into bed with Menelik."

"We've been over this, man," Lance said, as Harvey Kuenn moved Lund, who had walked, to third with a single to center.

"I know that," Jerry said. "What, you think I'm an idiot? This is like chumming the water. We're fishing for sharks here."

"How do we know when we catch one?"

Jerry whacked his scorecard. "Right here. You'll see."

A roar rose up from the crowd as Steve Souchock, of all people, hit a long opposite-field home run: 6–4 Tigers. "There's two," Jerry said. "On the right track."

"Three-run homer, Jerry. Lund and Kuenn were on."

"I mean two home runs in the game."

"Right. Sharks circling yet?"

"Don't you dare patronize me. Spicer has wet dreams about seeing what we're doing here. I told you, magic is real. Shut up and watch the game, and I'll show you."

Okay, Lance thought. He settled back and fell into the rhythm of the game. It turned into a slugfest, both teams firing doubles into the gaps, sharp singles through the box, and in the seventh Jerry nearly had a stroke when Kuenn ripped a long line drive just outside the foul pole in right. "Jesus," he said. "I thought for a minute this wasn't going to pan out. Way the ball's carrying today, I should know better. Say something about the Grail."

"Spicer said it was all about Thoth and Osiris."

"Spicer knows all kinds of stuff, but his problem is that he can only think like a poet. Remember, poets in this business disguise the truth. They come up with parables, metaphors, all that shit. This does all start with Thoth and Osiris, but that's just a story, too. The Egyptians got it from Ethiopia, way back before they started building pyramids. You really think that the Holy Grail is Osiris' pecker?"

"Man, I hope not. I don't want to spend the rest of my life with a shriveled-up Egyptian pecker in my hand."

"Hell no," Jerry said. "Only dick you want in your hand is your own."

Which was Lance's cue to get up and get more beer. He brought back hot dogs too, and thought, here I am sitting in Yankee Stadium. Beats the hell out of watching the Seals, that's for sure. Chalk that one up for New York. Be nice to see a ballgame without having to listen to loony conspiracy theories, though.

Top of the eighth now, and with one out Kuenn floated a home run to left, just over the fence into the Yankee bullpen. "Check and mate," Jerry said, marking it down. "I told you the ball was carrying right. Look at this." He held his scorecard out to

Lance and drew a triangle between the three Tiger home runs, with two long sides and one short.

"Spell it out for me, Jerry," Lance said.

"Sacred geometry. That's one reason baseball is magic, because it's all about angles and shapes. And this triangle here?" Jerry reached into his hip pocket and unfolded a piece of paper. "Here's a map of France. This is Chartres, this is Troyes, this is Charleville." He made three circles, and drew lines to connect them, and damned if the triangle didn't match the figure on the scorecard.

Is this proof? Lance thought.

"Chartres, Troyes, and Charleville," Jerry went on. "Cathedral and two important birthplaces: both Chrétien and the Knights Templar come from Troyes, and guess who was born in Charleville?"

"I said spell it out."

"Rimbaud, man, Rimbaud. Think that's an accident? And there's more. The Templars are maniacs for reproduction of shapes; they built stone churches all over Ethiopia on the model of Solomon's Temple. Now if they're in the New World, not too long ago, they can't just go around building stone churches. It's not Ethiopia. People will notice. So they take this triangle. One point is New York, an administrative and financial center like Troyes was. Did I mention that the Templars and their patrons in Troyes were Europe's first capitalists?"

Lance kept his mouth shut, not wanting to provoke another commie rant. Especially not in the bleachers at Yankee Stadium with the Yankees losing.

"Well, they were. The second point, the one that matches Chartres, is San Francisco. Think of the Monkey Block as the cathedral, a place where writing and politics come together. Mark Twain named Tom Sawyer for a fireman he went boozing with at the Monkey Block. It was full of writers and artists beginning right around the time that George Gibson should have taken the left turn at Albuquerque, and Spicer must have told you about Sun Yat-sen."

"Yeah, he did, and the Indian revolutionaries. So did someone write Ethiopia's constitution in Chartres?" As he asked the question, Lance had to acknowledge that if you bought into the Templar-cipher routine, the analogy was there. "Never mind," he said. "I get it."

"Okay. You take the angles, map them out onto North America, and guess where the third point falls?"

"Are you going to tell me it's Dexter?"

"Hell, no. Do you think these people are obvious? The third point is Wawa, Ontario. Little town up on the shore of Lake Superior. Canada, man, where the Templars hid the Grail. And even though your guess of Dexter is naive and dumb, it's closer than you might think. I wasn't kidding when I mentioned your mom last night. You want to get the real skinny, ask her about Wawa, Ontario."

Right, Lance thought. "I'll do that. But what does this mean right now?"

"It means they're here. Look around. Shouldn't be too hard to pick them out." Jerry turned, scanned the bleacher crowd. "There. That guy."

Behind them, against the back wall of the center-field bleachers, a lone figure stood. He was an old guy, gray hair cropped short and face deeply seamed, wearing a suit and hat. And maybe it was just that he'd caught Jerry's paranoia, but looking at the guy Lance got a feeling. He wasn't there for the game, at least not in the way that the rest of the crowd was. For him, baseball wasn't a sport; he scanned the crowd without ever looking at the field. Watching him, Lance had a sense that this was how a frog felt when a heron landed in his pond.

And standing maybe twenty feet to his left was Gwen.

Until then, he'd just been talking, just going along with crazy

Jerry K. Now it was real, and Lance wanted to run away. He'd gotten just far enough away from Dewey that he was starting to question what he'd learned there, and Jerry's comic-book secret societies just didn't stand up on their own, but there was Gwen. She wasn't looking at him, or at Jerry; she was in fact making a note on a scorecard that Billy Martin had just grounded out to short.

Lance turned back around and said, "Jerry, look quick. Just to the right of the old guy."

Jerry glanced over his shoulder, then put his head down. If the Yankee Stadium bleachers had come equipped with steering wheels, he'd have been pounding on one. "Okay. Here's what we do. You go, ignore the old guy. Talk to Gwen. She'll suggest you go with her somewhere, and you'll do it. I'll follow the old guy, see what he does. There's a bar in the West Village called the White Horse. One way or another, you should get Gwen there, and if I'm right, it won't be too hard."

"There's a bar in Berkeley called that," Lance said. "Spicer hangs out there."

"I'll just bet he does. The White Horse was the symbol of Saxon kings for a long time; it's tied up with the Arthur story in all kinds of ways you'll never see in Chrétien or Malory. The name's a big inside joke for all the pinheads who believe the Arthur shtick. They use the place to pass notes. She'll know where it is. I'll even bet you that the bartender pulls her drink before you sit down."

"Okay, so we go there. What then? Get to the part about my father."

"Lance, that old guy might be your father."

"What, him? He's got to be eighty."

"You saying you won't be able to get it up when you're sixty? I thought you were a real man." Jerry guffawed. "Leave the father bit to me. The old guy will lead me to him if he's around. I'll meet you at the White Horse at nine tonight. Get rid of Gwen by then, okay, and whatever else happens, you are under strict orders not to fuck her. Clear?"

"Jesus, Jerry."

"Clear?"

"Yes, clear. But I'm not clear on why I don't just walk up to the old guy and ask him where my dad is."

"Because he might just stick a goddamn knife in you, that's why. If your dad knows about Dwight's decision, he can do one of two things, right? He can either go with it, do what he can to push you ahead, or he can dance with who brought him. You've never met the guy, and he's already shown that Dwight is first on his list. You trust him? Even if he'd welcome you with open arms, you've got to consider that other people have heavy bets on your brother, and they won't be happy to see you making a run this close to the finish line. I'm saying play it cool. I told you not to come to New York, but you didn't listen. Listen now."

Lance didn't like it, but it made sense. "Okay," he said. "I'm going. Nine o'clock."

"Keep it in your pants," Jerry said.

Gwen was wearing a smile he didn't like as Lance climbed up the bleachers to meet her. "Interesting company you keep," she said.

"He said the same thing about you, only not so polite."

"Well, courtesy is something you have to be taught, isn't it?" She inclined her head to the right. "Do you want to meet my friend? I saw you noticing him."

"No, right now I'm more interested in talking to you. How about if we take a walk?"

"A walk in the Bronx. How romantic."

"I was thinking more like the Village."

She looked past him, down at Jerry. "Leaving your friend?"

"He wants to see the end of the game."

"All right. The Village it is."

They rode the length of the city, Lance watching its neighborhoods blend in the petri dish of the subway car: Negroes and Puerto Ricans in Harlem, then working types and occasional couples in thin ties and shiny dresses as they rattled underneath Lexington Avenue past Central Park. The clothes got poorer after Grand Central, where Lance had a powerful rush of emotion thinking of the old radio program. *A million private lives.* He looked over at Gwen, who was staring into space as if she did this every day. She'd spent some time here, long enough for the effect to wear off. They got off at Astor Place and walked west to Washington Square Park, the old radio teaser on an endless loop in Lance's head. New York had a way of making everyone anonymous, and in this city Lance was more anonymous than most. At least they belonged here, going home or to work or out to eat or to school. He was an interloper, here with a girl who belonged.

True in more ways than one. *Wild card,* Jerry had called him. Coming home from a useless war with a useless wound, he'd unwittingly thrust himself into the middle of a dynastic succession people had been killing each other over for centuries. Gwen was part of it, even if she didn't always like her part. He remembered her sad silence, the morning after they'd made love in San Francisco. How did it feel to be moved around like that?

Ask yourself, he thought. You know a little about that by now. Enough that people are paying attention. Heck, if they cared enough to try to kill you, they must be worried that you'll succeed.

I'm falling into the mythology, he thought. Lance Porter, one more story in the naked city. Nobody knows I'm here. It was kind of like how he'd felt in San Francisco, but he'd learned enough since then that he didn't feel lonely anymore. He'd seen his brother, and would soon meet his father, and the rush and bustle of New York was getting into him, infecting him with a strange enthusiasm. Yes. It would all work out. He was meant to be King.

At the southwestern corner of the park they walked through a small plaza crammed with people playing chess and backgammon, shouting at each other in more languages than he could keep track of. They turned left, down Macdougal Street, and it was like North Beach again. Lance half expected Spicer to stumble out of one of the bars they passed, and when they got to an intersection he glanced to his right expecting to see the Monkey Block. Strange. He shook it off and focused on finding his father.

To do that he'd have to talk to Gwen. Jerry might follow the old guy to the moon, and in the hour he'd already been with Gwen, they hadn't said much. Lance was itchy to get things moving.

"I hear there's a place called the White Horse here too," he said.

Gwen looked startled. "There is. Did you see the one in Berkeley?"

"Spicer told my fortune there."

"Oh, God. Tarot?" She shook her head. "Poets."

"So how about if we have a drink?"

"How about if we talk about where you've been this past week?"

"Gwen, please. Can we have a beer?"

"I'm serious, Lance. I missed you. You didn't come to see me."

The conversation was turning in the wrong direction. He tried to make a joke. "No talk without drink," Lance said. "We soldiers get thirsty."

She didn't smile. "Okay. Right this way."

A few minutes later they walked up to the White Horse Tavern. Seeing its sign gave Lance a chill even though he'd known it was coming. White horses made him think of the Lone Ranger, and cowboys were just knights with six-guns, right? It was all starting to get spooky. He could hear Jerry expounding on the Lone Ranger, the white knight with his Indian sidekick. *It all maps back onto the Templars and their Ethiopian sidekicks,* Jerry would say. *Remember, they used to think Ethiopia was part of India; do I have to spell it out?*

And maybe it was a measure of just how far Lance had been sucked into this that he could almost believe. If Chartres Cathedral, why not the Lone Ranger? Where did it stop?

Standing there on the sidewalk holding the door for Gwen, he could see all the way up Eighth Avenue, the buildings on either side fading into the city's heave of brown haze, and way off in the distance a hint of green. Suddenly the size of it stopped impressing him; it was too far beyond his experience to even register. He followed her inside.

Jerry was right about one thing, anyway: the minute they walked in the door, the bartender spotted Gwen and started mixing a whiskey sour. It was four o'clock, and maybe a dozen people were scattered around the bar's front room. Off the bar area were two other rooms with tables, but no fireplace and no dance floor. The difference between New York and Berkeley, maybe.

They sat at the bar, near the end away from the taps, and the bartender brought Gwen's drink. Lance ordered a draft beer. When he'd gotten it and gotten to know it a little, Gwen said, "Dylan Thomas died here a couple of months ago."

"Who?"

"A poet."

"Don't tell me," Lance said.

"I won't. He was just a drunk. Put away twenty-odd whiskeys and fell over. They took him up the street and he died the next day, I think."

"So he didn't die here."

"Well, no, but they're already saying he did. Makes a better story. I'm sure you're familiar with that impulse by now."

"Yeah," Lance said. "I've run across it. Tell me something. Is Gwen your real name?"

"Is Lance yours?"

"Lance David Porter. Dewey has the same middle name because we're twins. I tried Dave for a while when I was a kid, but it didn't stick."

"My name is Gwenivere Nicole Deschamps. You and I are the same, Lance. Born to this even if we never wanted it."

"You never wanted it?"

"What do you mean by *it*?" she asked. "The Grail? Being a queen? I don't know. I've seen enough to know it's not just a story. Enough to know for certain that I can't always let myself be limited to the role I'm supposed to play."

"Which apparently is Dwight's girlfriend."

The smile left her face. "*Was,* Lance. I *was* your brother's girlfriend. I haven't seen him in quite a while."

He couldn't tell if she was lying, and it drove him crazy. The people who were straight with him said all kinds of crazy things that no reasonable person would believe, and the people who lied to him seemed just ordinary. *Was.* What difference did it make whether he believed her? He couldn't step on his brother like that, past tense or present. "How is it you didn't manage to let me know that?"

"Are you serious? When we were on my couch and you said you were a virgin, did you really want me to tell you that I'd been seeing your brother? That's a little bit sanctimonious."

Lance didn't know what *sanctimonious* meant, but he didn't like the tone. "It wasn't right," he insisted. "You playing the winning horse, Gwen? Did Dewey tell you he didn't want the Grail, and you went looking for me?"

He said it to make her angry, but instead she looked stricken. "I don't expect you to believe this," she said, "but I don't have nearly that kind of say in things."

And what was that supposed to mean? "So you were told to

go find me and get me in the sack," Lance said, meaning it as a question but pleased when it came out more like an accusation.

"What if I was? Would you have turned me down if you knew? Don't you dare get up on a high horse with me. I was there, and you wanted me. You wanted me."

Yes, and he still wanted her. Even there in the White Horse, waiting for Jerry K. and distracted by the specter of the gaunt figure in the Yankee Stadium bleachers, Lance wanted her. If she suggested it, he'd go with her right then, just to forget. He wanted the sweep of her hair across his face, the touch of her hands on his scars, the secrets of her body wordlessly whispered in the San Francisco dark. The ache in his groin was sudden and painful; I could have her, he thought. I can say a word and have her. He opened his mouth.

Before he could speak, Gwen said, "Even if I was told, it became what I wanted for myself," and Lance's mouth was still open but he had no idea what to say. She was looking at him, dark eyes vulnerable and inviting, and what had been easy—what was easier than to take what was offered?—became impossible. Poised to speak, Lance hung torn between desires. Gwen, or what Gwen knew. Instinct murmured that he couldn't have both. For some reason he thought of Dwight, cross-legged on his rickety dock, looking out over the Atlantic sunrise, and it wasn't his betrayal that came to mind but Dwight's adamant calm: *I don't want any part of it.*

Renunciation.

"I have to find my father," Lance said, gambling.

A shadow of disappointment swept over Gwen's face. "He's not around here," she said, and looked away from him to find cigarettes in her purse. She lit one and blew smoke over the ember, casual again. Reserved. Hiding something.

"Dwight doesn't want the Grail," Lance said, not caring who heard. "I have to find my father."

"I'll bet Jerry took you to the baseball game," Gwen said, now cynical and teasing, "and then he spotted someone who he said was watching you, and said that person would know where your father was."

"Are you saying he was wrong?"

"I'm saying that Jerry Kazmierski thinks he knows more than he actually does."

Which was exactly what she—and Jerry—had said about Spicer. Lance was starting to accept ignorance as a universal truth. He didn't think he knew anything, but once in a while he had suspicions, and once in a while they were confirmed. "I'm supposed to meet him here at nine," Lance said. "He seemed a little nervous about you being around."

Her gaze dropped again. She stirred the lemon slice around the bottom of her glass. "Are you asking me to leave?"

Lance saw that she was genuinely hurt, and against all his better judgment he wanted to make her feel better. God, she was a puzzle. "I'm saying that putting the two of you in the same room isn't a great idea right now."

"Nine's a long way off yet," she said. "You sure we can't just enjoy each other's company a little?"

Now she was playing him. "Where's my father, Gwen?"

"I told you I don't know. I've never spoken to him. From what I understand, he stays in the same room with George Gibson every minute he's not in the bathroom. He figures that if he leaves Gibson alone, Gibson will start to think for himself or someone else will get to him. The problem with being the power behind the throne is you have to stay right there behind the throne. Believe me, Lance, if I could put you in touch with him I would. God knows someone needs to sort this mess out, and if Dwight has taken himself out of the running everyone would benefit from a little family reunion."

"Was the old guy at the game my dad?"

She rolled her eyes. "You want to know what happened at the game, Lance? Jerry saw someone, had a paranoid Templar fantasy that struck him like a revelation, and followed some retired pay-roll clerk home to Murray Hill. He's probably sitting on a trash can on Thirty-first Street right now congratulating himself, and if he's not doing that he's back at his apartment sucking down whiskey and feeling sorry for himself. Jerry Kazmierski's a drunk, in case you hadn't noticed."

Her teasing pissed him off. "Tell you what," Lance said. "I'll make you a deal. Let's go to Jerry's. If you're right and he's sitting there, you call the shots. I'll do what you tell me to do. If not, you tell me, no bullshit, what you know about all this. You're holding out on me, and you are not going to get between me and my dad."

"That sentimental streak will kill you, Lance." Gwen stubbed out her cigarette. "But you win. Talk to Jerry, let him poison you a little more. I'll see you around."

She got up and left him there. Lance waited to see if Jerry would breeze through the door right after she'd left, as he had in San Francisco, but the only people who came in during the next ten minutes were a group of guys in denim arguing about jazz. It was just past five; four hours to go. He nursed his beer and wished he had something to do other than stew and wait on Jerry. Even that stupid *Junkie* book. William Lee was probably writing about people he'd seen in the White Horse. Didn't heroin junkies call the drug horse? That fit. He'd feel a lot better about things if the people trying to pull his strings had to take time out to stick nee-dles in their arms. It was hard to be scared of junkies.

Four hours to go.

The bar clock read nine, and the White Horse was packed, but Jerry had yet to appear. Lance had tried to be careful, but what could you do when you were stuck in a bar waiting for a lunatic to tell you whether you could meet your father and arrange your coronation as a mythical king? He'd lost count of the beers a while ago, but judging from his posture he'd had a few. He straightened himself up and wondered how fast the bar clock was. Ten minutes? Surely no more than twenty.

So at twenty after nine, glass empty and no sign of Jerry, Lance waved for one last beer. Might as well have something to sip while he listened to Jerry rant. When the bartender brought it, Lance asked if a guy named Jerry came in often. Red hair, motormouth, et cetera.

"Jesus Christ," the bartender said. "You want to talk to that guy?"

"Is he in here a lot?"

"Too much. If I never see him again, it'll be too soon, but if he ain't here tonight you'll find him at Chumley's."

Lance got directions to Chumley's, scribbled on a napkin. "There's no sign," the bartender said, "just look for a door with EIGHTY-SIX on it."

"Good enough," Lance said. "Appreciate it."

"Pleasure. One thing: if you're a friend of this Jerry guy's, do him a favor. Next time he's in here, don't get him started with the Freemason garbage. I don't want to hear it."

"Will do." Lance drank his beer slowly, watching the crowd. The place was filled with people about his age, and again he had the sense that he was back in San Francisco—there was the guy shouting and waving what had to be a poem, over there a table of guys who might as well have been wearing signs that said QUEER, at the bar a string of older locals giving the whole scene the hairy eyeball. Any minute Spicer would walk in and boil the whole room down in a single cutting remark.

Spicer, Jesus. Just thinking about the guy made Lance want another beer. He got it and sipped, suddenly grateful that Jerry K. hadn't walked in. An afternoon just holding down the bar had done him good. Time to digest everything. In the past two weeks Lance had gone from a disabled Korea vet to, well, a knight questing for the Grail. There was no other way to put it. Spicer said so, Gwen had hinted at it, Jerry had his version, and Dewey sat there so calm, saying no like he was turning down a leaflet from a Jehovah's Witness. Any one of them might have gone crazy, might have lied to Lance out of spite. Would all four?

Didn't mean it was true, but Lance found himself believing it, believing that somewhere in the world there was a Grail, and that for almost nine hundred years people had been maneuvering to get it, and that somewhere along the line a barnstorming baseball player had stumbled over it, and that whoever had it now, Lance himself was next in line. And he wanted it to be true, wanted there to be a reason that his father had disappeared, wanted anything that meant he was more than just another vet with a bum leg and no clear idea of what he was doing next week.

The beer disappeared, and Lance weighed ordering another, but it was way after nine, and the place was about packed, and Jerry hadn't made an appearance. Time to look elsewhere.

He made his way through the Village, stopping at intersections to check the bartender's map. The street was easy enough to find, but Lance walked by the door three times before he noticed the iron 86 and went in. Chumley's was all bare wood and pictures of writers, and even though Lance fought it he caught himself thinking of the Black Cat's literary mural. All these places were the same. Too much alike, in fact. He didn't like it. He halted just inside the doorway, looking across the tables at the bar, and walked back out.

Fifteen minutes later he climbed the stairs to Jerry's floor, shaking off the light rain that had begun to fall. The door was open, but the door was always open, and when Lance saw Jerry snoozing on the couch with a book over his face and a dangling finger plugged into the neck of an empty whiskey bottle he said, "Jerry. Goddammit. The joke is getting old." The beers he'd had in Chumley's and the White Horse were wearing off, and he went to the fridge. No beer. He went back into the living room. "Hey," he said, and picked up the book.

Jerry's eyes were wide open, his tongue hanging out of his

mouth, a deep purple bruise circling under his jaw. He'd bitten into his tongue, and a dried trickle of blood meandered from the corner of his mouth to stain the frayed neck of his T-shirt. Stepping back, Lance put a hand to his mouth and hit himself in the chin with the book; he flung it away and sat down in the middle of the carpet. Get out, he thought. What if they're still around? But he stayed where he was, transfixed by Jerry's pale dead face.

Strangled, like Lance had strangled the hobo. The same bruises, the same hanging tongue and empty bloodshot eyes. A message.

A noise from the doorway startled him. He spun around and saw Gwen with one hand over her mouth, making a choked hiccupping sound like she was trying to talk and cry at the same time and couldn't quite manage either. Lance looked wildly around the room, and all of his terror exploded on Gwen. "You knew about this," he said. "Bitch. Did you show up here just so you could watch when I found out?"

"I came here to talk to him," she said. "Both of us were wrong, Lance, I swear I don't know what this is."

"This is Jerry!" he screamed. "Jerry Kazmierski, dead on his fucking couch, and you saw us together this afternoon, and I was with you when it happened. Do you think I'm that dumb, Gwen? Do you think I can't put all this together?"

Then they were screaming at each other, accusations and denials, and before he could stop himself Lance hit her. She went straight down onto the floor in the doorway and huddled there for a long moment while Lance stood trembling with remorse and fear. Somewhere behind the tingle in his palm and the hammering of his pulse, Lance in an eyeblink of panicked clarity realized that he could kill Gwen, kill her and be gone. This was New York. No one knew he was here.

Except whoever she'd talked to since she left him in the

White Horse. *All the cops around here are in on it,* Dewey had said. Was it that way in New York too?

"Look at the book, Lance," she said. Her hair hung over her face, and both her hands were splayed on the floor, and speaking she became a human being again, the woman who had made him a man, the woman who might know where his father was.

Lance found the book lying open on the floor in front of the radiator. He picked it up and read the title. *"Parzival.* By Wolfram von Eschenbach."

"Oh, oh no," Gwen moaned. "Oh no, Lance. We have to get out of New York."

They were most of the way to the garage where Lance had left the Plymouth before a fresh bloom of paranoia stopped Lance dead in his tracks. No way could he drive Jerry's car now; might as well soap the rear window with the word GUILTY. Gwen thought they should fly somewhere, but when Lance asked where she froze up and he got suspicious of her all over again. "The old guy who killed Jerry," he said. "He the guy who brings you orders from my dad?"

He was fishing, and he knew it, but she bit. "More often than not, yes," she snapped. "His name is Frank. But I didn't know he was going to kill Jerry, and I don't know for certain that he did. Do you want to argue about it on the sidewalk or should we maybe get moving?"

We. Should *we* get moving. Was he really going to take her with him, wherever he was going? Right then, Lance was agreeing with the last thing Jerry had said about her: she was poison. Whenever he ran into her, bad things happened.

On the other hand, she knew how to get in touch with his father. Was that just another part of her act? Lance didn't know enough to make a good decision. Dewey didn't know where their dad was. After the day's events Lance was ready to believe that *that* might be an act too: act uninterested, send your rival on a wild-goose chase, get him tangled up in a murder. It was smooth, if it was true . . . but Dwight was his brother. Lance had to trust somebody. He chose Dwight. So Jerry's ruse at the ballpark had smoked out a Templar, but something about the tail had gone wrong. What did that say about Gwen?

Again he was caught in the gap between suspicion and certainty. Meeting Gwen was never a coincidence; she'd been in the ballpark right when Jerry said someone would be. Was she the one trying to set him up?

Or was she really starting to fall for him?

And the other question that he'd been avoiding all night: what did he feel for her?

Lance pulled that one up by the roots before it could bloom. He couldn't start down that road. He'd done what he'd done, and he'd have to pay for it later, but right then there was the game. All that mattered was making the right move.

In the end it all came back to his father. If Gwen knew where he was, she might tell Lance. Without her, he had no way to go forward. So there it was. *We.*

Somewhere on the highway through Pennsylvania, Gwen asked him the question he'd been gnawing over himself. "If you're worried about the police," she said, "won't they figure you might go home?" She had a point, but Lance remembered Jerry's triangle, and then he remembered laughing when Jerry suggested that Lance might see what his mother knew about all this, and at that moment there was nothing in the world Lance wanted to undo more than his own reaction in the ballpark. Jerry was right. His mother would know something.

Gwen was against it, to the point of almost leaving when they stopped for gas. When she saw that Lance was prepared to leave her there in the parking lot of the all-night gas station, she gave in, and he knew that she wasn't just playing him. She needed him for something. Maybe it was like he'd first thought, that she was trying to ride the winning horse, but now that he'd begun to sort things out, now that he'd figured the rules of the game, Lance could play. "Fine," he said. "I'm sure you can find me when you want to."

So she got back in the car, and he filed that away too. For the moment he'd won, taken some kind of control of the situation. Gwen didn't want him to talk to his mother, but she didn't want to let him out of her sight, either. They didn't say much on the ride, the long eleven hours to Ann Arbor, ending at the Embassy Hotel late Friday night. The Embassy was a flophouse, with a standard collection of drunks and panhandlers loitering out front; he waded through them with Gwen and they checked in as Mr. and Mrs. Jack Spicer, giggling at the joke once they were in the elevator to the fifth floor. The sheer monotony of the ride had sapped the tension between them, and as they shut the door to their tiny room Lance again felt his bone-deep want for her. He waited for the backwash of guilt, but it didn't come. What if part of the game was to take what was offered? Ellie felt far away.

Quit justifying, he told himself. You're the one who didn't show up for Ellie when you were supposed to.

That brought on the guilt, and Lance spent some time watching Gwen and feeling shitty about himself. There was something satisfying about it, though. He'd been feeling more and more disconnected from everything that had been important to him two weeks before—Ellie, the future, working his way back into manhood was the simple way to put it. More and more he was concentrating on the Grail, imagining the physical rush of possessing it, coming to believe that he could change the world. That was the easy part, changing the world, Dewey would say. What's hard is changing it for the better. The Philosopher's Stone, transforming people into golden versions of themselves. A little guilt reminded him to keep focused, stay grounded.

She noticed him watching her, and with a tired but mischievous smile she stripped her clothes off. "We should probably relax a little after the trip, don't you think?" Gwen walked toward him, and he was completely at a loss whether to resist or tackle her right there—but she solved the problem for him by walking right by into the bathroom. "Me, I'm going to take a shower."

He'd been had. Criminy, was everything a game with her? Lance heard the water come on, and he had a brief impulse to just walk out and leave her there. It was too hard, always having to figure out what angle she was playing. Out the door, a couple of miles west on Huron, cut across Veterans' Park to Dexter Road, and more straight miles to home. Easy. He'd be banging on his mother's door at two or three in the morning. The idea seemed better and better; he could find out about Jerry's triangles and Wawa, Ontario, and Dad, all before morning, and then he could make some decisions. Could be he'd need to go back for Gwen; could be he'd learn something that would make that a bad idea. Either way, he couldn't be any more confused and hounded and scared, not to mention horny, than he was right then.

Steam from the bath floated out into the room. God, he wanted a shower. His escape fantasy crumbled at the simple physical desire to be clean. Wish I was a dog, he thought. I'd just sit down and take care of things myself. He stood in dirty shorts feeling the sweat congeal between his toes. This was for the birds. Gwen's in there wrinkling up like a prune, he thought, while I stand around too dumb and tired to take my boots off.

That did it; nothing like a quick stab of self-mockery to get him moving. Lance sat on the bed and unlaced his boots. The shower turned off, and a minute later Gwen stepped out of the bathroom, naked and toweling her hair. "Now that is more like it," she said. "Your turn."

What a cruel world it was when you wanted nothing more than a shower but were too goddamn tired to walk into the bathroom and turn the knobs, Lance thought. He peeled off his socks, then his shirt and pants, and fell back on the bed. "Can't do it," he said. "I'm beat."

"Come on, you'll feel better." Gwen sat next to him, hooked her fingers into the waistband of his shorts, and started to pull them down.

He stopped her. "Gwen, come on. All I want is sleep." And sex and truth and the Grail and Jerry alive again and my father and Ellie. That's all. "Just sleep."

She let go and patted both his thighs. "That's not what I meant. I just thought you'd feel better if you had a shower, but have it your way. Scoot over."

He did, barely, and she wriggled under the bedspread and sheet. "We'll be more comfortable if you come under too," she said, and he wasn't quite exhausted enough to not be alarmed. But he did it, and she turned on her side and nestled her rear into his hip, and just like that she was asleep and he was listening to the late-night traffic on Huron Street, tracing the cracks in the plaster ceiling like an explorer whose time has passed, hungering for just one more blank space where he might lose himself at last.

ARTHUR

Terra Salvaescha, Wolfram had called it. The Land of Salvation, where lay the Holy Grail. Already at the turn of the thirteenth century the message had been garbled. Looking out his window at the desolation of Harar, Arthur could think only of how fragile any certainty must be. Ethiopia, Europe had believed in the days when a certain Canon Raimbaud was pouring money into the rebuilding of Chartres Cathedral, was a land of kings and riches, a boundless fount of Christian might in the form of Prester John and his army. In fact, the Ethiopia of 1182, when Chrétien de Troyes had introduced the world to the cipher of the Grail, had been a stew of competing warlords and hill tribes—Christian, Jew, Muslim, and pagan alike—most of whom could not have named the emperor and would not have known he was scion of a usurper clan that took the testicles of its defeated enemies as trophies.

As did Menelik. Some things never changed.

Doubtless Menelik would want the Grail Bearer's stones as well—all three of them, ha ha—in the event the Lion of Judah could set his claws in that party and hold on. It seemed unlikely to Arthur, and he intended to make it more so.

Across the dusty street he saw Jerome, his black habit flapping in the dry wind. So. The arrangement was made.

Arthur went downstairs, paused to inspect the skins drying outside the office. The local stray dogs had pissed on dozens of them over the previous few weeks until he'd poisoned them all again. Not a kingly gesture, perhaps, but royal munificence must wait on becoming royalty. In the meantime stray dogs couldn't be allowed to ruin valuable skins.

Jerome was sitting outside at a café facing Harar's main square. He nodded as Arthur sat down. "Arthur. It is troubling, this use of evil means to holy ends."

How I could trouble you, Jerome, Arthur thought. "Father, a Jesuit should know better than most that results do much to justify distasteful actions."

It was a discussion they'd nearly had a dozen times before, and as always Jerome avoided it. "It is not for me to decide," he said. "The Society has determined that no Templar may possess the Grail."

Which they surely would if the Grail reached Axum. Menelik's new guns would keep the Italians at bay a little longer, but Ethiopia would fall, and when it did, the Knights of the Temple would have the run of Wolfram's *Terra Salvaescha*. To have them in control of the Ark would be catastrophe enough, from a Jesuit point of view; if they had Ark and Grail together, the consequences would be unthinkable.

In this, Arthur agreed with the Society, but for different reasons. The Templars could not have the Grail because Arthur Rimbaud was going to have it for himself. Jerome didn't know this, of course, and since Arthur's testicles were not yet decorating a spearpoint in Entotto he was fairly certain that Menelik didn't either. He had to move cautiously, though, slowly, even if desire for the Grail wracked him the way physical lust or the seductions of poetry once had.

The Grail. Lost for centuries in a gabble of poetic ciphers and furtive escapades, now found. It had been his father's quest, of that Arthur was certain. The Widow Rimbaud alone had not driven him back to Africa, though God knew she would have been enough for most men; he had used his posting in Algeria to gather legends, test them in the daylight of reason and evidence. Painstakingly he compiled his histories and commentaries, and within them he embedded the clues that had led Arthur to Axum. For this Arthur had Jerome to thank, for it was Jerome who had whispered to him from the shadow of a Stockholm circus tent in June 1877. *Jean-Nicolas Arthur Rimbaud, do you remember me?*

The mustache was gray, the high boots replaced by sturdy working shoes, but the face was the face of the traveler who had knelt to tell a six-year-old boy that fathers were kept in the heart. Arthur was then twenty-three.

It was time for him to take up his father's work, the traveler said, and Arthur spent the next year traveling on errands whose full purpose Jerome—for so the traveler called himself—withheld from him. Rome, Zurich, Marseilles, home to Charleville and Roche, then Hamburg, Genoa, Alexandria . . . with one hiatus. Go to your father before you go to Africa, Jerome had instructed, and Arthur did. He left the Marseilles coach at the base of St. Gotthard Pass and was escorted south to Dijon. The men he traveled with were silent, but Arthur had grown accustomed to silence. They crossed the pass on foot, descended to Airolo, and spent the night. Then on to his father.

The Captain did not rise from his bed, did not smile when his younger son came in. "Arthur," he whispered. "Jerome has sent you."

"Yes, Father." Arthur felt his father's gaze, peeling away the son's disguises and camouflages. "He has shown me your papers. Frederic and I used to read them, after you'd gone."

"So Jerome has told me. He has also kept me abreast of your other entanglements."

The tiniest hint of distaste, disappointment in those last words. Arthur felt the scar on his wrist, souvenir of Verlaine's despair, like a brand. He was twenty-four years old and notorious across France, but now he stood with the tears of a six-year-old in his eyes. "Was the work so important, Father, that Frederic and Isabelle and I had to be sacrificed to it?"

A long silence passed. At its end the Captain said simply, "I could not stay." With the words, Arthur felt something close off within him. He would be a son no longer.

"Tell me what Jerome sent me for," he said, and in his dying old soldier's voice the Captain did.

Arthur sailed for Alexandria two days after his father died. There he found what Jerome had wanted him to find, a Cypriot Jew in the bazaar who had once in his boyhood seen a certain cross on the side of a certain hill an hour from the benighted village of Xylophagou. Arthur ran a crew at the quarry there, keeping an eye out for the underground Templar citadel Jerome had believed was somewhere beneath the dirt and bedrock; the Knights had made their headquarters on Cyprus for a century and more, and Jerome was certain that their mania for reproduction had invisibly manifested itself. All over Abyssinia were churches built by white men after the pattern of the Temple in Jerusalem, with Templar crosses carved in their walls, and beneath the Dome of the Rock, beneath the Shettiyeh revered by Muslims, Jerome believed that the Templars had located the Grail. Solomon in his wisdom, according to Jerome, had mistrusted his son by the Queen of Sheba, a boy named Menelik, and to prevent Menelik from gaining control of the Ark's powers he removed something from it and cached it there, in that holiest of holy places. Then Jerusalem fell to Saladin, and the Templars came to Cyprus, and if Jerome was right the Grail came with them. So Arthur harangued his workers and wrote reports and blasted and blasted and blasted, and in his dreams he saw granite dust clearing from a detonation to reveal a space under the hill.

Instead he contracted typhoid fever after six months, and

was sent home to recuperate. Four months later he was back in Alexandria, and in April 1880 he returned to Cyprus to supervise the construction of the new British governor's residence at the summit of Mount Troodos. Again he blasted, again he dug, and again the island sickened him. For months he did not understand why, and then he discovered that one of his motley work crew had been slowly poisoning him. An Abyssinian.

It was, together with the tantalizing matrix of hints gleaned from his father's papers and his own travels across Europe, clue enough. Arthur beat the Abyssinian to death with a stone and covered the forty-three rugged kilometers to the port at Limassol in nine hours. In the harbor a ship was lumbering away from the pier; he stole a boat and rowed out to meet it as it swung around in the direction of Egypt. If the Grail had been in Cyprus, his assassin would have acted decisively; any day might have brought the discovery. The Abyssinian's patience indicated to Arthur that Cyprus was a wild-goose chase, but also that whoever was hiding the Grail didn't want searchers to know that it was gone. He was on the right track.

And now, ten years later, he was startled from his reminiscence by a shambling Englishman, just this side of albino, sitting at the table with him and Jerome.

"Arthur," Jerome said, "this is Nigel Braithwaite. I hope you will send him away. I hope there is some other path. But if you believe there is not, I will trust to your experience. He will see to what you require." He stood and left them, gathering urchins like burrs to his habit as he crossed the square.

"Both the blacks and the Arabs tell stories about you, Nigel Braithwaite," Arthur said in English. "I suppose that means there's some truth to them."

"Enough," Braithwaite said.

Arthur straightened in his chair. "The blacks say you can

change into a hyena; of course, they say that about me from time to time as well. The Arabs say that you can run a hundred fifty kilometers in a day and go a fortnight without water. Both of them say that you talk to the dead and can track a man you've never seen. True?"

Braithwaite shrugged.

"Very well. Monsieur Braithwaite," he said, "who is the Bearer of the Grail?"

Braithwaite looked again at Arthur. His finger lifted, held; then with a rush of breath he said, "George Gibson."

A name, at last. An American name? It could have been English as well, even Canadian, Australian. "How do you know this?" Arthur asked.

A shadow of a smile crossed the Hyena's round face. "Zareh is no quieter dead than she was alive," he said.

Arthur opened his mouth, shut it again when no words came out. Could this be a fraud? Could Wondemu and Menelik be conspiring against him? It seemed impossible. The old *kahen*'s meddling with alchemy raised Menelik's superstitious hackles; the Lion of Judah could not allow the practice of hostile magic in a country governed by Solomon's line. Solomon, of course, had been a magician, but Wondemu had sided with the desert clans against Menelik after the Emperor Johannes' death the previous year, mistrusting both Menelik's ambition and his ability to hold on to power. If there was to be Solomonic magic in Menelik's Ethiopia, it would be practiced by men of Menelik's choosing.

No, it had to be true. This Nigel Braithwaite spoke to the dead, and drew from them information neither Wondemu nor Arthur had been able to glean. "Where is this George Gibson?" Arthur asked.

"Africa," the Hyena said, his face without expression.

A lump formed in Arthur's throat. "Where in Africa?" he demanded, his voice pitched high with fear. Was this Gibson coming to meet Arthur in Harar, or did he mean to *return* the Grail? If

Arthur's rival was trying to complete the work he himself had abandoned and betrayed, he thought he would die of the irony if not the hungry lump in his leg.

"Where in Africa?" he said again.

Braithwaite shrugged. "Shall I go find him?"

"Yes," Arthur said fiercely. "Find him. And kill him. And conceal the Grail until you can return to tell me where it is."

Without another word Nigel Braithwaite pushed back his chair and walked away.

BOOK FOUR

———

Lance, the cup is heavy. Drop the cup!
JACK SPICER, "The Book of Gwenivere"

LANCE

THE SUN CAME UP, and Lance wasn't sure if he'd slept or not. Gwen had hardly moved all night, sleeping the sleep either of exhaustion or contentment, or maybe both. While he was in the army Lance had acquired the ability to fall asleep practically on command, but sometime during these last two weeks it had left him. He lay there with the room brightening around him, wondering what else he'd lost since coming home, reminded of the pitiless morning after he'd gone back with her in San Francisco, when the dawn had come looking for him and he'd wanted nothing more than to hide in darkness so Ellie would never see what he'd done. It was bullshit, he knew it, but Lance felt that over the night just past he'd atoned at least a little. It would have been natural to give in to his loneliness and Gwen's warmth—roll over, slide a hand along her thigh, feel her shift and open to him. So much easier than dealing with all the things that remained to be said between them. Instead he'd stared at cracks in the ceiling. Somewhere during the small hours he'd started wondering what he would say to his mom. He still hadn't settled on anything specific; the indecision was like writing letters and then stowing them in the pocket of his coat.

Time to get moving, at least as far as Dexter. Jerry K. had said go see his mom, and now that Jerry was dead the suggestion made a little more sense. Gwen was against it, so he'd decided to side-step her for the day. He got up, waited to see if Gwen would stir, and when she didn't he dressed quickly, grabbed his boots, and tiptoed out of the room. She could have been listening to him, but if she was willing to pretend sleep, he was willing to believe it. They'd have it out soon enough.

Lance put on his boots in the hotel lobby and walked out onto Huron Street. With the morning clerk watching him between scornful drags on a cigarette in a mother-of-pearl holder, hunger hit Lance along with the sun. He'd pass out in a ditch if he tried to walk out to Dexter with his stomach growling like it was.

There'd been a diner just up a couple of blocks on Fourth, Bill's Coffee Cup. Lance walked that way, past the stores not yet open on this Saturday morning, suffused with the presence of Ann Arbor. It had always seemed remote and mysterious to him, this big town with its thousands of students, its ivied buildings and distracted professors and high-end clothing stores. What did people do in Ann Arbor? They talked, it seemed to him. They sat in rooms lit by dusty shafts of sunlight and they talked about things that people outside the walls had long since stopped caring about. Like the Holy Grail.

Some lecture I could give, Lance thought, and swung through the door into Bill's.

Half an hour later, toast crusts and smeared yolk were all that remained of Bill's breakfast special. Lance leaned his elbows on the counter and rubbed at the bridge of his nose. Fatigue was getting to him; all the meal had done was clot his blood, make him feel like a bear ready to crawl into its den and wait out the winter. Jerry K. was dead, and Lance was to blame. If the cops found him . . . Dewey had said that the cops around Peggy's Cove were Templars. Would they have the same setup in Dexter? And if their father hadn't bought into Dewey's renunciation, would he have Lance arrested?

Some betrayals were too awful to consider. My father wouldn't do that, Lance thought. He chose Dewey, okay, but he never rubbed it in my face. He cared that much.

Dewey was the one who'd told him.

He was on the edge of crying. Two years ago I was in high school, he thought, and I believed my brother was dead, and I believed Ellie and I would graduate and get married and have kids and I'd teach them how to throw a baseball and fish in the river. What's left?

Only what you take for yourself.

Okay then. Lance paid for his eggs, stood up, and nearly had a heart attack when Bill's door opened with a jingle and one of Ann Arbor's finest walked in. "Morning, Karl," the counterman said.

"Teddy," the cop said. He saw Lance looking at him and nodded. "Good citizen, how does this day find you?"

The cop's badge read K. AUFDEMBERGE. He sure looked German, with his sunburn, fat head, and cropped blond hair. "Looks to be a good one," Lance said.

"That it does," Aufdemberge said. "I was up all night transporting a suspect up north, but seeing a morning like this almost makes it worthwhile."

His gunbelt creaked as he sat on the stool to Lance's left. A cup of coffee appeared in front of him, and he lit a cigarette, and Lance wondered what in the holy hell he was doing still standing there. If he talked, his nervousness might make the cop suspicious. If he bugged out, same thing. There was no good way out.

Gwen would know what to do, he thought. This is what she's good at.

Around the butt of his smoke, Aufdemberge said, "Back from the war?"

Was everyone going to ask him that? "Yes sir," Lance said. "Just a couple of weeks ago."

"Gave 'em hell, right?"

"Some. They gave some of it back." Lance tried to grin. It felt like putting on a mask.

"Couldn't be too bad," Teddy the counterman said. "Here you are, walking and talking and scarfing down my eggs."

This is where I'm supposed to say *You should see the other guy*, Lance thought. Another mask. He couldn't do it.

"Yeah, it could be worse," he said.

Aufdemberge sat and smoked his cigarette, the wrinkles around his eyes deepening and smoothing as he inhaled and let the smoke trickle from his nose. Without meaning to Lance followed the motion with his eyes, and his heart did another flip when he saw a squared cross with flared arms tattooed on the back of the cop's right hand, between the stubby thumb and the first finger that was missing a joint. Aufdemberge noticed him noticing.

"Ever think about joining the force?" he said. "Good work for an ex-serviceman."

"Yeah, I have." It was true. The leg, though, the goddamn leg. The leg had screwed everything up.

"You ever stop thinking and start doing, come around the station and ask for me. Karl Aufdemberge," the cop said. He winked, and Lance's stomach rolled over.

"Okay," he said. "I'll do that."

Aufdemberge nodded and sipped his coffee. Teddy set a plate of steak and eggs in front of him. Lance felt like he ought to say something else. "Thanks for the tip, Sergeant."

"Can always use good people on our side," Aufdemberge said, and saluted Lance with his fork, and Lance got the hell out of Bill's and started walking.

That could have been anything, he told himself as he walked out Huron Street through the Old West Side. Just a cop stopping in for breakfast before he starts his shift. Simple friendly conversation. Lance was jittery enough that he could interpret a menu ten different ways.

The tattoo screamed conspiracy, though. It looked like a German Iron Cross, but not quite. Fatter. Just like the one on the hobo's dead hand, lying in the trackside weeds. Abruptly possessed by the spirit of Jerry, Lance spun out all kinds of deranged scenarios about ex-Nazis and Knights Templar until after an hour or so he caught himself and decided that the sun was getting to him. It couldn't be later than eight, but he was sweating, and he hadn't had a shower since Nova Scotia. He must look like a bum. He sure felt like one.

To test the hypothesis he turned around and stuck out his thumb. It took a while, but before he'd gotten too far past the park a flatbed truck stopped to pick him up. A prick-eared dog in the cab barked and snarled at Lance, and the driver semaphored that Lance should ride on the bed, which was fine with him. He hopped up, leaned against the cab, and watched the cow pastures go by. Fifteen minutes later the truck ground to a halt at the stoplight in front of the IGA in Dexter, and Lance jumped off. He waved his thanks for the ride, but the driver rattled away without ever seeing him.

The minute Lance's feet hit the pavement on Main Street, he felt better. This was home. Across the street was Sportsman's Bar, where Mom took him and Dewey for the fish fry every Friday; another block west, across Warrior Creek, was the drive-in, where Ellie had worked as a carhop for a while. Somewhere past the bridge was the track that led to the Tree of Many Roots. Lance got a sudden yen to head out there, just to see what would happen. He imagined a sign carved into the trunk telling him where to find Ellie; that's how it would have been if he and Dewey and Jerry K. had been telling themselves the story when they were kids. Stories. Spicer would head out there, divine some loony oracle from the roots, and claim it was the same thing he'd read about in a book on Egypt or Phoenicia. Just like Tom Sawyer, claiming that he and Huck had to dig Jim out of slavery with spoons because he'd read it in a book somewhere. That was what being a crazy poet got you. Everyone else had to live in the real world. In the real world there was a yellow house with the shades drawn even on a summer morning, and a lonely woman sitting in her favorite chair with her lamp and her book and her ashtray on a stand and her glass of iced tea leaving rings on the end table. In the real world the neighbor kid hadn't been around to mow the lawn, and the flower beds in front of the house were overgrown, and there were weeds growing up through cracks in the driveway that nobody had bothered to patch.

She could be dead, Lance thought as he came up the block to the house he'd grown up in, unconsciously stepping over the cracks in the sidewalk just like he'd always done. He passed the spruce tree he'd nearly killed himself crashing into on his bike one summer, and the storm drain that always stopped up in spring rains to form a pool that filled up with huge balls of worms. He stepped up onto the porch and reflexively slid a hand into the mailbox, coming up with a phone bill and a bank statement. He knocked on the door and opened it, and there was his mother, exactly as he'd imagined her. She looked up, startled out of her reading, and her face was so full of astonished joy he hated himself for waiting so long to come home, and hated himself all over again for what he was going to have to put her through. But Jerry K. was dead, and Ellie was gone, and the Holy Grail gleamed just beyond Lance's reach.

"Mom," he said, and she started crying. He squatted in front of her, took her hands. She pulled them away and found a box of tissues next to the lamp. When she'd dabbed at her eyes and settled down some, he said, "I'm sorry. I should have come home sooner."

She shook her head. "No, it's not that. I'm just so happy to see you, Lance. I'd have done the same thing if you'd come here straight from the train station. You look good, I was thinking you'd look hurt somehow even though it was just your leg." She sniffed, touched the tissue to her nose, and threw it away.

"Well, I could show you my new tooth," he said, and she laughed a little. He saw that her pitcher of iced tea was nearly empty, and took it into the kitchen. A large jar of sun tea stood on the windowsill over the sink. "Is this ready?" he called.

She said it was, and he filled the pitcher, and then refilled the ice trays, happy to be doing something familiar. For a little touch of occasion, he found the wood serving tray on top of the refrigerator and set the pitcher and two fresh glasses on it, along with a bowl of sugar and a teaspoon. Coming back into the living room, he set the tray on the end table, and like a little boy he gloried in his mother's smile as he poured for both of them and stirred in her sugar. Then he settled on the couch. "You look so good," his mother said again. "I didn't mean to cry."

"Cry all you want, Mom. It's okay."

"No, I'm all done." She put her book on the arm of the chair and lit a cigarette, then leaned back and let out a long smoky sigh. Home, Lance thought, and like she was reading his mind she said, "Are you going to stay here?"

He hadn't thought about it. "Not right away. Still have some things I have to do." He thought of Gwen, and all of his problems jumped back into the front of his mind. "Maybe after it's all done." The King and the Queen Mother, he thought. But there had to be a Queen.

"Mom," he said, "there's a couple of things I have to ask you, and before I do I have to tell you something."

She got that intense look that Lance had only seen on the faces of mothers expecting bad news about their children. "Tell me what?"

He didn't know how to cushion it, so he just opened his mouth. "Dewey's alive. I talked to him three days ago."

For a long time she looked at him, and at first he thought she was just too stunned to speak, but as the silence went on he started to think that she wasn't surprised enough, and as soon as the thought appeared it wouldn't go away. He held himself back even as it solidified into certainty, and when she still hadn't said anything he clamped down on the sudden riptide fear that seeped into him and waited a little more. She sat in her chair, cigarette burning down in her fingers. He noticed small details about her, minute changes since he'd last seen her more than a year ago: a little more gray in the hair, lines around the mouth a little deeper, a little more weight around her hips. Age, like anyone else's age, but right then it seemed to Lance that her slow aging was more like the erosion of wind and water on an ancient sculpture, a blurring of surface that preserved and even enhanced the strength of the shape within.

I don't want to know this, Lance thought. "Mom?"

She leaned forward and stubbed out her cigarette. "I'm glad you talked to him," she said.

When he was ten years old, Lance had walked out on a dead tree limb on a dare from Jerry Kazmierski. One step, two steps, and just when he thought that he was going to win Jerry's prized Charlie Gehringer card, the branch moved, and for the first time in his memory Lance experienced that terrible moment when you realize you're about to fall and you know it's going to be a bad one and you're putting your hands out to break the fall but you know you're going to land badly, and you have that split second to hope, or maybe pray, that it won't hurt too much. This was that moment all over again, that lurching desperate suspended moment when direction deserted you and the only thing in the world you knew for certain was that a hard landing was coming.

"You knew," he said, praying she would deny it. If she denied it he would believe her.

She looked at him, and in her face he saw that he wouldn't be spared.

"How much of this do you want, son?" she said.

"Jerry Kazmierski is dead, Mom," he said, wanting to make

her part of it. "And if I'd been with him I think I'd be dead too. You better give me all of it."

That coldness again, coming over him, walling him off from the young boy's pain that cried out from the place in his mind where he was still seeing Dewey's shirt and shoes on the weedy bank of Warrior Creek. This was the game, fine. He was ready to play. As she began, he grew colder yet, her words falling on him like a gently lethal ice storm, gradually armoring him against the boy he once had been.

GEORGE

AFTER THE ITURI, George figured that anything else would be a picnic. The local chief's name was Mpiga, and after a routine shakedown he got bored when he figured out that George didn't have anything of value. Except the Grail, and George nearly had a coronary when Mpiga demanded to see what was in George's pouch. "Just a knife and my lucky rock," he said, because he couldn't think of anything else. Mpiga held out his hand, and George had no choice but to untie the pouch and hand it to him. The chief took out the knife, picked at the wire grip, tested the blade. Then he shrugged and put it back, saying something to one of his attendants, who translated for George: "Mpiga say you go now. You nothing for him, he nothing for you."

"Fair enough," George said. There was an easy trail along the western shore of Lake Albert, boats everywhere with Europeans in them, and he figured that one of them would give him a ride down the Nile until he could hop off and cut across to the base of the Abyssinian plateau.

He was right. Before he'd walked an hour, a white man sitting in the rear of a long trading canoe shouted at him from the lake. "You, there! Where you headed?"

"Abyssinia," George called back, provoking a delighted guffaw.

"A long way from here, mate, but I can get you as far as Khartoum unless Abdullah kills us along the way." The canoe steered into the shallows, and George splashed out to meet it.

The pilot's name was Timothy Crews. He'd once been attached to General Gordon's army, but had gotten out—"deserted, not to put too fine a point on it"—before Gordon was massacred with his army at Khartoum. "Then the bloody Mahdi died not six months later, and now Khalifa Abdullah's in charge. A man you can do business with, even if he does thieve and pillage enough to keep up appearances. You say you're going to Abyssinia?"

"That's right."

Crews looked George up and down. "And where'd you come from?" He pointed at the vine George was still using for a belt. "Those don't grow around here. Rubber vine, isn't it? Those are money back in the Congo. Leopold's got his men whipping the niggers to tap every rubber vine between Lake Victoria and Stanleyville; he has their hands cut off if they don't move fast enough. Some of the more enterprising niggers have taken to just cutting off people's hands and turning them in for bounty, to prove they're keeping the locals in line even if they're not."

This washed across George, scouring away the thin scabs that had formed over his memories of the Congo. Visions of the dying boy, the villages reduced to ash and the ghostly clinking of rifle shells, the little girl's body drifting on the current rose up to choke him. All of it stood between him and the promise he'd made to Yishaq on the shores of the Atlantic. He hadn't thought it would be easy, not exactly, but on the other side of it George had the notion that he'd lost something not even Martha could bring back. He had eaten the bitterness of the journey to give him strength, and now he'd had a year of his life and more to digest that bitterness, take it within him and feel it in his fingers, his gut, the way his eyes saw the colors of Africa. Without knowing it, George had promised Yishaq the sacrifice of George Gibson, who had once thought no farther into the future than the next summer playing for the Detroit Wolverines. In return for that sacrifice, George had the gift of knowing that nothing he had done, nothing he could do, would change anything he saw.

Except perhaps return the Grail. That one thing he could put right.

Crews saw the look on George's face. "You know what I'm talking about, then." George nodded. "Was you with Stanley?"

"No," George said. "I came from Stanleyville by myself."

"You—" Crews looked as if he couldn't decide whether to laugh or be insulted. "You walked from Stanleyville? Through the jungle? You don't mind me saying, mate, that's about the worst whopper I ever heard, and around here you hear some big ones. Stanley himself lost two hundred men on the way, and he had guns. You're telling me you just strolled all that way?"

"That's what I'm telling you."

Crews shook his head. "You stick to that story, then. I won't tell you any different."

The canoe glided across the glassy water of Lake Albert to the headwaters of the White Nile, powered by eight Africans who chanted the rhythm of their stroke. A few miles down, they came to rapids, and Crews called a halt. "We'll camp here, portage in the morning, get on our way," he said. "Few days, you'll have a choice to make. You can either come with us down to Khartoum, go back up the Blue Nile, take your chances that way, or you can cut across the Sennar. Never been there myself, but I know there's caravans. You could hook on with one. What did you do before you walked across the Congo by yourself?"

"I'm a baseball player," George said.

"Baseball? Like cricket? Good Lord, mate, where do you think you're going to find a game in Abyssinia?" Crews shook his head. "You don't want to tell me what you're doing here, that's your business, but if you want to make it in Africa, George my friend, you're going to have to learn to tell a better lie. Baseball," he snorted, and left George to organize the camp for the night.

They ate well, better than George had eaten since stealing the sack of food from Stanley's rear detachment: real beef, real bread, real whiskey. George ate until his stomach hurt, drank until he couldn't feel his lips, fell asleep on the banks of the Nile and kept falling.

Some time later—although that isn't exactly right, he's dreaming and everything in the dead-land happens right now—motion on the other side of the river captures George's attention. A hyena, yellow and spotted and carrying its head low to the ground, is pacing him along the far bank. He stops, and it does too, dropping back on its haunches to gaze at him.

"What you doing, dog?" George says. The hyena cocks its head, unleashes a hoarse bark, and stands, its mouth now open in a grinning pant. When its saliva drips onto the ground, it rolls like beads of mercury down the bank into the river.

George starts walking again, past booming rapids above which mist hangs shimmering like the Northern Lights, and which make only a distant rumble, as if they were still around several bends of the river and George was hearing them before they came into view. Then more flat water, and the hyena pacing him easily, grinning as it trots ahead a little way and then doubles back to match his progress. Ahead George can see the mountains, and he mutters under his breath, "If you can cross that river, old dog, how come you haven't done it yet?" He goes on as the banks of the river grow steeper and more broken, climbing without sweating, jumping without having to breathe hard, and then he reaches the top of a bluff hanging over the outside of a sweeping curve in the river. Looking to his right, he can see the starlit ribbon all the way to the horizon, and the hyena pacing back and forth on the opposite side. In the other direction, mountains loom over him—like home, he starts to think, but no, these naked black crags are nothing like the sharp swooping ridges of the Rockies. These mountains aren't beautiful. No snow streaks their slopes, no trees wash them in dark green or fall yellow. They are, George thinks, exactly what mountains should be in the land of the dead.

He looks back to the river. The hyena is gone. He knows it is following him, and this knowledge spurs George to begin climbing again, leaving the river's vast valley for the naked foothills where, for the first time in the land of the dead, he feels a breath of wind. Other sounds, too, catch his attention as he works his way up a narrow canyon and emerges onto a rocky saddle between two peaks: animal sounds, as if a million invisible creatures are scrabbling and scurrying in the crevices that mark the canyon walls like runes carved by giants. What lives in the land of the dead? George asks himself, and covers his ears knowing that the way he has asked the question guarantees that it can have no answer. The wind is howling now, but like the roar of the rapids its sound is strangely diminished. It is a sound of remembered winds, and the gusts that buffet George as he crosses the spine of the black mountains push at him with the force not of reality, but memory.

I am not really here, he thinks. I remember wind, so there is wind; I remember lizards and rabbits slinking through canyons, so I hear them now. This is the truth of the land of the dead, that it collapses memory and experience into a single sense of present.

And when I leave here, George thinks, I will never be able to explain the feeling in quite that way.

Below him, the mountains subside like storm-driven waves after the storm has passed. Beyond the last ridge of foothills, an empty plain stretches as far as George can see. Which way to go?

"The boy said the place would speak to me," George says, and his own voice has now acquired the tinny resonance of memory. He looks at himself, expecting to see right through his feet to the naked gravel below, and sees that the pouch hiding the Grail is now on his left wrist. "All right, then," he says, and begins his descent out of the mountains, bearing to the left whenever the choice presents itself.

He has been walking on the plain for some time when it occurs to him to wonder where the hyena has gone. He stops and turns in a complete circle, but even the mountains are lost in the distance now, and all he can see in any direction is the flat dirt of the plain and its sparse vegetation that seems to be that same dirt grown up to look like plants. Are there buffalo in Africa? he thinks, and there are, in a herd that blackens the plain in front of him. No, not buffalo; shouldn't those be zebras, or gazelles? But the buffalo are still there as George walks again, weaving his way between them and inhaling their prickly stink. He is oddly grateful for the smell; it seems real, more real even than he himself.

And then the buffalo scatter and George is left alone on the plain with the hyena again pacing him, out on the edge of his field of vision. He shivers with the sudden certainty that somewhere in the real world, the living world of sunshine, of savanna and wind that smells of water, a hyena is trotting across Africa, pausing every so often to put its nose in the air and give out its giggling bark. "You smell the Grail, don't you, dog?" George calls out.

The hyena lifts its head and yips in answer.

"Well, you go on and meet me, then," George challenges it. "I'm going to Axum, you mangy hound, and you meet me there!"

The hyena's giggle fades with a rolling wind that blows the plain's dirt plants into a blinding haze of dust. George throws an arm up over his eyes, starts to plunge ahead into the storm, then stops. Better to stay put than go running off and get lost. Dust grits in his mouth, and he spits until his mouth is too dry to muster any saliva. His eyes burn and water, his neck itches where the wind forces dust down his collar, he sneezes as the storm works its way into his nose. A gust of wind knocks him to his knees.

Go, a voice says out of the storm. *This land is angry that you have spoken to the land above. If you stop now, you will stay here forever.*

George cries out in fear and lurches to his feet. Blind and choking, he begins to run, terrified with every step that he will break his ankle in a rut or fling himself over a cliff that appears suddenly from the wavering horizon. With every staggering step his fear multiplies. Then he is screaming like a horse in a burning barn, the scream interrupted only when—after an impossibly long time—he has to draw breath and he realizes that he is no longer choking on dust.

A woman stands before him when he lowers his arm and blinks the dust from his eyes. "George Gibson," she says.

George moans at her, unable to form words.

"George Gibson," she says again.

This time George nods. "Yes," he rasps, and the word loosens the dust in his throat. He begins to cough, great sobbing hacks that eventually clear his throat while shaking caked dust from his hair and clothes. The woman touches him and he cries out, falling away from her. "You touched me," he whimpers. "Does that mean I'm dead?"

"It only means that you are here," the woman says gently.

George is too afraid to look anywhere but into the woman's luminous dark eyes. She seems kind. "Where is here?"

"You are still in the land of the dead," she says, and George shudders. She touches his forehead, and his body stills. "But you do not belong here. Time now for you to leave."

His mouth is open for a long time before George can make himself speak. "How?"

"Do not ask me, George Gibson. I am only Zareh, and Zareh is only able to speak to you because of what you carry. Ask the Grail, and it will show you the way to return."

"Zareh," George says. "You're—" His voice fails him again as he recognizes her from the beach.

"He is my son, yes."

"Where is he?"

"We are all here, George Gibson. Some of us you see, some are hidden from you." Zareh steps away from him, and behind her George sees a castle on the plain. Like the plants, it seems to have formed itself of the dust that still eddies in the aftermath of the storm.

"Is that where I'm going, Zareh?" he asks, but even as her name leaves his mouth she is gone. At the same time, the hyena lopes around the corner of the castle and sits like a watchdog at its front gate.

Anger, hot and living and welcome, surges through George. "All right, dog," he growls. "All I've seen since I came here, you think a dog can stop me? You just come on and try."

Three days later Crews' canoe came to a settlement at Kusti, pausing to trade bits of junk for other bits of junk. "You want to strike out across the Sennar," Crews said, "this is the place to do it."

George thought about it. He'd save time, that was for sure, but that hyena . . . he'd dreamed about it every night since meeting Crews, and each time it loped up the opposite bank of the river to sit and watch him with its idiot grin. Someone was following him, or something. Maybe it was better to keep on this side of the river.

What would he do if Crews decided to camp on the eastern bank, though? He hadn't so far, George gathered because he didn't trust the Dinka chiefs who ran the eastern side as much as he trusted Khalifa Abdullah, who controlled the western banks. But that wasn't much to go on. George watched the Dinkas who gathered to see the canoe passing down the river, wondering if one of them was the hyena in his dreams. They all looked to be about seven feet tall, with spears taller yet, and red sashes tied over one shoulder to cover their privates. Any one of them, George thought, could kill him without breathing hard.

"How far is it to Khartoum?" he asked Crews.

"Week or so. We'll be stopping more often to trade with Abdullah's chiefs along the way. Must make sure we're thoroughly swindled before we get to Khartoum, where we can get bilked for good and all." Crews shook his head in disgust. "This is a terrible place. I hate it. All slaves and Mohammedan lunatics and niggers waving spears at the sahibs with Maxim guns. Can't wait to get out of here, go back to England. Or I guess I could go to America, couldn't I? Join all the Irish, head for New York or Boston. Time to get out of here, that's certain. You're going to Abyssinia, my advice is to get it done now, mate, and if you don't get killed along the way keep right on going to Cairo and get home. Africa's only fit for dead men."

"This is going to sound like a strange question," George said, "but which bank are you camping on between here and there?"

"I told you, I don't trust the bleeding Dinkas as far as I could throw a piano. Unless I hear Abdullah's gone mad, we'll be staying on his side of the river."

George nodded. "Guess I'll ride along to Khartoum, then, if it's all the same to you."

"Be my guest," Crews said. "Always glad of a white man to talk to, even if he's as big a liar as you are."

Khartoum had recovered from the Mahdi's siege four years before, but George still hated it. Slave caravans coming and going, beggars in the streets, smoke from burning garbage, and aloof from it all the few Europeans in their white suits drinking tea on balconies. Across the river to the east sat Omdurman, where Khalifa Abdullah passed his days plotting to expel the British and having his feet rubbed by a harem of women too fat to stand upright. The whole place had the feeling of living under a sentence of death. Either Abdullah would raise an army and destroy Khartoum again, or the British and French would go to war over Egypt, in which case a French army would storm up the Nile. George didn't stay any longer than he had to, especially since Khartoum sat on the inside edge of the confluence of the Blue and White branches of the Nile, on the same side where the hyena came every night in George's dreams.

Crews took him aside before they parted company for good, giving him a blanket and a new pair of boots. "This is for the story," he said. "I'll be able to drink free for months on the American baseball player who walked across bloody Africa."

"It's all the truth," George said.

"So much the better. I still don't believe you, mate, but if you're telling the truth it's one for the books, that's certain."

Crews shook George's hand and got back to haggling over the cloth and ivory he'd brought down from Mpiga's side of Lake Albert.

There were no boats going up the Blue Nile, so George took a ferry across to the far bank. Keep the dog inside the confluence as long as you can, he told himself. If it hasn't crossed yet, maybe it won't until you get into Abyssinia. Belly full and feet throwing a party inside the new boots, he started walking.

Pretty soon the Sennar forced him into a change of strategy. George thought he'd been hot before, in a Colorado summer and even worse in the stifling humidity of the Congo, but the Sennar sun was like nothing he'd ever felt. It hammered right through the top of his skull, boiling his brain in its own juices. He was hallucinating before he knew it, and he barely made it to the shadow of a tree by the river, where he could wait out the day and travel in the cool of the evening. He watched birds, elephants, buffalo, zebras, crocodiles; he tried to ignore the flies that settled over him the minute he stopped moving. The blanket Crews had given him kept most of them off, but under it he felt like he was in a hot spring made of his own sweat. Still, it was better than the flies—though not by much—and night couldn't come soon enough. He slept a little, and woke up feeling swollen and more fatigued than when he'd dropped off. Look on the bright side, he told himself. This ain't the Ituri.

Which was true. No matter how sunburned and miserable he got trekking across the parched Sennar scrub, George no longer wished for death. He did wish that the dead would leave him alone, though. They'd come back when he'd left Tim Crews' boat in Khartoum and begun walking again, and now he drew them the way a corpse draws flies—or hyenas, he thought with a shudder. They came to be near the Grail; it was the hole at the center of a whirlpool, with the worlds of living and dead smeared together around it. The pressure of existing in this center crushed George, a bit at a time, the way the sun beat him down in the day, until he was raving with desire just to put the Grail down. Whether he was still alive or had died in the water off Oak Island two years ago, he just wanted to be rid of it. I'm alive, I'm dead, I'm a hyena, I'm a nigger, he thought. Where did I go?

Days passed. Around him, the swelling grassland and dry forests of the Sudan started to break up into foothills. The Blue Nile narrowed and flowed faster, broken by rocks the way the Colorado was, back in Glenwood Canyon where George's father had taken him once to see the Hanging Lake. George imagined Lake Tana, source of the Blue Nile, a bowl of clear water with a trickle running out of one side that tumbled from the Abyssinian highlands to flood Egypt every summer. He didn't care whether Lake Tana really looked like that, he was beyond caring what things really looked like, he had no idea whether he'd ever see things as they really were again. He'd given up on the world. Hadn't he walked across the bottom of the Atlantic Ocean after catching a ride with an Egyptian god? Hadn't he seen black hands rising through sand, driven from their rest by the promise of a child's touch? Hadn't he sweated and wept his way up the Congo and Aruwimi and down the Nile and up the other Nile, with the dead more real than the living and a spotted hyena tracking him on the other side of the water? What did the world mean after that?

Flanking him, their silent steps raising the dust of their bodies, the dead marched in the corner of his eye. When he was tired or sad, which was nearly all the time, he might catch a solid glimpse that made him turn to see—and then they were gone, leaving behind only the pressure of their eyes on his back. They couldn't be following him. He was no general, he was no King. He was just a baseball player in the wrong place at the wrong time, walking across Africa because a dead Abyssinian Jewish boy had asked him to.

If I set down the Grail and keep walking, will you leave me alone?

Yishaq?

He couldn't. He was almost there. Just up over these mountains, turn north, keep the river on his right. Then he could lay down the Grail and go home.

Sometimes he fell asleep in midstep, coming to a stop and sagging to the ground in a slow-motion fall. Then he saw the hyena, pacing across the river, and he said in his sleep: come on, dog. It ain't just you and me; it's you and me and them. But when he stretched his arm out over the ranks of dead souls, they were gone, and he awoke on his side or on his knees, face in the dirt like a praying Muslim. Alone except for the river and the miles of rocks between him and the Abyssinian plateau.

He begged food from trading caravans while he was still in the flatlands, but the road petered out in the gorges and George lived on what he could find or kill. Some of the Nile pools held oysters that put him in mind of New England, from the time he'd passed through before heading north to Canada. When he couldn't find oysters he could always rely on his arm. A little patience and a stone equaled a goose, knocked down from the reedy shores along the edge of the river. Sometimes he cooked these geese, sometimes he didn't; either way they were a big step up from the beetles in the Ituri jungle, and when he let fly at them his spirits lifted with the memory of a hard peg from the outfield, a runner tagged out trying to take an extra base on a sharp single. The snap of his arm, the flight of the stone: I'll get home again, he thought. When I'm playing for the Wolverines or the Brown Stockings and some of the guys start talking about how hard they had it when they were kids, won't this just button their lips. I ate oysters from the Nile, walked across Africa by myself. When he'd eaten, he drank and washed in the river, closing his eyes in case he looked up and saw the little girl in the water, ants in her eyes, asking him why he hadn't come a little sooner, just a little sooner, and his faith fell away from him again, leaving just the miles before him and the dead behind.

The walls of the gorge closed in, and for days at a time he couldn't stay on the riverbank. He climbed when he had to, skirting the windy rim of the canyon and enduring until he could descend into the riverside warmth again. He was Jim Bridger, Jedediah Smith, a mountain man, traveling with no desire for fame, no explorer's journal or samples, just his two legs and the Grail thumping against his hip with every step. The higher he got, the colder he was, and he was glad for the blanket and new shoes. Even with them, some nights his mind got foggy from the cold and he huddled over the Grail like it was a fire, feeling the press of the dead around him, feeling the transparency of his body to them, as the glow of the Grail passed through him to kindle in their hungry eyes. When his teeth stopped chattering he knew it was time to move again.

The day he topped the massif was like the day he'd spotted Lake Albert, an upsurge of delirious joy at the sight of level ground. Abyssinia! He'd made it! Lake Tana couldn't be far, and Axum couldn't be far beyond it. He stopped at a village of thin, sharp-faced people who wouldn't talk to him. They kept looking over his shoulder—whether at the dead or just expecting other white men, he didn't know, and he was too tired to care. He recognized the look on their faces, too frightened to be kind. When they offered him food to leave, he took it and went on.

He came to the shores of the lake a week or a month later, he couldn't tell, and after what had happened on the Congo and through the Ituri he wasn't sure time was moving for him the way it did for everyone else. The Grail twisted two worlds together, and here before him was the source of the Blue Nile, the lake that brought life to Egypt. He slept that night waiting for the hyena to giggle at him from across the marshy stream, wondering if it would pick its way through the muddy shallows, but his dreams held only the dead, and in his sleep he muttered, *All right then, dog. You come on around the lake and meet me. Then we'll see.* He kept alert during the days that followed, waiting for the hyena and wondering what it would look like in the real world, whether he would recognize it, whether it too was drawn to the Grail or whether it wanted only him.

He walked with a map of Africa in his mind. The dead gathered their ranks behind him, and the closer he got to Axum, the closer they pressed. George spent more and more time lost in a hallucination that he was in Colorado. Great mountains reared up in the east, and the rolling foothills he traveled might have been in the basin between Fairplay and Salida. Except for the jackals and the baboons and the black-and-white bearded monkeys, and the strange birds that hovered over the canyons. Why was Colorado full of baboons and dead Negroes? he thought occasionally, and usually had the presence of mind to stop and rest when he was that far gone. By the time he walked into Axum, his new boots flapping at the heel and Crews' blanket long since fallen into shreds, he would have killed his own mother to be rid of the ghosts. To distract himself he wrote another letter to Martha, in the margins of a poem called "Vigil."

> Dear Martha,
>
> I am almost there. Part of Abyssinia reminds me a little bit of Colorado, El Dorado Canyon maybe. Except African. I see baboons and once in a while a giraffe, and I've seen lions, and there are hyenas everywhere. Some safari I could have had now that I'm out of the jungle finally. I know I have been gone a long time, and I shouldn't tell you this but I wouldn't blame you a lot if you had found another. But the only reason I can tell you that is because I don't believe you have. I think of you all the time. When I come back I promise I'll even be nice to that dumb cat in your dad's barn.

He looked at that last bit and couldn't figure out why he'd written it. With a shrug he shut the book and went on.

Axum was like every other town he'd passed through in Abyssinia, a forlorn collection of huts gathered around a small center of stone buildings. The one difference was the church, which looked like the pictures George had seen in his history books. Thomas à Becket, he thought. He was a monk, right? But he couldn't remember the rest of the lesson.

At the front door stood a shriveled African with a beard down to his belt buckle. He held out a staff to block George's way and said something in whatever language they spoke around there.

"I have to go in," George said. "This is where the Ark is, right?"

It occurred to him that maybe he should have been more discreet, and the priest's reaction sure made it seem that way. When he heard the word *Ark* the old man straightened up and unleashed such a gabble that George wouldn't have understood it even if it had been in English. A crowd of other priests, or maybe monks, every one with a long beard and a long stick, burst out of the doorway to get their two cents in, and George backed away. "You don't understand," he said. "I have to put this back." He tore the pouch loose from his belt and waved it at them. "Do you know what's in here?"

They didn't care. One of them swung his staff, cracking George a good one on the elbow, and he almost swung back except he was outnumbered and Christ he was tired, how long had it been since he slept in a bed, anyway? He kept backing away, across the little square with a well that faced the church, and when he butted up against an old stone wall he sat down, dejected and beat and not knowing what to do next. Yishaq, he thought. Talk to me. You didn't tell me anything about this.

"Ahoy, mate." A gangly, moon-faced fellow with what looked like a lethal sunburn clapped George on the shoulder. "Problem with the monks?"

"I'll say." George looked the man up and down. British missionary? It would explain the native dress. He didn't talk like a missionary, though, and he wasn't wearing a collar. Not for the first time, George felt way out of his depth. A year ago, he'd never been farther from Central City than trips to Denver three or four times a year. Now he was in Africa, of all places. Almost all the way to Egypt.

"Everything's so different," he said.

"Different from where?" The Englishman's watery blue eyes stared unblinking at George. "Come on, lad. It's a dry country, but I'll wager we can find a drink if we look in the right places." He nodded at George. "Nigel Braithwaite."

"George." They walked down the street, passing a sprawling ruin overgrown with sorghum and almond trees. Women filed through it to descend stairs cut into the hillside, at the bottom of which was a rectangular reservoir. Towering over the ruins, stone obelisks still told their stories to whoever understood. Pieces of those that had fallen lay like the skeletons of snakes among the exposed building foundations. "Queen of Sheba's palace," the Englishman remarked as they passed. He was still staring at George. "Over this hill here, I know a Bedouin who'll sell us a drop."

"Excuse me."

Now a French accent, George thought as he stopped and turned around. This Axum sure is a cosmopolitan place for a hick town in Ethiopia.

"Your name isn't, by any chance, George Gibson?" The Frenchman smiled between the handlebars of his mustache and reached to take George's hand. He had a funny cross tattooed on the hand.

"Piss off, friend." Nigel stepped in front of George. Michel never looked at him. His gaze remained fixed on George as, with a motion that chilled George to the base of his soul, he casually flicked a knife from his cuff and thrust it upward into Nigel's belly.

Without a word, George turned tail and ran into the ruins. I saw him on Oak Island, he thought. That's the guy who killed Yishaq. He's been following me since then. Dodging the women who waited in line to fill their water jars, he risked a glance over his shoulder. Michel was pursuing him, and Nigel was struggling to get up from his hands and knees. George ran around to the other side of the reservoir, then scrambled his way up the hill. I got someone else killed, he thought. Just like on Oak Island.

Michel caught him at the top of the hill, in the middle of a rock-strewn meadow that sloped away from Axum into a broad valley. One second George was running, hoping there really were Bedouins on the other side of the hill, and the next he'd slammed face-first into the ground. Michel's knee ground into his back. "The Grail," he panted into George's ear, his breath hot and reeking of onions. "Give it to me and walk away."

"Fine," George said. "I never wanted it anyway." He'd fallen with his arms tucked under him, and now he worked his right arm loose until Michel could see the pouch. "There it is."

"Well done, Monsieur Gibson," Michel said. "I prefer not to kill when I do not have to." His weight shifted off of George's back as he reached over to cut the pouch free.

Whip-fast, George rolled to his left, lashing the pouch around like he was turning on an inside fastball. And the sound of the Grail breaking Michel's jaw even sounded like the good old crack of a baseball smoked out into right-center field. George let his momentum carry him to his feet. "You killed Yishaq when you didn't have to, you son of a bitch," he said.

Michel squatted to retrieve his knife. "*Oui,*" he said indistinctly, unable to fully close his mouth. "A mistake." Blood flowed freely over his lower lip, dripping from his chin into the grass. "Which I rectify now," he finished, and advanced toward George.

A throaty snarl rose from behind a boulder just to George's left, and as he turned to look Nigel Braithwaite came leaping over the rock, blood staining his robe in a wide fan from waist to hem. He landed on Michel and bore him to the ground, sinking his teeth into the back of the Templar's neck. The sight stretched George's mind a little too far, and all he could think was: no way he's a missionary. Missionaries didn't bite people after they'd been stabbed in the gut. He backed away until he tripped over a bush and went sprawling down the hill, skidding to a halt about twenty feet down the slope. He started to get to his feet and noticed of all things a priest in full black habit clambering down on his trail.

Jesus, was everyone in Axum after him? George looked over his shoulder. No Bedouins. Nothing but grazing cattle and a yellow dog nipping after them when they wandered. The dog put him in mind of the hyena that had followed him across the land of the dead; would it show up next?

"Mister Gibson," the priest said.

"Stay away from me," George warned.

"Mister Gibson, we have no time for foolishness. Those two up there might kill each other, but if one of them wins he will be along shortly. My name is Jerome."

"You aren't with the church up there?" George said suspiciously.

"No, no." Jerome laughed. "I come from the south. Never been here."

"Then why are you here now?"

"Looking for you. Rimbaud—"

"Rimbaud!?" George was about to take off running again when Nigel Braithwaite came slinking over the crest of the hill, his head low, chuckling in his throat at the sight of George on the slope below him.

Exactly the way the hyena had, when he'd first noticed it across the underworld river.

Jerome said something that sounded like a curse. He pulled a skull covered with some kind of sticky black sludge from his robe. "Zareh, fight like a Jew now," he said, and threw the skull at Braithwaite.

Braithwaite caught the skull, and then went rigid as it bit down on his left thumb. The blood leaking from his gut spotted the dusty ground. He bared his teeth and bit back, his canines scraping across its cheekbone, and then he was thrown violently to the ground, which rose to embrace him. Earthquake, George thought, but something was wrong with him, he couldn't feel the motion of the earth, and all at once he realized that it wasn't the earth that rose but a thousand black arms, clawing into the world of the living to get a grip on Nigel Braithwaite.

"They have watched him," Jerome said, and George understood. The hyena.

Braithwaite was borne into the air from the sheer press of the hands that gripped and tore at his body. He moved faster than the eye could follow, but there was only one of him, and the entire hillside erupted with bodies, forcing life back into themselves for the one moment it would take to protect the Bearer of the Grail. In a moment Braithwaite was gone, lifted up and torn to pieces as if on a wind, and then the storm receded and the hillside was as it had been, the bushes that clung to it spotted with blood. Only the skull remained, still smeared with the tar that also grimed Jerome's fingers. He went to it. "Free, Zareh," he said, kneeling. "For this last favor I thank you." Then he crushed the skull with a stone.

He got up and tossed the stone down the hill. "You, George Gibson," he said, facing George and pointing a crooked finger. "You cannot always wait for others to act for you."

George realized that he'd been standing petrified since Braithwaite had appeared at the top of the slope. "I didn't . . . I couldn't kill anyone," he said. "What . . . ?" He couldn't finish the question.

"A mass grave. One of the Emperor Johannes' raids of pacification. Africa is lousy with such places. He would have killed you, this Braithwaite," Jerome said. "And Rimbaud still might."

George nodded. "Why did you help me?" he asked.

"The Arabs have a saying: *The enemy of my enemy is my friend.* Rimbaud endangers us both."

"Oh." George kept thinking about Braithwaite, blowing apart like leaves in the wind.

Jerome clapped his hands. "Hey! Listen. You have a choice. Rimbaud is ill; he has left Harar. I think he has gone back to France, or will soon. The way is clear to you: you may try to return the Grail, but the Ark may not accept you. Or you may run. Take the Grail back to America and guard it. You are no King."

"I don't want to be King." George looked at the pouch dangling from his wrist, and wished for the millionth time that he could just flip it down the hillside like Jerome had the rock he'd used to break Zareh's skull. The wish was as faded as belief in the tooth fairy. He knew better now.

"That does not matter," Jerome said. He gathered up the hem

of his robe and climbed to the top of the hill, pausing there to call back down to George. "I do not know what will happen to you, George Gibson, but you must bear the burden you have been given. Bear it until I return for you. Then you may finish your work." With that he turned and walked back toward Axum, leaving George alone with the lowing cattle and the bodies under the earth, his army returning to its rest.

LANCE

A MOTHER ALWAYS has reasons for her lies. You'll never know this, but it's true. I have lied to you all your life. Best to get that right out front.

When I was sixteen, I ran away from home. My father had been dead for three years, and I was a headstrong girl who didn't see eye to eye with your grandmother. She was a strong woman, but a narrow one, and the more she tried to hold me down the more I hit back. I started going with older boys, I drank. I smoked cigarettes in front of her, and girls didn't smoke cigarettes then. Only women's-rights types smoked, and then just to let everyone know they were independent, they didn't care. And I guess that's why I did it.

I started going with colored boys too, down to the dance halls in the black parts of Ypsilanti, where we were living then. I even went into Detroit sometimes, down into the Black Bottom where they said any white girl would be raped and killed and thrown in the river. When my mother found out about it, she threatened to send me away to a reform school, and I cursed at her and told her to go ahead and do it, I'd just run away. I said all kinds of things just to hurt her because she didn't understand, and every time she'd say at the end, Fine, just go then, whore around with the niggers, and I'd go down with some boy to some place and watch the dancing and singing. Knowing I could never really be part of it, that unless you went through every day being on the wrong side of the color line you couldn't understand. But I wanted to, and I took advantage of the boys who wanted to be seen squiring a white girl because I wanted people to see my mother at the grocery and say *There's Amelia Porter, her girl Vera goes with niggers.* That was how I could hurt her the most, and that's what I was foolish enough to want to do.

There was a spring night in 1932, April I think, when I came home to find her waiting for me with a bag packed on the floor next to her. There's a change of clothes and twenty dollars, she said. I have taken about all I'm going to take from you. Either you straighten yourself out or you get out from this house.

Well, I was sixteen and prideful, and I'd gone too far to take a step back, so I picked up the bag and said, All right then. That's the last you'll see of me, and you can go to hell. And I walked out the door.

I started to go to this boy's house, down on the south side of Michigan Avenue where the colored neighborhoods were, but while I was walking I started to cry thinking about what I'd done, and I knew that I was just playacting, that I didn't care about that boy any more than he really cared about me, and I just sat down on the curb with my little bag and cried. But you can only cry for so long. After a while you have to get up and do something, so I turned around and walked over to the bus station on Cross Street, and I got a ticket on the next bus for the farthest south twenty dollars would take me, which was Nashville. I didn't care what would happen when I got there, just so long as I got there. I'd change my name, get a job cleaning or sewing clothes, it didn't matter. I was running *away,* not running *to.* On the bus trip a fat old man sat next to me and felt up my leg all night, and I sat there like a stone and let him do it. He offered me two dollars to do something for him, and I got off at the next stop, which was Columbus, Ohio. It was the first time I'd ever been out of

Michigan, and I remember being surprised that everything was the same. And I mean everything: there I was, away from my mother and on my own, and still no idea what I would do or where I was going.

I walked out to the edge of town, just to be moving, and there was a carnival setting up. I had three dollars left from my bus ticket, and I waited until afternoon when the carnival opened. Something about the crowd and the touts yelling out and the smell of cotton candy made me feel good, I don't know why, so I spent the whole day wandering up and down the midway on the trampled grass, watching boys win ribbons for their girls, and I was as lonely as any girl has ever been, and I liked it.

Later on in the evening I was walking by one of the show tents and the tout was arguing with the girl who sold cigarettes. She said something I won't repeat and threw her tray down in front of him, and before she'd gotten ten steps away I was over there quick as lightning and picked up the tray. Looks like you need a cigarette girl, I said. Reckon I do, he said, but what's your daddy gonna say? My daddy's dead, I said, and my mama don't care what I do. He grinned and said, Sounds like you're cut out for the job, kid. He offered me ten dollars a week and I took it, and it's a cliché but it's true. Just another girl who ran away to join the circus.

Well, I found out right away that the job involved more than selling cigarettes and breath mints to folks who came to watch The Great Vizier Tamburlaine. The tout's name was Milt, and every night when I came to his tent to settle up he made advances, and he let me know right off the bat that I couldn't say no if I wanted to work the next day. I kept my virtue, but there wasn't much else I kept. I'm sorry to tell you this, but that's the way it was.

We toured north as the weather got warmer, going up through Indiana and Illinois and Wisconsin and then Minnesota, and as June went along we followed the northern shore of Lake

248 — ALEXANDER C. IRVINE

Superior, going along through Thunder Bay and Nipigon and all the other towns up that way, and then down around toward Sault Ste. Marie. But I never got there, because one Friday we set up in this little mining town called Wawa. We wouldn't have stopped except it was Friday and the miners would be getting paid, so we spent the day pasting up bills advertising all the shows and when we opened up at one o'clock there was a crowd waiting to get in.

By this time I'd figured out that Milt's deal wasn't as good as it sounded back in Columbus. He didn't just expect me to be friendly, he found some excuse or other to cheat me out of my ten dollars nearly every week. Either I miscounted my take every night and he had to take it out of my wage, or he charged me for a new outfit, or something else, on and on. I'd been with the show two months and hadn't more than five dollars in my pocket; let me tell you, home was starting to look pretty good.

Anyway, we were in Wawa, and people there were mighty glad to see us. Tamburlaine's show involved lots of fortune-telling and some magic, rabbits from a hat, ring tricks and such. His big finale was sawing a woman in half, and you should have heard Milt complain about having to haul the mirrors around. Twice that summer we had to change the show because the mirrors broke on the road and we couldn't get new ones in time. Tamburlaine's real name was Mathieu Riendeau. He was a drunk old French-Canadian from Quebec who used to be a lumberjack, and the best thing I can say about him is that he never laid a hand on me. For all I know he was queer, but that doesn't matter. What I'm getting to is the last show we did that night.

The tent was jammed, positively bursting with miners and their girls and townies who had scraped together ten cents to see the show, and some Indians from the reservation outside of town. It being Friday night, they were all liquored up, and my rear end was black and blue from the pinching by the end of the night. The only two gents in the place who didn't belong were right against the back wall of the tent, by the entrance. They were wearing suits and ties, which caught my attention right away—you didn't see many people dressed like that at carnivals in the summer of 1932—so I made sure they had what they needed. Truth is I used them as kind of a break, chatting them up a little when I needed relief from the rest, and let me tell you I could chat a gent up back then. I was a good-looking girl, and I'd had the whole summer to learn to use what I had. So when one of them called me over toward the end of the show, I hustled.

They were both of them about fifty, but handsome in the way that money can give you even if you don't have it naturally. I had on my smile, and I leaned over to show them the tray, if you take my meaning, and you could have plain knocked me over with a feather when one of them dropped a fifty-dollar bill on the tray and took a cigarette. Tamburlaine was in the middle of his finale, sawing some drunk Indian girl into pieces on the stage, and I said I couldn't change his bill.

That's fine, he said, and I remember thinking he must have been from Quebec; he had the accent. It's yours, he told me. And there are ten more waiting if you will meet my brother and me when the show is over.

What I said next is the one thing in my life I wish I could take back. I was desperate and full of hate the way you can only get when you're alone and poor and don't have much hope of improving either, and before I could take a breath to speak I was already out of Wawa, out of the carnival and into the big wide world with five hundred and fifty dollars in my pocket. That doesn't excuse it, but that's where I was.

I'll go with you, I said. But I want something else.

Name it, he said.

That bald stinking bastard who took your money when you came in? That's Milt. You give me that five hundred dollars and you kill that sonofabitch, I said.

He glanced at his friend, then back at me. Both of them with little smiles like I'd just pleased them no end. Just the kind of girl we're looking for, the friend said. It's a deal.

And I walked away from them, just like that, and put up with the miners and all the other suckers who were whooping and hollering when the Indian girl stood up and wasn't sawed to pieces after all. Tamburlaine gave his closing speech, same as he always did, and for those couple of minutes I got to carry around this secret feeling of being in control of myself for the first time in my life. When the tent had emptied out, I went out the back way to where Milt's office was, in a little trailer. The gent who'd first called me over was standing outside the door, and his friend was just then coming out.

It hit me what had just happened, and even if Milt had been a lecherous conniving bastard, knowing what I'd done made me feel dirty. I never even knew his last name. Plus now that it was done, I couldn't help but think that maybe they'd do the same thing to me once they'd taken what they wanted. As bad as the carnival had been, now I was a murderer, and I'd put myself at the mercy of men who had money and were willing to kill strangers. The midway was still full, and I could have run, could have screamed, but I was a sixteen-year-old girl. Who was a hick Canadian cop going to believe? So I swallowed hard and went with them.

We got into a car and drove around the north side of town, then up a winding little track that came out into a turnoff at the top of a waterfall. When we stopped, I'd gone from rage to despair, and I asked them their names. I guess I figured that if they'd tell me their names, maybe we'd be more than just strangers, and what we were about to do would be more than just money changing hands.

The gent who'd called me over at first said he was Raymond, and the other fellow, the one who'd killed Milt, was his brother Philippe. Philippe held the door for me as I got out, and I stood there, still in my little cigarette-girl outfit, and I said Please don't hurt me.

What's your name? Raymond asked me, and I told him, and he said Don't worry, Vera. As of tonight, you are the most important woman in our lives.

For some reason that scared me more than anything else that had happened so far, and I was this close to just hoofing it back down the road. But they walked away from the car into a space in the trees, a little clearing surrounded by big overhanging pines. They turned back to me, and Raymond said Vera, will you join us?

I did, and they each took one of my hands, and Philippe said We make this a sacred grove tonight, Vera. It is Midsummer's Eve, and the trees watch over us, and the river listens.

My hands started to shake, and they stepped a little away from me. Philippe and I have been at odds for a long time, Raymond said. If I told you we were Kings, it would be a lie, but you can believe that our offspring will be. To put our dispute to rest, we have agreed that we will lie with the same woman, and the child of that union will inherit what we have contested.

Now I might have been scared, and I might have been just a girl, but you could never have said that I held my tongue. That's crazy, I said.

Yes, crazy, Philippe said. So crazy that if you want to change your mind, we'll drive you back into town right now. You can keep the fifty dollars we've already given you. Is that what you'd like?

Back into town, where Milt was dead and old Tamburlaine would have noticed I'd been gone. Some offer. Now I knew why they were smiling when I thought I was sweetening my end of the deal. Let me see the money, I said, just to say something, and just like that Raymond took a roll bigger than I'd ever seen out of his pocket and scattered the bills in the grass. It's more than we offered, he said. Vera, listen to me. We don't command. We offer. We offer you a child, and we offer to take care of you until that child is of age. Are you afraid because we killed your tout? If our feud is not settled, more men will die. You can settle it.

So you want me to carry a King, I said. Don't I have to be some kind of aristocrat?

Exactly the opposite, Raymond said. The only competing interests here are ours, and we need to keep it that way. Now decide, if you please. It's almost midnight.

I decided.

Afterward, they drove me down to Sault Ste. Marie, the Michigan side, and dropped me off at the bus station. Along with the money they gave me a card with an address on it, and said that if I ever needed anything I should write there, and they'd see that I got it. They asked me where I was going, and I said home, then I changed my mind. Dexter was a little small to be a single girl raising a baby. Ann Arbor, I said.

A place named for trees, Philippe said. Perfect.

A few hours later I got onto a bus, and nine months later, right on the first day of spring, I had you and your brother, and the first thing I thought was, Won't this just be a kick in the teeth when I tell them. I brought you home to the little apartment I had on Arch Street, in one of the student neighborhoods where people weren't too judgmental, and I wrote them about you two. Ten days later I got a check for three thousand dollars and a note asking whether you were identical or fraternal twins. Well, even then I could tell you apart, so I said fraternal, and the next letter I got just said *Congratulations*. And that was it until the day Dwight disappeared twelve years later. When I needed money I wrote and the money came. When you were four years old I bought this house so you'd have a yard to play in, and I thought they'd forgotten about whatever it was they wanted to settle. I took care of you boys, and when you started asking about your father I made up a story, and then the day after Dewey went missing there was a letter from them. All it said was *We have chosen. Dwight is safe. Continue to write if you need anything.*

The hardest thing I ever did was not tell you, Lance. I used to wake up out of a sound sleep and go to your bedroom door because I just couldn't stand to see what it did to you, thinking your brother was dead and blaming yourself. Then every time I stopped myself because my first responsibility was to raise you, and what would happen if I did tell you? How would a teenage boy understand? So I kept quiet, and I kept lying, and if you hate me for it that's your right but I want you to know that I still think it was the right thing to do.

So. There you have it. I'm not sure how it squares with whatever your brother said, but that's the truth as far as I know it. Now you tell me one thing, son to mother: would you have done anything different?

Lance took the question in, waited for it to seep through the ice. He was calm, remote, falling and not caring what would happen when he finally hit. My father's name is Raymond, my father's name is Philippe, he thought. From a billion narrowed down to two, but never one.

"Have you heard from them since I came home from Korea?" he asked.

"Answer my question, Lance."

"You answer mine."

She shrank into herself, settling deeper into the chair and looking away from him at the cigarette in her hand. "Thank you for making the tea," she said. "I'll remember that."

"Have you heard from them, Mom?"

"Yes," she said. "A couple of days after you called, I got a letter asking me to let them know if a girl named Gwen came around. You know her?"

Lance didn't answer. His mother got up and went down the hall into her bedroom. Lance heard her open a drawer. When she came back, she had a card in her hand. She held it out, and Lance took it. It was about the size of a playing card, embossed along its borders with a pattern of roses and crosses like the tattoo on the cop he'd talked to that morning. He looked at the address: Mahone Bay, Nova Scotia.

Ice. He was all over ice, and black water inside.

"Here's one more thing," his mother said. He held out a hand, and she dropped a gold coin into it. On one side, a man with the head of a bird, in the flat profile he remembered from a grade-school history unit on the Pyramids. On the other side, a figure with limbs spread like the famous Da Vinci sketch and slight gaps at all the joints, as if it had been dismembered and put back to-gether on a table. "That's the coin they flipped to decide who would go first," his mother said. "I thought you should have it."

There was terrible pain in her voice and it drove like a spike through the ice, and into him. "I didn't come here to judge you," Lance said.

"Well, you are," she said.

He put the coin and card in his pocket. "Put yourself in my shoes, Mom."

"Put yourself in mine."

He thought that one over. "I don't know what I would have done. But I don't know what else you could have."

"That's right," she said.

Lance thought some more. "Can you give me a ride to Ann Arbor?"

She insisted on driving the '35 Ford she'd had since Lance and Dwight were in kindergarten, and since he didn't have the road to absorb his attention Lance fidgeted all the way. He'd meant to have her take him straight to the hotel, but as they got into town Lance got a sudden impulse. "Show me the apartment, Mom," he said.

She kept on down Huron, then turned down Main to

Packard. They skirted the southern part of the campus, and she turned onto a side street of big old houses, pulling to a stop about halfway up the block. "Right there," she said. "The front part of the third floor."

He looked up at the windows, wanting to remember something of the place, but nothing came. "There was a grad student down on the first floor who used to watch you two when I had to run errands," she said. "Her name was Rose. She was studying medieval literature, and she used to teach you Latin words. I don't suppose you remember any of that."

"No, I don't," Lance said. It made him sad, and he regretted the side trip. Everything he learned about his childhood made him feel fake—but it was fake. In the past two weeks he'd done a lifetime of becoming himself, and he crushed the nostalgia under a renewed determination to claim everything he'd been denied. All of it until now was just a story. The Grail was real, and it waited for him in Nova Scotia.

"I got a letter yesterday," his mother said. "If you're planning to go back to Nova Scotia, you might want to take in a little of the Lake Superior shoreline first."

There was a lapse of ten seconds or so before Lance caught on. "You heard from Dewey," he said.

"He said it's all arranged. This is about Ellie, isn't it?"

Lance nodded.

"You listen to me, son. If your brother managed to get Ellie away from wherever she was, he might have just taken a knife pointed at you and turned it toward himself."

"I know," Lance said.

"Everything you do from here on out is going to kill someone. Remember that, and remember that whatever happens, you owe your brother. He stepped out of your way, and that means that if you don't follow through, he'll be first on the shit list of whoever does come out on top."

"You think she's really there?"

She thought it over. "Yes. If I had to guess. Today's the summer solstice, which is when you and Dwight were conceived. To your father, it might seem like a good time to make some new matches. But this is no time for guessing. As of right now, you don't get to make any mistakes. Ellie's probably in Wawa, but you damn well better be asking yourself why."

The old Ford thumped into gear, and five minutes later they were in front of the hotel. Lance got out and leaned down to talk to her through the window. "I'll come see you when everything's sorted out," he said.

"Is there a girl named Gwen waiting for you in there?" his mother asked, in a tone that let him know she already knew the answer. When he didn't answer, she shut off the engine and said, "I want to meet her."

"I don't know if that's a good idea, Mom."

"I don't know if it is, either, but that's what I want."

Lance went inside and up to the room. Gwen was sitting on the side of the bed, and he had the feeling she hadn't moved in a while. He'd half expected her to be gone, and now that she wasn't he had a new problem. How was he going to tell her that he was going north to find Ellie with her along? What would she do if she didn't go with him? With a prickle of fear he remembered the cop in Bill's, and with the memory came his mother's voice: *Everything you do from here on out is going to kill someone.*

"There's something I haven't told you," she said.

"You don't say." He stood there holding the door open. "Tell me later. Right now my mom wants to meet you."

She got up and came with him, quiet and resigned. Lance's mother was standing on the sidewalk next to her car. She looked Gwen up and down, and Gwen stood there looking at the ground. All the air had gone out of her since last night, and goddamn right, Lance thought. What exactly was she going to tell him that he hadn't heard already from his mother? Gwen had lost the chance to give him her version first.

"Your name is Gwen?" Lance's mother asked.

Gwen nodded.

"Let me tell you something, Gwen. Look at me."

Gwen did.

"I have been you, girl," Lance's mother said. "It never stops when you want it to."

She held Gwen's gaze a little longer, then looked at Lance. "Your babysitter, Rose. Right before we moved out to Dexter, I came home from the dentist and she asked me if I'd named you for Sir Lancelot. No, I said, I read a book when I was little about a girl who fell in love with a boy named Lance Lincoln, and I always liked the name. She was wondering because you'd gotten mad at a wooden puzzle you were working and smashed all the pieces with a hammer, and she said that was just like Lancelot to smash your way through a problem without taking the time to work it out. She called you a hotheaded little knight, and you sure were. You make sure you've learned better."

Gwen was looking at him. The world was a broken record, Lance thought, little pieces of conversations replaying themselves in different mouths. At the moment, with Ellie so close, he was in no mood for retread advice. "I'll come see you, Mom," he said.

She kissed him on the cheek. "Listen to your mother," she said. "And I'm not your mother," she added to Gwen, "but you listen to me too." Then she got back into her car and drove away.

ARTHUR

THE SOLE GOOD THING about a crisis, Arthur thought, was that it considerably narrowed the number of possible reactions. He'd waited a week since giving Zareh's skull to Jerome, not asking why Jerome wanted it since he thought he already knew. It couldn't be that Jerome wanted to consult with Wondemu; he was enough of a Jesuit to feel nothing but scorn for the *kahen's* brand of sorcery. The only other possibility was that Jerome thought it necessary to subject the skull to some other variety of divination. Arthur felt himself being moved aside, which suited him; it would clarify the situation still further, and if Jerome underestimated him that made it all the easier to get what he wanted.

He put it to himself simply: either I respond correctly or I die. His hand fell to his thigh, tracing through the fabric of his trousers the lump growing above his knee. He'd had no word from Nigel Braithwaite, no word from Jerome, no word from Michel; the last two had likely turned against him, and who knew what the Hyena had gotten up to? Only one way remained to track down the Grail. It might not work, might in fact cost him his life, but there was no other decision to make.

I will survive, Arthur resolved. Again. Quickly he wrote a note and left it where Cesar Tian would find it in the morning;

then he stood and made his way upstairs, hoping to get some sleep before first light, when he would have to leave for Entotto. Menelik would no doubt be pleased to see him. Arthur would spin out the story of the Bearer insofar as he knew it, leaving out the Hyena. Perhaps leaving out Wondemu as well; there was no reason to bring down Menelik's anger on the *kahen,* who might well prove useful long after Menelik's power had crested and waned. What Arthur had to offer was Jerome and Michel, and he would trade both of them for decisive action on Menelik's part. It was time to apply force where guile had failed.

His sleep was thin and troubled, and he awoke when a shadow blocked the moonlight streaming across his face. Opening one eye a crack, Arthur saw a robed figure reflected in the iron-framed mirror on his bureau, circling the bed. He kept still against the surge of adrenaline, watched the curve of a long dagger emerging from the folds of the robe. The edge of the assassin's blade gleamed in the moonlight.

So it begins, Arthur thought. The hand holding the dagger was black. Would Michel have sent an Abyssinian when the Templars had no dearth of skilled murderers? Unlikely. Jerome? Was that possible? Now that he had Zareh's skull, was he moving for himself? Or had Menelik outmaneuvered Arthur again, perhaps striking an alliance with Jerome? These possibilities raced through his mind as the assassin crept silently to the side of his bed and reached the knife across toward the hollow below Arthur's jaw.

As he lunged, Arthur rolled off the side of his bed away from the stroke, at the same time sweeping his pillow up behind him. The pillow snagged the dagger's handle, jerking it free of the assassin's grasp. It clattered against the bureau and fell to the floor. Arthur threw the pillow aside and scooped up the knife, holding it before him as the assassin drew another blade and came slowly around the bed. The room's creaky floorboards made no sound under his feet.

Arthur had never been much of a fighter, and with his leg barely able to carry his weight his chances against a trained assassin weren't worth the stuffing of his slashed pillow. But I will survive, he thought. I have killed a man with a stone, and I have touched the Ark, and I will survive.

"Did Michel send you?"

No answer. The assassin advanced another step, more careful now. Arthur swiped his knife in a broad arc between them. His adversary backed up and flipped his own weapon so the blade rested between thumb and forefinger.

Now, Arthur thought. Before the assassin's knife had fallen back to his hand, Arthur seized the mirror from his bureau and flung it edge-on at the man's head. The mirror struck squarely above the assassin's right ear, snapping his head back. In that moment Arthur lunged toward him, crying out at the flaring agony in his knee. He jammed his knife into the assassin's neck, jerking it free and pounding it home again. They crashed together into the wall, grunts of pain whistling between gritted teeth; the assassin struck at Arthur with his reversed knife, and its blade slashed his fingers as the hilt ground into Arthur's ribs. Again Arthur stabbed him, this time above the collarbone, and blood spurted over his arm. He struck again and again, until the man lay silent beneath him and the pumping of blood from the base of his neck slowed to a dying trickle.

"Too confident," Arthur panted into the dead man's ear. "All of you. Too confident."

He raised himself slowly, already planning his next actions. The body could go in the alley behind the house; the entry carpet could be burned with the robe and the towels Arthur would use to sop up the blood. Harar was a dangerous place for white men. No police would come calling, and if they did, Cesar Tian would be able to plead genuine ignorance.

Then, away. Plans had changed; an Abyssinian assassin threw open the question of Menelik's involvement. There would be no trip to Entotto. If Arthur left in an hour and got fresh horses on the way, he might make it to Lake Tana in five days.

It wasn't until halfway through the ride to Lake Tana, as Arthur was heaving his saddle onto the dappled back of a fresh horse in the mountain village of Habro, that it occurred to him that the assassin was only the second man he'd ever killed. It seemed as if there must have been more. The thought rumbled through his exhausted mind like a distant peal of thunder, promising the lightning of repercussions to come. God knew he had seen enough men die, in Europe, on the long sea voyage to Java with the Dutch army, and these last years in Africa; but only once had he killed a man himself, and then as now his victim would have been an assassin. This is supposed to be a Rubicon of some sort, he mused, climbing onto the horse and continuing west as the sky lightened behind him, and I've crossed it twice without taking account. Once you kill a man . . . what? What was different?

Nothing, he decided. I protected myself, just as I would have ducked into a doorway to escape the rain. There is no difference.

The flat crack of a gunshot destroying the horse he'd left spurred Arthur on toward Bahar Dar.

It was four days, not five, and six horses dead behind him before Arthur reached Bahar Dar, where the same knock-kneed fisherman's son rented him the same fraying *tankwa* and he paddled out of the hippopotamus-infested marshes onto the same midnight-blue rippling dangerous water. Even the weather was the same here in the highlands, the Switzerland of Africa: air light and cool on the skin, sun warm and blinking off a million tiny waves. Yes, lake, he thought as he stroked north, I believe you would very much like to swallow me, and I would go down smoothly, weighted down by ten kilos of gold. You hate my incompleteness, the charade of my Kingship, my powerless wasted body; and so do I, and risk every day the remains of my life for a reward so grand I am unable even to dream of it. You hate me because I am usurper, Zagwe, because here at the source of the floods that brought life to the builders of the Pyramids I assume a legacy better laid at the feet of another man. Do not blame me yet, lake, because unlike that centuries-ago party of monks I have not brought the Ark across your waters. And do not blame me because the Ark too is incomplete. I pledge my life to your waters that I will complete it. Once I have saved myself.

Foolish oath. If he was unable to fulfill it he would die, and what then of penalties, of shame?

If I had known this would happen, Arthur thought, would I have touched the Ark? I told Wondemu that I couldn't imagine wishing to die, but to act knowing that one of the possible consequences is death—this is courting death, casting the gauntlet of self at its feet. I lie even to myself.

Each trip up the great escarpment that separated Lake Tana's watershed from the arid coastal plain, each daylong paddle back and forth across Tana's hungry waters took a little more from Arthur than he could replace. He was no longer young, and years in the African sun seeking fortune aged one more quickly than quiet years in Parisian cafés writing poetry and seducing wealthy matrons—or their daughters, or their sons—with spells only available to young men and the volcanic energy of genius. Ah, for the life of quiet dissipation, Arthur thought as the *tankwa* waddled around a spit of land and moved east toward Tana Kirkos. The sedentary life I so laughingly insulted when once I was a poet, and mocked the sedentaries' pockmarks, their eyes circled with green rings, their swollen fingers clenched around their thighs. I have hardly been sedentary these last years, but I look like them just the same. The breeze at his back now, he stroked harder, feeling sweat evaporate off the back of his neck and drinking deep the

sensation—rarer and rarer these last months—of his body, working and at his command for a little while longer.

This time, Wondemu was waiting for him on the shore, and
he helped Arthur drag the *tankwa* clear of the water. "To see the
face of your rival," Wondemu said, "needs more than a mouse's
life."

"Nothing like an enemy to show the face of a rival," Arthur
answered. He turned away from Wondemu's puzzled expression
and went back to the water's edge. Removing his shoes and
rolling the right leg of his trousers to midthigh, Arthur took a
deep breath and stepped into the lake. He stood ankle-deep as the
water's elemental anger rode coldly up his legs into his groin, settling like a freezing blade in his balls. Sand shifted under his feet
as the lake eddied around him, hungry to pull him deeper. "Not so
fast," said Arthur, hoarse with the pain. From his belt he drew the
assassin's knife meant for him and slashed open the swelling on his
leg, opening his body to the lake.

"You will bring an earthquake," Wondemu quavered behind
him. Arthur ignored the *kahen,* watching as the blood running
down his leg exploded into froth upon touching Tana's waters. He
endured the pain for a full minute, until his blood had made
churning clouds around his feet and he thought his testicles
would drop off like hailstones. Then he unstoppered a wineskin
and bent to fill it with the lake's anger and his own life. The water
surged away from the neck of the wineskin, but Arthur had bled
too much, and he grimaced with satisfaction as the empty skin
bloated with bloody frothing water. When he had drawn several
liters and his hands were so numbed by the lake's chill that he
could barely keep his grip on the skin, he stepped back out of the
water, leaving bloody footprints on the beach.

He looked at his feet; dark purple, toenails split, white
patches of frostbite riming the cuticles. His hands weren't much
better, and he thought that the next time he took a piss it might
move him to tears, and God knew what would grow in the Nile

delta next spring. But he had mastered the lake for the moment. At least this afternoon, he would turn its hatred of him to his own purposes.

"Tell me this will work, *kahen*," he said to Wondemu, who had retreated to the shelter of the rocky bluffs as a storm began gathering over the western reaches of the lake. "The lake should hate my rival as much as me, no? Unless he's Abyssinian?"

"It should be so," the *kahen* replied. "But I would not have staked my life on this belief."

"I stake my life every time I ask a question," Arthur said. "Someone tried to assassinate me four nights ago. It might have been the Order, or Menelik. The lake is my only friend at the moment." He handed Wondemu the wineskin.

"Rimbaud, all the days of your life you have never had a friend," Wondemu said. Arthur ignored him.

In the laboratory Wondemu set the wineskin on the table and went to a chest filled with dried herbs. "You—particularly you—cannot bleed in here," he said. "It will distract the spirits too much." Working swiftly, before the lake water and Arthur's blood burst the skin, he mixed a poultice and bandaged Arthur's leg. The pain from the gash faded with supernatural speed, surprising Arthur.

"*Kahen,*" he said. "Did Jerome bring Zareh's skull here?"

Wondemu fiddled with his preparations. "I hope you are ready for this." He opened a teak box next to the bowl he'd drowned the mouse in at Arthur's last visit. "I do not envy you your passage back across these waters, Monsieur Rimbaud."

That was something Arthur hadn't considered. Would he be stranded on the island until a vessel more substantial than the *tankwa* arrived to take him back? Nothing to be done, he decided. All he could do at this point was survive from hour to hour.

Wondemu set the skull from the box in the bowl, then mixed the black sludge again and poured it over the skull. When he unstoppered the wineskin, a gout of bloody water spurted out of it

onto the table, and the *kahen* held on to the skin with some difficulty. Arthur sat, his frostbitten hands cradled in his lap as
Wondemu emptied the wineskin into the bowl. Steam immediately erupted from the bowl, obscuring the skull and rising in a
column to the vaulted ceiling as the wineskin slowly drained. A
dry clicking filled the room, and Arthur looked around perplexed
until he realized that the skull must have been trying to speak before it had risen to the surface.

From the clearing steam, a whispered voice began to mutter,
all hissing consonants at first. Gradually the vocalizations became
words, and as the skull floated around to face Arthur it said, "You
presume, poet."

"I presume to save my life," Arthur answered calmly. "Answer
my questions, Zareh. I know your son is dead: who, then, is the
Bearer now? And who is my rival?"

"This is not Zareh. You don't recognize my voice? Arthur, I am
saddened."

So much sarcasm from a dried sphere of bone. Arthur hesitated, then made the connection. "Michel?" He shot a look at
Wondemu, who would not look at him.

"The plotter outplotted," the skull said. "I have much time to
consider the ironies."

"Never mind, Michel. We have all turned on one another, and
now you will tell me. I have bled into the lake and captured its
waters. You will tell me."

"Bleeding into the lake, you have given it voice. I can only tell
what it allows."

Arthur stood and leaned his face close to the skull, smelling
his own blood in the bowl. "We will stay here as long as I can
bleed, Michel. If the lake hates me, it must hate my rival too, and
I will destroy him. Show me his face."

"Ah, Arthur Rimbaud, that I can do." Fresh steam rolled from
the skull's eye sockets and hung like a thunderhead over the table.
"Look on his face, and then let me go."

Lamplight scattered in the cloud of steam, filling the laboratory with light like a foggy sunrise. Outside it began to rain, and drops from the church's leaky roof pattered on the stone floor. "You see how the lake will find its way to you," Michel's skull said, but Arthur barely heard; a face resolved itself from the interplay of light and water.

A young man, younger than Arthur, perhaps only of an age with Yishaq, who had been not quite nineteen when Arthur had sent him to France. He was kneeling on a hillside, face dusty and streaked with tears. A handsome, square-jawed man, wearing the coarse canvas of an explorer's porter. Something about him shouted *American* at Arthur, but how could an American be the rival? "Michel," he said, "who is this?"

"His is the only face you need to see, Arthur Rimbaud." As the skull spoke, raindrops fell through the cloud, tearing the image into wisps of steam.

"Answer my questions. Is he American? Where is Yishaq?"

"Yishaq, he comes. He comes with a man wearing the face of a bird." The rain was falling harder through the ceiling now, and Wondemu scrambled to cover his books and open decanters. Thunder boomed over the church, nearly drowning out Michel's final words: "You see, Arthur Rimbaud, how the lake will have the last word with you. Do not call me again." The skull sank, slopping black fluid and a film of bloody water over the edge of the bowl.

Arthur looked up to find Wondemu frowning at him. "Michel's skull? Where did you get it?"

"Your friend Jerome. I had to clean it when he brought it to me."

All coming apart, Arthur thought. Too many desires, too many men with their jealousies and their ambitions and their sins. "You couldn't have thought Michel would just play Zareh's role, *kahen*. What game are you playing?"

"I play no games. Now you know what you came to learn.

Leave. Go back to Harar, go back to France, go to hell and die there."

"I might just do that. But before I do, I might write a letter to Menelik, and a hundred soldiers will arrive to dangle your jewels from their spearpoints."

Wondemu laughed at him. "You flee from assassins, you don't even know your Templar patron is dead at the hands of your Hyena, and still you vomit threats at me. Once I feared you, Rimbaud. Now I think I must have been a child."

Arthur didn't respond. Was it true? Had he come so far only to lose in the final moments? He might get off the lake, might make his way to Axum, but even if he did George Gibson might have come and gone. He felt his ambition leaking away. I am thirty-six years old, he thought. My body is broken and dying. The goal I staked my life on recedes before me. What remains?

Wondemu sighed. "In the next room," he said, "the ceiling is not so leaky. Come and let's see to your hands and feet."

The Ides of March, and children crying in the streets of Harar like Caesar's mistresses. But it is not your friends that have betrayed you, waifs, Arthur thought. It is me. And I in turn have been betrayed by George Gibson. The day was bright, the sky's color leached away by the ferocity of the sun. Nothing grew because no rain had fallen since Arthur had returned from Lake Tana. He felt himself slowly wasting, shriveling as the land around him shriveled, mimicking its brittle brown lifelessness. These past months he had begun to understand what it meant to die.

From his bed he could see Harar's central plaza. Women thrust the swollen bellies of their children at any European who passed, sharp-ribbed dogs dragged their dusty tongues through the streets in search of water or sniffed dispiritedly around the empty racks that had once stretched drying skins. But the skins were long since stolen and eaten, the wells and streambeds dried up, the Europeans withdrawn to their houses where their meals would not start riots.

This, Arthur thought, is what it means to be King. To die the death of one's land, even one's adopted land. In France it would be spring, low clouds in the hills and chilly rainstorms sweeping across his brother's fields in Charleville. His sister would go to the market wearing the long coat he'd given her before leaving for Java, one hundred years ago by African reckoning. And Jean-Nicolas Arthur Rimbaud lay sweating in his bed, a tumor bulging from his knee like a gnarled lump grown from a tree that has lost a branch. He took a sip of water and let it trickle slowly down his throat.

There was a knock at the door, and Cesar Tian came in, his shirt unbuttoned to reveal runnels of sweat meandering through the thick black hair matting his chest. He scratched at his sagging belly. "Rimbaud. Someone to see you."

"Cesar, I'm hardly in shape to do business. What does he want?"

Cesar shrugged. "His name is Michel Deschamps."

Arthur struggled up to lean back against the headboard of his bed, wincing as he tried to move his leg. "Michel, is it? Send him in." This ought to be good, he thought. A dead man with no head, clumping up the stairs past a puzzled Cesar Tian. I hope it is Michel. That would at least enliven this terrible boredom, this waiting to die in a country that cannot die soon enough.

Cesar stepped back and Jerome came in to sit in a chair next to Arthur's bed. He looked exactly the same as he had twelve years before, when he'd stepped out of the shadows to set Arthur on his father's path.

"Cesar," Arthur said, "could you get me some water?"

"No, I'll get it," Jerome said. Cesar nodded his thanks and went back downstairs.

"Very droll," Arthur said. Jerome placed the full pitcher on Arthur's nightstand, sat on cushions next to the wall.

"In times such as these, one takes humor as it comes."

"Someone tried to assassinate me," Arthur said when he'd wet his throat. "In this room."

"Only one, eh?"

The two men looked at each other for a moment.

"So far." Arthur poured himself another glass of water. The sound of it gurgling from the pitcher seemed to him like the wet rattle of his assassin's last breaths.

"Well, it is as I said. They have their own ideas, you know, about who should be King." Jerome sighed and poured water for himself, then looked toward the window, where a shouting match had erupted in the square.

Emotion caught in Arthur's throat. "I am glad to know it wasn't you," he said.

"I too am glad you know that," Jerome said quietly.

"They have little to worry about from me," Arthur said bitterly. "I don't believe I'll live out the year, and I haven't any idea where the Grail is. Three months ago I sent the Hyena after it, but I haven't heard from him. He might as well be dead too, for all the good he's done me."

Jerome was looking at him with one eyebrow raised. "I hate to be sanctimonious, but I believe I expressed reservations in this regard at the beginning."

"Please, Jerome. What have you come to tell me? Did you kill Michel yourself?"

Jerome didn't look upset. "No. I saw it done, and if I could have prevented it I would have. Michel was corrupted by his desires, and he has passed that corruption on to his sons. They will have their say in these affairs." He lapsed into thought. "Hm. Well, Rimbaud. Perhaps you should have played Menelik's game according to his rules."

What he means is *Once you decided to take it for yourself, all bets were off,* Arthur thought. Something here was not as it seemed, but the fatigue coming over him had sapped his ability to think.

Jerome did not condemn him, and Arthur was saddened—and surprised by his sadness. I have not repaid his belief in me, he thought.

It didn't matter. The Hyena was dead, the Grail was God knew where, and if Menelik wanted to have Arthur killed, there was little Arthur could do about it. He'd been lucky the first time, no question. For that matter, Jerome could strangle him then and there.

Of course he wouldn't, though. Jerome was there. Jerome he could trust. A flush of optimism suffused him.

"Jerome," he said. "If this George Gibson is alive and Yishaq turned on me, the Grail is likely to be in Axum. Gibson may be trying to return it."

"Arthur, still you're deceiving yourself. It is lost, don't you understand that? Perhaps you might have had it once, but now it is lost."

He drifted in and out of sleep for the rest of the day, finally waking up when nightfall brought cooler temperatures and the faintest stirring of a breeze. Outside the only sound was the occasional dog barking, sharp against the rustling of dead leaves. *Bring me the Grail, Jerome.* Which was foolish. Even if Jerome found Gibson, even if he bothered to search, Arthur was too ill to go to Axum. His body was running down, an unwound clock. An unwatered plant withering in the killing Shoa drought.

It was time to leave Africa. If he was to die, he would die in France. Tomorrow he would begin making arrangements.

Arthur found that he couldn't muster much anxiety. His body was collapsing around him, and with it the steely resolve that had driven him since he'd first gone to Paris—how many years ago? It was odd to acknowledge this feeling, Arthur found; but he had at some point crossed a threshold from believing he would survive to resigning himself to death. *All my life I have believed in power,* he thought. When I wrote poetry, it was to find the language that would give me power over myself, give me power over the world. But power over language is not power over the world, because no one spoke the language I did. Power over the world is found in the world, and when I stumbled across the track of the Ark and began searching for the Grail, I thought I had found this power. Mistaken, mistaken again; what I found instead was one more way for the world to exert its power over me.

Something always hovered just beyond his grasp. He had learned languages, written poetry, joined armies and bands of explorers, traveled parts of the world few Europeans had ever seen, but always with the awareness that what he was looking for danced just beyond his ambition. I have lived many lives, Arthur thought, and soon I will die my only death.

But I will not die here.

He rolled onto his side so he could see the stars through his window. All the things he had done were like different names for a constellation, searches taken by different routes to arrive at a destination that could be understood only by experience. This is the final weakness of language, Arthur thought, that it cannot be a thing, and it is my final weakness that I cannot be the thing I imagined was possible. Once I thought I could make language. Then I thought I could make myself. And after it all, am I anything more than a dog that lies in the shade to die?

Gazing out the window, Arthur realized he didn't know the names of any of the stars he could see. Only the Milky Way, the ancients' road to heaven, linked him to the life he remembered in France. In France he had been able to believe in himself, but Africa allowed no belief but in itself, and in coming to Abyssinia Arthur had given himself over to it. No man can be King of Africa, he thought. It has humbled even me.

In humility, though, was a certain kind of power. I know what I can do now, Arthur thought, and what I cannot.

BOOK FIVE

———

What you don't understand are depths and shadows
They grow, Lance, though the sun covers them in a
   single day.

JACK SPICER, "The Book of Gwenivere"

LANCE

HE WAS STARTING to think that Gwen just didn't like to talk in cars. They'd been on the road for two hours, passing Flint and Saginaw and following U.S. 23 north through a part of his home state Lance had never seen, and she hadn't said a word. Hadn't asked where they were going, hadn't brought up whatever it was she'd been about to tell him back in the hotel. So they drove in an unbearable silence that neither of them wanted to break because things were only going to get worse. Lance watched a tractor rattling along a dirt access road next to the highway. They'd left the factory towns of southern Michigan behind and were now surrounded by farm country, fields thick with corn and other crops Lance didn't recognize. He'd never been very good at plant names. It crossed his mind that he'd have to brush up if he was to become the Fisher King, represent the fertility of the land, et cetera; wouldn't do to have a King who couldn't tell wheat from soybeans.

When he got loosey-goosey about the whole thing, that was a sure sign that he wasn't taking it seriously. Behind everything Jerry and Spicer and Dewey had told him was a single idea that Lance was only now starting to get hold of: the stories of the Grail were like Grimm fairy tales, simple stories of right and wrong designed to stick in the mind and keep alive some kernel of a greater truth. Spicer had sneered at his own idea that the Grail might be a kind of switch that when flipped brought out all that was best about humankind, but Lance had begun to wonder if maybe he wasn't right. A spiritual transmutation, the lead of the twentieth century alakazaamed into some wonderful Golden Age: that was worth fighting for. And fight for it people did, he thought, himself included. He'd already killed one man, had thought about killing the girl who now sat morosely beside him staring out at passing fields, had without thinking about it decided that he would kill anyone who got between him and Ellie.

Was he ready to make the same decision about the Grail? Didn't absolute power corrupt absolutely? What if the kind of person who had the steel to take the Grail was also exactly the kind of person who shouldn't have it?

It's not ours to take, Dewey had said, and that train of recollection led to Ethiopia again. Cradle of humanity, where the first humans had left the trees and hit the road that led to agriculture and writing and television and the atomic bomb. According to Jerry, the Egyptians had gotten their Osiris story from Ethiopia; in their version of those stories, an Ethiopian queen named Aso was among the plotters who imprisoned Isis so they could kill her brother; according to the Ark legend, the Queen of Sheba—an Ethiopian woman with disfigured feet—had come to Solomon, been healed in the presence of the Ark, and laid the groundwork for her son to steal it. Out of the mishmash of stories in Lance's head rose a cartoon image of an Ethiopian woman with Joe Stalin's mustache and uniform, limping around with addled fantasies of dominion. Something Jerry would have appreciated.

Which drained the humor right out of the situation. If Jerry or Spicer or whoever was right that Solomon had modeled the Ark tabernacle on the shrine the Egyptians had built to house the parts of Osiris' body they could recover, it all started to fit together a little too neatly. Add the Templar stories, Arthur legends, and the associated weirdness about the Philosopher's Stone, and it all started to seem like thousands of years of people retelling myths that they believed without knowing what ancient secrets the stories really disguised. And now, on the longest day of the year, Lance was tooling north toward a reenactment of his own conception. Another story retold though only partially understood.

He couldn't avoid talking to Gwen any longer. Where to start, he wondered, and after deliberating long enough to drive himself crazy he opened his mouth and said, "So when you said my father wasn't in New York, were you talking about my father or Dwight's?"

Her head snapped around, and Lance had a rush of angry glee. After all the times she'd known what he was going to say before he said it, at last he'd nailed her. "Oh, you didn't know?" Already he was ashamed of himself, but he piled it on. "Dewey and I have different fathers. My mom whored herself out to two guys so she could get out of working for a carnival. Merging the line, getting behind a single heir, right? A good strategy, but my mom laid two eggs that month and oh shit there are still two good candidates. Which one got you involved? I'm starting to put some things together here. What if you were one of those guys, and you agreed with your brother to choose an heir, and for whatever reason the two of you settle on your nephew. For the sake of argument we'll call him Dwight. And then what if you started feeling a little out of touch now that the decision had been made? Maybe you'd get a girl involved, a relative of yours, not too close but close enough that you could count on her to know what's good for the family. We'll call her Gwen. Her job is to be the perfect royal match, and at the same time she'll be your pipeline to the new King. Good politics. But then your son, who you've left at home to just be a regular ignorant Joe, joins the army and picks up a Fisher King wound on the same day that the world's worst dictator, who by the way also has a little problem with his feet, finally gives up the ghost? Times are changing, the last sixty years have been a historical shithole, but now the accidental King is getting old and maybe your nephew isn't the best guy for the job anymore. So you tell the lovely and talented Gwen Deschamps that maybe she should take a look at this new guy Lance. Only trouble is, he's already got a girlfriend, and she's onto at least part of what's going on. So you get the girlfriend out of the way. You don't kill her because who knows, she might be useful later, but you whisk her away and leave a trail of just enough bread crumbs to get this Lance guy interested. Maybe you even put a bug in an unhappy poet's ear. Presto—Lance is dancing to your tune, and your nephew can go off and read books and stare at the ocean for the rest of his life for all you care. Tell me when I get it wrong, Gwen, okay?"

She was looking out the window again. In a small voice she said, "Sounds like you've got most of it."

"I thought so."

They were approaching the town of West Branch, and the needle on the gas gauge was leaning way to the left. Lance pulled up to the pumps of an Esso station. The attendant appeared. "Quite a number you done to the front end there, bud," he said.

"You should see the other guy," Lance said.

While the pump jockey was filling the car and checking the oil, Lance got out and took a leak. He felt better now that he'd finally hammered together a story out of all the floating elements he'd heard since the first time he'd laid eyes on Spicer two weeks ago. Control at last, and God it felt good. It even showed in the figure he saw in the men's-room mirror: slightly taller than average, filling out from hospital thinness, angular jaw needing a shave, army cap covering blond hair darkening toward brown as childhood receded from the features of the face. Eyes still clear and blue, just beginning to wrinkle around the edges, nose straight with a nick across the bridge from a bit of shrapnel, unremarkable mouth over a chin with a little cleft. He washed his face, wet and combed his hair, and grinned into the mirror, thinking: *This is the face Ellie will see.* All things considered, he thought he looked pretty good.

He stepped out of the men's room feeling like a million bucks. Gwen was waiting for him, smoking a cigarette, her purse over her shoulder. "So let me guess," she said. "We're going north because your mother told you where to find Ellie."

"That's the plan," he said.

"I see. To quote one Lance Porter: how is it you didn't manage to let me know about this? Were you just waiting to see whether we'd shake hands, or were we supposed to fight for you?"

"I don't know, Gwen. Maybe I just hadn't thought it all the way through yet."

"Bullshit," she said. "All the time you spend complaining about how you're being led around by the nose, and now you're doing the same thing to me. You callous bastard."

"Doesn't feel so good when you're on the receiving end, does it?"

"That's all I've ever been, is on the receiving end. The one time in my life I tried to make a decision on my own was when I took you home in San Francisco. That was my way of doing what your brother did, opting out. I didn't want to be good material for a dynastic marriage. I wanted to fall in love."

This stopped him dead. Was she saying she was in love with him? Was that what she'd wanted to tell him earlier that day in the hotel room?

No. It couldn't be. A little too perfect, wasn't it? One more game.

"I'm already in love, Gwen. You knew that going in." You knew it was a snake when you picked it up, he thought, and a moment later realized he'd put himself in the role of the snake.

"Yes I did. And now I'm cutting my losses. Thanks for the ride, Lance Porter. I'll see to myself now."

She hiked her purse up on her shoulder and glared at him, daring him to challenge her, and even though he wanted more than anything just to be rid of her, something about Gwen's show of lonely courage touched Lance. Did he really have any right to be angry at her? Anything they'd done, they'd done together.

"What will you do?" he asked her.

"You don't get to ask me that. You don't get to make yourself feel better before you waltz off and see your girlfriend."

She was right. Lance was sorry he'd asked. Time to walk away, he thought, but he couldn't quite leave it there. "I'll take care of you," he said. "Once this is all over, I'll make sure you're okay."

"Don't you dare," she said. "Already it's changing you, Lance. Everything you're doing is out of hurt, and it can't work that way. One day you'll wake up and realize that you're just like George Gibson, only you won't even know who's pulling your strings."

"No. Gibson was never supposed to be part of this. I am. The whole goddamn history ends now. It's mine to take, and I'm going to take it, and then you'll see." The bravado in his voice made him feel ridiculous, but he couldn't tell Gwen what he was really feeling, which was a pleading almost like prayer, a desperate desire to believe that he could transform himself into someone worthy of the Grail.

"I hope that's true," she said, but he could tell she had no faith in him. "One more thing before I go. Jerry Kazmierski was killed to warn *me* away, not you. That was my message from Frank about what was going to happen if I chose you instead of letting your father choose Dwight for me. I did it anyway. I chose you because I was hoping you wouldn't want the Grail, that it could just be us." She shrugged, and Lance caught a glimpse of the cynical city girl, but she couldn't maintain it. "This is what I get. If you go on being the same self-centered little boy you've been so far, you're going to die. Do what's right, Lance."

She walked away from him then, down the road toward the center of town, and Lance paid for his gas and drove on. He passed her and looked into his rearview mirror hoping she'd at least wave, but she gave no sign that she'd seen him, and he kept going, confused by how much he still had to say to her and sad that he'd never get to say it.

Did he have to break one woman's heart to have another? The nagging sense that he'd been wrong about Gwen dogged Lance as he drove on north. How much about her was real? She might have been in on Jerry's murder, or she might be right that the message was meant for her. She might be working for Dewey's father, or she might just have gotten herself in too deep. There was no way to know because in the end Lance couldn't trust her. The only certainty he had left was Ellie.

Lance clung to the idea of her, and grew more certain again. He was doing what was right, and despite what his mother had said, Gwen knew how to take care of herself. He told himself that over and over until he believed it.

He stopped for a burger in Mackinac City, looking at the mighty bridge as he ate. Like the water below and the sky above, it was blue, and as he drove across it Lance felt like he was crossing a magical span between the confusion of his past and the clear beckoning destiny of Ellie. Night was falling when he crossed into Canada at Sault Ste. Marie, and it was after eleven when he stopped at the intersection where the new Trans-Canada Highway would pass through the outskirts of Wawa. He went on, relying on his mother's recollections to get him to where Ellie must be: through the quiet town, to the hills bordering it on the east, up the narrow dirt road next to the river until he saw the turnout and heard the rumble of the waterfall.

He pulled off the road, and his hands started to shake. To the right of the turnout there was a clearing in the pines, and in the clearing was a picnic table, and sitting on the picnic table was Ellie Patterson, chin in her hands, looking away from the car in the direction of the river. The Plymouth's headlights lit her up as if she were on stage. Behind her, the trunks of the pines also caught the light, but between them the darkness seemed artificially deep. She didn't move, and there was no wind to bend the branches that in the cone of light looked like a roof. Lance shut off the car and killed the headlights. When he got out of the car, the tremor left his hands. He felt strong, purposeful, rooted. His leg didn't hurt. The earth under his boots was soft with moss and fallen needles. He sat next to Ellie on the picnic table and took a long, slow breath. The scent of her mingled with the smells of water and stone and pine sap, and he'd known it would happen but still the conjured memory of the Tree of Many Roots overwhelmed him. He forgot what he'd meant to say.

"I wish you'd come to see me in California, Lance," Ellie said.

"Me too," he said, and it was true, but at the same time he was wondering what would have been different. If he'd heard the whole Grail story from Ellie instead of Spicer and Jerry, he might have been more likely to believe it right off. Jerry might still be alive. He wouldn't have had to freelance everything; they could have put together a plan to protect themselves.

Maybe I'd have met my father by now, Lance thought. Maybe I wouldn't have hurt Gwen.

Or maybe we'd all be dead.

"So what are we supposed to do here, Ellie?" he asked her. "Are there guys with knives in the bushes?"

She looked at him, and he knew he'd screwed up. "If you think I'd let that happen, I've been wrong about you, Lance," she said. "What happens here is we make some decisions. Your father and your uncle are busy killing off your rivals, and when they're not doing that they're pressuring Dwight to change his mind. The man who dropped me off here said that we should meet them three days from now. You met him. He's a policeman in Ann Arbor."

Karl Aufdemberge, Lance thought, remembering the sunburn and the offer to join the force back in Bill's Coffee Cup. Ellie had been right under his nose. "You've been home this whole time?"

"In jail in Ann Arbor. They came to get me in Berkeley, right after you got out of the hospital. Charged me with plotting violent attacks against American interests; don't you love it?" She smiled bitterly. "Karl said they were being generous. He said they wanted us to have some time together first. While he was taking me up to Wawa, he even let me know that you were home and that you were okay."

"First," he repeated.

"Meaning that they're willing to accept you. And meaning that if we don't do what they want, they're going to kill George Gibson. Then they're going to kill your brother and they're going to kill you and they're going to kill me. That's what they do when they're uncertain. They kill people."

"Like Jerry," Lance said softly. "Jesus, Ellie. What do we do?"

"We're going to save lives, Lance. We're going to do what they want us to do. You're going to be King, and I'm going to be Queen, and we're going to fight them. The world can't take another sixty years like the last sixty."

He was amazed at her certainty, at her strength. She took his hand and said, "You have to make yourself worthy of this. I never wanted to be a Queen. I wanted to stay with you. Man and woman. Just ordinary people." She put her other hand over her mouth, and he wondered what she was holding back. Then she brushed her hair back and said, "I guess Gwen probably said some of the same things."

And that was all. Just like that she let him know that she knew what he'd done, and just like that she dismissed it. Yes, Ellie, he thought. I will make myself worthy. "I'm sorry," he said. It was pitiful, but it was all he had.

She squeezed his hand and scooted off the table, tugging Lance along with her to the center of the clearing. "When your mother first told me about this, I was disappointed more than anything else. Not at her; she did what she had to, and if it was wrong God knows she's beat herself up enough since then. I was disappointed at the way it would happen between us. We don't get to choose. It's not just you and me. Shouldn't this just be about you and me?" She was crying, but fiercely, and when she started to unbutton her blouse Lance covered her hand with his.

"Ellie, stop," he said.

She shook her head and tried to pull her hand free. "We have to. Enough people have died. Do you want another George Gibson? Can you live with that?"

"No." He held on to her hand. "Ellie, listen. This isn't about who's more worthy to have the Grail. It's about who can take it. The only thing we have going for us is that I can. This is a game, and that's our trump, and I know how to play it."

Still she was shaking her head, and Lance let go of her hand long enough to put his hand on her cheek. "If we do this," he said, "we're already playing their game. Believe me, they'll know. If we don't, we keep them wondering. We've got three days. You can get a lot done in three days."

The last sentence came out in a tone Lance had never heard in his voice before. Ellie heard it too, and looked up at him with fear in her eyes. She's changed, Lance thought, and now she's seeing that I have too. A terrible sense of loss welled up in him, a mourning for all that they might have had, and on the heels of that came cold fury at the people who had done it.

"None of this is worth anything if you turn into your father," Ellie said.

"How can I turn into someone I've never met?" Lance said.

"Easy. You play a role. You know all the stories now. There are plenty of roles to play."

Lance heard her, but Jerry and Dwight were louder in his head. Spiritual transformation, Dwight had said, and Jerry went on and on about belief. They were both wrong, Lance realized. If it was about belief, Solomon would never have done what he did. He knew it was about wanting, and about power, and right then Lance wanted that power more than anything else he'd ever wanted. It was his to take, and he knew what was right, and he was by God going to have his revenge on the people who had forced him into this. He would prove himself to his father. Spiritual transformation was for people who didn't have assassins on their trail.

Lance kissed Ellie, there at midnight on Midsummer's Eve. "That's a promise," he said. "When we're together, it'll be on our own terms."

Now there was a little breeze, and the rustle of the pines came up to answer the constant rush of the waterfall. Lance kept his face close to Ellie's, closing his eyes, knowing that as long as it was just the two of them together under the trees he was safe but also knowing that the moment would have to break and that he would have to break it. He stretched it out as long as he could, but the cold was settling over him again, and this time it wouldn't leave until he'd made sure they were all safe. Permanently. Dwight would stay on his rickety dock, Gwen and Spicer would prop up the bars of North Beach, and Lance would hold the Grail up to his father and say *Look. Look what I have done.* He swore to himself that it would happen.

Then Lance did something he'd never done before. He lied to Ellie. "I'm not going to play a role," he said. "I'm going to play the game."

GEORGE

JEROME CAME FOR HIM on the equinox. George had done nothing but sit in the room he'd found across the street from the ruins of a tomb. He got up in the morning, looked out at a stone obelisk and a weedy rectangle of stones surrounding the central mausoleum. From his window he could see the Maryam Tsion church. Somewhere in there was the Ark. He went downstairs, ate the fierce orange stew called *kai wat,* took some flatbread back upstairs to ride out the rest of the day. Three or four times a day he convinced himself that Jerome wouldn't be back. If a knock came on the door, it would be Rimbaud, and one more time George would have to fight for his life. He waited, and looked within himself, trying to figure out if he would be up to killing a man.

When the knock came, George was at the window watching a parade led by one of the priests from the church. The priest carried some kind of icon, and the people behind him chanted and crossed themselves every so often. That night there would be a feast, and some kind of procession out to Makeda's tomb, a couple of miles outside of town. None of it was exactly Christian as far as George could tell, but what did he know? He didn't have a gold cup in his pouch, either.

He opened the door and Jerome came in. "George Gibson," Jerome said. "Today we find out."

"I hope so," George said.

They waited until the parade was over and the priest had gone back into the church. Jerome led, and knocked on the door. The priest appeared, then looked from Jerome to George and back. He stood aside.

They passed between rows of benches through a broad stone hall, decorated with muddy frescoes and hung with tapestries dimmed by centuries of smoke. A door stood open before them, and inside it was an altar, and behind the altar a second door. "I go no farther," Jerome said. The Abyssinian priest stopped too.

George took a deep breath and went on. He put a hand on the latch of the inner door and felt again the presence of the dead all around him, gathered to watch his final test. As he stepped across the threshold, he could see them, and when his right foot touched the stones of the Holy of Holies, he felt the world fall away from him and knew he was dying again, the way he had died in Boma, riding down into the underworld on the soul of a murdered boy. He shut his eyes and sat carefully on the floor. His ears started working again first, and the faint crackle of the torches came into focus. That is outside, George thought, struggling to order the sounds assaulting him. Outside me. I can hear my heart pumping, my breath in my throat. That is inside. He opened one eye, waited for the sparkling haze to resolve itself into the torch flames that he knew were there. Opened his other eye.

I am alive, he thought, and dead. I exist in this world and the other.

It would make quite a story, if he ever had anyone to tell it to.

Four torches burned at the corners of a square stone dais. Beyond them George could see no walls, only the shifting ranks of the dead and the spectral shadows they cast in the torchlight. On the dais sat a large rectangular box, filigreed with gold and stamped with images that wouldn't stay in focus. Two stone pillars bracketed the box, and George thought there were hieroglyphs carved on them, but when he looked toward the box his eyes hurt. He had a sense of great weight pressing in on him from every direction.

With great effort he stood. So this is it, he thought. The Ark of the Covenant. He'd imagined it differently; bigger, and crusted with gems or something, like a treasure chest from a medieval romance. Here it was, though. A wooden crate about the right size to carry baseball bats, covered with stamped gold like a wooden ceiling hidden behind stamped tin. "Okay," George said softly. He took the Grail from its pouch.

Light blazed from the seam between the Ark's lid and its walls. The figures on its sides seemed to catch the light and carry it with them as they processed across George's field of vision. He squinted, and had an uncomfortable moment of recollection. Hadn't the Ark incinerated entire armies, and fried up whoever looked at it? Was he about to burn away into ashes for the priest to chuckle over the next time he came in to freshen the torches? George froze as the light played across him, shone through him. He could see the veins in his hands and the shadows where his arm bones disappeared into the cuffs of his shirt. I'm not burning, he thought. But I reckon I will whenever it decides to quit playing nice.

He held the Grail out in front of him, cupped in both hands. "I don't want this," he said. "I've seen too much already."

The Ark's cover lifted back, flooding the room with blinding, dangerous light. George felt the light enter him, shiver him into atoms that only it held together. "No disrespect," he whispered, able to think of nothing else. "Don't hurt me. I'm just giving it back." He stepped to the dais, reached into the Ark, and laid the Grail gently into the light. He thought he saw bits of broken stone, and then it seemed as though the stones were sculpted into the shape of a body. The light filled George and blinded him, electrified him with the awareness of annihilation. From around him came the murmurs of the assembled souls. No, don't hurt me, George thought. I might swear once in a while, but I don't steal and I don't—

He shut his eyes so tight they hurt, but the light intensified. He could feel himself coming apart, dissected and searched for sin, and silently he began to plead: no, not Yishaq, I didn't know, and not the girl in the Ituri, I'm sorry, I'm sorry so sorry but I didn't get there soon enough, if I'd known I would have run, please, I would have run—

Darkness fell with a weight that brought George to his knees thinking he'd been killed. Shaking, sobbing, he brought his hands up, felt that through the tears and snot he still had a face, and his face told him that he still had hands. Daring to open his eyes, he looked at the floor, expecting the featureless brown-gray dust of the land of the dead. When he saw the dark red stones of the chamber floor, he had to touch them. They were cool, and real, and he felt the porous rock absorb the tears from his fingers.

Alive, he thought. His heart leapt, physically moved in his chest, with relief and joy. Home. He could go home to Martha. He'd discharged his errand, squared his debt to Yishaq.

The torches still burned in a square, but now the square defined the boundaries of a small room. The Ark still stood on the dais, but the pillars at its head and foot were smooth. The room smelled of incense and damp stone. George turned away from the pedestal and stood. The door he'd come through stood open. Through it he could see the antechamber with its small altar, and beyond that the door that led back into the world. He took a step toward the door, and the pouch at his belt swung with a familiar weight.

"No," he said, but when he reached into the pouch, his fingers closed around the familiar smooth surface of the Grail. "No," he said again, turning back to the Ark, and then he cried out as the symbols on its sides blinded him. It had given him one chance,

George realized as he stumbled back into the doorway, and found him wanting. It would not give him another. He fell through the door into the antechamber and rolled onto his stomach, hiding his face from the terrible light.

Someone kicked him in the side, and George yelped, scrambling to his feet. The Abyssinian priest, changed into long black robes and a flat-topped cap, poked George in the chest with the butt end of a wooden staff. He spat out a furiously unintelligible stream of words and poked George again.

"I—I don't know," George stammered. He held out the pouch. "I'm trying to give it back."

The priest's eyes widened and he took a step back. "Take it," George said, following him. "I don't want it." The priest shook his head violently and jabbed George with his staff.

"Rimbaud," he said, and spit on the floor.

"No, not Rimbaud. Don't you speak English?"

"Out," the priest said. "Get out."

"Where's Jerome?" George tried to hold his ground, but the priest kept prodding him with his staff, and before he knew it he'd been shoved right out onto the street. Jerome was gone, everyone was gone except the dogs and the beggars who wouldn't look him in the eye, and George was walking again. Walking across Africa because he didn't know what else to do.

LANCE

Dwight was fixing his bicycle when Lance and Ellie pulled up, just as the sun was hitting the ocean. "So you did it," he said when they got out of the car.

"What are you, some kind of pervert?" Lance said. "Some things are private."

The joke hung there long enough that Lance wished he hadn't said anything.

Dwight didn't smile. "I think you know what I mean."

"Everything's taken care of, little brother."

Ellie walked up to Dwight and hugged him before going inside. Lance had a feeling she didn't trust him, maybe because Lance had refused to play along back in Wawa, but he was damned if his first time with Ellie was going to be a command performance, and right then he didn't have time to care. They'd spent nearly twenty-three hours on the road. Lance hadn't slept. He was wound tighter than a watch spring. Right then he felt like he might never sleep again.

"I'm going to take it, Dewey," Lance said. "Can I trust what they say?"

"How should I know?"

"Well, according to Mom, you're the one who got Ellie loose."

"Don't make me a part of this. All I did was tell Dave what I'd told him a million times in the last six months, with a new twist. Instead of just telling them no, I put in a little recommendation for you, and dropped a pretty broad hint that you'd be more likely to listen to them if you could see Ellie again."

"Mom thinks you put a gun to your head," Lance said.

Dewey shrugged. "We've all got guns to our heads. I just want this over. You want it, it's yours. Let's go inside and work out how."

First they ate, sitting on the dock as the sky darkened around them and the wind shifted to come up off the water. Lance was jumpy with questions, but his brother and Ellie both told him to shut up until they'd finished eating. So he sat, working through his cheeseburger and potato salad, trying to take the edge off with a beer. It didn't work; the food sat in his stomach like an anchor, making his body feel sluggish even in the midst of his jitters. He tried to distract himself by observing Ellie and Dwight, getting a sense of what they were thinking, but there too he was frustrated. Here they were about to engineer the succession of the Holy Grail, and they were picnicking and talking about Dwight's plans to paint his house if it didn't rain over the next couple of days. He wanted to scream at them that they all might die.

What stopped him was that he didn't believe it. All of them were going to come through just fine. Lance was the wild card, and the time had come to play himself. He'd worked out the plan during the drive from Wawa. All he needed now were two things from Dewey.

Dinner polished off at last, they went inside, cleaned up the kitchen, and sat around the table. "Okay," Dwight said. "Tell me."

"Jerry K. is dead."

It took too long for Dwight to respond, and Lance pressed. "I went to New York. I told him I wanted to see Dad. We went to Yankee Stadium, and guess who showed up? Gwen and an old guy in a suit. I went with Gwen and Jerry was going to follow the old guy. That night I came back to his place and he was dead on his couch with a copy of *Parzival* over his face. But that afternoon he'd told me I should go see Mom, and I was about ready to do that when guess who showed up again? Gwen."

"I see Dave with an old guy in a suit," Dwight said, sounding like he was really thinking about something else. "Frank, he calls him. They're both old, really. Dave gives Frank hell all the time for the way he dresses, for smoking in their car, anything. They don't like each other much, but they spend a lot of time together. They both work for Dad, that's pretty clear."

That squared with what Gwen had said. Lance waited until he was sure Dewey had worked out what Jerry's death meant for him—now he was completely isolated. If Lance didn't gain the Grail, someone would come looking for Dewey sooner rather than later.

"About Dad," Lance said. "They said to meet us there in three days. Any ideas why?"

Ellie looked sharply at Lance, but Lance was focused on Dewey, who did exactly what Lance wanted him to do. "*They?*" he said.

"I had to make sure, Dewey," Lance said.

"What did you mean by *they*?"

Lance laid the story out exactly as his mother had told it. When he was done, he took the address card from his pocket and flipped it onto the table. "There's two of everything except this," he said. "Two fathers, two guys who do our fathers' dirty work, so on. Two of us. This is where Mom was supposed to write when she needed something."

Dwight slid the card toward himself and looked at the address. He leaned back in his chair, tilted his head back, covered his face with his hands. "I should have known," he said through his hands. "I don't know the exact number, but the farmhouse where George Gibson played his last game is on that road."

That was the last piece of the puzzle, snapping perfectly into place. "We've both been played, Dewey," Lance said. "That's why we need to get everything on the table. When we go to take the Grail, we have to know what to expect. All five of the people we're dealing with are old. We're young. We have to take sides."

"So why are you asking about three days?" Dewey asked. He sat forward again. Lance could see the strain on his face. Me, I'd be breaking windows, Lance thought. Dewey just says koans in his head and puts it all in a box.

"Right now it's almost twenty-four hours from when they started the clock," Lance said. "I'm not waiting for the three days. The more unexpected we are, the better. For all I know, one of our fathers sent the guy who tried to kill me in San Francisco. Could be your dad to get me out of the way, could be my dad to make sure you got the Grail and his investment in Gwen wasn't wasted. Either way, they might do it again, and that house is a perfect place."

"The Perilous Chapel," Ellie said. Lance and Dwight looked at her.

"Gibson jokes about it," she said. "He doesn't think much is funny anymore, but he comes back to that one."

"You've talked to him?" Dwight asked.

"No, that's what Aufdemberge said. He's been there, checking in with your fathers. He said they never leave the house because they're too afraid that one of them will get too much influence over Gibson. Dave and Frank have to go there to meet them every so often."

"So they're waiting for us," Dwight said.

So this was his family—a house full of crazy recluses. "They said three days for a reason," Lance insisted. "What do they need three days for?"

"These are your father and uncle, Lance," Ellie said quietly. "Is it so hard to believe that they just wanted to give us a few days?"

Lance looked at Dewey. "Yeah. It is."

"Don't do this for me, big brother," Dwight said. "I told you, I'm out of it."

"I'm doing it for all of us," Lance said. "They set the time because they wanted something to be right when we came. So here's what we're going to do. We'll wait the three days, but then I'm going alone. Even if they're watching us here, they won't know what happened between Ellie and me back in Wawa. One of the last things Spicer told me was that I should use uncertainty. I think he was right."

"And what if they kill you?" Ellie asked.

"Then maybe you and Dewey will find out soon enough to get away and do something about it."

"No," Dwight said. "Whatever happens. No."

"How far is the farmhouse?" Lance asked.

Dwight frowned. "Five or six miles. I don't drive much."

"What's to stop them from coming here once you've left?" Ellie asked.

Lance realized he was stuck. "If they have me, and it's me they want, maybe they'll leave you alone," he said, but he didn't believe it and he could tell they didn't either. *Every decision you make from here on out will kill someone,* his mother had said. At that moment, the realization that she'd been right was almost enough to make him walk away from the whole thing. That wouldn't work, though. Ellie had said as much by the waterfall, and Dwight had to know it too. He had to go through with it. The only decision was how.

"For all we know, they could come here tonight," he said.

"That's ridiculous, Lance," Ellie said. "If all they wanted was to kill us, they could have done it by now."

"No, they couldn't. Not while they don't have someone else ready. Gibson is old, and our fathers are old, and unless they want to hand the Grail over to someone outside the immediate family, Dewey and I are it. They have to deal with us."

"With you, you mean," Dwight said.

"Right. With me. Which is why I think I should go alone at first. The less they know, the better."

Echoes of Spicer again, but Lance knew the only uncertainty he was playing on was Ellie's and Dwight's. He was lying again. "Look," he said. "Let's talk about it again in the morning."

Dwight gave Ellie and Lance the bed. He took a sleeping bag and headed to the back yard, which made Lance nervous. "I'm going to worry about you out there," he said, but Dwight just shrugged.

"They aren't thinking about me right now," he said. "You two get some sleep." He eased the door shut behind him. Lance watched his brother go out onto the dock, unroll the bag, and crawl into it. Man, he thought. Dewey must sleep like a log. I'd roll right off into the water.

If he slept at all, which he didn't think he would, wherever he ended up.

Ellie came up behind Lance and linked her hands around his waist. "It's okay if you want to sleep in the bed too," she said, a little shyly.

He leaned back into her, reached up to run his fingers through her hair. "After," he said. "When it's just us."

She rested her forehead on his shoulder. "Lance," she murmured. "It's never going to be just us."

Yes it is, he thought. The last of his indecision fell away.

He turned around and kissed her, trying not to think about how much it felt like a goodbye. "I'm going to sit up for a little while. Still jittery from the road."

"Okay," she said, relenting but not agreeing. "Don't stay up all night."

Lance said he wouldn't, and she went into the bedroom. He looked back outside. Dewey was already asleep. Lance turned out all the lights in the house except for a table lamp next to the couch. He sat paging through one of Dewey's books on Zen. *Life is suffering,* he read.

Everybody knew that.

There is an end to suffering, he read, and thought, Yes. There will be.

From where he sat he could see part of the bedroom door. No light shone from inside the room. He turned out the lamp to be sure, and then sat in the darkness. Time passed. He heard Ellie shift and sigh.

It was time. Lance got up to squat next to his duffel bag at the end of the couch. Slowly he unzipped it and dug the canvas-wrapped bundle from under his clothes. Holding it in the crook of his elbow, he went out the front door. He stopped a few steps from the house and waited. No light came on. Dwight didn't come around from the back of the house, Ellie didn't open the door. He counted to a hundred and then started walking.

ARTHUR

"Arthur."

He stirred, cried out. "Give it to me!"

"Arthur, wake up!"

It was his sister, Isabelle. Arthur opened his eyes, saw the hospital room and her tear-streaked, fearful face. He looked down, where the bedsheet draped crookedly over his remaining leg. "I have to go back," he said.

"What, home again?" Isabelle's hands fluttered, as if like the rest of her they could think of no way to pacify him. "After what you suffered on the journey down here? And the police might come for you in Roche; they're still asking about your desertion."

"Not Roche. Not Charleville. Not home." Arthur groaned and gritted his teeth as the pain reawakened. It seemed that with his leg gone, the agony he carried had simply dispersed itself through the rest of his body. His right arm was nearly useless, and he thought his left leg was beginning to swell. What have I to fear from police? he thought. It's been thirteen years since I was in an army. "I have to go back to Africa," he grated.

Isabelle gasped. "Africa! In your condition? Arthur, you barely survived coming back to Marseilles; how will you make a voyage to Africa?"

"It will save me," he said stubbornly.

"God will save you, my brother," Isabelle said. She sat and folded her hands. "Nothing else."

He was awake now, enough to take a little pleasure at puncturing his sister's piety. "If God is all that will save me," Arthur said, "I had better get on with dying. Don't you think that would be best, sister?" He was crying now, and he swiped angrily at the tears. "I shall go under the earth, and you will walk in the sun."

"You mustn't speak that way. The doctors say you will be cured."

"The doctors know shit," Arthur spat. "Doctors, nuns, chaplains; shit on them all! They spend their days buggering each other while men die in their beds, while infection breeds in their sterile hospital." Grunting with the effort, he turned himself onto his left side, facing away from Isabelle. "Let me die, sister. It's the only thing worth doing that I can still manage."

After a pause, he heard Isabelle get up and go to the door. "I'll come back when the nuns bring you supper," she said carefully, and shut the door.

Alone; this was best. A man who died surrounded by family and friends had a responsibility to them, had to make sure they didn't feel too bad about his death. It's not so bad, one had to say. Really, I expected worse. No, thank you, I'm comfortable.

Shit, all of it.

The truth was that dying was best done alone. A man had enough to do facing death without mitigating the experience for a squadron of mooning relations.

Once it had become a foregone conclusion, death had lost much of its terror for Arthur. And why not? He'd done almost nothing but think about it, ever since the day four years before when he'd determined to have the Grail for himself, dooming himself to a Kingship that would never be crowned. And since leaving Abyssinia in April, Arthur realized, he'd been expecting death nearly every day, as if it would come to exact revenge for his abandonment of his adopted, uncrowned kingdom. He often dreamed of Yishaq, and occasionally of George Gibson, and every so often his yearning to know what had become of the Grail seemed to seep into his dreams. Then he visualized Jerome, skulking across some forsaken landscape—a Kenyan swamp, an Arctic snowscape, a trackless forest somewhere in Canada. Fleeing whatever pursuit he might imagine, and waiting for Arthur to die.

Well, Jerome, Arthur thought. If that's what you're doing, you don't have long to wait. Soon I'll be out of your way, and my claim will no longer concern you.

And that was fine. Arthur sighed, grimaced as pain pulsed outward from his left hip. He rolled onto his back. *Yes, that's fine.* Power to those who can use it. It was never for me. I spent my life searching for it, and it is time I learned to cut my losses. Even if I could go back to Africa, track down Jerome or this Gibson and reclaim the Grail . . . what? What would I do? Menelik is starting a war with the Italians, the Boers are rebelling in the Transvaal, God knows what other bloodshed is brewing. What would I do, make it rain in Shoa? What difference would that make, if those who didn't starve would instead be gutted by Italian bayonets?

Looking death in the face made a man want to recognize certain truths, Arthur thought. And one of those was that his destiny had always been to seek, not to find. Very well.

His door opened, and Arthur closed his eyes. "Go away, Isabelle," he said. "It's not time yet for supper."

"Mister Rimbaud?"

Spoken in English. With an American accent.

Arthur opened his eyes, feeling again as he had when Isabelle had shaken him free of his dream. A rangy young man, his hair a tangle of brown curls, his shoulders nearly as wide as the door frame, stood a few feet from Arthur's bed. "George Gibson," Arthur said. "What a surprise."

"You speak English," Gibson said. "First Frenchman I've seen who will admit to it. I've been looking for you since March. Eight months."

March, Arthur thought. Jerome's visit. He must have come straight to see me from Axum. What lovely irony.

Arthur's attention fixed on a pouch dangling from Gibson's right wrist. He had tied that very pouch around Yishaq's wrist four years ago, instructing him to carry the Grail in no other receptacle. Now it swung with real weight as Gibson looked over his shoulder into the hall.

"You have at least an hour before those damned nuns will bring supper, Mister Gibson," Arthur said. "I would get up, but as you see . . ." He indicated the flat spot under the sheet where his right leg should have been.

"Oh," Gibson said.

"You've come to kill me, I suppose?" Arthur's mouth twitched in a painful smile. "Not unexpected. I wouldn't want any obstacle between myself and the Kingship. A question first, though, if I might: how did you survive both the Hyena and Michel?"

"Kill you?" Gibson's face, so different from what Arthur had dreamed, nonetheless acquired exactly the expression Arthur had dreamed onto it. Like a steer in the instant after the sledgehammer falls.

"Please, Mister Gibson. I am crippled and dying, not stupid."

Gibson started to speak, then cleared his throat. He dipped into the pouch and removed the Grail.

Arthur's mouth fell open as its light flowed through the room, seeming to settle like quicksilver on the bed and pool in the hollow left by his amputated leg. Tiny, almost sexual sounds escaped his throat at the feeling. "Oh," he said, "oh."

"I came to give it to you," Gibson said. "If I didn't, it'd be the same as killing you."

It was Arthur's turn to look like a slaughtered bull. "Give it to me?"

Vistas unfolded at the speed of thought, where five minutes ago Arthur's mental landscape had collapsed into a canyon wide enough for only a single man to pass. And where that canyon had been blocked by Death, patiently awaiting Arthur's approach. I can grow old, he thought. I can marry, I can have children, I can see them married. I can watch the new century dawn.

I can make it rain in Shoa.

Arthur closed his eyes again. It was easier to think that way, easier to imagine oneself alone. He could take the Grail and send the American boy back to wherever he'd come from.

He could, he could, he could.

Even with his eyes closed, Arthur could see the radiance of the Grail, playing across his face. He could feel its light soaking into his bones—healing him, he wondered, or just masking the pain?

He could hear Gibson holding his breath.

"No," Arthur said. He lifted his right arm as if to fend Gibson off.

"No?"

"My leg," Arthur lied. "The King is supposed to be wounded, but this is . . . extreme, I think, is the word." He looked at Gibson and smiled weakly.

"I don't want it," Gibson said. "I'm not even sure what it is. Isn't it supposed to be a cup?"

"Stories," Arthur said. "There are more stories than truths." The smile still creased his face. It felt good to smile.

"I don't want it," Gibson said again.

"Go, Monsieur Gibson. If you did not kill Michel, he will come looking for you. If you did, his sons will take his place. The Grail draws pursuit. Hide yourself, my friend. Hide yourself, and do what you can."

Arthur closed his eyes once more, a King ending an audience. After a while, Gibson's feet scuffed on the floor as he turned. I did not always live well, Arthur thought as the footsteps faded down the hall.

But I can die well.

Morning sun shone through the narrow hospital window. "One tusk. Two tusks. *Allah kerim,*" Arthur said, and died.

And stands on the shore of a river, a stone gate towering above him. At the gate, a figure he recognizes. "So it is you," he says.

Jackal-headed Anubis, behind a stone pedestal on which rests a papyrus scroll, nods. "As you wished," he says. "Through the gate."

On the other side, a stone corridor with only faint stars for a roof. Arthur walks, feeling two feet beneath him, but when he looks down all that meets his eyes is the floor of dead brown dust. Raising his head again, he sees that the corridor is lined with people, their heads turning as he passes. He sees his baby sister in his father's arms, Baudelaire, his servant Djami, Dmitri Righas who worked for Alfred Bardey in Harar. "Dmitri, Djami," he says. "The famine?"

They make no answer, and Arthur passes by.

At last he reaches a doorway. Yishaq and Zareh wait there, push the door open. Arthur cannot turn his head, but he feels them behind him as he walks out onto a gray beach made from the meal of ground bones. His feet sink in over the ankles, and a terrible chill grows in his legs.

"And you," he says. Osiris, who like the Nile died and lived again with the seasons, nods; at his left hand Thoth, keeper of knowledge, dips his ibis beak at Arthur's approach. The two halves of the coin, life and knowledge. Like Anubis, Thoth holds a reed pen over a curling sheet of papyrus. Before them, a scale taller than Arthur stands on a pyramid sunk into the earth.

Arthur walks slowly to the scale. "Have I chosen this as well?"

Osiris holds up a hand. "Jean-Nicolas Arthur Rimbaud. Confess."

Arthur hesitates. "I have not," he begins, and stops. What have I not done? he thinks to himself. "I have not," he says again.

"Confess," Osiris commands.

Two halves of the coin, but when looking at one the other is obscured. How is a man to live on the narrow edge invisible to both? "I have not," Arthur says, "failed to learn from my errors. I have not died in the same way that I lived."

"The scales will tell," Osiris intones. "Your soul."

His soul is in Arthur's hands, a shimmering stone outlining Arthur's body in its silvery light. The Grail, he thinks.

And begins to understand.

"Like you," he says to Osiris, "I wanted to live again."

"The scales judge," Osiris says, and Arthur places his soul in the left-hand pan. The scales tip, ever so slightly, in that direction. Yishaq steps around Arthur, stoops to gather a handful of the beach. He works it in his hands, lets it fall away to reveal a white feather. "Ma'at," Osiris says. "Jean-Nicolas Arthur Rimbaud, your soul is weighed against that which brought order into the chaos of the world."

Yishaq lays the feather in the right-hand pan. Arthur hears a tidal roar behind him as something immense beyond imagining rears itself out of the lightless ocean. I know how this story ends, he thinks, and the scale tips back.

It stops, hanging just short of horizontal. Arthur exhales, letting go.

"Pass," in the voice of his father, and Arthur does, through the impotent jaws of the Eater of the Dead, beyond into the oblivion that in the end was his desire.

BOOK SIX

———

It is repose in the light, neither fever nor languor, on a
   bed or on a meadow.
It is the friend neither violent nor weak. The friend.
It is the beloved neither tormenting nor tormented. The
   beloved.
Air and the world not sought. Life
—Was it really this?
—And the dream fades.

ARTHUR RIMBAUD, "Vigils"

No kingdom will be saved.

JACK SPICER, "The Book of the Death of Arthur"

LANCE

HIGH CLOUDS WISPED across the face of the gibbous moon. Lance stopped five hundred yards from the farmhouse, scouting for lights anywhere along the stretch of road. To his left, the short reach between the mainland and Oak Island glimmered. The sun would come up just to the right of the island, he thought, working out the best place to position himself. There wasn't much cover on the strip of land between the road and the water, but if he was smart he wouldn't need much. On the other hand, the far side of the farmhouse property ended in forest, and it was off to the side of the house. People on the porch would be looking away from him.

He walked another half a mile before cutting off the road into the woods. A little stream ran just inside the tree line; he followed it until it bent to the left, away from the house, then worked his way through the undergrowth to the edge of the cleared part of the property. The land hadn't been planted in years, from the look of it. Not even hayed, since there were young trees beginning to creep out from the woods. From where he was, he could see five windows, two upstairs and three on the ground floor. Bedrooms up, kitchen and living room down, was his guess. He'd be able to see into any of them once they turned on the lights. He sat at the base of a gnarled Dutch elm, working his rear around until he'd settled in a position he could keep for hours. His watch read three o'clock almost on the nose. Midsummer in Nova Scotia, the sky would start to brighten around four. He'd have a better idea of how to proceed once whoever was in the house started to move around.

An hour passed, and Lance didn't move except to twitch away bugs. The silence was broken only by the steady wash of the ocean and the occasional rustle of a small animal behind him in the forest.

The first thing he always noticed about the approach of dawn was how color reappeared in the world. Before you could really say the sky was brighter or the stars were beginning to fade, you noticed color. Green crept into the moonlit gray of the leaves, and the barn behind the farmhouse reddened.

Lance laid the oilcloth on the ground and untied it. Eyes still on the house, he put the rifle together by touch. As his hands took over, he felt emotion draining out of him. Cold again. It was good to be cold. His fingers grazed the gouges in the rifle's stock from the mortar shell that had ended his war. Such a delicate balance, probability: any one of the fragments that had chewed a piece from the stock might have tumbled a little differently, plowed into his intestines or his bladder or a kidney. Half an inch to either side, he thought, resting a fingertip in a triangular pock where the inside of his pinkie knuckle would grip when he aimed. Half an inch and I bleed to death, down there in the mud and the cold water.

Instead he was feeling the first light of the day on his face one more time. The smell of gun oil cut through the rising scents of earth and sea and the awakening fragrance of some flower he couldn't see. The rifle fell together in his hands.

You don't forget this, Lance thought. The feeling of a bright beautiful morning, a coming day during which you will kill men you don't know, and maybe die yourself. The shells from his pocket clicked into the magazine, one two three four.

A light came on in the house, upstairs. Five minutes later, another, at the back of the ground floor, what he figured was the kitchen. Old men rose early, and everyone there was old. Frank from Yankee Stadium, Dave who kept an eye on Dwight, George Gibson, all of them. Bringing everything to a head because this was their last chance to determine their successors. Lance ran the cloth over the rifle, his drill sergeant's voice in his head: *If you're hit, nobody can pick you up and use you, but your clean rifle might save another man's life.* Smoke rose from the farmhouse's chimney and he realized that during the past hour the ground's chill had seeped into him. He hoped he wouldn't have to run anytime soon.

The bang of a screen door reached him, and someone came out onto the porch. From three hundred yards, identification was an iffy business, but the guy fell right into the description Dewey had given of Dave, the guy keeping tabs on him, the one who relayed messages from his father. He was barefoot and cowlicked, wearing a river driver's shirt and dungarees. Lance ticked the front sight on the Garand ahead a couple of notches, looked up at the leaves to get a sense of the wind. There was a very slight off-shore breeze. He chambered a round and brought the rifle to his shoulder, centered it on the bottom button of the shirt, held steady when Dave turned to look out at the water, giving Lance his profile and also a look at the butt of a gun tucked into the small of his back. Three hundred yards with negligible crosswind wasn't a tough shot. Pow, Lance thought. It felt right. Shooting people was easy when they didn't know you were there; he could take the guy right now.

He wondered if there was a dog. What kind of dog would guard the Grail? He thought of Cerberus. He didn't like his chances against a giant three-headed magical dog, that was for sure, so best not to think about it. Too much time devoted to the unknowable just drew attention from the things that could be controlled.

Lance rested the rifle in his lap again. No point shooting when he was still pretty sure there was another guy in there. His father and Dewey's would be in with Gibson; Dewey and Gwen had both said that, and Ellie had heard the same from the cop. But Lance was getting a pretty good sense of the game. He was willing to take odds that the old guy in the suit from Yankee Stadium was somewhere inside as well. They'd all be keeping each other in sight, and Dewey had said they spent a lot of time together. No wonder; while the two brothers spent their time figuring out how to stick knives in each other, their vassals were smart to keep an eye on one another. Could even be they were cooking something up on their own.

It was worth waiting a few minutes to find out for sure.

Again he wondered who or what else might be inside. Other Templars? He couldn't get all of them. With Frank it was personal: he'd killed Jerry. And Dave wasn't just enjoying the view. He and Frank might be playing the whole situation from their own angle, and with both of them gone Dad and Uncle would *know* that Lance wasn't playing by the rules they'd written. While the rest of the world stumbled around looking for a gold cup or Jesus Christ's family tree, Lance was going to go into this ramshackle farmhouse and take what was his. As of today, it was his house. Two shots, lay down the rifle, and walk in. That would be enough of a statement.

Someone was moving in the kitchen. Lance looked hard, but couldn't see enough of the figure to pin it down. Then the kitchen was empty again, the screen door banged, and there he was. The guy who had killed Jerry Kazmierski. Frank. He wasn't wearing a suit this morning, but he was still dressed sharper than his colleague. Or partner. His chinos were ironed, his shirt collar buttoned down, his hair wet and combed. He held a mug in one hand, drew a cigarette from his pocket and lit it. Dave leaned forward to rest his elbows on the porch railing. From time to time Frank turned to his left to tap his cigarette into an ashtray; each time Lance had a moment's perfect view of his back, but only as long as the cigarette lasted. Dave was giving Lance the hollow under his right arm, tougher but still plenty to work with.

Here we go, Lance thought. He brought the rifle up again, breathing slow in time to his heartbeat: three beats in, three beats out, feeling the twinkle of sunrise on his face through the branches of the trees. To do what was right, sometimes you had to do what was wrong. That much he'd learned in the army. Now he had to save himself, save his brother and Ellie and maybe even Gwen. Raymond and Philippe wouldn't give it to him. Other rivals would appear, or Dewey would change his mind, and in the end it didn't matter. This once, he would be chosen, and to be chosen he had to choose himself.

Inhale, exhale, pause. In the stillness between heartbeats Lance squeezed the trigger.

GEORGE

AT THE CRACK of the rifle, George was already dying, because a man begins to die at the moment he can measure the remainder of his life. And a dying man remembers:

The Atlantic Ocean pitched and rolled past the *Beauchamp*'s hull, breaking over its forward gunwales. George sat bundled in a deck chair, looking once in a while up at the night sky, hoping for a break in the clouds, but no stars showed themselves, and even the half-moon was just a pale smudge dropping toward the western horizon. He couldn't sleep—hadn't been able to sleep the whole voyage—and when the shipboard saloon had closed half an hour before, George had come out on deck rather than return to his stifling stateroom. He wanted to be outside, watching, with no idea what it was he watched for. Keeping a vigil. Looking for a sign.

The Grail rested in the pocket of a peacoat he'd stolen in Marseilles. He might be better off looking like a sailor if the Templars came looking for him. He held it in his hand, feeling its strange energy. What do you do? he asked it silently. And what am I supposed to do with you?

Am I supposed to be responsible for every dying boy in Africa because I went barnstorming to Nova Scotia?

I can't do it, George thought. Can't. How can I even face all the things I'm supposed to fix?

In three or four hours, after the sun came up, he would reach New York. From there, what? *Hide yourself,* Jerome had said, but from who? And where? How could he hide when he didn't know who would be looking for him? George took a long swallow from the bottle he'd purchased from the bartender, welcoming whiskey's heat on this cold night. He could get to New York drunk, just get on the first train he saw—even he wouldn't know where he was going—take the Grail out into the wilderness somewhere, and sit until a successor came along.

"Martha," George said. "Martha, Martha."

As soon as he got to New York he would send her the book with his letters written in it. A memento of his travels. She'd get it, and wonder about him, and then he'd show up and take her with him. It was a big world, just how big he'd spent the last three years finding out, and the two of them would run away and hide.

Won't be playing much baseball any time soon, he thought, cracking a grim smile at the thought of sliding into third base with the Holy Grail in the back pocket of his uniform. So how can I marry her? Can I ask her to follow me out into the hinterlands somewhere, waste her life sitting on this Grail like a blackbird duped into hatching a cuckoo's egg? His smile twisted into a pained grimace, and George began quietly to sob, alone on the deck of a French steamer, twenty-two years old with no idea of where to carry the burden chance had placed on him. Wish I'd never heard of Oak Island, he thought. Or Rimbaud or the Holy Grail. He could live without a home, he could live without base-ball; but how was he going to live without Martha Ciccarelli?

Nobody had the right to ask him to do this. He could throw the damned Grail right over the railing here, leave it on the bottom of the North Atlantic. Go back and explain to Mr. von der Ahe why he'd had to leave the Maroons so suddenly; he'd be angry, but George knew how good a baseball player he was. If Mr. von der Ahe had a brain in his head, he'd be playing George in center field next spring.

He wouldn't do that, though, if George didn't ask him. And George couldn't ask him unless he got rid of the Grail.

"I never asked for it," he said. "I never wanted it." He struggled to his feet, kicking over the whiskey bottle, and wobbled forward to the *Beauchamp*'s bow. A sailor on watch, observing him from his station on the bridge, shoved open a window and called out in French. "I don't understand French," George sang out, full of sudden intoxicated glee at the prospect of being rid of the Grail. "It's Tuesday morning, I don't understand French, and I don't want the goddamned Grail!" He climbed over a huge coil of rope, slipped, and fell on his behind. "Icy up here," he muttered to himself, squinting at the bow railing. He could easily throw the Grail from here.

"No, boy," he said to himself, imitating his father. "These things oughta have some ritual to 'em, dammit." Right, ritual. George got laboriously to his feet again, skidded his way across the deck to the very point of the bow railing. He looked down at the foam where the *Beauchamp* cut across the ocean's surface. "How deep are you, ocean?" he called out.

Ritual, he reminded himself. "Right," he nodded, "ceremony. Here; I do hereby declare that on Tuesday the thirtieth of damn November, eighteen hundred and ninety-one, at—" He checked his watch. It was still on Marseilles time, but the hell with it. "—ten o'clock in the morning, I realized that this whole Grail business was better off in Davy Jones' locker than in George Gibson's pocket." He swayed, clutching the railing, as the *Beauchamp* plowed through a trough. Freezing seawater sprayed over George and he whooped, shaking it off. "Here you go, then, Grail. Hope you like mud."

George drew a bead on a line of waves to starboard, just visible in the faint moonlight. It was getting stormy, the waves getting bigger and picking up froth at their tips. He hefted the pouch, felt how heavy the Grail really was. Unnaturally heavy, considering it was only about the size of a baseball. Someone shouted at him in French; he looked back and saw the watchman picking his way across the icy deck. "Whoops, hurry up," he said, and took a step backward, leaning back like he was ready to throw out a runner trying to score from second on a sharp single up the middle.

The ship pitched forward, cresting a wave, and at the same time George's foot slipped. He flailed backward, one leg up in the air and the other skidding across the ice, and when the *Beauchamp*'s prow punched into the trough at the bottom of the rolling wave, George bounced up off the deck and a torrent of water smashed him into the railing. Agony stabbed through his right leg, and he sucked in an involuntary lungful of ocean. He felt the bow rise again, and as the water drained off the deck, it sucked him halfway between the chains linking the rail posts. I didn't mean it, I didn't mean it, he thought, sounding in his head like a little boy who has accidentally set the barn on fire, and he clutched the Grail tightly to his chest. With his left hand he caught the chain and held on as the rest of the water sluiced across him and fell like rain into the waves.

Someone jerked at George's injured leg. "Stop! Oh Jesus, stop!" he screamed as the watchman dragged him back onto the deck, screaming back in French as he hauled George to his feet and half-carried him back to the relative shelter of the bridge overhang. *"Idiot! Aliene!"* was the only bit George caught out of the whole barrage, and as he choked and vomited up seawater, he found himself nodding. "I'm surely an idiot," he gasped. "Not an alien, though. I'm going home." Then he tried to sit up, and the wave of pain from his leg nearly made him faint. When he managed to fight off the nausea and focus his eyes, all he could do was shake his head at the crooked mess the railing had made of his leg.

"Damn, George Gibson, but you are stupid," he said, talking to himself as the watchman ran for the ship's doctor. "After all this, you thought you could just get rid of it. Well, I guess the ocean had different ideas." He was laughing by the time the doctor arrived, and only stopped to say "ouch" when the sawbones stuck a needle in him.

George woke up in a hospital bed with a view of a lawn that ran between the building and a busy street. His leg, encased in plaster from toe to hip, hung from a pulley bolted into the ceiling. A curtain cut him off from the rest of the room. On the other side, George heard someone shift on a bed, settle into a new position with a pained whisper. His tongue scraped on the roof of his mouth, and he thought he'd give his left arm for a glass of water. Then his leg started to hurt again. Thirsty and in mounting pain, George tried to relax; he looked out at the people walking or being wheeled across the lawn, waiting for someone to come check on him.

After a vague length of time—George's head seemed to be stuffed full of red ants and broken glass, and his eyes still wouldn't hold focus for very long—a tubby nurse who reminded George of his aunt Sylvia came bustling into the room. She checked the tension in George's traction wires and asked him how he felt.

"Could use a glass of water," George rasped.

"Of course, Mister . . ." The nurse glanced at the chart hanging from the foot of George's bed. "I'm sorry, but we don't have your name recorded here."

"Ciccarelli." George spelled it. "Martin Ciccarelli."

"Hm. Excuse my saying so, but you don't look Italian."

George smiled. "All those Huns and Vandals passing through, I suppose." It was what Martha's father always said when people questioned his red hair.

The nurse chuckled and wrote the alias on George's chart.

"I'll get you a glass of water and find the doctor so he can tell you about your leg."

She returned right away with the glass of water, then left George alone to wait on the doctor. He drank the water slowly, savoring it, letting it clear his head a little. It was nice, George thought, having someone take care of you. If he could just relax here for a week or so, out of the way . . . but that wouldn't be smart. Time to go west. Templars might skulk through the door at any moment.

The Grail. George had a nauseating moment of panic as he realized that it wasn't on his wrist. He tried to remember what had happened to it on the ship, but couldn't. Had it fallen overboard, been washed into the Atlantic by that last wave? No, he remembered holding on to it even when the ship's doctor had given him the injection. So where was it? Craning his neck, George saw a small bureau in the corner near his bed. Above it, his coat hung from a peg on the wall. Lord Almighty, George said to himself, I hope no orderly stole it. For his sake.

The doctor came in, paused to check on George's sleeping roommate, then poked his bald head around the edge of George's curtain. "How are you feeling"—he too shot a quick look at George's chart—"Mister Ciccarelli?"

"Better after having a drink." George shifted, tried to sit up and found that the traction wires were too tight to allow him to scoot up higher on the bed.

"Is there much pain from your leg?"

"Well, it's not much like a hot bath," George said. "But I reckon I can tolerate it."

"Good man." Sunlight reflecting from the lenses of his spectacles, the doctor came around the side of George's bed, poked at the side of his head. "How about here?"

George realized his head was bandaged. "Hadn't noticed it," he said.

"Well, it's fairly superficial. Some stitches above your ear, and a dozen or so in the cartilage of the ear itself." The doctor leaned his considerable bulk over George's bed, held up a finger. "Follow this, please." George focused with an effort as the finger traced some invisible doctor-pattern in the air. "Well, I don't believe there's any real cranial trauma," the doctor said. "But your leg is quite another matter. I've set the femur, which was fractured just above the knee, and done what I could to stabilize the patella, which was dislocated and I believe also fractured. If the degree of swelling is any indication, there is considerable damage to the connective tissues in the knee. Do you have any family or friends in the area? I understand you sustained this injury on a ship."

George shook his head. "I'm traveling back west."

"Not for at least a month, you're not. It'll be that long before you can walk farther than the nearest washroom. And I'm afraid, Mister Ciccarelli, that you'll have a limp for the rest of your life. The reason I ask about relations is that you'll be undergoing a prolonged convalescence, but you needn't stay here for all of it."

"No, nobody I know here." George fell silent, thinking. The doctor turned to go. "Hold on one second, Doctor. Can you do me a favor?"

"I'll certainly try." The doctor flashed a perfect bedside smile.

"There's a, a good-luck charm in my coat pocket. At least I think that's where it is," George said. "It's from my girl back in," he coughed, "Montana."

"Montana?" The doctor looked through George's coat. "You're quite a traveler, Mister Ciccarelli."

George couldn't disguise the depth of his relief when the doctor's search yielded the brown leather Grail pouch. "Yes, sir," he said, taking the pouch and tying it around his right wrist. "I've been around a bit. Europe, Africa, Canada. Haven't been home in . . . goodness. More than three years."

"Africa. Gone exploring, were you? Big-game hunting?"

"A little bit of both, you might say." George held the Grail in both hands, a sense of well-being spreading through him. His head was clearing, and it seemed like the pain in his leg had let up a bit.

"Quite a journey," the doctor said. "You get some rest now; I'll check on you later in the afternoon."

George waited until he was gone, then took the Grail from its pouch and spent a long time just looking at it, letting it soothe him and clear his head so he could think. Behind the curtain, his roommate stirred and mumbled in his sleep.

Look at me, George thought. In a hospital bed, like Rimbaud, with my leg a mess, like Rimbaud's. Try and try, but there's no getting away from destiny.

At least he wasn't dying. He'd never play baseball again, but he wasn't dying.

Baseball. Was it that easy to let go? He tried the idea on again: he'd never play again. It was sad, but only a little. Amazing. He was going to have to get to know himself all over.

"Seems I'm stuck with you," he said softly to the Grail. "So let's see what you can do." He unwound the bandage from his head, felt the stubbled scalp where they'd shaved his head to stitch him up. The cut was maybe an inch long, with five stitches holding it closed. His ear was a bit worse; it felt like the top of it was completely split in two, and the stitches went right through to the back. "All right, Grail," George said. "Go ahead and fix those up, but first we need to get at this leg." He sat up as far as he could, feeling an unaccustomed stretch in his suspended hamstring. Out of shape, he thought. The wire holding up his leg led to a spool anchored to the wall over George's head. He reached up, found the release, and cranked his leg down until his heel rested on the rail at the foot of the bed.

"Now we'll see," he said. He pressed the Grail against his forehead. "Come on, Grail. I need to be traveling, and I need you to help me out."

His leg grew hot inside the cast, and a fierce itch attacked the skin around his knee, as if all the red ants had crawled down from

George's head to bedevil his leg. And George could have sworn that the Grail's strange glow, like winter light in cold water, was seeping from the edges of the cast, shooting up past his toes to decorate the ceiling, glistening on the sterile white of his bedsheet. He was healing, and a delighted smile broke across his face as the Grail cooked his leg back together with its living gray heat. The pain began to recede.

"I'll be running from here to Denver pretty soon, eh, Grail?" Still grinning like a fool, George ran the Grail up and down the length of his leg. "Yes, sir. Places to go."

Ten minutes later, his clothing bundled in his arms, George stumped across his room and peeked out into the hallway, where a trio of nurses was just rounding the corner and coming toward his room. His leg still hurt like the dickens, but the Grail had quit doing whatever it was doing, and there was no time to waste. I'll heal up better over time, he thought. A few feet down the hall, an open door revealed a storage closet. Storage closets, thought George, must have plaster saws in 'em. I got to get this thing off. He waited until the nurses passed and the hall was empty, then dragged himself across to the closet like Ahab stumping from port to starboard.

It took another ten minutes to saw off the cast, and then George struck his first real obstacle when he tried to dress. Apparently the doctors had cut off his pants, which now flapped in his hands like he'd split all their seams at once. "Damn," George said. He limped to the back of the closet, hoping for some kind of lost and found. Nothing.

Then inspiration struck. He put on his shirt and coat, then stole back into his room. His roommate, one Cyrus Kirkendall, was still snoring away, both of his legs hung in a traction rig. There was room in Kirkendall's trousers for two of George, especially after all the traveling he'd done, but they would have to do.

He was ready to stagger out the door when it opened and the Templars came in.

· · ·

At the second shot, he reached for the brittle thong that had held the Grail on his hip all these sixty-four years. It snapped as he untied the knot, and he held the pouch in his hand, wondering what the Grail looked like when no one saw it, or what it would look like under the gaze of a person completely without belief or desire. Until a few days ago, George had always thought he would be able to ask Dwight Porter that question. A perfectly groomed empty vessel, that was Dwight. Raymond and Philippe had done that work well, even if things had gotten more complicated since Dwight's brother had come home with the mark. Or maybe even before that; George couldn't help but think that the leggy brunette, Gwen, hadn't just caught Dwight's eye at the farmer's market.

He'd made it a hobby these past few years to try to figure out which one of the Deschamps brothers fathered which Porter boy. He'd never seen either boy; but Raymond and Philippe didn't look all that different from each other, so it would likely be hard to judge just on looks. Ray was a little taller, dressed better, and had aged into a sack of bones who still gave off an unhealthy vitality; Phil dressed like a lumberjack and had put on weight in his later years. But both of them had the same dishwater hair and pale blue eyes. All the same, George had made his guesses over the years, and right now he supposed that Ray was Lance's father. That would explain why Ray was so ticked off when Gwen hit the hay with Lance—so much for his plan to get a piece of the Grail even if Phil's son became the next King.

That was his current theory, anyway, and anyway it was all just guesswork, and none of it mattered now because both Ray and Phil were dead out on the porch, and Lance Porter was coming for his birthright while Dwight did whatever Dwight did in his little weatherbeaten shack over in Peggy's Cove.

Now, at the end of his life, George wished he had a better

grasp on the situation, but it was a feeble wish. He hadn't had much energy for anything but remorse in a long time.

They took him straight out of New York, up the coast on a private train to Portland, Maine, and then on a ship across to Yarmouth, Nova Scotia, a sailor's town bursting with saloons and cathouses, noise all night, but they only stayed long enough to get another train up the coast, and then George was right back where it had all started. For a long time they stayed in Halifax, keeping a close eye on him. He couldn't even take a leak without one of them outside the door. After a while, some weeks, he guessed they'd figured he'd had enough time to get a handle on the situation, because they sat him down and said it was time for him to make some choices.

George didn't recognize the Frenchman who started the conversation. He was a terrible mess, scarred all over his face and hands, missing an eye and a big part of his lower lip and joints from a couple of his fingers, but he was in charge. He introduced George to a pair of brothers, Raymond and Philippe. "These are angry boys," the Templar said. "They cannot have the Grail, and you got their father killed in Axum."

"Who was that?" George asked, and knew as soon as the words got out of his mouth. Michel's sons. Things were going to get a lot worse. He looked again at the chewed-up mess of a Templar who was leading the discussion, and he knew it was a bad idea, but he said, "Looks like Nigel Whatsisname got a piece of you too."

The Templar gave him the thinnest of smiles. "Joke while you can," he said.

Ray and Phil were just boys then, twelve or thirteen, but it was clear right away that they were in charge, and the scarred Templar was right, they were mad and determined to take it out on George. They would prefer not to kill him, they said, because circumstance had made him King, and to kill a King would bring them a great deal of trouble. All of their rivals would know immediately, and there would be massacres.

George had seen enough on Oak Island, let alone in Africa, to know that they didn't have quite as much compunction as they were letting on. "I'd just as soon keep that as a last resort myself," he said.

"Very well," Raymond said. "Here is the arrangement. You think of us as your regents, or viziers, or seneschals, you pick the word. But you sit on the throne and do what we tell you."

The only one of those words George knew was *regent*. This twelve-year-old kid with a French accent was showing him up, and it made him mad, but he kept his cool. "What are you going to tell me?"

"Nothing," Philippe said. "You're going to do just exactly nothing. You sit there and keep the seat warm while we get the succession arranged."

Then they told him about the Ras Tafari, just that past summer born to Menelik's brother. He was a likely prospect, they thought, but Rimbaud's friend Jerome had already tangled himself up in Menelik's court and would likely be appointed tutor to the boy as soon as he was old enough to learn. An African king would be better, they said. The Grail comes from there, and Ras Tafari is of Solomon's line. It was the same problem they had dealt with for nearly eight hundred years—Zagwes and Solomonids circling each other until they found the Grail and were in a position to use it. "Now we are in that position," Philippe said, "thanks to you. What if we told you that as soon as the Ras Tafari achieves his majority, you can relinquish the Grail to him and go back to your life?"

Seventeen years, George thought. I'll be thirty-nine. Martha will have found someone else if she hasn't already. Not that he had much choice.

"Is that how it works?"

Raymond leaned forward. "You should hope so."

Some kids, George thought. They'd kill him as soon as spit, but whether he'd just slipped on the *Beauchamp*'s deck after lugging the Grail ten thousand miles, or the Grail had known what was coming and bound itself to him on its own, he had it. That was keeping him alive. He was King, and Michel's boys could keep hold of him, but they couldn't have the Grail for themselves until he was out of the way. Could he really give it up? The Ark hadn't taken it from him. Maybe it would be different if a real King showed up.

George was twenty-two years old. Even at thirty-nine, he'd have a good part of his threescore and ten left. They'd been waiting since the Crusades. Another seventy years was a sneeze to them. There was only one thing he could do.

And if things worked out the right way, he'd come out smelling like a rose. Maybe he could do some good when they weren't looking, and then when this Ras Tafari came along he'd hand the Grail off and go back to Colorado. Give the Grail back to someone who wanted it and deserved it.

Yishaq would have been a better King, George thought. The Grail belonged to him more than any of them.

The thought returned to him often over the next sixty years. He read George Washington Williams' dispatches from the Congo, reprinted in the Halifax papers, and everything he'd seen there came up on him like he was right there in the river again, feeling the little girl slip away into the current. He was just as helpless in Nova Scotia as he'd been in Africa. And that kind of helplessness, once he'd felt it, never quite let go of him again. Baskets of hands, the price paid for gaskets and bicycle tires. He walked in Halifax, and every rubber tire he saw seemed like it was made of African bodies. He started talking to Yishaq again.

Leave them, Yishaq said. What is the threat of death weighed against the good you might do?

Nothing took the soul from a man like realizing he was weak. You confronted the weakness like it wasn't part of you, you hatched plans, you imagined getting on a boat in Halifax Harbor and making the trip to London and then Cairo and then back in Africa couldn't you make things a little better? But that's all George did, think and imagine, because the weakness was as much a part of him as his ability to see when the bottom was about to fall out of a spitball, as the way he had once felt himself making the turn around first even before he'd swung and heard the effortless crack of the bat. Once George had thought he was strong because he played baseball.

Now he went years at a time without thinking of Martha.

They taunted him. Maybe they figured that, if he was really planning anything, a little chafing would make him do something stupid. Articles about the Congo appeared in his room, photographs of massacres in India and famines in the Horn of Africa, all the separate hells created by white men in the lands of brown men. It got to George, all the nights he spent choking down the acid in his stomach and—once Ray and Phil bought the farmhouse where he'd played his last game of baseball—looking out at the black lump of Oak Island. Wondering, all the time, wondering what he might do if he didn't spend all his time convincing himself he had to do nothing.

George asked Ray and Phil if maybe something shouldn't be done, maybe not about the Congo or the German slaughter in South-West Africa or the Zulus dying in the Transvaal, but what about the natural disasters? Wasn't that what it was all about? Kids dying of cholera after a flood, starving when the crops failed in the desert lands? He was supposed to restore the land, wasn't he?

Maybe he was and maybe he wasn't, they said. "Would the Grail even respond to you?" Ray asked him once, around 1900, and George realized he was afraid to find out. If he tried to do something and it didn't work, they'd kill him. He was sure of it.

If he'd been a man he'd have said the hell with it. The hell with Ray and Phil, he'd take the Grail back to Africa himself. Or he'd have gotten out of bed early one morning, with the sun just cresting the ocean horizon, and asked something of the Grail. End this famine, stop this war—or just let me put this burden down. Let me put it down. Let me go home to Martha.

He hadn't done any of that. The Ark had refused him, and deep down inside George thought the only reason he still had it was because of Yishaq, who had never completely left. My soul used to be clear, George thought, and now it's like stained glass the color of Yishaq. I fail his example, and fail, and fail.

Now Ras Tafari was Haile Selassie, Emperor of Ethiopia. Whatever Ray and Phil had planned for him hadn't worked out. It didn't matter. Ray and Phil were dead. George would be soon. He was an old man with pains in his legs, unable to turn his head to the right, nearly blind in his left eye. His knuckles had begun to kink up with arthritis, and when he woke up in the morning— when he slept at all—his heart raced until he sweated. Time was running out for him, here in the front room of the farmhouse with its green-and-white velvet wallpaper, its ugly watercolors of Walt Wallace's spinster aunts, and its piano that no one had played since George had been there.

The porch steps creaked. The front door opened. Sunrise backlit the figure of Lance Porter, and George squinted, hoping to resolve his question. Ray or Phil? George leaned forward in the chair where he'd spent most of the last ten years or so, since he'd really started to feel old. He could almost feel the presence of Ray and Phil in the room, there on the couch that sat against the wall under the front windows. He'd watched them grow into men and then grow old, patiently waiting for their plans to bear fruit. Several times they'd nearly killed each other, and right after the Great Depression struck, when they were both old enough to take a longer view of things, they'd realized they had to work together. So in true Templar fashion, they'd mapped a replica of Champagne onto the New World, and left George alone in the house for a week. That had been his last chance to work himself free of their control, free of his own cowardice, and he hadn't taken it. Nineteen thirty-two: Hitler was a loudmouth crank in Munich, Stalin still just a Party cog with provincial roots. George hadn't heard of either yet. What might he, or the Grail, have been able to do?

What he did was fry eggs, look out the window, and try to explain to Yishaq why he was doing nothing. It could be worse, he said. If I tried something and it didn't work, they'd know. Wouldn't they? People must be watching from somewhere. And then they'd kill me, and who would take the Grail in my place?

Roosevelt, Yishaq suggested. He is powerful, he knows about Oak Island, his legs are diseased. He is a man other men can believe in.

Again the fantasy: out the door and down the road. Did Pitblado with his bird's head still sail his little boat around the island? Would he take George across the Gulf of Maine to Campobello Island, where Roosevelt summered?

What if he wouldn't? And what if Roosevelt wouldn't take it, wouldn't see George once he got there?

It could be worse, he insisted. Yishaq did not answer.

When Ray and Phil came back they exuded a confidence George hadn't seen in a long time. That had lasted for years, and then in 1945 he'd started to hear about his successor. It was a good time to consider such things, said Ray and Phil. The atomic age was upon them. Seismic changes would shake the next generation. And maybe they were right; George had a brief interlude of optimism. Things couldn't get any worse. It was always darkest before the dawn, right? Maybe the Bomb was just the growing pains of a new age, and this kid Dwight Porter would lift George's burden and let him die.

Eight years later, this morning, George's optimism had died with the pair of rifle shots that announced Lance Porter's . . . coup, was the only word for it. Oddly, his resignation made him feel better about his inaction. See, Yishaq, he said. If the alternative to me was a guy like this, a guy so torn up about his dad that he'll do anything to get out from under his pain, it could have been worse.

Yishaq did not answer.

Lance Porter shut the door behind him. Could be either, George thought. He's rangy like Ray, but something about the set of his shoulders, that's Phil.

"Where'd you hit 'em?" he asked.

"You George Gibson?" Lance looked around the room. "Where's my father? And Dewey's dad, where's he?"

"Don't be in such a hurry, kid," George said. "Where'd you hit 'em?"

"The taller guy, Frank, just inside the right shoulder blade," Lance said. "The breeze died, so I was a little off center. The other guy, in one armpit and out the other."

"Good shooting," George said. "Probably they had time to admire it too, for just a second. It's the kind of thing a dad can take a little pride in."

LANCE

ALL AROUND LANCE the terrible clarity of the world, within him the intolerable clarity of knowing. Ice. He waited for time to begin moving again, for Gibson to crack a smile at what had to be a joke. The room waited in perfect stillness. Lance's heart beat, once. He waited for time to begin moving again, to begin wearing away the razored edges of his transgression that—as he stood motionless in George Gibson's living room—carved belief and faith away from his wailing soul. Names marched through his mind, as if the wandering finger of memory was tracing its way down the family tree of story. *We guess at fatherhood through resemblance*—but King Solomon, changing his appearance to seduce the Queen of Sheba; Uther Pendragon, enchanted by Merlin to enter Igraine's bed; Lancelot's father, conceiving a son under an obscuring spell. Again and again.

His soul calved into the black water of despair. His father, Dewey's father, lost. Ellie, lost. Dewey, lost. Lance himself, found but in the finding condemned to know and to not forget.

Hadn't they warned him, Gwen and Jerry and Ellie? Even his mother? Despair fractured into rage and sorrow; they'd known, they'd seen it coming, and they'd let him go.

Dwight, Lance thought. He did this. He walked me straight into it. And just as quickly he despised himself for thinking it.

"You can't be all that surprised, now, can you?" George Gibson said, the cataract in his left eye shining like silver in the morning light. Now he did give Lance a smile, the smile of a man looking up to notice that he is no longer alone in his self-loathing. "Pieced the rest of the story together well enough to figure out what you had to do to get in here, didn't you? And somehow you figured a way not to notice the rest."

It's not like that, Lance wanted to say. What stopped him was the possibility that it *was* like that, that part of him had known and acted not out of a sense of destiny but out of pure greed and animal hate. He remembered vowing to himself *This ends here*—but here, when it mattered, Gwen was right; whether he'd meant to or not, he had committed the unpardonable sins. Another list of names: Oedipus, Alexander the Great, Caligula.

Sound started to leak from his mouth. Lance bit down on it, swallowed. In the wake of everything else followed shame, for his lie to Ellie, for his brusqueness with his mother, for what he'd thought about his brother moments before, for what he'd done moments before that.

All that remained was to go through with it. He walked across the room to George Gibson and said, "Give me what I came for."

"The thing you and I have in common," Gibson said, "is that both of us are only strong when we're driven by our worst flaws."

"Give it to me," Lance said.

Gibson didn't move. "I tried to give it to Rimbaud," he said. "In the end, he didn't want it."

Lance reached down and took the cracked leather pouch from the old King's hands. He upended it over his own cupped palm, and out spilled a stone. He waited for the shock, the flood of power and rightness, the blaze of entering the lineage he'd been born to.

The stone rested in his palm, slightly warm from Gibson's touch.

Lance closed his hands over the stone, closed his eyes, willed himself to accept it. Willed it to accept him.

He opened his eyes. "I said give it to me."

"You've got it," Gibson said. "Except you don't. Work on that for a while."

Something in Gibson's face caught Lance's attention. The folds of his old man's flesh, the watering eyes and sloping shoulders—behind it all was a shadow, flitting just outside Lance's focus. Younger, darker, distant.

He saw Lance staring and said, "He never completely left. When something like that happens to you, it keeps happening after it's over."

A car engine downshifted on the road, and Lance heard the crunch of tires on the gravel shoulder in front of the house. Two dead men on the porch, a rifle in the woods—if it was one of the local cops Dewey had mentioned, Gibson had already won. And wouldn't that be easier? Wouldn't it be easier if he could just be taken away, left to be alone with his memories? They might kill me, Lance thought. The idea struck him like hope. I could die now, he thought. Forget the failure, forget the body of my father and the betrayal of Ellie's belief in me.

Footsteps coming up to the porch, then a pause. Lance could envision them, heavy men like Karl Aufdemberge, unsnapping their holsters, one of them standing off to the side of the door while the other took a deep breath before charging through into whatever awaited them. The back of his neck felt hot, and he wished they would do it, just kill him and cover it up, erase him from the world so Ellie and Dwight would never know. He held his breath, held the stone, and prayed to die the way he'd screamed to live four months ago.

The screen door creaked on its hinges. With the sound came a smell that tipped Lance back into the unbearable now. He remembered pine and stone and water, the feel of her hand in his, the hard curving ridge of a button pressing into the side of his finger, the rise and fall of a living body. Ellie.

Hope fled him, left him alone and defenseless. He could not turn to face her. He heard someone else come in behind her, and knew it was Dewey. The only two people he had left. "Ellie," he said. The word came out empty, even though it tore him apart to say it, devastated him to admit she was there to witness what he'd done. He tried again: "Dewey." Nothing. He had nothing. The two words that meant more to him than any other, and they fell from his mouth and died in the pale light with George Gibson sitting and taking it all in. He put the stone back in the pouch, weighed it in his palm, saw in front of him the long and desolate years he'd condemned himself to spend alone with this weight. He would grow old, and someone would come to take it from him, and then he would die enclosed by memories of all that he'd sacrificed for the weight of a stone.

Give it to Dewey, he thought, and hated himself for the thought. No. Dewey had made his choices, Lance had made his.

But something was there, maybe just the illusion of hope. Lance seized on it, and all at once he knew. He turned to Ellie and Dwight. Justifications came to mind, and withered just as quickly under the heat of what he saw in their faces. Spiritual transformation, yes; Lance had been transformed. The stone in his hand told him exactly how.

Out the window, past the faces of brother and beloved, the bright green of the field between the house and the road. For Gibson, it had all started here and here it was ending. *In baseball, you're always trying to get back home, and every time you do the score is different.* Spicer had said that, in the diner, the morning after Gwen, before Lance's damnation.

Something about it worked at his mind. Always trying to get back home. And another line from a story, drifting up from one of Jerry's all-night monologues: *Sir Knight, you shall not enter. Go back to your own country, for you are surely no companion of the Quest.* Lancelot's failure.

I have taken the Grail, Lance thought. Now it is mine to do with as I please.

"Ellie," he said, still unable to look at her. "I need you to come with me."

In the corner of his eye he could see the slow shake of her head. "No, Lance. Not like this."

"Ellie. Please. I can't do this alone."

She did not answer.

"Dewey," Lance said. "All of us together. I have to ask you."

"As witness," Dwight said. "Just as witness."

"As witness," Lance agreed. He turned to Gibson. "You too." If he could no longer prove anything to his father, he'd take the man who had known his father best.

Morning sunlight was warm on the porch as they filed out through the front door. Raymond Deschamps lay at the top of the steps, his dead face turned toward Mahone Bay and the green bristle of Oak Island. His cigarette had burned down between his fingers. Philippe Deschamps had crumpled into the railing and come to rest sitting with the side of his face pressed into the supporting posts. Lance and Dwight paused, looking at the dead men, and simultaneously asked, "Which one was he?"

Gibson kept going. He held on to the banister and descended the porch steps carefully, getting both feet on each before stepping down to the next. He avoided the blood that had spilled onto the top step; avoided too the bloody prints of Lance's boots on the unfinished planks of the porch itself.

"They never said, and I never figured it out," he said when he'd gotten to the ground. Lance and Dwight looked at each other. Ellie followed Gibson. After a moment, the Porter brothers fell in behind them. The group moved as if they all knew where they were going but were praying for a reason not to go there.

As they crossed the road, Gibson said, "Top of the fifth, I hit a ball would have gone right over our heads here. Landed twenty, thirty yards out in the water. Road was just a dirt track then. We played on it." He looked over his shoulder and pointed to the left of the house, his finger shaking a little but on a line toward the spot where Lance had fired two shots fifteen minutes before. "Home plate was over there, about a quarter of the way between here and the trees. Old Ev Tillbury, he hit a foul fly that bounced off the roof of the house. You should have heard Wallace kick up a fuss about having to reshingle." He chuckled, wheezing a little. "Roof was already in damn worse condition than anything a baseball could do."

He trailed off as they crossed the drainage ditch on the seaward side of the road. Everyone except Lance walked more slowly now, through weeds and shoreside brush, and by the time they'd come out on the beach Lance was well in the lead. He stopped and watched a dying wave sink into the sand at his feet, leaving behind bursting bubbles of foam and tumbled strands of seaweed. Lance stood there thinking about what Spicer had said about baseball being a rite, thinking too that once out of the house and free, George Gibson had turned into the kind of garrulous old man he'd have become if he'd never seen the Grail. The thought sank into him, rearranged other thoughts around it.

Dwight was standing next to him. "Your show, big brother," he said. "I don't steal boats in broad daylight."

"You won't need to," Lance said. His hand came out of his pocket with the gold coin his mother had given him. He curled his index finger around its rim and skimmed it out over the flat water between Crandall's Point and the island. It skipped twice, then curved over to its left and disappeared without a splash.

Nothing changed. The sun still shone, the sand was still cool under his feet.

Then a small sailboat tacked into view around the northern shore of the island. At its tiller stood a heavy man in a white suit, and just as Lance had seen a darker and younger face ghosting behind the sagging visage of George Gibson, he now saw a bird's head with a long curving beak flickering around the sailor's own head the way a movie flickered when the projector wasn't playing fast enough. He kept his gaze steady on the sailor as the boat cut into the channel breeze and slowly closed toward them. It halted a few feet from the shore even though wind still stiffened its sails.

"Four," said the sailor—*ferryman,* Lance found himself thinking, echoing another echo. "And only one of you has paid."

"For all four of us," Lance said. "It's a short trip."

Pitblado laughed. His head jutted forward at Lance, startling him. "Four, then," he said.

They splashed out. The water was barely shin-deep where the boat rested, and the boat barely rocked as Lance held on to the gunwale and first Ellie, then Dwight, and then Gibson hoisted themselves over the side. Dwight and Ellie had to help Gibson, but once he was aboard he looked at Pitblado and smirked. "Put on weight, haven't you?"

Pitblado ignored him. He watched Lance, and as Lance rolled himself onto the boat Pitblado changed. Aboard his vessel he was Thoth, and he held Lance's gaze in a steady regard that stripped Lance bare and inscribed every sin he'd ever committed on his skin.

"Don't judge me yet," Lance said.

The gaze held Lance a moment longer, and then Thoth shrugged and the boat heeled to its left, toward the island.

They stepped onto the shore of Oak Island at Smith's Cove. The remains of the coffer dam used to uncover the artificial beach were still visible in the slack tide. When they got to shore, Lance looked back. Pitblado was Pitblado again, and George Gibson sat against the bow railing. "This is as far as I go," Gibson said. "I can't look at that hole again." He lifted a hand to George, and with him an African ghost hailed Lance, wordlessly commanding him. I obey, Lance thought. He inclined his head and watched the boat turn out into the bay. It sailed south, through the bay and out of sight around Crandall's Point.

Now all that remained was the Grail. Lance turned away from the water, followed the path he remembered walking with Dewey—only days ago? They crossed weedy ground long since stripped of oaks and any other trees. That entire part of the island had been denuded in the quest for what he held in his hand. A hundred yards or so inland, about halfway across a narrow neck of island that pointed out into the bay—back toward Europe, it occurred to Lance—gaped a sandy-banked hole, filled to within eight or ten feet of its edge with still black water. Lance stopped when he was close enough to see his own shadowed face reflected in the water. To his right, Dewey; to his left, Ellie. Both of them looked at him.

This is what a newly crowned King does, Lance thought. He returns to the source of his power and awaits a sign, an oracle to legitimize him. Canterbury, Mecca, Jerusalem, Thebes. He searched himself, and found that a shadow of his belief remained, like a childhood fear of the dark never completely shed. I join a tradition that goes back farther than anyone can trace, he thought, back to the flowering of the race, back to the time when we first gathered in the Rift Valley and started to explain to each other why the seasons changed, why the rains sometimes came and sometimes failed. I forced my way into those stories, like my father and grandfather did, like the Abyssinian traitor did when he founded my line.

He had no right, but it was more right than I ever had.

Lance saw the face behind George Gibson's face, the dark ghost of history overwritten through centuries of retellings, erasures, lies, failures of valor and discretion alike. *Palimpsest* was the word Jerry had used, somewhere in Nebraska or Illinois, while Lance drowsed against the Plymouth's window. Every white face a palimpsest written on dark paper.

If it was all true . . .

Somewhere there must be waiting a strong black King who would someday come to claim what had been stolen from him. Maybe he had already been born; maybe Hiroshima and Dachau and the gulags were the birthing pangs of a new world. Lance wanted to believe it. But maybe George Gibson was to blame for the last sixty years, at least partially, and maybe Lance Porter would be no better.

He was asking the wrong question again. It didn't matter whether he would be a good King. It only mattered that he had no right. And maybe it mattered that when they told Lance Porter's story, the telling just might mean that another man wouldn't have to do what Lance had done.

Are you listening? he thought. I obey. He raised his hand and dropped the Grail into the black water.

It disappeared with a small splash. Ripples fanned out, then quickly subsided, and a minute after Lance opened his hand the water was still again. He saw himself, his reflection coming back together as the water stilled. He saw Dwight and Ellie. He saw the sky. All of it looked the same. Lance waited to feel something, but all that came was a question. Was it enough? He was frozen again—not ice this time, just a man waiting, maybe forever, to learn whether he leveled the scales.

Dwight took a step toward him. An endless moment later, so did Ellie.

ABOUT THE AUTHOR

ALEXANDER C. IRVINE has won the Crawford Award for best new writer, which is given by the International Association for Fantastic in the Arts. He won awards for best first novel from *Locus Magazine* and the International Horror Guild as well, and he was a finalist for the Campbell Award for best new writer. His short fiction has appeared in Salon.com, the *Vestal Review, Fantasy & Science Fiction, Alchemy,* and *The Year's Best Science Fiction,* among others. He has been nominated for a Pushcart Prize for his short story "Snapdragons." Irvine lives in Maine with his wife and two children.